THE WORLD'S BEST
FAIRY TALES

A READER'S DIGEST ANTHOLOGY

THE WORLD'S BEST FAIRY TALES

Edited by
BELLE BECKER SIDEMAN

Illustrations by
FRITZ KREDEL

The Reader's Digest Association, Inc.
Pleasantville, New York   Montreal

The acknowledgments that appear on page 448 are
hereby made a part of this copyright page.

Library of Congress Catalog Card Number 79-89496
ISBN 0-89577-077-6 (Volume Two)
ISBN 0-89577-078-4 (Set)

Printed in the United States of America

Tenth Printing (Two-Volume Edition), April 1991

CONTENTS

JORINDA AND JORINGEL

ONCE UPON a time there was a castle in the middle of a deep forest where an old woman lived quite alone, for she was an enchantress. In the daytime she changed herself into a cat or an owl, but in the evening she became an ordinary woman again. She was able to entice animals and birds to come to her castle, and then she would kill and cook them.

If any youth found himself within a hundred paces of the castle, he became rooted to the spot and could not stir till the woman set him free. If a pretty girl came inside the magic circle, the old enchantress changed her into a bird and locked her up in a wicker cage. She had seven thousand such cages in the castle, each containing a rare bird that had been a happy, carefree young girl.

Now, there was once a maiden called Jorinda, who was very beautiful. She was betrothed to a youth named Joringel, and their greatest delight was to be together. One summer evening, the two went for a walk in the forest. It was calm and peaceful under the trees, and the fading sunlight glinted on the dark green leaves.

"How beautiful this place is!" sighed Joringel. "But we must take care not to come too close to the witch's castle."

They wandered on, hand in hand, and, without knowing why, they began to feel sad and forlorn. In a nearby tree a turtledove sang its plaintive lament. They looked around, quite confused, for they did not remember their way home. Jorinda began to weep and sob, overcome by a strange fear. Joringel tried to comfort her, but he, too, felt something ominous in the air around them.

Half the sun was still above the mountain and half had dropped behind it when Joringel looked through the trees and saw the old wall of the witch's castle near them. He was terrified.

In the last rays of the setting sun, Jorinda sank to the ground and began to sing:

> My little bird with throat so red
>   Sings sorrow, sorrow, sorrow;
> He sings to the little dove that's dead,
>   Sings sorrow, sor——jug, jug, jug.

Joringel looked at Jorinda. Right before his eyes she had been changed into a nightingale and was singing "Jug, jug, jug."

An owl with glowing eyes flew three times around

her and screeched three times, "Tu-whit, tu-whit, tu-whoo." Joringel could not stir. He stood like a stone—he could not weep nor speak nor move hand or foot.

Now the sun had disappeared. The owl flew into a bush, and immediately an old, bent woman came out of it. She was yellow-skinned and thin and had large red eyes and a hooked nose which met her chin. She muttered to herself, caught the nightingale that had once been Jorinda and carried it away in her hand.

Joringel stood speechless and motionless until at last the woman returned and said in a gruff voice, "Good evening, young man. When the moon shines on the basket in my castle you will be freed."

And suddenly the moon broke through a cloud and Joringel was free. He fell on his knees before the old woman and implored her to give him back his Jorinda. She said he would never see Jorinda again, and then she went away. He called after her, he wept, but all in vain. "What is to become of me?" he cried.

After a while he found a way out of the forest and came to a strange village. There he took employment as a shepherd and stayed on herding sheep for a long time. He often went back to the castle, but never too close. Then one night he dreamed that he found a blood-red flower, in the center of which lay a beautiful pearl. He plucked it, and in the castle everything he touched with the flower was freed from the enchantment and thus he rescued his lovely Jorinda.

When Joringel awoke he set out to find such a flower. He roamed through woods and valleys and crossed steep mountains in his search. For eight days he did not give up hope, and on the ninth, early in the morning, he found it. In the center of this flower was a large dewdrop, as big as the most lovely pearl.

He traveled day and night with the flower till he arrived at the castle. This time, when he came within a hundred paces, he was still able to move, and he continued on till he reached the gate. Delighted at his success, he touched the great gate with the flower, and it sprang open. He entered, passed through the court-yard and then stopped to listen for the singing of the birds. At last Joringel heard the melodious chirping and followed the sounds until he found himself in the great hall of the castle. And there was the enchantress, with her thousands of birds in their wicker cages.

When she saw Joringel, she went into a rage and breathed out poison and gall at him, but she could not move a step toward him. He took no notice of her and looked at the thousands of cages filled with birds. How was he to find Jorinda among them? While he was considering, he saw the old witch pick up a cage and steal toward the door—but he sprang after her and touched her and the cage with his flower, making her powerless to work enchantment ever again. And the little nightingale stepped out of the wicker cage and became Jorinda, more beautiful than before.

Then Joringel walked all around the room, touching each cage with his magic flower. One by one the birds were released and turned back into lovely maidens. When they were all freed, Joringel went home with his Jorinda, and they lived a long and happy life.

JAKOB AND WILHELM GRIMM, TRANSLATED BY MAY SELLAR

PUSS IN BOOTS

A CERTAIN MILLER had three sons, and when he died the sole worldly goods which he bequeathed to them were his mill, his donkey and his Cat. This little legacy was very quickly divided up, and you may be quite sure that neither notary nor attorney were called in to help, for they would speedily have grabbed it all for themselves.

The eldest son took the mill, and the second son took the donkey. Consequently, all that remained for the youngest son was the Cat, and he was not a little disappointed at receiving such a miserable portion.

"My brothers," said he, "will be able to get a decent

living by joining forces, but for my part, as soon as I have eaten my Cat and made a muff out of his skin, I am sure to die of hunger."

These remarks were overheard by Puss, who pretended not to have been listening, and said very soberly and seriously, "There is not the least need for you to worry about your share, Master. All you have to do is to give me a pouch and have a pair of boots made for me so that I can walk in the woods."

Now this Cat had often shown himself capable of performing cunning tricks. When catching rats and mice, for example, he would hide himself among the grain and hang downward by the feet as though he were dead. Therefore his new master felt some hope of being assisted in his miserable plight.

On receiving the boots which he had asked for, Puss gaily pulled them on. Then he hung the pouch around his neck and, holding the cords that tied it in front of him with his paws, he sallied forth to a warren where rabbits abounded. Placing some bran and lettuce in the pouch, he stretched out and lay as if dead. His plan was to wait until some young rabbit, unlearned in worldly wisdom, should come and rummage in the pouch for the eatables he had placed there.

Hardly had he lain himself down when things happened as he wished. A stupid young rabbit went into the pouch, and Master Puss, pulling the cords tight, killed him on the instant.

Well satisfied with his capture, Puss departed to the King's palace. There he demanded an audience and was ushered upstairs. He entered the royal apartment and bowed profoundly to the King. "I bring you, sire," said he, "a rabbit from the warren of the Marquis of Carabas (such was the title he invented for his master), which I am bidden to present to you on his behalf."

"Tell your master," replied the King, "that I thank him and am pleased by his attention."

Another time the Cat hid himself in a wheat field, keeping the mouth of his pouch wide open. Two partridges ventured in, and by pulling the cords tight he captured both of them. Off he went and presented them to the King, just as he had done with the rabbit. His Majesty was not less gratified by the brace of partridges, and handed the Cat a present for himself.

For two or three months Puss went on in this way, every now and again taking to the King, as a present from his master, some game which he had caught. There came a day when he learned that the King intended to take his daughter, who was the most beautiful princess in the world, for an excursion along the riverbank.

"If you will do as I tell you," said Puss to his master, "your fortune is made. You have only to go and bathe in the river at the spot which I shall point out to you. Leave the rest to me."

The so-called Marquis of Carabas had no idea what plan was afoot, but did as the Cat directed.

While he was bathing, the King drew near, and Puss began to cry out at the top of his voice: "Help! help! The Marquis of Carabas is drowning!"

At these shouts the King stopped the carriage. He recognized the Cat who had so often brought him game, and bade his escort go speedily to the help of the Marquis of Carabas.

While they were pulling the poor Marquis out of the river, Puss approached the carriage and explained to the King that while his master was bathing robbers had come and taken away his clothes, though he had cried "Stop, thief!" at the top of his voice. As a matter of fact, the rascal Puss had hidden them under a big stone. The King at once commanded the keepers of his wardrobe to go and select a suit of his finest clothes for the Marquis of Carabas.

The King received the Marquis with many compliments, and, as the fine clothes which the latter had just put on set off his good looks, for he was handsome and comely in appearance, the King's daughter found him very much to her liking. Indeed, the Marquis of Carabas had not bestowed more than two or three respectful but sentimental glances upon her when she fell madly in love with him. The King invited him to enter the coach and join the party.

Delighted to see his plan so successfully launched,

the Cat went on ahead and presently came upon some peasants who were mowing a field. "Listen, my good fellows," said he, "if you do not tell the King that the field which you are mowing belongs to the Marquis of Carabas, you will all be chopped up into little pieces like mincemeat."

In due course the King came along and asked the mowers to whom the field on which they were at work belonged. "It is the property of the Marquis of Carabas," they all cried with one voice, for the threat from Puss had frightened them.

"You have inherited a fine estate," the King remarked to Carabas.

"As you see for yourself, sire," replied the Marquis, "this is a meadow which never fails to yield an abundant crop each year."

Still traveling ahead, the Cat came upon some harvesters. "Listen, my good fellows," said he, "if you do not declare that every one of these fields belongs to the Marquis of Carabas, you will all be chopped up into little bits like mincemeat."

The King came by a moment later and wished to know who was the owner of the fields in sight.

"It is the Marquis of Carabas," cried the harvesters.

At this the King was more pleased than ever with the Marquis.

Preceding the coach on its journey, the Cat made the same threat to all whom he met, and the King grew astonished at the great wealth of the Marquis of Carabas.

Finally Master Puss reached a splendid castle, which belonged to an ogre. He was the richest ogre that had ever been known, for all the lands through which the King had passed were part of the castle domain.

The Cat had taken care to find out who this ogre was and what powers he possessed. He now asked for an interview, declaring that he was unwilling to pass so close to the castle without having the honor of paying his respects to the owner. The ogre received him as politely as an ogre can and bade him sit down.

"I have been told," said Puss, "that you have the power to change yourself into any kind of animal—for example, that you can transform yourself into a lion or an elephant."

"That is perfectly true," said the ogre, curtly, "and just to prove it you shall see me turn into a lion."

Puss was so frightened on seeing a lion before him that he sprang onto the roof—not without difficulty and danger, for his boots were not meant for walking on tiles.

Perceiving presently that the ogre had abandoned his transformation, Puss descended and admitted having been thoroughly frightened. "I have also been told," he added, "but I can scarcely believe it, that you have the further power to take the shape of even the smallest animals—for example, that you can change

THE WORLD'S BEST FAIRY TALES

yourself into a rat or a mouse. I confess that to me it seems quite impossible."

"Impossible?" cried the ogre. "You shall see!" And in the same moment he changed himself into a mouse, which began to run about the floor. No sooner did Puss see it than he pounced on it and ate it.

Presently the King came along and, noticing the ogre's beautiful mansion, desired to visit it. The Cat heard the rumble of the coach as it crossed the castle drawbridge and, running out to the courtyard, he cried, "Welcome, Your Majesty, to the castle of the Marquis of Carabas!"

"What's that?" cried the King. "Is this castle also yours, Marquis? Nothing could be finer than this courtyard and the buildings which I see all about. With your permission we will go inside and look around."

The Marquis gave his hand to the young Princess and followed the King as he led the way up the staircase. Entering a great hall they found a magnificent banquet there. This had been prepared by the ogre for some friends who were to pay him a visit that very day. These friends had not dared to enter when they learned that the King was there.

The King was now quite as charmed with the excellent qualities of the Marquis of Carabas as his daughter. The latter was completely captivated by him. Noting the great wealth of which the Marquis was evidently possessed, and having quaffed several cups of wine, the King turned to the Marquis, saying, "It rests with you, whether you will be my son-in-law."

The Marquis, bowing very low, accepted the honor which the King bestowed upon him. The very same day he married the Princess.

Puss became a personage of great importance and gave up hunting mice, except for amusement.

CHARLES PERRAULT, TRANSLATED BY A. E. JOHNSON

THE EMPEROR'S NEW CLOTHES

MANY YEARS ago there lived an Emperor who was so fond of new clothes that he spent all his money for them. He did not care about his soldiers, he did not care about the theater; he only liked to go out walking to show off his new clothes. He had a costume for every hour of the day; and just as they say of a king, "He is in the council chamber," they always said of him, "The Emperor is in his dressing room."

Life was very gay in the great city in which the Emperor lived. There was always something going on and every day many strangers came to visit. One day two swindlers arrived who announced that they were weavers and knew how to manufacture the most beautiful cloth imaginable. Not only were the texture and pattern uncommonly beautiful, but the clothes which were made from it had the wonderful quality of becoming invisible to anyone who was not fit for his office or who was unpardonably stupid.

"My, oh, my," said the people. "Think of that!"

"Those must indeed be splendid clothes," said the Emperor to himself. "If I wore them I could find out which men in my kingdom are unfit for the offices they hold. I could distinguish the wise men from the fools! Yes, this cloth must be woven for me at once." And he gave both the weavers money so that they could begin their work.

They set up two weaving looms and pretended they were working, but actually the looms had nothing on them. They also demanded the finest silk and the best gold thread, which they put into their bags, and worked at the empty looms till late into the night.

"I would certainly like to know how much cloth they have woven," said the Emperor. But he remembered, when he thought about it, that whoever was a fool or unfit for his office would not be able to see the material. Now he certainly believed that he had nothing to fear for himself, but he wanted first to send somebody else in order to see how he stood with regard to his office. Everybody in the whole town knew what a wonderful power the cloth had, and all were curious to see how incompetent or stupid their neighbors were.

"I will send my old and honored minister to the weavers," said the Emperor. "He can judge best what the cloth is like, for he has great intellect and no one understands his office better than he."

Now the good old minister went into the hall where the two men sat working at the empty looms. Dear me! thought he, opening his eyes wide, I can see nothing! But he did not say so.

Both the weavers begged him to be good enough to step closer, and asked him if the cloth were not of beautiful texture and lovely colors. They pointed to the empty loom, and the poor old minister went forward rubbing his eyes. But he could see nothing, for there was nothing to see.

"Dear, dear," he said to himself, "can I be stupid? I have never thought that, and nobody must know it! Can I be unfit for my office? No, I must certainly not say I cannot see the cloth!"

"Have you nothing to say about it?" asked one of the weavers.

"Oh, it is lovely, most lovely!" answered the old minister, looking through his spectacles. "What a texture! What colors! Yes, I will certainly tell the Emperor that it pleases me very much."

"We are delighted to hear that," said both the weavers, and thereupon they named the colors and explained the making of the pattern. The old minister paid great attention so he could tell it all to the Emperor when he went back to him, which he did.

The deceitful pair now wanted more money, more silk and more gold thread to use in their weaving. They put it in their own pockets and went on as they had before, working at the empty looms. The Emperor soon sent another worthy old statesman to see how the weaving was progressing and whether the cloth would soon be finished. It was the same with this gentleman as with the other old minister; he looked and looked, but because there was nothing on the looms he could see nothing.

"Is it not a beautiful piece of cloth?" asked the two men, as they described the splendid material which was not there.

Stupid I am not, thought the man, so it must be that I am not fitted for my good office. It is strange, certainly, but no one must be allowed to notice it. And he praised the cloth which he did not see, and expressed his delight at the beautiful colors and the splendid texture.

"Yes, it is quite beautiful," he said to the Emperor.

Everybody in the town was talking of the magnificent cloth.

Now the Emperor wanted to see it himself while it

was still on the loom. With a great crowd of select followers, including the two worthy statesmen who had been there before, he went to the cunning workmen now weaving more busily than before, but without fiber or thread, of course.

"Is it not splendid!" said both the old statesmen. "See, Your Majesty, what a texture! What colors!" And they pointed to the empty looms, for they believed that the others could see the cloth quite well.

What! thought the Emperor, I can see nothing! This is indeed horrible! Am I a fool? Am I not fit to be Emperor?

"Oh, very beautiful," he said aloud. "It has my gracious approval." And he nodded pleasantly and examined the empty looms, for he would not say he could see nothing.

His whole court around him looked and looked and saw no more than the others, but they said like the Emperor, "Oh, it is beautiful!" And they advised him to wear the new and magnificent clothes to be made of it for the first time at the great procession which was soon to take place. "Splendid! Lovely! Most beautiful!" went from mouth to mouth.

Everyone seemed delighted, and the Emperor gave the two impostors the title of Court Weavers to the Emperor.

Throughout the night before the procession was to take place, the weavers were up and working by the

light of more than sixteen candles. People could see that they were very busy finishing the Emperor's new clothes. They pretended they were taking the cloth from the loom, jabbed the air with huge scissors and sewed with needles without thread. At last they said, "Now the clothes are finished!"

The Emperor came himself with his most distinguished courtiers, and each weaver lifted up his arms as if he were holding something, and said, "See, here are the breeches! Here is the coat! Here is the cloak!" and so on. "These clothes are so comfortable that one would imagine one had nothing on at all. But that is the beauty of it!"

"Yes," said all the courtiers, but they could see nothing, for there was nothing there.

"Will it please Your Majesty to take off your clothes," said the weavers, "then we will dress you in the new clothes, here before the mirror."

The Emperor removed his clothes, and the weavers placed themselves before him as if they were putting on each part of his new clothing which was ready, and the Emperor turned and examined himself in front of the mirror. "How beautifully they fit! How well they are made!" said everybody. "What material! What colors! Such a gorgeous suit!"

"They are waiting outside with the canopy which is held over Your Majesty in the processions," announced the Master of Ceremonies.

"Look, I am ready," said the Emperor. "Doesn't it fit well!" And he turned again to the mirror to see if his finery was on properly.

The courtiers groped on the floor as if they were lifting up the train. Then they pretended that they were holding something in the air. They would not have it said that they could see nothing.

So the Emperor went along in the procession under the splendid canopy, and all the people in the streets and at the windows said, "How gorgeous are the Emperor's new clothes! The train fastened to his dress, how beautifully it hangs!"

No one wished to admit that he could see nothing, for then he would have been unfit for his office or else a fool. Never before had the Emperor's clothes met with such approval as had these.

"But he has nothing on!" said a little child.

"Just listen to the innocent child!" said the father, and each one whispered to his neighbor what the child had said.

"But he has nothing on!" the whole town shouted at last.

The Emperor could not help but hear, and he began to realize that the people were right. But I must go on with the procession now, he thought. And the courtiers walked along still more uprightly, holding up the train which was not there at all.

HANS CHRISTIAN ANDERSEN, ANDREW LANG COLLECTION

BILLY BEG AND HIS BULL

ONCE UPON a time there was in Ireland a King and Queen, and they had one son, Billy Beg. The Queen gave Billy a Bull that he was very fond of, and it was just as fond of him.

After some time the Queen died, and she put it as her last request to the King that he never part Billy and the Bull; and the King promised that, come what might, come what may, he would not. After his wife died, the King married again, and the new Queen didn't take to Billy Beg, and no more did she like the Bull, seeing himself and Billy so thick. But she couldn't get the King on any account to part Billy and the Bull, so she consulted with a hen-wife—a woman who raises chickens—to see what they could do about separating the two.

"What will you give me," says the hen-wife, "and I'll very soon part them?"

"Whatever you ask," says the Queen.

"Well and good then," says the hen-wife. "You are to take to your bed, making pretend that you are sick with a complaint, and I'll do the rest of it."

And, well and good, to her bed she took, and none of the doctors could do anything for her or make out what was her complaint. So the Queen asked for the hen-wife to be sent for. And sent for she was, and when she came in and examined the sick Queen, she said there was one thing, and one thing only, which could cure her.

The King asked what was that, and the hen-wife said it was three mouthfuls of the blood of Billy Beg's Bull. But the King would on no account hear of this, and the next day the Queen was worse, and the third day she was worse still and told the King she was dying and he'd have her death on his head. So, rather than that, the King had to consent to Billy Beg's Bull being killed.

When Billy heard this, he got very down in the heart and he went doithering about, and the Bull saw him and asked what was wrong that he was so mournful. So Billy told the Bull what was wrong with him, and the Bull told him to never mind but to keep up his heart, for the Queen would never taste a drop of his blood.

The next day, then, the Bull was to be killed, and the Queen got up and went out to have the delight of seeing his death. But as the Bull was being led up, says he to Billy, "Jump up on my back till we see what kind of a horseman you are."

Up Billy jumped on his back, and with that the Bull

leaped nine miles high, nine miles deep and nine miles broad and came down to earth with Billy sticking between his horns.

Hundreds were looking on, dazed at the sight, and through them the Bull rushed and over the top of the Queen, killing her dead, and away he galloped to where you wouldn't know day from night or night from day, over high hills, low hills, sheepwalks and ox trails, the Cove of Cork and old Tom Fox with his bugle horn.

When at last they stopped, the Bull says to Billy, "Put your hand in my left ear, and you'll get a napkin that, when you spread it out, will be covered with eats and drinks of all sorts, fit for the King himself."

Billy did this and, when he spread out the napkin, ate and drank to his heart's content. When he was finished, he rolled up the napkin and put it back into the Bull's ear.

"Now," says the Bull, "put your hand into my right ear and you'll find a bit of a stick. If you wind it over your head three times it will be turned into a sword and give you the strength of a thousand men besides your own, and when you have no more need of it as a sword, it will change back into a stick again."

Billy did all this, and the Bull said, "At twelve o'clock tomorrow I'll have to meet and fight a great bull."

Billy then got up again on the Bull's back, and they

started off and away to where you wouldn't know day from night or night from day, over high hills, low hills, sheepwalks and ox trails, the Cove of Cork and old Tom Fox with his bugle horn.

There, Billy's Bull met the other bull, and both of them fought, and the like of their fight was never seen before or since. They knocked the soft ground into hard and the hard into soft, the soft into spring-wells, the spring-wells into rocks and the rocks into high hills. They fought long, and Billy Beg's Bull killed the other and drank his blood.

After the fight, Billy took the napkin out of the Bull's ear again and spread it out and ate a hearty good dinner.

Then says the Bull to Billy, says he, "At twelve o'clock tomorrow, I'm to meet the brother of the bull that I killed today, and we'll have a hard fight."

Billy got up on the Bull's back again, and the Bull started off and away to where you wouldn't know day from night or night from day, over high hills, low hills, sheepwalks and ox trails, the Cove of Cork and old Tom Fox with his bugle horn.

There he met the brother of the bull that he killed the day before, and they set to and they fought, and the like of the fight was never seen before or since. They knocked the soft ground into hard, the hard into soft, the soft into spring-wells, the spring-wells into rocks and the rocks into high hills. They fought long, and at last Billy's Bull killed the other and drank his blood.

And then Billy took the napkin out of the Bull's ear once again and spread it out and ate another good, hearty dinner.

Then says the Bull to Billy, says he, "At twelve o'clock tomorrow I'm to fight the brother of the two bulls I killed—he's a mighty, great bull, the strongest of them all. He's called the Black Bull of the Forest, and he'll be a match for me. When I'm dead," says the Bull, "you, Billy, will take with you the napkin, and you'll never be hungry; and the stick, and you'll be able to overcome everything that comes in your way; and take out your knife and cut a strip of the hide off my back and make a belt of it, and as long as you wear it you cannot be killed."

Billy was very sorry to hear this, but he got up on the Bull's back again, and they started off and away to where you wouldn't know day from night or night from day, over high hills, low hills, sheepwalks and ox trails, the Cove of Cork and old Tom Fox with his bugle horn.

And sure enough, at twelve o'clock the next day they met the great Black Bull of the Forest, and both of the bulls commenced to fight, and the like of the fight was never seen before or since. They knocked the soft ground into hard ground, and the hard ground into soft, and the soft into spring-wells, and spring-wells

into rocks, and the rocks into high hills. And they fought long, but at length the Black Bull of the Forest killed Billy Beg's Bull and drank his blood.

Billy Beg was so vexed at this that for two days he sat over his Bull, neither eating nor drinking but crying salt tears all the time.

Then he got up, and he spread out the napkin and ate a hearty dinner, for he was very hungry from his long fast. After that, he cut a strip of the hide off the Bull's back and made a belt for himself and, taking it, the bit of stick and the napkin, he set out to seek his fortune.

He traveled for three days and three nights till at last he came to a great gentleman's place.

Billy asked the gentleman if he could give him employment, and the gentleman said he wanted just such a boy for herding cattle. Billy asked what cattle would he have to herd and what wages would he get. The gentleman said that he had three goats, three cows, three horses and three donkeys that he fed in an orchard, but no boy who went with them ever came back alive, for there were three giants—brothers—who came to milk the cows and goats every day and always killed the boy who was herding. If Billy wanted to try, they wouldn't fix the wages till they'd seen if he came back alive.

"Agreed, then," said Billy. So the next morning he got up and drove out the three goats, the three cows, the three horses and the three donkeys to the orchard, and commenced to feed them.

About the middle of the day, Billy heard three terrible roars that shook the apples off the trees, shook the horns on the cows and made the hair stand up on Billy's head, and in comes a frightful big giant with three heads who begins to threaten Billy.

"You're too big for one bite," says the giant, "and too small for two. What will I do with you?"

"I'll fight you," says Billy, says he, stepping out to him and swinging the bit of stick three times over his head; whereupon it changed into a sword and gave him the strength of a thousand men besides his own, and he up and killed the giant.

When it was evening, Billy drove home the three goats, three cows, three horses and three donkeys, and all the vessels in the house weren't able to hold all the milk the cows gave that night.

"Well," says the gentleman, "this beats me, for I never saw anyone come back alive out of there before, nor the cows with a drop of milk. Did you see anything in the orchard?" says he.

"Nothing worse than myself," says Billy. "What about my wages now?"

"Well," says the gentleman, "you'll hardly come out of the orchard alive tomorrow. So we'll wait till after that."

Next morning his master told Billy that something

must have happened to one of the giants, for he used to hear the cries of three every night, but the night before he had heard only two crying.

That morning after breakfast, Billy drove the three goats, three cows, three horses and three donkeys into the orchard again and began to feed them. About twelve o'clock he heard three terrible roars that shook the apples off the trees, shook the horns on the cows and made the hair stand up on Billy's head, and in comes a frightful big giant with six heads, and he accuses Billy of killing his brother.

"You're too big for one bite," says he, "and too small for two. What will I do with you?"

"I'll fight you," says Billy, swinging his stick three times over his head and turning it into the sword which gave him the strength of a thousand men besides his own, and he up and killed the giant.

When it was evening, Billy drove home the three goats, three cows, three horses and three donkeys, and what milk the cows gave that night overflowed all the vessels in the house and, running out, turned a rusty wheel in a mill that hadn't been turned for more than thirty years.

If the master was surprised at seeing Billy come back the night before, he was ten times more surprised at seeing him now.

"Did you see anything in the orchard today?" says the gentleman.

"Nothing worse than myself," says Billy. "What about my wages now?"

"Never mind about your wages," says the gentleman, "till tomorrow, for I think you'll hardly come back alive again," says he.

Well and good. Billy went to his bed, and, when the gentleman rose in the morning, says he to Billy, "I don't know what's wrong with two of the giants; I heard only one crying last night."

When Billy had had his breakfast that day, he set out to the orchard, driving before him the three goats, three cows, three horses and three donkeys; and sure enough about the middle of the day he hears three terrible roars, and then in comes the last giant, this one with twelve heads on him; and if the other two giants were frightful, surely this one was ten times more so.

"You villain, you," says he to Billy, "you've killed my two brothers, and I'll have my revenge on you now. You're too big for one bite and too small for two. What will I do with you?"

"I'll fight you," says Billy and, waving the bit of stick three times over his head, he up and killed the third giant.

That evening he drove home the three goats, three cows, three horses and three donkeys, and the milk of the cows had to be turned into a valley, where it made a lake three miles long, three miles broad and three miles deep, and that lake has been filled with salmon and white trout ever since.

The gentleman wondered now more than ever at seeing Billy back the third day alive. "You saw nothing in the orchard today, Billy?" says he.

"No, nothing worse than myself," says Billy.

"Well, you're a good, mindful boy and I couldn't do easy without you," says the gentleman. "I'll give you any wages you ask for in the future."

The next morning, says the gentleman to Billy, "I heard none of the giants crying last night. I don't know what has happened to them."

"I don't know," says Billy, "they must be sick."

"Now, Billy," says the gentleman, "you must look after the cattle today again, while I go see the fight."

"What fight?" says Billy.

"It's the King's daughter is going to be devoured by a fiery dragon if the greatest fighter in the land, whom they have been feeding specially for the last three months, isn't able to kill the dragon first. And, if he's able to kill the dragon, the King is to give him his daughter in marriage."

"That will be fine," says Billy.

Billy drove out the three goats, three cows, three horses and three donkeys to the orchard that day again; and the like of the people who passed him on their way to the fight between the man and the fiery dragon Billy never witnessed before. They were in coaches and carriages, on horses and donkeys, riding and walking, crawling and creeping.

"My good little fellow," says a man that was passing to Billy, "why don't you come to see the great fight?"

"What would take the likes of me there?" says Billy.

But when Billy found them all gone, he saddled and bridled the best black horse his master had, put on the best suit of clothes he could find in his master's house and rode off to the fight after the rest.

When Billy arrived, he saw the King's daughter with the whole court about her on a platform before the castle, and he thought he had never seen anything half so beautiful. The great warrior who was to fight the dragon was walking up and down on the lawn before the Princess, with three men carrying his sword and everyone in the whole country gathered there looking at him.

But when the fiery dragon came up, with twelve heads on him, and every mouth of them spitting fire, and let twelve roars out of him, the warrior ran away and hid himself up to the neck in a well of water, and they couldn't get him to face the dragon.

Then the King's daughter asked if there was no one who could save her from the dragon and win her in marriage. And not a person stirred.

When Billy saw this, he tied the belt of the Bull's

hide around him, swung his stick over his head and, after a terrible fight, killed the dragon.

Everyone then gathered about to find out who the stranger was. Billy jumped on his horse and darted off rather than let them know, but just as he was getting away, the King's daughter pulled a shoe off his foot. The warrior who had hidden in the well of water came out and, cutting the heads off the dragon, he brought them to the King and said that it was he, in disguise, who had killed the dragon. And he claimed the King's daughter.

But the Princess tried the shoe on the warrior and found it didn't fit him, so she said that he wasn't the right man and that she would marry no one, only the one the shoe fitted.

When Billy got home, he changed his clothes and had the horse in the stable and the animals all in before his master arrived.

The master began telling Billy about the wonderful day, and about the warrior hiding in the well of water, and about the grand stranger who had come down out of the sky in a cloud, riding on a black horse, and had killed the fiery dragon and then vanished into a cloud again.

"And," says he, "Billy, wasn't that wonderful?"

"It was, indeed," says Billy, "very wonderful."

After that, it was given over the whole country that all the men were to come to the King's castle on a certain day so that the Princess could try the shoe on each one of them; and whoever it fitted she was to marry.

When the day arrived, Billy was in the orchard with the three goats, three cows, three horses and three donkeys, as usual, and the like of all the crowd that passed that day going to the King's castle to get the shoe tried on, he never saw before. They went in coaches and carriages, on horses and donkeys, riding and walking, crawling and creeping.

They asked Billy was he not going to the King's castle, but Billy said, "Arrah, what would be bringing the likes of me there?"

At last, when all the others had gone, there passed an old man with a very scarecrow suit of rags on his back, and Billy stopped him and asked if he would swap clothes.

"Just take care of yourself, now," says the old man to Billy, "and don't be playing your jokes in my clothes, or maybe I'd make you feel the weight of this stick."

But Billy soon let him see it was in earnest he was, and both of them swapped suits.

Then off to the castle started Billy, with the suit of rags on his back and an old stick in his hand, and when he got there he found all in great commotion trying on the shoe. But it was of no use—the shoe did not fit any of them.

The King's daughter was going to give up in despair, when a ragged boy, who was Billy, elbowed his way through the crowd and said, "Let me try it on; maybe it will fit me."

The people, when they saw him, began to laugh at the sight of him, and "Go along out of that," says they, shoving and pushing him back.

But the King's daughter saw him and called on them by all manner of means to let him come up and try on the shoe.

So Billy went up to the Princess, and the people looked on, almost breaking their hearts laughing at the conceit of it.

But to the dumbfounding of them, the shoe fitted Billy as nicely as if it had been made with his foot for the form. So the King's daughter claimed Billy as her husband.

He then confessed that it was he who had killed the fiery dragon; and when the King had him dressed in a silk and satin suit, with plenty of gold and silver ornaments on the front, everyone gave out that his like they never saw before.

Billy was married to the King's daughter, and the wedding lasted nine days, nine hours, nine minutes, nine half-minutes and nine quarter-minutes, and the two of them have lived happily and well from that day to this.

OLD IRISH TALE,
RETOLD BY VERONICA S. HUTCHINSON

LITTLE ONE EYE, LITTLE TWO EYES
AND LITTLE THREE EYES

HERE WAS once upon a time a one-eyed woman who had three daughters. The eldest was called Little One Eye, because she had only one eye in the middle of her forehead; the second was called Little Two Eyes, because she had two eyes like other people; and the youngest was called Little Three Eyes, because she had three eyes, and her third eye was also in the middle of her forehead.

But because Little Two Eyes did not look any different from other children, her sisters and mother would say to her, "You, with your two eyes, are no better than common folk. You don't belong to our family." They pushed her here, threw her wretched clothes there and gave her to eat only the little that they left. They were about as unkind to her as ever they could be.

It happened one day that Little Two Eyes had to go out into the fields to take care of her goat. She was still hungry because her sisters had given her so little to eat, and she sat down in the meadow and began to cry. She

told to go along with Little Two Eyes when she drove the goat to pasture, to see whether anyone brought her food and drink.

Now when Little Two Eyes was setting out, Little One Eye came up to her and said, "I will go into the field with you and see if you take good care of the goat and if you drive him properly to get grass." But Little Two Eyes knew what Little One Eye had in her mind, and she drove the goat into the long grass and said, "Come, Little One Eye, we will sit down here and I will sing you something."

Little One Eye sat down. She was tired by the long walk to which she was not accustomed and by the hot day, and when Little Two Eyes began to sing:

> Little One Eye, are you awake?
> Little One Eye, are you asleep?

she shut her one eye and fell asleep. When Little Two Eyes saw Little One Eye was asleep, she said:

> Little goat, bleat,
> Little table, appear,

and sat down at her table and ate and drank as much as she wanted. Then she said again:

> Little goat, bleat,
> Little table, away,

and in the twinkling of an eye everything had vanished.

Little Two Eyes then woke Little One Eye, and said, "Little One Eye, you meant to watch and, instead, you went to sleep. In the meantime the goat might have run far and wide. Come, we will go home." So they went home. Little Two Eyes again left her dinner untouched. Little One Eye could not tell her mother why, and said as an excuse, "The fresh air made me so tired I fell asleep."

The next day the mother said to Little Three Eyes, "This time you shall go with Little Two Eyes and watch what she does out in the fields and whether anyone brings her food or drink."

So Little Three Eyes went to Little Two Eyes and said, "I will go with you and see if you take good care of the goat and if you drive him properly to get grass."

But Little Two Eyes knew what Little Three Eyes had in mind. She drove the goat into the tall grass and said to Little Three Eyes, "Sit down here, I will sing something for you." Little Three Eyes sat down; she was tired by the walk and the hot day. And Little Two Eyes sang the same song again, but instead of singing as she should have:

> Little Three Eyes, are you asleep?

she sang, without thinking:

> Little Two Eyes, are you asleep?

And she went on singing it.

The two eyes of Little Three Eyes fell asleep, but the third, which was not spoken to in the little rhyme, did not fall asleep. Of course Little Three Eyes shut that eye also, to make it seem as if she really was asleep, but her third eye kept blinking and could see everything quite well.

When Little Two Eyes thought Little Three Eyes was sound asleep, she said her rhyme:

> Little goat, bleat,
> Little table, appear,

and ate and drank to her heart's content. Then she made the table go away again by saying:

> Little goat, bleat,
> Little table, away.

But Little Three Eyes had seen everything. Then Little Two Eyes came to her, woke her and said, "Well, Little Three Eyes, have you been asleep? You watch well! Come, we will go home."

When they reached home, Little Two Eyes did not eat again, and Little Three Eyes said to their mother, "I know now why that proud thing eats nothing. When she says to the goat in the field:

> Little goat, bleat,
> Little table, appear,

a table stands before her, spread with food much better

than what we have. When she has had enough, she says:

Little goat, bleat,
Little table, away,

and everything disappears. I saw it all. She made two of my eyes go to sleep with a little rhyme, but the one in my forehead remained awake, luckily!"

Then the envious mother cried out to Little Two Eyes, "Will you fare better than we do? You shall not have the chance to do so again!" She fetched a knife and killed the goat.

When Little Two Eyes saw what her mother had done, she went out full of grief and sat down in the meadow weeping bitter tears. Again the wise woman stood before her and said, "Little Two Eyes, why are you crying?"

"Have I not reason to cry?" she answered. "My mother has killed the goat which spread the table so beautifully before me when I said the rhyme. Now I must suffer hunger again."

The wise woman said, "Little Two Eyes, I will give you a good piece of advice. Ask your sisters to give you the heart of the dead goat. Bury it in the earth before the house door. That will bring you good luck."

Then she disappeared, and Little Two Eyes went back home and said to her sisters, "Dear sisters, do give me something of my goat. I ask nothing more than its heart."

They laughed and said, "You may have that if you want nothing more."

Little Two Eyes took the heart and in the evening, when all was quiet, buried it before the house door as the wise woman had told her. The next morning, when they all awoke, there stood a most wonderful tree, which had leaves of silver and fruit of gold growing on it—more lovely and gorgeous than anything they had ever seen in their lives.

But only Little Two Eyes knew that the marvelous gold and silver tree had sprung from the heart of the goat, for it was standing just where she had buried it in the ground.

Then the mother said to Little One Eye, "Climb up, my child, and break us off some fruit from the tree." Little One Eye climbed up, but just when she was going to take hold of one of the golden apples, the bough sprang out of her hands. And this happened every time, so she could not break off a single apple, however hard she tried.

Then the mother said, "Little Three Eyes, do you climb up. With your three eyes you can see much better than Little One Eye." So Little One Eye slid down, and Little Three Eyes climbed up. She was no more successful than her sister. Try as she might, the branches of golden apples sprang out of her hands. And at last the mother grew impatient and climbed up herself, but she was even less successful than Little

One Eye and Little Three Eyes in catching hold of the fruit and only grasped at the empty air.

Then Little Two Eyes said, "I will try just once; perhaps I shall do better."

The sisters called out, "You with your two eyes will no doubt succeed!"

Little Two Eyes climbed up, and the golden apples did not jump away from her. They behaved properly so that she could pluck them off, one after the other, and brought a whole apronful down with her. The mother took them from her. But instead of treating poor Little Two Eyes better, as they should have, they were jealous that only she could reach the fruit and were still more unkind.

One day, when the three were standing together by the tree, a young knight came riding along. "Be quick, Little Two Eyes," cried the two sisters. "Creep under this so you shall not disgrace us."

They put poor Little Two Eyes beneath an empty cask and pushed under with her the golden apples which she had plucked.

When the knight, who was a very handsome young man, rode up, he was amazed to see the marvelous tree of gold and silver and said to the two sisters, "Whose is this beautiful tree? Whoever will give me a twig of it shall have whatever she wants." Then Little One Eye and Little Three Eyes answered that the tree belonged to them and they would certainly break off a twig for him. They went to a great deal of trouble, but in vain. The twigs and fruit bent away from their hands every time.

Then the knight said, "It is very strange that the tree should belong to you and yet you cannot break anything from it!"

But they insisted the tree was theirs. While they were saying this, Little Two Eyes rolled a couple of golden apples from under the cask so they lay at the knight's feet. She was angry with Little One Eye and Little Three Eyes for not speaking the truth.

When the knight saw the apples he was astonished and asked where they had come from.

Little One Eye and Little Three Eyes answered that they had another sister, but she had been hidden away and could not be seen because she had only two eyes, like ordinary people.

But the knight demanded to see her and called out, "Little Two Eyes, come forth."

Little Two Eyes came out quite happily from beneath the cask.

The knight was astonished at her great beauty and said, "Little Two Eyes, I am sure you can break off a twig for me from the tree."

"Yes," answered Little Two Eyes, "I can, for the tree is mine."

So she climbed up and broke off a small branch with its silver leaves and golden fruit without any trouble at all and, leaning forward, she gave it to the knight.

Then he said, "Little Two Eyes, what shall I give you for this?"

"Ah," answered Little Two Eyes, "I suffer hunger and thirst, neglect and sorrow, from early morning till late in the evening. If you would take me with you and free me from this, I should be happy!"

Then the knight lifted Little Two Eyes onto his horse and took her home to his father's castle. There he gave her beautiful clothes and food and drink, and because he loved her so much he married her.

When the handsome knight carried Little Two Eyes away with him, the two sisters at first envied her good luck. "But the wonderful tree is still with us, after all," they said. "Although we cannot break any fruit from it, everyone will stop and look at it and will come to us and praise it. Who knows whether we may not reap a harvest from it?"

But next morning the tree had vanished and their hopes were gone. When Little Two Eyes looked out of her window there the tree stood, to her great delight.

Once two poor women came to the castle to beg alms. Little Two Eyes looked at them and recognized both her sisters, who had become so poor they had to beg bread at her door. But Little Two Eyes bade them welcome and was so good to them they both repented of having been so unkind to their sister.

JAKOB AND WILHELM GRIMM, TRANSLATED BY MAY SELLAR

THE RED SHOES

THERE WAS once a little girl, a dainty and pretty little girl, but because she was very poor she always went barefoot in summer, and in winter wore heavy wooden shoes which made her insteps very red, dreadfully red.

In the heart of the village lived an old shoemaker's widow. She sewed a pair of shoes as well as she possibly could out of strips of old red cloth. They were rather clumsy, but she meant well, and she wanted them to be a present for the little girl. The little girl's name was Karen.

On the very day her mother was buried, Karen was given the red shoes and wore them for the first time. They were not really suitable for mourning, but as she had no others she walked in them, bare-legged, behind the poor pine coffin.

Suddenly a large old carriage drove up with a large old lady in it. She looked at the little girl and, feeling very sorry for her, she said to the parson, "Let me take the little girl and I'll look after her."

Karen thought that it was all because of the red

shoes, but the old lady said they were hideous and had them burned. However, she gave her some neat new clothes and had her taught to read and sew. People said she was pretty, but her mirror said, "You are more than pretty, you are lovely."

Now the Queen happened to travel through the country, and she had her little daughter with her—naturally she was a princess. People soon flocked to the palace to see them, and Karen was among the crowd. The little Princess stood at the window in a snow-white dress to let herself be admired. She was wearing neither a train nor a golden crown, but she had on a pair of beautiful red morocco shoes. Of course they were far nicer than the ones the shoemaker's widow had made for little Karen. There could be nothing in the world like a pair of red shoes!

When Karen was old enough to be confirmed, she had new clothes and was to have new shoes as well. The fashionable shoemaker in town took the measure of her little feet. He fitted her in his own house, where lovely shoes and shiny leather boots were arranged in great glass cases. The display was very attractive, but it gave no pleasure to the old lady, whose eyesight was rather weak. Among all the shoes was a pair of red leather ones exactly like those the little Princess had worn. How beautiful they were! In fact, the shoemaker said that they had been made for a nobleman's daughter but they had not fitted very well.

"I suppose they are patent leather, they're so shiny," said the old lady.

"Yes, they are shiny," said Karen. The shoes fitted her and they were bought, but the old lady did not know they were red, or she would never have allowed Karen to wear them for her confirmation. However, that's what happened.

Everybody looked at Karen's feet when she walked up the aisle of the church toward the chancel. It seemed to her as if those old pictures on the wall, those portraits of clergymen and their wives with ruffs and long black garments, fixed their eyes upon her red shoes. She thought of nothing else when the rector laid his hand upon her head and spoke to her of Holy Baptism, the Covenant with God, and told her that she was now a grown-up Christian.

The organ played a solemn melody, the children sang with their lovely voices, and the old choirmaster sang, but Karen could think of nothing but her new red shoes.

By the afternoon everybody had informed the old lady that Karen had worn red shoes, so she told Karen that it was very naughty of her and not at all the proper thing to do, and that thereafter whenever she went to church she must wear black shoes, even if they were her oldest pair.

The following Sunday there was Holy Communion, and Karen looked at the black shoes and she looked at the red ones—she looked at the red ones again, and finally put them on.

It was beautiful sunny weather. Karen and the old lady followed the dusty path through the cornfield. At the church door stood an old soldier with a crutch and a funny long beard that was more red than white; in fact, it was practically red. He bowed right down to the ground and asked the old lady if he might dust her shoes. Karen also put out her little foot. "My, what beautiful dancing shoes!" said the soldier. "Stick on tightly when you dance!" and he slapped the soles with his hand.

The old lady gave the soldier a penny and went into the church with Karen.

Everyone stared at Karen's red shoes, and all the portraits stared, and when Karen knelt at the altar and put her lips to the gold chalice, she thought only of the red shoes—it seemed to her as if they were floating before her eyes. She forgot to sing the hymn and she forgot to say the Lord's Prayer.

Then everyone left the church, and the old lady got into her carriage. Karen was about to step in after her when the old soldier said, "Look at the pretty dancing shoes!" And Karen could not keep her feet still. She just could not resist dancing a few steps, and when once she had begun, her feet continued to dance—it was as if the shoes had gained control over them. She danced around the corner of the church—she could not help herself. The coachman had to run after the girl, take hold of her and lift her into the carriage, but her dancing feet kicked the nice old lady violently. Finally they took her shoes off and her legs were still.

At home the shoes were put away in a cupboard, but Karen could not resist looking at them now and then.

Soon after this, the old lady lay ill and the doctors said that she could not live. She needed constant attention and careful nursing, and this was naturally Karen's duty. But a big ball was being given in town and Karen was invited. The little girl looked at the old lady, who in any case could not live, and then she looked at the red shoes—for she thought there could be no sin in doing that—and she put on the red shoes, thinking there was no sin in doing that, either. Then she went off to the ball and started dancing.

When she wanted to turn to the right, the shoes danced to the left; when she wanted to dance up to one end of the room, the shoes danced down to the other; they danced down the stairs, through the streets and out of the town gate. Dance she did, and dance she must, straight out into the dark forest.

She saw something shining between the trees, and because of its face she thought it was the moon, but it was the old soldier with the red beard, who nodded to her and said, "Look at the pretty dancing shoes!"

Filled with terror, Karen tried to kick off the red shoes, but they stuck to her feet. She tore off her stockings, but the shoes had grown fast to her feet, and so dance she did, and dance she must, over field and meadow, in rain and sunshine, by day and by night. It was most horrible at night. She danced through the gate of the churchyard, but the dead did not dance in there; they had something far more sensible to do. She tried to sit down on the grave of a pauper where bitter tansy grew, but for Karen there was neither rest nor peace, and as she danced toward the open church door, she saw an angel standing there with long white robes and white wings reaching from his shoulders right to the ground; his face was grave and severe, and in his hand he held a broad and shining sword.

"Dance thou shalt!" he said. "Dance in thy red shoes till thou art pale and cold, till thy body shrivels to a skeleton! Dance from door to door, and wherever proud, conceited children live, thou shalt knock at the door till they hear thee and fear thee! Dance, I command thee, dance!"

"Have mercy!" shrieked Karen. But she did not hear what the angel answered, for the shoes carried her through the gate, into the fields, along the highway and byway, dancing, ever and ever dancing.

One morning she danced past a door she knew well. Inside, a hymn was being sung and a coffin was carried out covered with flowers. Then she realized that the old lady was dead, and she felt that she herself was forsaken by all and accursed by the angel of God.

Dance she did, and dance she must, dance through the dark night. The shoes carried her on over stump and thorn; she was scratched till she bled; she danced across the heath to a lonely little house. She knew that the executioner lived there, and she tapped with her finger on the windowpane and cried, "Come out! Come out! I can't come in, for I'm dancing!"

And the executioner said, "You don't seem to know who I am. I chop off the heads of wicked people, and I can feel my axe beginning to quiver."

"Don't chop off my head," said Karen, "for then I can never repent of my sin, but chop off my feet with the red shoes on!"

Then she confessed her sin, and the executioner chopped off her feet with the red shoes on, and the shoes danced away with the little feet still in them over the fields into the depths of the forest.

Then he made her a pair of crutches and taught her a hymn—the one that penitents always sing. She kissed the hand which had wielded the axe, and went away across the heath.

"I have suffered enough because of the red shoes," she said. "Now I will go to church and show myself to everyone." And she went quickly to the church door, but when she arrived there the red shoes were dancing in front of her so that she became very frightened and turned back.

The whole week through she was very sad and shed

See page 58

61

many bitter tears, but when Sunday came she said, "There, now, I have suffered and struggled long enough. I think I am just as good as many of the people who sit in church and hold their heads high." She set forth confidently, but no sooner did she reach the churchyard gate than she saw the red shoes dancing in front of her again, and she was terrified. She turned back, away from the church, and repented of her sin with all her heart.

Then she went to the rectory and begged to be taken into service there. She would be hardworking and do all she could—the wages were not important if only she might have a roof over her head and be with good people. The rector's wife felt sorry for Karen and took her into her service. Karen was serious and industrious. She sat quietly and listened in the evening when the rector read aloud from the Bible. The little children were very fond of her, but when they spoke of frills and finery and of being as beautiful as a queen, she would shake her head.

The following Sunday when they went to church they asked her to go with them, but with tears in her eyes she looked sadly at her crutches. The others went to hear the Word of God. Left alone, she went into her tiny room. It was just big enough for a bed and a chair. She sat down with her hymnbook in her hand, and while she was reading it devoutly, the wind carried the organ notes from the church straight into her room.

She raised her face, all wet with tears, and said, "Lord, help me!"

Then the sun shone brightly, and the angel of God in white robes, the same one whom she had seen that other night at the church door, stood before her. Instead of the sharp sword, he held a beautiful green branch covered with roses. He touched the ceiling with it, raising it high up, and a golden star appeared; then he touched the walls and they opened wide. She saw the organ, she saw the old pictures of the clergymen and their wives and she saw the congregation seated in their flower-decorated pews, singing from their hymnbooks. For the church itself had come to the poor girl in her narrow little room, or was it she who had been brought to the church? She sat in the pew with the people from the rectory, and when they had sung the hymn, they looked up and nodded to her, saying, "It was right of you to come, Karen."

"It was by God's mercy that I came," she said.

The music of the organ pealed forth, and the voices of the children's choir rang out in mellow and lovely tones. The bright rays of the sun streamed warmly through the window to the pew where Karen sat. Her heart was so filled with the sunshine of peace and joy that it broke, and the sunbeams carried her soul to Heaven. And no one there questioned her about the red shoes.

HANS CHRISTIAN ANDERSEN, TRANSLATED BY PAUL LEYSSAC

THERE WERE once upon a time five-and-twenty tin soldiers—all brothers, for they were made out of the same old tin spoon. Their uniforms were red and yellow; they shouldered arms and looked straight ahead. The first words they heard in this world, when the lid was taken off their box, were, "Hurrah! Tin soldiers!" This was shouted by a little boy as he clapped his hands. They had been given to him because it was his birthday, and he began setting them out on the table. Each soldier was exactly like the next, except one, who had been made last when the tin was running short. There he stood as firmly on his one leg as the rest did on two and he is the one who became famous.

There were many other playthings on the table. But the nicest of all was a pretty little castle made of cardboard, with windows through which one could see into the room. In front of the castle stood some little trees surrounding a tiny mirror which looked like a lake. Wax swans were floating about, and were reflected in the glass. That was all very pretty, but the prettiest was a little lady who stood in the open doorway of the castle. She, too, was cut out of paper, but she had on a dress of the finest gauze, with a scarf of narrow blue ribbon around her shoulders. The ribbon scarf was fastened in the middle by a glittering paper rose almost as large as her head. The lady had both her arms outstretched, for she was a dancer, and one leg was raised so high behind her that the tin soldier couldn't see it and he thought that she, too, had only one leg.

That's the wife for me! he thought; but she is so grand and lives in a castle, while I have only a box with four-and-twenty others. This is no place for her! But I must make her acquaintance. Then he stationed himself next to a snuffbox on the table. From there he could watch the dainty lady, who continued to stand on one leg without losing her balance.

When night came all the other tin soldiers were put into their box, and the people of the house went to bed. Then the toys began to play at visiting, dancing and fighting. The tin soldiers rattled in their box, for they wanted to be out, too, but they could not raise the lid. The nutcrackers played at leapfrog and the slate pencil ran about the slate. There was so much noise that the canary woke up and began to talk to them—in poetry, if you please! The only two who did not stir from their places were the tin soldier and the little dancer. She remained on tiptoe, with both arms outstretched. He stood steadfastly on his one leg, never moving his eyes from her face.

The clock struck twelve, and crack! Off flew the lid of the snuffbox. But there was no snuff inside, only a little black imp—that was the charm of it. "Hello, tin soldier!" said the imp. "Don't look at things that aren't intended for the likes of you!"

But the tin soldier took no notice and seemed not to hear him.

"Very well, very well! Wait till tomorrow!" said the imp, peevishly.

When it was morning and the children were up, the tin soldier was put on the windowsill. Whether it was the wind or the little black imp, I don't know, but all at once the window flew open and out fell the little soldier, head over heels, from the third story window! That was a terrible fall, I can tell you! He landed on his head with his leg in the air, his gun wedged between two paving stones.

The nursery maid and the little boy rushed down to look for him but, though they were so near they almost stepped on him, they did not see him. If the tin soldier had only shouted, "Here I am!" they would certainly have found him, but he did not think it right to shout, when he was in uniform.

Then it began to drizzle. Soon the drops came faster, and there was a regular downpour. When it was over, two little boys came along.

"Just look!" cried one. "Here is a tin soldier! Let's send him sailing."

So they made a little boat out of newspaper, put the tin soldier in it and made him sail up and down the gutter. Both the boys ran along beside him, clapping their hands. What great waves there were in the gutter and what a swift current! The paper boat tossed up and down, and in the middle of the stream it went so fast that the tin soldier trembled. But he remained steadfast, showing no emotion and looking straight in front of him, shouldering his gun. Suddenly the boat passed into a long tunnel that was as dark as his box had been. "Where can I be now?" he wondered. "Oh, dear! This is the black imp's fault! Ah, if only the little lady were sitting beside me in the boat, it could be twice as dark for all I'd care!"

Then there came along a great water rat that lived in the tunnel.

"Where's your passport?" asked the rat. "Out with your passport!"

But the tin soldier was silent and grasped his gun more firmly. The boat sped on and the rat behind it. Ugh! How he gnashed his teeth as he cried to chips of wood and straw: "Catch him, catch him! He hasn't paid the toll! He hasn't shown his passport!"

The current became swifter and stronger. The tin soldier could already see daylight where the tunnel ended. In his ears there sounded a roaring enough to frighten any brave man. Just imagine! At the end of the tunnel the gutter emptied into a great canal that was just as dangerous for him as it would be for us to go down a waterfall.

It came nearer and nearer; on went the boat, the poor tin soldier keeping himself as stiff as he could. No one could say of him afterwards that he had flinched. The boat whirled three, four times and became filled to the brim with water. It began to sink! The tin soldier was standing up to his neck in water. Deeper and deeper sank the boat. Softer and softer grew the paper. Now the water was over his head. He was thinking of the pretty little dancer, whose face he would never see again, and there sounded in his ears, over and over:

> Forward, forward, soldier bold,
> Death's before thee, grim and cold!

The paper came apart, and the soldier fell right through—but at that moment he was swallowed by a great fish! Inside it was even darker than in the tunnel. It was really very close quarters! But the steadfast little tin soldier lay full length, shouldering his gun.

Up and down swam the fish, then it made the most dreadful contortions and suddenly became quite still. It was as if lightning had passed through it; the daylight streamed in and a voice exclaimed, "Why, here is the little tin soldier!" The fish had been caught and taken to market, then sold and brought into the kitchen,

See page 66

69

where the cook had cut it open with a great knife.

She picked up the soldier between her fingers and carried him into the room, where everyone wanted to see the hero who had been found inside a fish. The tin soldier was not at all proud. They put him on the table and—what strange things do happen in this world—the tin soldier was in the same room in which he had been before! He saw the same children and the same toys on the table. There was the same grand castle with the pretty little dancer. She was still standing on one leg with the other high behind her. She too was steadfast. That touched the tin soldier. He was nearly ready to shed tin tears, and that would not have been fitting for a soldier. He looked at her, but she said nothing.

Suddenly one of the little boys picked up the tin soldier and, for no reason, threw him into the stove. Doubtless the little black imp in the snuffbox was at the bottom of that, too.

There the tin soldier lay and felt a truly terrible heat. Whether he was suffering from real fire or from love he did not know. All his color had disappeared. Whether this had happened on his travels or whether it was the result of trouble, who can say? He looked at the little lady, she looked at him, and he felt that he was melting. He remained steadfast with his gun at his shoulder.

Then a door opened, the draft caught up the little dancer, and off she flew like a sylph to the tin soldier in the stove, burst into flames—and that was the end of her! The tin soldier melted down into a small lump, and next morning when the maid was taking out the ashes, she found him in the shape of a heart. There was nothing left of the little dancer but her gilt rose, burned as black as a cinder.

HANS CHRISTIAN ANDERSEN, ANDREW LANG COLLECTION

SNEGOURKA, THE SNOW MAIDEN

ONCE UPON a time a peasant named Ivan had a wife called Marousha. They had been married many years, but they had no children. This was a great sorrow to them. Their only pleasure was watching the children of their neighbors.

One winter day, when fresh white snow lay deep everywhere, Ivan and his wife watched the children playing in it, laughing loudly as they played. The children began to make a beautiful snowman, and Ivan and Marousha enjoyed seeing it grow. Suddenly Ivan said, "Wife, let us go out and make a snowman, too!"

Marousha was ready. "Why not?" she said. "We may as well amuse ourselves a little. But why should we make a big snowman? Let us make a snow child, since God has not given us a living one."

"You are right," said Ivan, and he led his wife outdoors.

There in the garden by their house they set to work to make a child of snow. They made a little body, and little hands, and little feet. When all that was done, they rolled a snowball and shaped it into a head.

"Heaven bless you!" cried a passerby.

"Thank you," replied Ivan.

"The help of Heaven is always good," said Marousha.

"What are you doing?" asked the passerby.

"We are making a snow girl," said Marousha.

On the ball of snow which stood for a head they put a nose and a chin, and they made two little holes for eyes.

Just as they finished their work—oh, wonder of wonders!—the little snow maiden moved! Ivan felt a warm breath come from her lips. He drew back and looked: the snow maiden's sparkling eyes were blue, and her lips, rosy now, curved in a lovely smile.

"What is this?" cried Ivan, making the sign of the cross.

The snow maiden bent her head and the snow fell from now golden hair, which curled about her soft round cheeks. She moved her little arms and legs in the snow as if she were a real child.

"Ivan! Ivan!" cried Marousha. "Heaven has heard our prayers." She threw herself on the child and covered her with kisses.

"Ah, Snegourka, my own dear snow maiden," she cried, and she carried her into the house.

Ivan had much to do to recover from his surprise, and Marousha became foolish with joy.

Hour by hour, Snegourka, the snow maiden, grew both in size and in beauty. Ivan and Marousha could not take their eyes away from her.

The little house, which had held such sadness, now was full of life and merriment. The neighboring children came to play with the snow maiden. They chattered with her and sang songs to her, teaching her all they knew.

The snow maiden was very clever. She observed everything and learned quickly. When she spoke, her voice was so sweet that one could have gone on listening to it forever. She was gentle, obedient and loving. In turn, everyone loved her. She played in the snow with the other children and they saw how well her little hands could model things of snow and ice.

Marousha said, "See what joy Heaven has given us after these many years."

"Heaven be thanked," replied Ivan.

At last the winter came to an end, and the spring

sun shone down and warmed the earth. The snow melted, green grass sprang up in the fields, and the lark sang high in the sky. The village girls went about singing:

> Sweet spring, how did you come to us?
> How did you come?
> Did you come on a plow, or on a harrow?

Although the other children were gay with spring, and full of song and dance, the snow maiden sat by the window looking sadder and sadder.

"What is the matter with you, my dear child?" asked Marousha, drawing her close and caressing her. "Are you not well? Why aren't you happy?"

"It is nothing, Mother," answered the snow maiden. "I am quite well."

The last snow of the winter had now melted and disappeared. Flowers bloomed in every field and garden. In the forest, the nightingale poured out its song and all the world seemed glad, except the snow maiden, who became sadder still.

She would run away from her friends and hide from the sun in dark corners, like a timid flower under the trees. She liked best to play by the water, under shady willow trees. She was happiest at night and during a storm, even a fierce hailstorm. When the hail melted and the sun broke forth again—she began to weep.

Summer came, with ripening fields, and the Feast

of St. John was soon to be celebrated. The snow maiden's friends begged her to go with them to the forest, to pick berries and flowers.

The snow maiden did not want to go, but her mother urged her, even though she, too, felt afraid.

"Go, my darling, and play. And you, children, look after her well. You know how much I love her."

In the forest the children picked wild flowers and made themselves wreaths. It was warm, and they ran about singing, each wearing a crown of flowers.

"Look at us!" they shouted. "Come play with us," they urged the snow maiden. "Follow us."

They went on, dancing and singing. Then all of a sudden they heard, behind them, a sigh.

They turned and looked. There was nothing to be seen but a fast-melting little heap of snow. The snow maiden was no longer among them.

They called and called and shouted her name, but there was no answer.

"Where can she be? She must have gone home," they said.

Back they ran to the village, but no one there had seen her either.

During the next day and the day following, everyone searched. They went through the woods and looked through every thicket, but no trace of the little snow maiden was to be found.

Ivan and Marousha felt that their hearts would

break, and for a long time Marousha cried, "Sne-gourka, my sweet snow maiden, come to me!"

Sometimes Ivan and Marousha thought they could hear the voice of their child. Perhaps, when the snow returned, she would come back to them.

TRADITIONAL RUSSIAN TALE, RETOLD BY VIRGINIA HAVILAND

THE THREE LITTLE PIGS

THERE WAS an old Sow with three little Pigs, and as she had not enough to keep them, she sent them out into the world to seek their fortune.

The first that went off met a man with a bundle of straw and said to him, "Please, man, give me that straw to build me a house."

Which the man did, and the little Pig built a house with it.

Presently along came a Wolf, who knocked at the door, and said, "Little Pig, little Pig, let me come in."

To which the Pig answered: "No, no, by the hair of my chinny chin chin."

77

The Wolf answered to that: "Then I'll huff, and I'll puff, and I'll blow your house in."

So he huffed, and he puffed, and he blew the house in, and ate up the little Pig.

The second little Pig met a man with a bundle of twigs and said, "Please, man, give me those twigs to build a house."

Which the man did, and the Pig built his house. Then along came the Wolf and said, "Little Pig, little Pig, let me come in."

"No, no, by the hair of my chinny chin chin."

"Then I'll puff, and I'll huff, and I'll blow your house in."

So he huffed, and he puffed, and he puffed, and he huffed, and at last he blew the house down, and he ate up the little Pig.

The third little Pig met a man with a load of bricks and said, "Please, man, give me those bricks to build a house with."

The man gave him the bricks, and he built his house with them. So the Wolf came, as he did to the other little Pigs, and said, "Little Pig, little Pig, let me come in."

"No, no, by the hair on my chinny chin chin."

"Then I'll huff, and I'll puff, and I'll blow your house in."

Well, he huffed, and he puffed, and he huffed, and he puffed, and he puffed; but he could not get the house down. When he found that he could not, with all his huffing and puffing and huffing, blow it down, he said, "Little Pig, I know where there is a nice patch of turnips."

"Where?" said the little Pig.

"In Mr. Smith's home field, and if you will be ready tomorrow morning I will call for you, and we will go together and get some for dinner."

"Very well," said the little Pig, "I will be ready. What time do you mean to go?"

"Oh, at six o'clock."

Well, the little Pig woke up at five and got the turnips before the Wolf came—which he did about six—and said, "Little Pig, are you ready?"

The little Pig said, "Ready! I have been and come back again, and got a nice potful for dinner."

The Wolf felt very angry at this, but thought that he would catch the little Pig somehow or other, so he said, "Little Pig, I know where there is a nice apple tree."

"Where?" said the Pig.

"Down in the big park," replied the Wolf, "and if you will not deceive me I will come for you at five o'clock tomorrow, and we will get some apples."

Well, the little Pig bustled out the next morning at four o'clock, and went off for the apples, hoping to get back before the Wolf came; but he had farther to go and had to climb the tree, so that just as he was

climbing down from it, he saw the Wolf coming, which, as you may suppose, frightened him very much.

When the Wolf came up he said, "What! Little Pig, are you here before me? Are they nice apples?"

"Yes, very," said the little Pig. "I will throw you down one." And he threw it so far that, while the Wolf had gone to pick it up, the little Pig jumped down and ran all the way home.

The next day the Wolf came again and said to the little Pig, "Little Pig, there is a fair in the town this afternoon. Will you go?"

"Oh yes," said the Pig, "I will go. What time shall you be ready?"

"At three," said the Wolf. The little Pig went off before the time, as usual, and arrived at the fair. He bought a butter churn, which he was going home with when he saw the Wolf coming. Then he could not tell what to do. He got into the churn to hide, and by so doing turned it around, and it rolled down the hill with the Pig in it, which frightened the Wolf so much that he ran home without going to the fair. He went to the little Pig's house and told him how frightened he had been by a great round thing which came down the hill past him.

Then the little Pig said, "Hah, I frightened you, did I? I had been to the fair and bought myself a butter churn, and when I saw you, I got into it and rolled down the hill."

Then the Wolf was very angry indeed and declared that he would eat up the little Pig and he would come down the chimney after him. When the little Pig saw what he was about, he hung up a pot full of water and made a blazing fire, and, just as the Wolf was coming down, took off the cover of the pot, and in fell the Wolf. So the little Pig put on the cover again in an instant, boiled the Wolf up and ate him for supper, and lived happily ever afterwards.

OLD ENGLISH TALE, RETOLD BY JOSEPH JACOBS

THE SHOEMAKER AND THE ELVES

THERE WAS once a shoemaker who, through no fault of his own, had become so poor that at last he had only enough leather left for one pair of shoes. That evening he cut out the shoes which he intended to begin upon the next morning and, since he had a good conscience, he lay down quietly, said his prayers and fell asleep.

In the morning when he had prayed as usual and

was preparing to sit down to work, he found the pair of shoes standing finished on his table. He was amazed, and could not understand it in the least.

He took the shoes in his hand to examine them more closely. They were so neatly sewn that not a stitch was out of place, and were as good as the work of a master.

Soon after, a purchaser came into the shop. He was very pleased with the shoes and paid more than the ordinary price for them, so that the shoemaker was able to buy leather for two pairs with the money.

He cut them out that evening, and the next day with fresh courage was about to go to work; but he had no need to, for when he got up, the shoes were finished, and buyers were not lacking. These gave him so much money that he was able to buy leather for four pairs of shoes.

Early next morning he found the four pairs finished, and so it went on; what he cut out at night was finished in the morning, so that he was soon again in comfortable circumstances and became a well-to-do man.

Now it happened one evening not long before Christmas, when he had cut out shoes as usual, that he said to his wife, "How would it be if we were to sit up tonight to see who it is that comes to lend us such a helping hand?"

The wife agreed, and so they lit a candle and hid themselves in the corner of the room behind the clothes which were hanging there.

At midnight came two little naked men who sat down at the shoemaker's table, took up the cut-out work and began with their tiny fingers to stitch, sew and hammer so neatly and quickly that the shoemaker could not believe his eyes. They did not stop till everything was quite finished and stood complete on the table; then they ran swiftly away.

The next day the wife said to the shoemaker, "The little men have made us rich, and we ought to show our gratitude. They run about with nothing on and must freeze with cold. Now I will make them shirts, coats and vests, and will even knit them some thick stockings, and you shall make them each a pair of shoes."

The husband agreed, and in the evening when they had everything ready they laid out the presents on the table and hid themselves to see how the little men would behave.

At midnight they came skipping in and were about to set to work. But instead of the leather already cut out they found the charming clothes. At first they were surprised, then excessively delighted. With the greatest speed they put on and smoothed down the pretty clothes, singing:

> Now we're dressed so fine and neat,
> Why cobble more for others' feet?

Then they hopped and danced about, and leaped

over chairs and tables and out of the door. From that time on, the little men came back no more, but the shoemaker fared well as long as he lived and had good luck in all his undertakings.

OLD GERMAN TALE, COLLECTION OF
KATE DOUGLAS WIGGIN AND NORA ARCHIBALD SMITH

DOCTOR KNOW-IT-ALL

ONCE THERE was a peasant and he was very poor. All he had in the world was a patch of woodland, a two-wheeled cart and a pair of oxen to pull it. From time to time he chopped down some of his trees, cut them up into logs and carted them into the village. If he was lucky enough to find a buyer for the wood, he would sell it for two dollars a load.

One day, this peasant Fish—for that was his name —took his oxcart full of wood to the village and sold it to a doctor. While Fish was standing at the open door waiting for his two dollars, a powerful smell of rich, savory food reached his nostrils. He peeped in at the door. There was the doctor's dinner laid out on the table, all steaming and ready to eat: soup and roast, juicy vegetables, a frosted cake and a dish of luscious fruit such as peasant Fish had never even laid eyes upon before.

Oh! thought the poor man. If I could only be a doctor too, and eat such heavenly dinners.

This set him thinking. After the doctor had given him his two dollars for the wood, the peasant lingered in the doorway, twirling his cap this way and that; and at last he asked whether he might not learn to be a doctor also.

"Well, and why not?" the doctor said to him. "It's easy enough."

"And how would one go about doing that, now?" asked Fish.

"First of all," said the doctor, "you must sell your two oxen and the cart. With that money you must buy some fine clothes. You must also buy a few medicine bottles, pills and capsules, salts, salves and so on. Next you must get yourself a book—one of those ABC books will do, the kind with the picture of a rooster inside. And last of all, you must get a board with the words I AM DOCTOR KNOW-IT-ALL painted on it, and you must nail it over your door."

Fish did all this. Over his door hung the newly painted sign, in his room was a shelf full of medicine bottles and on his table was the ABC book. He himself

was so fine and grand he felt like someone new. With his spectacles, his long-tailed coat, his watch and his pointed beard, he really looked as if he knew it all. He was ready to start, but day after day went by and nothing happened: there he sat among his salves and pills with not a thing to do.

At last someone came, and a lord, no less. This lord had been robbed of a big sum of money, and when he saw the sign I AM DOCTOR KNOW-IT-ALL, he said to himself, "That's just the fellow I want. If he really knows it all, he will surely know who has stolen my money."

He knocked at the door, and when Fish heard him he straightened his spectacles, gave a pull at his watch chain, put on his tall hat, but took it off again and at last opened the door.

"So you are Doctor Know-It-All," said the rich lord.

"Oh, yes," said Fish.

"I want you to find my stolen money," said the lord. "Can you come with me now to my palace?"

"Yes, indeed," said Fish. "And my wife, Gretl—may she come, too?"

"Certainly," said the lord; so they all stepped into his coach and drove off.

It was the dinner hour when they reached the lord's palace, and he invited Fish and Gretl to join him at the table. They all sat down, and when the first servant came in with a dish of soup, Fish whispered to his wife, "Look, Gretl, that is the first."

He meant that this was the first course being served, but the servant, who had overheard him, thought he meant this was the first thief who had stolen the lord's money. As he really was one of the thieves, he became worried, and when he reached the kitchen he said to his fellow servants, "Things will go ill with us, now that this Doctor Know-It-All is around here. Just think! As soon as he set eyes on me, he told his wife I was the first thief!"

The other servants gasped in alarm, and when the bell tinkled for the next course, the second servant hardly had the courage to go into the dining room. But what could he do? It was his turn to serve. He tried to look innocent as he entered with a dish of steaming food, but Fish leaned over to his wife and whispered, "See, Gretl, that's the second."

He meant this was the second course, but the servant thought that he himself was meant, and his knees knocked together as he rushed back to the kitchen.

When the third servant came in with still another dish, it was the same. Fish nudged his wife, whispering, "And that, Gretl, is the third."

The third servant, his hair standing on end, set the dish on the table and dashed into the kitchen as fast as he could. Luckily for the thieves, the lord had noticed nothing, for he had been too busy thinking up some way of putting Doctor Know-It-All to the test, and now he said, "Doctor, here is the fourth servant with a covered dish. If you really know it all, you should be able to guess what is in the dish."

Poor peasant Fish! How should he know what was in it? He looked and looked at the covered dish; and at last, seeing he was caught, he said, "Oh, you poor Fish. You're done for!"

As luck would have it, there was a fish in the dish! And the lord cried, "Well, well, Doctor, you've guessed it! Now I know you can find my stolen money."

He was in a fix, the peasant Fish, and no mistake about it. He was still racking his brains for something to say when the fourth servant, who was just leaving the room, winked meaningly at him. Fish excused himself from the table and followed the man into the kitchen. The servants, looking greatly frightened, said, "Oh, Doctor, you told your wife we were the thieves who stole my lord's money, and it's true. But we'll give it all back to him and we'll reward you besides, if you'll only promise not to tell on us."

Fish promised to keep their secret, and they showed him where the stolen money was hidden. When he returned to the dining room, he cleared his throat and stroked his beard, saying, "Hm, hm! So you want to know what's become of your money, my lord. Hm, hm! Well! I'll have to consult my book about that."

He sat down and spread the ABC book on his knees.

Then he put his spectacles on his nose and, with an important air, began to look for the picture of the rooster. Meanwhile, the servants were curious to know whether Doctor Know-It-All would really keep their secret, so the fifth servant was sent in to listen. He sneaked in on tiptoe and hid in the oven.

All this time, peasant Fish or Doctor Know-It-All—whichever you wish to call him—was still flipping pages back and forth in his ABC book, but he couldn't find the picture of the rooster. At last he lost his temper and shouted, "You rascal! I know you're in there, and I'll find you yet!"

The servant who was in hiding thought that he was the "rascal." He jumped out of the oven, yelling, "Hulla! The man knows everything!"

Doctor Know-It-All, who had found the rooster at last, looked pleased, closed his ABC book and cleared his throat again. "Hm, hm!" he said. "Yes. Well, well! And now as to your stolen money, my lord, I can show you just where it is."

He led the lord to the place where the servants had hidden the money, saying, "You see, my lord. Here it is, every penny of it."

The lord was pleased—so very pleased, in fact, that he grabbed a great handful of gold, pressed it into Fish's hands and said, "Well done, my good Doctor, and my undying thanks to you. I will spread your fame far and wide."

This he did, too; and from that time on, Fish and his good wife Gretl lived in wealth and ease, had plenty of good food to eat and rode about town in a fine carriage.

JAKOB AND WILHELM GRIMM, TRANSLATED BY WANDA GÁG

THE SIX SWANS

A KING WAS once hunting in a great wood, and he hunted the game so eagerly that none of his courtiers were able to keep up with him. When evening came on he saw that he had lost his way and was quite alone. He sought a way out of the forest, but could not find one. Then he saw an old woman with a shaking head coming toward him.

"Good woman," he said to her, "can you not show me the way out of the wood?"

"Oh, certainly, Sir King," she replied, "I can do that, but only on one condition. If you do not fulfill my request, you will never get out of the wood and will die of hunger."

"What is the condition?" asked the King.

"I have a daughter," said the old woman, "who is so beautiful that she has not her equal in the world and she is well worthy of being your wife. If you will make her Queen, I will show you how to get out of the wood."

The King, in his anguish of mind, consented, and the old woman, who was indeed a witch, led him to her little house where her daughter was sitting by the fire. She received the King as if she were expecting him, and he saw that she was certainly beautiful.

But somehow the girl did not please the King, and he could not look at her without a secret feeling of horror. As soon as he had lifted the maiden onto his horse, the old woman showed him the way. Soon the King reached his palace, and the wedding was celebrated there.

Now, the King had already been married once and had by his first wife seven children, six boys and one girl, whom he loved more than anything in the world. But because he was afraid that their new stepmother might not treat them well, he put them all in a lonely castle that stood in the middle of a wood. It lay so hidden, and the way to it was so hard to find, that he himself could not have reached it had not a wise woman given him a spool of thread which possessed a marvelous property: when he threw it before him it unwound itself and showed him the way.

But the King went so often to visit his dear children

that the Queen became annoyed with his absences. She grew more and more curious, and decided to discover what he did alone in the wood. So she gave his servants a great deal of money, and they betrayed his secret to her and also told her of the spool of thread which alone could point out the way. She did not rest till she found out where the King guarded the spool. Then she made some little white shirts and, as she had learned from her witch mother, sewed an enchantment in each of them.

And one day, when the King had ridden off, she took the little shirts and went into the wood, and the spool showed her the way. The boys, who saw someone in the distance, thought it was their dear father coming to see them and they rushed out to meet him joyfully. Then she threw a white shirt over each one, which changed them all into swans, and they flew away over the forest.

The Queen went home quite satisfied and thought she was well rid of her stepchildren. But of the King's daughter she knew nothing, because fortunately the child had not run out of the castle to meet her.

The next day the King went to visit his children and he found no one but his daughter.

"Where are your brothers?" he asked her.

"Alas, dear Father!" she answered. "They have gone away and left me all alone." And she told him that, looking out of her window, she had seen all of her brothers flying over the wood in the shape of swans.

The King mourned for his sons and, since he was afraid of losing his daughter also, he decided to take her with him. But she was afraid of the stepmother and begged the King to let her stay just one night more in the castle in the wood.

The poor girl thought: My home is no longer here. I will go and seek my brothers. And when night came she went deep into the forest. She walked all through the night and the next day, till she could go no farther for weariness.

Then she saw a hut, went in and found a room with six little beds. She crept under one of them, lay down on the hard floor and was going to spend the night there.

Just before sunset she heard a rustling sound and saw six swans flying in the window. They stood on the floor and blew all their feathers off, and then they stripped off their swan skins like shirts. Overjoyed as she recognized her brothers, the girl crept out from under the bed.

And her brothers were no less delighted to see their little sister again, but their joy did not last very long.

"You cannot stay here," they said to her. "This is a den of robbers."

"Could you not protect me?" asked the sister.

"No," they answered. "For just a quarter of an hour

after sunset do we regain our human forms. After that, we are changed into swans again."

Then the little sister cried and said, "Can you not be freed?"

"Oh, no," they said, "the conditions are too hard. You, our dear little sister, could not speak or laugh for six years and in that time must make six shirts for us out of starflowers. If a single word comes out of your mouth, all your labor would be in vain, and we would remain under the spell."

When the brothers had said this, the quarter of an hour came to an end, and they flew away through the window as swans.

The maiden determined to free her brothers even if it should cost her her life. She left the hut, went into the forest, climbed a tree and spent the night there. The next morning she came down, collected starflowers and, returning to the tree, began to sew. She could speak to no one and she had no wish to laugh, so she sat there, looking only at her work.

When she had lived there some time, it happened that the King of another country was hunting in that forest, and his hunters came to the tree in which the maiden sat. They called out to her and asked, "Who are you?"

But she gave no answer.

"Come down to us," they called, "we will do you no harm."

She shook her head silently. As they pressed her further with questions, she threw them a golden chain from her neck. But they would not leave off, and she threw them her belt, and when this was no use, her garters and then her dress. The huntsmen would still not leave her alone, but climbed the tree, lifted the maiden down and led her to the King.

The King asked, "Why are you in that tree?"

But she answered nothing.

He asked her in all the languages he knew, but she was as silent as a fish. Because she was so beautiful, however, the King's heart was touched and he was overcome with a great love for her. He wrapped her up in his cloak, placed her before him on his horse and brought her to his castle. There he had her dressed in rich clothes, but not a word could be drawn from her. He seated her by his side, and her modest ways and behavior pleased him so much that he said: "I will marry this maiden and none other in the world."

And after some days he married her. Now the King had a wicked mother who was displeased with the marriage and said terrible things of the young Queen.

"This girl is not worthy of a King," she said.

After a year, when the Queen had her first child, the old mother took it away from her. Then she told the King that the Queen had killed their baby. The King could not believe it and would not allow any harm to be done her. And his wife sat quietly sewing at the

THE WORLD'S BEST FAIRY TALES

shirts, apparently not troubling herself about anything.

The next time she had a child the wicked mother did the same thing, but the King would not believe her. He said, "She is too sweet and good to do that."

But when the third child was taken away, and his wife was again accused and could not utter a word in her own behalf, the King was obliged to give her over to the law, which decreed that she be burned to death.

When the day came on which the sentence was to be executed, it was the last day of the six years in which she could not speak or laugh. The six shirts were done, except for the left sleeve of the last. As she was being led to the stake, the Queen laid the shirts on her arm and, when she stood on the pile of sticks and the fire was about to be lighted, she looked around her and saw six swans flying through the air. Then she knew that her release was at hand and that she could free her dear brothers from enchantment. Her heart danced for joy.

The swans fluttered around her and hovered so low that she could throw the shirts over them. The swan skins fell off, and her brothers stood before her—living, well and handsome. Only the youngest had a swan's wing instead of his left arm because his shirt-sleeve had not been finished. They embraced and kissed each other, and the Queen went to the King, who was standing by in great astonishment.

"Dearest husband, now I can speak and tell you that I am innocent and have been falsely accused."

She told him of his old mother's deceit and how she had taken the three children away and hidden them. Then the children were fetched, to the great joy of the King, but the wicked old woman came to no good end.

And the King and the Queen, their children and her brothers lived for many years in happiness and peace.

OLD GERMAN TALE, ANDREW LANG COLLECTION

DICK WHITTINGTON
AND HIS CAT

DICK WHITTINGTON was a very little boy when his father and mother died; so little, indeed, that he never knew them nor the place where he was born. He strolled about the country as ragged as a colt till he met with a wagoner who was going to London. He gave Dick leave to walk all the way by the side of his wagon without paying anything for his passage. This pleased little Whittington very much, as he wanted to see London.

He had heard the streets were paved with gold and he was more than willing to get a bushel of it. But how great was his disappointment, poor boy, when he saw the streets covered with mud instead of gold and found himself in a strange place without a friend, without food and without money.

Though the wagoner had the charity to let him walk by the side of the wagon for nothing, he parted hastily from Dick when they came to town, and the poor boy was, in a short time, so cold and so hungry that he wished himself in a good kitchen and by a warm fire in the country.

In his distress he asked charity of several people, and one of them with a sneer bade him, "Go to work for an idle rogue."

"That I will," said Whittington, "with all my heart. I will work for you if you will let me."

The man, who thought this savored of impertinence —though the poor lad intended only to show his readiness to work—gave him such a blow with a stick that he cut his head so the blood ran down. In this situation, and fainting for want of food, he lay down at the door of Mr. Fitzwarren, a merchant, where the cook saw him. Being an ill-natured woman, she ordered him to go about his business or, she declared, she would scald him. At this moment, Mr. Fitzwarren came from the Exchange and began also to scold the poor boy, bidding him to work.

Whittington answered that he should be glad to work if anybody would employ him, and he would be able to if he could get some food, for he had eaten nothing for three days, and he was a poor country boy who knew nobody.

He then endeavored to get up, but he was so weak he fell down again, which aroused such compassion in the merchant that he ordered the servants to take Dick in and give him meat and drink and let him help the cook to do any work she had to give him. People are often too apt to reproach beggars for being idle but give themselves no concern to find them work or to consider whether they are able to do it, which is not true charity.

Whittington would have been happy in this worthy family had he not been bumped about by the cross cook, who was always roasting or basting; and when the grill was idle she employed her hands upon poor Whittington! At last, Miss Alice, his master's daughter, was informed of this and took compassion on the boy and made the servants treat him kindly.

Besides the crossness of the cook, whose name was Cicely, Whittington had another difficulty to overcome before he could be happy. There was, by order of his master, a lumpy bed placed for him in a garret, but rats and mice often ran over the poor boy's nose and disturbed him in his sleep. After some time, however, a gentleman who came to his master's house gave Whittington a penny for brushing his shoes. This he put into his pocket, and the next day, seeing a woman in the street with a cat under her arm, he ran up to ask the price of it. Because the cat was a good mouser, the woman wanted a great deal of money for it, but on Whittington's telling her he had but a penny in the world and wanted a cat badly, she let him have it.

Whittington concealed his cat in the garret, for fear she should be beaten by his enemy the cook. Puss soon killed or frightened away the rats and mice so the poor lad could now sleep as soundly as a top.

Soon after this, the merchant, who had a ship ready to sail, called for his servants, as his custom was, that they might offer something they had to sell on the voyage. Whatever they sent was to pay neither freight nor custom, for he thought justly that God Almighty would bless him the more for his readiness to let the poor partake of his fortune.

All the servants appeared except poor Whittington, who had neither money nor goods to try his luck. But his good friend Miss Alice, thinking his poverty kept him away, ordered him to be called. She then offered to lay down something for him, but the merchant said that would not do—it must be something of his own— upon which Whittington said he had nothing in the world but a cat which he had bought for a penny that was given to him.

"Fetch the cat, boy," said the merchant, "and send her along."

Whittington brought poor Puss and delivered her

to the captain with tears in his eyes, for he said he
should now be disturbed by the rats and mice as much
as ever. All the company laughed at this but Miss
Alice, who pitied the boy and gave him some coins to
buy another cat.

While Miss Puss was being tossed by the billows at
sea, poor Whittington was being severely beaten at
home by his tyrannical mistress the cook, who used
Dick cruelly and made such mockery of him for sending
his cat to sea that at last the unhappy boy determined
to run away from his place and, having packed up the
few things he had, he set out very early on the morning
of Halloween. He traveled as far as Cheapside, and
there sat down on a stone to consider what course he
should take. While he was thus ruminating, the Bow
Bells, of which there were six, began to ring, and he
thought their sounds addressed him in this manner:

> Turn again, Whittington,
> Thrice Lord Mayor of London.

"Lord Mayor of London!" said he to himself.
"What would one not endure to be Lord Mayor of
London and ride in such a fine coach? Well, I will go
back again and bear all the pummeling and ill-usage of
Cicely rather than miss the opportunity of being Lord
Mayor!" So home he went, and happily got into the
merchant's house and about his work before Cicely
made her appearance.

The ship which had the cat on board was a long time at sea and, at last, by contrary winds, was driven onto a part of the coast of Barbary inhabited by Moors unknown to the English. The people received the voyagers with civility; therefore, the captain sent some of his goods to the King.

The King was so pleased that he asked the captain and Mr. Fitzwarren's business agent, who always traveled with the boat, to come to his palace, which was about a mile from the sea.

Here they were placed, according to the custom of the country, on rich carpets flowered with gold and silver, with the King and Queen seated at the upper end of the room. Dinner was brought in, which consisted of many courses; but no sooner were the dishes put down than an amazing number of rats and mice came from all quarters and devoured everything in an instant. The agent, in surprise, turned around to the notables and asked if these vermin were not offensive to them.

"Oh, yes," they said, "very offensive. The King would give half his treasure to be freed of them, for they not only destroy his dinner, as you can see, but they also assault him in his chamber, and even in bed. He has to have a guard in his room while he is sleeping for fear of them."

The agent jumped for joy. He remembered Dick Whittington and his cat; and he told the King he had a creature on board the ship that would dispatch all these rats and mice immediately. The King's heart heaved so high at the joy this news gave him that his turban dropped off his head.

"Bring this creature to me," said he. "If she will do what you say I will load your ship with gold and jewels in exchange for her."

The agent, who knew his business, set forth the merits of Miss Puss. He told His Majesty that it would be inconvenient to part with her, for, without her, rats and mice might destroy the goods in the ship— but to oblige His Majesty he would fetch her.

"Run, run," said the Queen. "I am impatient to see the dear thing."

Away flew the agent, and another dinner was prepared in his absence. He returned with the cat just as the rats and mice were devouring that also. He immediately put down Miss Puss, who killed a great number of them.

The King rejoiced greatly to see his old enemies destroyed by so small a creature, and the Queen was highly pleased and desired the cat to be brought near that she might look at her. The agent called, "Pussy, pussy, pussy!" and she came to him. He then presented her to the Queen, who started back. She was afraid to touch an animal who had made such havoc among the rats and mice. However, when the agent stroked the cat and said, "Pussy, pussy," the Queen

also touched her and cried, "Putty, putty," for she had not learned English.

He then put the cat down on the Queen's lap, where, purring, she played with Her Majesty's hand and then sang herself to sleep.

The King, having seen the exploits of Miss Puss, and being informed that her kittens would stock the whole country, bargained with the captain and agent for the ship's whole cargo, and then gave them ten times as much for the cat as for all the rest—on which, taking leave of Their Majesties and other personages at court, they sailed with a fair wind for England.

In London, morning had scarcely dawned when Mr. Fitzwarren rose to count over the cash and settle the business for that day. He had just entered the counting house and seated himself at the desk, when somebody came, tap, tap, at the door. "Who is there?" said Mr. Fitzwarren.

"A friend."

"What friend comes at this unseasonable time?"

"A real friend is never unseasonable," answered the caller. "I come to bring you good news of your ship *Unicorn*."

The merchant instantly opened the door, and who should be there but the captain and agent, with a cabinet of jewels and a bill of lading, for which the merchant lifted up his eyes and thanked Heaven for sending him such a prosperous voyage. Then they told

him the adventures of the cat, and showed him the
cabinet of jewels which they had brought for young
Dick Whittington. Upon which he cried out:

> Go, send him in, and tell him of his fame,
> And call him Mr. Whittington by name.

When some who were present told Mr. Fitzwarren
this treasure was too much for such a poor boy as
Whittington, he said: "God forbid that I should de-
prive him of his due; it is his own and he shall have
it to a penny."

He then sent for Mr. Whittington, who was clean-
ing the kitchen and would have excused himself from
going into the counting house, saying his master's
room was swept and his shoes were dirty and full of
hobnails. The merchant, however, made him come in
and ordered a chair to be set for him. Upon which,
thinking they intended to make sport of him, as had
been too often the case in the kitchen, he besought his
master not to mock a poor simple fellow who intended
no harm, but let him go about his work.

The merchant, taking him by the hand, said, "Indeed, Mr. Whittington, I am in earnest with you and
wish to congratulate you on your great success. Your
cat has procured you more money than I am worth in
the world, and may you enjoy it long and be happy!"

At length, being shown the treasure and convinced
that all of it belonged to him, he fell upon his knees

and thanked the Almighty for his providential care of such a poor and miserable creature. He then laid all the treasure at his master's feet, but Mr. Fitzwarren refused to take any part of it and told Dick he heartily rejoiced at his prosperity and hoped the wealth he had acquired would be a comfort to him and would make him happy.

Dick Whittington then applied to his mistress and to his friend Miss Alice, who both refused to take any part of the money, but Miss Alice told him she was gladdened by his good success and wished him all felicity. He then gave gifts to the ship's captain, the agent and the ship's crew for the care they had taken of his cargo. He likewise distributed presents to all the servants in the house, not forgetting even his old enemy the cook, though she little deserved it.

After this, Mr. Fitzwarren suggested Mr. Whittington send for the necessary people to advise him how best to dress himself like a gentleman, and made him the offer of his house to live in till he could provide himself with a better one.

Now it came to pass, when Mr. Whittington's face was washed, his hair curled and he was dressed in a rich suit of clothes, that he turned out a genteel young fellow. Since wealth contributes much to give a man confidence, he soon grew to be a sprightly and good companion, so much so that Miss Alice, who had formerly pitied him, now fell in love with him.

When her father perceived the two young people had this good liking for each other he proposed a match between them, to which both cheerfully consented, and the Lord Mayor, aldermen, sheriffs, the Company of Stationers, the Royal Academy of Arts and a number of eminent merchants attended the ceremony and were elegantly treated at an entertainment made for that purpose.

History further relates that they lived very happily, had several children and died at a fine old age. Mr. Whittington served as Sheriff of London and, as the Bow Bells had told him many years before, was three times Lord Mayor.

The last year of his mayoralty he entertained King Henry V and his Queen, after his conquest of France, upon which occasion the King, in consideration of Mr. Whittington's merit, said, "Never had king such a subject." On hearing this, Mr. Whittington replied, "Never had subject such a king." His Majesty, out of respect for his host's good character, conferred the honor of knighthood on him soon after.

For many years before his death, Sir Richard constantly fed a great number of poor citizens and built a church and a college, to which he gave a yearly allowance for poor scholars. He also gave liberally to St. Bartholomew's Hospital and other public charities to help the people of London.

OLD ENGLISH TALE, ANDREW LANG COLLECTION

RAPUNZEL

ONCE UPON a time a man and his wife were very unhappy because they had no children. These good people had a little window at the back of their house which looked into the most lovely garden full of all manner of beautiful flowers and vegetables; but the garden was surrounded by a high wall, and no one dared to enter it, for it belonged to a witch who possessed great power and who was feared by the whole world.

One day the woman stood at the window overlooking the garden and saw there a bed full of the finest salad greens called rampion. The leaves looked so fresh and green that she longed to eat them. The desire grew day by day, and just because she knew she couldn't possibly get any, she pined away and became pale and wretched. Then her husband grew alarmed and said, "What ails you, dear wife?"

"Oh," she answered, "if I don't get some rampion to eat from the garden behind the house, I know I shall die."

The man, who loved her dearly, said to himself,

"Come! Rather than let your wife die you shall pick her some rampion, no matter the cost." So at dusk he climbed over the wall into the witch's garden and, hastily gathering a handful of rampion leaves, he returned with them to his wife. She made them into a salad, which tasted so good that her longing for the forbidden food was greater than ever. If she were to know any peace of mind, there was nothing for it but that her husband must climb over the garden wall again and fetch her some more. Again at dusk over he went, but when he reached the other side he drew back in terror, for there, standing before him, was the old witch.

"How dare you," she said, with a wrathful glance, "climb into my garden and steal my rampion like a common thief? You shall suffer greatly for your rashness."

"Oh," he implored, "please forgive my boldness; necessity alone drove me to the deed. My wife saw your rampion from her window and had such a desire for it that she would certainly have died if her wish had not been gratified."

Then the witch's anger was a little appeased, and she said, "If it's as you say, you may take as much rampion away with you as you like, but on one condition only—that you give me the child your wife will shortly bring into the world. All shall go well with it, and I will look after it like a mother."

The man in his terror agreed to everything she asked. As soon as the child was born, the witch appeared and, having given it the name of Rapunzel, which in that country means the same as rampion, she carried it off with her.

Rapunzel was the most beautiful child under the sun. When she was twelve years old the witch shut her up in a tower, in the middle of a great forest, and the tower had neither stairs nor doors, only high up at the very top a small window. When the old witch wanted to visit the girl she stood underneath and called out:

Rapunzel, Rapunzel,
Let down your golden hair.

For Rapunzel had wonderful long hair, and it was as fine as spun gold. Whenever she heard the witch's voice she loosened her braids and let her hair fall down out of the window. This became a ladder for the old witch to climb straight up to the top of the tower.

After they lived like this for a few years, it happened one day that a Prince was riding through the woods and passed by the tower. As he drew near it he heard someone singing so sweetly that he stood spellbound and listened. It was Rapunzel, in her loneliness trying to while away the time by letting her sweet voice fill her solitude. The Prince longed to

see the owner of the voice, but he sought in vain for a door in the tower. He rode home, but he was so haunted by the song he had heard that he returned every day to the woods and listened. One day, when he was standing thus behind a tree, he saw the old witch approach and heard her call out:

> Rapunzel, Rapunzel,
> Let down your golden hair.

Then Rapunzel let down her braids, and the witch climbed up by them.

"So that's the staircase, is it?" said the Prince. "Then I, too, will climb it and try my luck."

On the following day, at dusk, he went to the foot of the tower and cried:

> Rapunzel, Rapunzel,
> Let down your golden hair.

And as soon as she had let down the marvelous golden ladder the Prince climbed up.

At first Rapunzel was terribly frightened when a man came in, for she had never seen one before. But the Prince spoke to her kindly and told her at once that his heart had been so touched by her singing he felt he should know no peace of mind till he had seen her. Very soon Rapunzel forgot her fear, and when he asked her to marry him she consented at once.

For, she thought, he is young and handsome, and

I'll certainly be happier with him than with the old witch. So she put her hand in his and said: "Yes, I will gladly go with you, only how am I to get down out of the tower? Every time you come to see me you must bring a skein of silk with you, and I will braid it into a ladder. When it is finished I will climb down by it, and you will take me away on your horse."

They arranged that, till the ladder was ready, he was to come to her every evening, because the old woman was with her during the day. Each time the Prince came he brought some silk.

The old witch, of course, knew nothing of what was going on, till one day Rapunzel, not thinking of what she was about, turned to the witch and said, "How is it, good mother, that you are so much harder to pull up than the young Prince? He is always with me in a moment."

"Oh, you wicked child," cried the witch. "What is this I hear? I thought I had hidden you from the whole world and in spite of it you have managed to deceive me."

In her wrath she seized Rapunzel's beautiful hair, wound it around and around her left hand and then, grasping a pair of scissors in her right, snip, snap, off it came, and the golden braids lay on the ground. And, worse than this, she was so hardhearted that she took Rapunzel to a lonely desert place and there left her to live in loneliness and misery.

But on the evening of the day in which she had taken poor Rapunzel away, the witch fastened the braids onto a hook in the window, and when the Prince came and called out:

> Rapunzel, Rapunzel,
> Let down your golden hair,

she let them down, and the Prince climbed up as usual.

Instead of his beloved Rapunzel he found the old witch, who fixed her evil, glittering eyes on him and cried mockingly, "Ah, ah! You thought to find your lady love, but the pretty bird has flown and its song is mute. The cat caught it and will scratch out your eyes, too. Rapunzel is lost to you forever—you will never see her again."

The Prince was beside himself with grief, and in his despair he jumped right down from the tower and, though he escaped with his life, the thorns among which he fell pierced his eyes. Then he wandered, blind and miserable, through the forest, eating nothing but roots and berries and weeping and lamenting the loss of his lovely bride.

So he wandered about for a year, as wretched and unhappy as he could be, and at last he came to the desert place where Rapunzel was living. Suddenly he heard a voice which seemed strangely familiar to him. He walked eagerly in the direction of the sound, and, when he was quite close, Rapunzel recognized him and fell on his neck and wept. Two of her tears touched his eyes, and in a moment they were healed, and he could see as well as ever before. Then he led her to his kingdom, where they were welcomed with great joy, and they lived happily ever after.

JAKOB AND WILHELM GRIMM, TRANSLATED BY MAY SELLAR

ALADDIN AND
THE WONDERFUL LAMP

THERE ONCE lived a poor tailor who had a son called Aladdin, a careless, idle boy who would do nothing but play all day in the streets with other idle little boys. This so grieved the father that he died; yet, in spite of his mother's tears and prayers, Aladdin did not mend his ways.

One day, when he was playing in the streets as usual, a stranger asked him his age and if he were not the son of Mustapha the tailor.

"I am, sir," replied Aladdin. "But he died a long while ago."

On this, the stranger, who was a famous African

magician, fell on his neck and kissed him, saying, "I am your uncle and I knew you from your likeness to my brother. Go to your mother and tell her I am coming."

Aladdin ran home and told his mother of his newly found uncle. "Indeed, child," she said, "you have no uncle by your father's side or mine."

However, she prepared supper and bade Aladdin bring home the man who called himself his uncle. He came laden with wine and fruit and presently he knelt and kissed the place where Mustapha used to sit. He told Aladdin's mother not to be surprised at never having seen him before, as he had been forty years out of the country.

The African magician then turned to Aladdin and asked him his trade, at which the boy hung his head, while his mother burst into tears. On learning that Aladdin was idle and would learn no trade, he offered to take a shop for him and stock it with merchandise. The next morning he bought Aladdin a fine suit of clothes and took him all over the city, showing him the sights, and brought him home at nightfall to his mother, who was overjoyed to see her son so finely dressed.

Next day the magician led Aladdin into some beautiful gardens a long way outside the city gates. They sat down by a fountain, and the magician pulled a cake from his pocket, which he divided between them. They then journeyed onward till they had almost reached the mountains. Aladdin was so tired that he begged to go back, but the magician beguiled him with pleasant stories and led the boy on in spite of himself.

At last they came to two mountains divided by a narrow valley. "We will go no farther," said the false uncle. "I will show you something wonderful; but first you gather up sticks while I kindle a fire."

When the fire was lit the magician threw on it a powder he had with him, at the same time saying some magical words. The earth trembled a little and opened in front of them, disclosing a square, flat stone with a brass ring in the middle to raise it by. Aladdin became so frightened that he tried to run away, but the magician caught him and gave him such a blow that it knocked him to the ground.

"What have I done, Uncle?" he asked piteously.

Whereupon the magician said more kindly, "Fear nothing, but obey me. Beneath this stone lies a treasure which is to be yours, and no one else may touch it, so you must do exactly as I tell you."

At the word "treasure," Aladdin forgot his fears and grasped the ring as he was told, saying the names of his father and grandfather. The stone came up quite easily and steps appeared.

"Go down," said the magician. "At the foot of those steps you will find an open doorway leading into three large halls. Tuck up your trousers and go through them without touching anything, or you will die instantly. These halls lead into a garden of fine fruit trees. If you should wish any of the fruit you may gather as much as you please. Walk on till you come to a niche in a terrace where stands a lighted lamp. Pour out the oil it contains and bring it to me."

He then drew a ring from his finger and gave it to Aladdin, telling him that it would protect him from any evil he might meet.

Aladdin found everything as the magician had said. He gathered some fruit off the trees and, having got the lamp, arrived at the mouth of the cave.

The magician cried out in a great hurry, "Make haste and give me the lamp." This Aladdin refused to do until he was out of the cave. The magician flew into a terrible passion and, throwing some more powder on the fire, muttered something, and the stone rolled back into its place, sealing Aladdin inside.

The magician instantly left Persia for Africa, which plainly showed that he was no uncle of Aladdin's but a cunning sorcerer who had read in his magic books of a wonderful lamp which would make him the most powerful man in the world. Though he alone knew where to find it, he could only receive it from the hand of another. He had picked out the foolish Aladdin for this purpose, intending to get the lamp and kill him afterward.

For two days Aladdin remained in the dark, crying and lamenting. At last he clasped his hands in prayer,

and in so doing rubbed the ring, which the magician had forgotten to take from him.

Immediately an enormous and frightful genie rose out of the earth, saying, "What wouldst thou with me? I am the slave of the ring and will obey thee in all things."

Aladdin fearlessly replied, "Deliver me from this place," whereupon the earth opened, and he found himself outside. As soon as his eyes could bear the light he went home, but fainted on the threshold. When he came to himself he told his mother what had passed, and showed her the lamp and the fruits—in reality precious stones—which he had gathered in the garden. He then asked for some food.

"Alas, child," his mother said, "I have nothing in the house, but I have spun a little cotton and will go and sell it."

Aladdin bade her keep her cotton, for he would sell the lamp instead. As it was very dirty she began to rub it, that it might fetch a higher price. Instantly a hideous genie appeared and asked what she would have.

She fainted away, but Aladdin, snatching the lamp, said boldly, "Bring me something to eat!"

The genie returned with a silver bowl, twelve silver plates containing rich meats, two silver cups and a bottle of wine.

Aladdin's mother, when she came to herself, said, "Whence comes this splendid feast?"

"Ask not, but eat," replied Aladdin. So they sat at breakfast till it was dinner time, and Aladdin told his mother what had happened when he had rubbed the lamp. She begged him to sell it and have nothing to do with genies.

"No," said Aladdin, "since chance has made us aware of its virtues, we will use it and the ring likewise, which I shall always wear on my finger." When they had eaten all the genie had brought, Aladdin sold one of the silver plates, then another and another. When none were left, he had recourse to the genie, who gave him another set of plates, and thus he and his mother lived for many years.

One day Aladdin heard an order from the Sultan proclaiming that everyone was to stay at home and close his shutters while the Princess, his daughter, went to and from the bath. Aladdin was seized by a desire to see her face, which was very difficult as she was veiled. He hid himself behind the door of the bath and peeped through a chink.

The Princess lifted her veil as she went in, and looked so beautiful that Aladdin fell in love with her at first sight. He went home quite changed and his mother became frightened. He told her he loved the Princess and could not live without her and meant to ask for her in marriage. His mother, on hearing this, burst out laughing, but Aladdin at last prevailed upon her to go before the Sultan and carry his request. She fetched a napkin and laid in it the magic fruits from the enchanted garden, which sparkled and shone like the most beautiful jewels. She took these with her to please the Sultan and set out, trusting in the lamp.

The Grand Vizier and the lords of council had just gone into the hall as she entered and placed herself in front of the Sultan. He, however, took no notice of her. She went every day for a week and stood in the same place. When the council broke up on the sixth day the Sultan said to his Vizier, "I see a certain woman in the audience chamber day after day, carrying something in a napkin. Call her tomorrow that I may find out what she wants."

Next day, at a sign from the Vizier, she went up to the foot of the throne and remained kneeling till the Sultan said to her, "Rise, good woman, and tell me what you want." She hesitated, so the Sultan sent away all but the Vizier and bade her speak freely, promising beforehand to forgive her for anything she might say.

She then told him about her son's violent love for the Princess.

"I prayed him to forget her," she said, "but in vain; he threatened to do some desperate deed if I refused to go and ask Your Majesty for the hand of the Princess. Now I pray you to forgive not me alone but my son Aladdin."

The Sultan asked her kindly what she had in the

napkin, whereupon she unfolded the jewels and presented them.

He was thunderstruck, and turning to the Vizier, said, "What sayest thou? Ought I not to bestow the Princess on one who values her at such a price?"

The Vizier, who wanted her for his own son, begged the Sultan to withhold her for three months, in the course of which he hoped his son would contrive to make him a richer present. The Sultan granted this and told Aladdin's mother that, though he consented to the marriage, she must not appear before him again for three months.

Aladdin waited patiently for quite a while, but after two months had elapsed, his mother, going into the city to buy oil, found everyone rejoicing and asked what was going on.

"Do you not know," was the answer, "that the son of the Grand Vizier is to marry the Sultan's daughter tonight?"

Breathless, she ran and told Aladdin, who was overwhelmed at first, but presently bethought him of the lamp. He rubbed it, and the genie appeared, saying, "What is thy will?"

Aladdin replied, "The Sultan, as thou knowest, has broken his promise to me, and the Vizier's son is to have the Princess. My command is that tonight you bring hither the bride and bridegroom."

"Master, I obey," said the genie.

Aladdin then went to his chamber where, sure enough, at midnight, the genie transported the bed containing the Vizier's son and the Princess.

"Take this new-married man," Aladdin said, "and put him outside in the cold and return at daybreak."

Whereupon the genie took the Vizier's son out of bed, leaving Aladdin with the Princess.

"Fear nothing," Aladdin said to her. "You are my wife, promised to me by your unjust father, and no harm shall come to you."

The Princess was too frightened to speak and passed the most miserable night of her life, while Aladdin lay down beside her and slept soundly. At the appointed hour the genie fetched in the shivering bridegroom, laid him in his place and transported the bed back to the palace.

Presently the Sultan came into the chamber to wish his daughter good morning. The Vizier's unhappy son jumped up and hid himself, while the Princess would not say a word and was very sorrowful.

The Sultan sent her mother to her, who said, "How comes it, child, that you will not speak to your father? What has happened?"

The Princess sighed deeply, and at last told her mother how, during the night, the bed had been carried into some strange house, and what had happened there. Her mother did not believe her in the least but bade her rise and consider it an idle dream.

The following night exactly the same thing happened, and next morning, on the Princess' refusing to speak, the Sultan threatened to cut off her head. She then confessed, bidding him ask the Vizier's son if it were not so. The Sultan told the Vizier to ask his son, who admitted the truth, adding that, dearly as he loved the Princess, he would rather die than go through another such fearful night, and he wished to be separated from her. His wish was granted, and there was an end of feasting and rejoicing.

When the three months were over, Aladdin sent his mother to remind the Sultan of his promise. She stood waiting to see the Sultan, and he, who had forgotten Aladdin, at once remembered him and summoned his mother. On seeing her poverty, the Sultan felt less inclined than ever to keep his word and asked advice from the Vizier, who told him to set so high a value on the Princess that no man could come up to it.

The Sultan then turned to Aladdin's mother, saying, "Good woman, a Sultan must remember his promises and I will remember mine, but your son must first give me forty basins of gold brimful of jewels, carried by forty black slaves, led by as many white ones, splendidly dressed. Tell him that I await his answer."

The mother of Aladdin bowed low and went home, thinking all was lost. She gave Aladdin the Sultan's message, then said, "He may wait long enough for your answer!"

"Not so long, Mother, as you think," her son replied. "I would do a great deal more than that for the Princess." He summoned the genie, and in a few moments the eighty slaves arrived and filled up the small house and garden.

Aladdin made them set out to the palace, two and two, followed by his mother. They were so richly dressed, with such splendid jewels in their belts, that everyone crowded to see them and the basins of gold they carried on their heads.

The procession entered the palace and, after kneeling before the Sultan, stood in a half-circle around the throne, each man with his arms crossed, while Aladdin's mother presented them to the Sultan.

"Good woman," said the Sultan, "return and tell your son I wait for him with open arms."

She lost no time in telling Aladdin, bidding him make haste. But he first called the genie. "I want a scented bath," he ordered, "and a richly embroidered robe, a horse surpassing the Sultan's and twenty slaves to attend me. Besides these I desire six slaves, beautifully dressed, to wait on my mother; and lastly, ten thousand pieces of gold in ten purses."

No sooner said than done. Aladdin mounted his horse and passed through the streets, the slaves strewing gold as they went. Those who had played with him in his childhood knew him not, he had grown so handsome.

When the Sultan saw him, he came down from his throne, embraced him and led him into a hall where a feast was spread, intending to marry him to the Princess that very day. But Aladdin refused, saying, "I must build a palace fit for her," and took his leave.

Once home, he said to the genie, "Build me a palace of the finest marble, set with jasper, agate and other precious stones. In the middle you shall build me a large room with a dome, its four walls of massive gold and silver, each side having six windows whose lattices—except for one, which is to be left unfinished—must be set with diamonds, emeralds and rubies. There must be stables and horses and grooms and slaves. Go and see about it!"

The palace was finished by the next day, and the genie transported him there and showed him all his orders faithfully carried out, even to the laying of a velvet carpet from Aladdin's palace to the Sultan's. Aladdin's mother then dressed herself carefully and walked to the palace with her slaves. The Sultan sent musicians with trumpets and cymbals to meet them, and the air resounded with music and cheers.

Aladdin's mother was taken to the Princess, who saluted her and treated her with great honor. That night the Princess said good-bye to her father and set out on the carpet for Aladdin's palace, his mother beside her, and followed by one hundred slaves. She was charmed at the sight of Aladdin, who ran to receive her.

"Princess," he said, "blame your beauty for my boldness if I have displeased you."

She told him that, having seen him, she willingly obeyed her father in this matter. After the wedding had taken place, Aladdin led her into the hall where a feast was spread, and she supped with him, after which they danced till midnight.

Next day Aladdin invited the Sultan to see the palace. On entering the hall with the four-and-twenty windows, with their rubies, diamonds and emeralds, he cried, "It is a world's wonder! There is only one thing that surprises me. Was it by accident that one window was left unfinished?"

"No, sir, it was by design," returned Aladdin. "I wished Your Majesty to have the glory of finishing this palace."

The Sultan was pleased and sent for the best jewelers in the city. He showed them the unfinished window and bade them fit it up like the others.

"Sir," replied their spokesman, "we cannot find jewels enough."

The Sultan had his own gems fetched, which they soon used, but to no purpose, for in a month's time the work was not half done. Aladdin, knowing that their task was in vain, bade them undo their work and carry the jewels back, and the genie finished the window at his command. The Sultan was surprised to receive his gems again and visited Aladdin, who showed him the window finished. The Sultan embraced him, the envious Vizier meanwhile hinting that it was the work of enchantment.

Aladdin had won the hearts of the people by his gentle bearing. He was made captain of the Sultan's armies and won several battles for him, but remained modest and courteous as before and lived thus in peace and contentment for many years.

But far away in Africa the magician remembered Aladdin, and by his magic arts discovered that Aladdin, instead of perishing miserably in the cave, had escaped and had married a Princess, with whom he was living in great honor and wealth. He knew that the poor tailor's son could only have accomplished this by means of the lamp. So he traveled night and day till he reached the capital of Persia, bent on Aladdin's ruin. As he passed through the town he heard people talking about a marvelous palace. "Forgive my ignorance," he said, "what is this palace you speak of?"

"Have you not heard of Prince Aladdin's palace," was one man's reply, "the greatest wonder of the world? I will direct you if you have a mind to see it."

The magician thanked the man and, having seen the palace, knew that it had been raised by the genie of the lamp, and he became half mad with rage. He determined to get hold of the lamp and again plunge Aladdin into the deepest poverty.

Unluckily, Aladdin had gone hunting for eight days,

which gave the magician plenty of time. He bought a dozen copper lamps, put them into a basket and went to the palace, crying, "New lamps for old!" and followed by a jeering crowd.

The Princess, sitting in the hall of four-and-twenty windows, sent a slave to find out what the noise was about. The slave came back laughing, so the Princess scolded her.

"Madam," replied the slave, "who can help laughing to see an old fool offering to exchange fine new lamps for old ones?"

Another slave, hearing this, said, "There is an old one on the cornice there which he can have."

Now this was the magic lamp, which Aladdin had left there, as he could not take it hunting with him. The Princess, not knowing its value, laughingly bade the slave take it and make the exchange. She went and said to the magician, "Give me a new lamp for this."

He snatched it and bade the slave take her choice, amid the jeers of the crowd. Little he cared, but left off crying his lamps and went beyond the city gates to a lonely place, where he remained till nightfall, when he pulled out the magic lamp and rubbed it. The genie appeared and at the magician's command carried him, together with the palace and the Princess in it, to a lonely place in Africa.

Next morning the Sultan looked from the window toward Aladdin's palace and rubbed his eyes, for it was gone. He sent for the Vizier and asked what had become of the palace. The Vizier was lost in astonishment. He again put it down to enchantment; and this time the Sultan believed him, sending thirty men on horseback to fetch Aladdin in chains. They met him as he was riding home, bound him and forced him to go with them on foot.

The people, however, who loved him, followed, armed, to see that he came to no harm. He was carried before the Sultan, who ordered the executioner to cut off his head. The executioner made Aladdin kneel, bandaged his eyes and raised his scimitar to strike. At that instant the Vizier, who saw that the crowds had forced their way into the courtyard and were scaling the walls to rescue Aladdin, called to the executioner to stay his hand. The people, indeed, looked so threatening that the Sultan gave way and ordered Aladdin to be unbound, and pardoned him in the sight of the crowd.

Aladdin begged to know what he had done.

"False wretch!" said the Sultan, "come hither," and showed him from the window the place where his palace had stood. Aladdin was so amazed that he could not say a word.

"Where is the palace and my daughter?" demanded the Sultan. "For the first I am not so deeply concerned, but my daughter I must have and you must find her or lose your head."

Aladdin begged for forty days in which to find her, promising, if he failed, to return and suffer death at the Sultan's pleasure. The Sultan granted his request, and Aladdin went forth sadly from the palace. For three days he wandered about like a madman, asking everyone what had become of his palace, but they only pitied him. He came to the banks of a river and knelt down to say his prayers before throwing himself in. In so doing he rubbed the magic ring he still wore. The genie he had seen in the cave appeared and asked his will.

"Save my life, genie," said Aladdin, "and bring my palace back."

"That is not in my power," said the genie. "I am only the slave of the ring; for that you must ask the slave of the lamp."

"Even so," said Aladdin, "but thou canst take me to the palace and set me down under my dear wife's window." He at once found himself in Africa, under the window of the Princess, where he fell asleep from sheer weariness.

He was awakened by the singing of the birds, and his heart was lighter. He saw plainly that all his misfortunes were owing to the loss of the lamp and vainly wondered who had robbed him of it.

That morning the Princess rose earlier than she had since she had been carried into Africa by the magician, whose company she was forced to endure once a day. She, however, treated him so harshly that he dared not live there altogether. As she was dressing, one of her women looked out and saw Aladdin. The Princess ran to open the window. Hearing her there, Aladdin looked up. She called him to come to her, and great was their joy at seeing each other again.

After he had kissed her, Aladdin said, "I beg of you, Princess, before we speak of anything else, for your own sake and mine, tell me what has become of an old lamp I left on the cornice in the hall of four-and-twenty windows, when I went hunting."

"Alas," she said, "I am the innocent cause of our sorrows," and told him of the exchange of the lamp.

"Now I know," cried Aladdin, "that we have to thank the African magician for all this! Where is the lamp?"

"He carries it about with him," said the Princess. "I know, for he pulled it out of his robe to show me. He wishes me to break my faith with you and marry him, saying that you were beheaded by my father's command. He is forever speaking ill of you, but I only reply by my tears. If I persist, I doubt not that he will use violence."

Aladdin comforted her and left her for a while. He changed clothes with the first person he met in the town, and after buying a certain powder returned to the Princess, who let him in by a little side door.

"Put on your most beautiful dress," he said to her, "and receive the magician with smiles. Lead him to believe that you have forgotten me. Invite him to sup with you and say you wish to taste the wine of his country. Now listen while I tell you what else to do."

She listened carefully to Aladdin and, when he left her, arrayed herself gaily for the first time since leaving Persia. She put on a belt and headdress of diamonds, and seeing in a glass that she looked more beautiful than ever, received the magician, saying to his great amazement, "I have made up my mind that Aladdin is dead and that all my tears will not bring him back to me, so I am resolved to mourn no more and therefore invite you to sup with me. But I am tired of the wines of Persia and therefore desire to taste those of Africa."

The magician flew to his cellar, and the Princess put the powder Aladdin had given her in her cup. When he returned she asked him to drink her health in the wine of Africa, handing him her cup in exchange for his as a sign she was reconciled to him.

Before drinking, the magician made a speech in praise of her beauty, but the Princess cut him short, saying, "Let us drink first, and you shall say what you will afterward." She set her cup only to her lips, while the magician drained his to the dregs and thereupon fell back, lifeless.

The Princess then opened the door to Aladdin and flung her arms around his neck, but Aladdin held her off, bidding her to leave him, as he had more to do. He then went to the dead magician, took the lamp out of his vest and bade the genie carry the palace back to Persia. This was done, and the Princess in her chamber felt only two slight shocks and little thought she was at home again.

The Sultan, who was sitting in his bedchamber mourning for his lost daughter, happened to look up and rubbed his eyes, for there stood the palace as before! He hastened forth, and Aladdin received him in the hall of the four-and-twenty windows, with the Princess at his side. Aladdin told him what had happened and showed him the dead body of the magician, that he might believe. A ten days' feast was proclaimed, and it seemed as if Aladdin might now live the rest of his life in peace, but it was not to be.

The African magician had a younger brother, who was, if possible, more wicked and cunning than the elder. He traveled to Persia to avenge his brother's death and went to visit a pious woman called Fatima, thinking she might be of use to him. He entered her cell and clapped a dagger to her breast, telling her to rise and do his bidding on pain of death. He changed clothes with her, colored his face like hers, covered it with her own veil and murdered her that she might tell no tales.

Then he went toward the palace of Aladdin, and all the people, thinking he was the holy woman, gathered around him, kissing his hands and begging his blessing.

When he reached the palace there was such a noise that the Princess bade her slave look out the window and ask what was the matter. The slave said it was the holy woman, curing people of their ailments by her touch, whereupon the Princess, who had long desired to see Fatima, sent for her.

On coming to the Princess, the magician offered up a prayer for her health and prosperity. When he had finished, the Princess made him sit by her and begged him to stay with her always. The false Fatima, who wished for nothing better, consented, but kept his veil down for fear of discovery.

The Princess showed him the hall and asked him what he thought of it.

"It is truly beautiful," said the false Fatima. "In my mind it wants but one thing."

"And what is that?" said the Princess.

"If only a roc's egg," replied he, "were hung up from the middle of this dome, it would be the wonder of the world."

After this the Princess could think of nothing but a roc's egg, and when Aladdin returned from hunting he found her in a very ill humor. He begged to know what was amiss, but she told him that all her pleasure in the hall was spoiled for the want of a roc's egg hanging from the dome.

"If that is all," replied Aladdin, "you shall soon be happy."

He left her and rubbed the lamp, and when the genie appeared, commanded him to bring a roc's egg.

The genie gave such a loud and terrible shriek that the hall shook. "Wretch," he cried, "is it not enough that I have done everything for you, but you must command me to bring my master and hang him up in the midst of this dome? You and your wife and your palace deserve to be burned to ashes for this request, but I know it does not come from you but from the brother of the African magician whom you destroyed. He is now in your palace disguised as the holy woman Fatima—whom he murdered. He it was who put that wish into your wife's head. Take care of yourself, for that man means to kill you." So saying, the genie disappeared.

Aladdin went back to the Princess, saying his head ached and requesting that the holy Fatima should be fetched to lay her hands on it. But when the magician came near, Aladdin, seizing his dagger, pierced him to the heart.

"What have you done?" cried the Princess. "You have killed the holy woman!"

"Not so," replied Aladdin, "but a wicked magician," and told her of how she had been deceived.

After this Aladdin and his wife lived in peace. He succeeded the Sultan when he died, and reigned for many years, leaving behind him a long line of kings.

ARABIAN NIGHTS, TRANSLATED BY ANTOINE GALLAND

THE THREE BEARS

ONCE UPON a time there were three Bears who lived together in a house of their own in a wood. One of them was a little, small, wee Bear; and one was a middle-sized Bear; and the other was a great, huge Bear. Each of the Bears had a porridge pot: a little pot for the little, small, wee Bear; and a middle-sized pot for the middle Bear; and a great pot for the great, huge Bear.

Each of the Bears had a chair to sit in: a little chair for the little, small, wee Bear; and a middle-sized chair for the middle Bear; and a great chair for the great, huge Bear. And they each had a bed to sleep in: a little bed for the little, small, wee Bear; and a middle-sized bed for the middle Bear; and a great bed for the great, huge Bear.

One day, after they had made the porridge for their breakfast and poured it into their porridge pots, they walked out into the wood while the porridge was cooling, so that they might not burn their mouths by beginning to eat it too soon. And while they were walking, a little girl called Goldilocks came to the house. First she looked in at the window and then she peeped in at the keyhole; and, seeing nobody in the house, she turned the handle of the door. The door was not fastened, because the Bears were good bears who never did anybody any harm, and never suspected that anybody would harm them. So Goldilocks opened the door and went in; and well pleased she was when she saw the porridge on the table. If she had been a thoughtful little girl, she would have waited till the Bears came home and then, perhaps, they would have asked her to breakfast; for they were good bears—a little rough, as the manner of bears is, but for all that very good-natured and hospitable. The porridge looked tempting, and little Goldilocks set about helping herself.

So first she tasted the porridge of the great, huge Bear, and that was too hot for her. And then she tasted the porridge of the middle Bear, and that was too cold for her. And then she went to the porridge of the little, small, wee Bear and tasted that; and that was neither too hot nor too cold, but just right, and she liked it so well that she ate it up.

Then Goldilocks sat down in the chair of the great, huge Bear, and that was too hard for her. And then she sat down in the chair of the middle Bear, and that was too soft for her. And then she sat down in the chair of the little, small, wee Bear, and that was neither too hard nor too soft, but just right. So she seated herself in it, and there she sat till the bottom of the chair fell out, and down she went plump onto the ground.

Then Goldilocks went upstairs into the bedchamber in which the Three Bears slept. And first she lay down upon the bed of the great, huge Bear, but that was too high at the head for her. And next she lay down upon the bed of the middle Bear, but that was too high at the foot for her. And then she lay down upon the bed of the little, small, wee Bear; and that was neither too high at the head nor at the foot, but just right. So Goldilocks covered herself up comfortably and lay there till she fell fast asleep.

By this time, the Three Bears thought their porridge would be cool enough; so they had come home to breakfast. Now Goldilocks had left the spoon of the great, huge Bear standing in his porridge.

SOMEBODY HAS BEEN AT MY PORRIDGE!

said the great, huge Bear, in his great, rough, gruff voice.

And when the middle Bear looked at hers, she saw that the spoon was standing in it, too.

SOMEBODY HAS BEEN AT MY PORRIDGE!

said the middle Bear, in her middle voice.

Then the little, small, wee Bear looked at his, and there was the spoon in the porridge pot, but the porridge was all gone.

SOMEBODY HAS BEEN AT MY PORRIDGE, AND HAS EATEN IT ALL UP!

said the little, small, wee Bear, in his little, small, wee voice.

At this, the Three Bears, seeing that someone had entered their house and had eaten up the little, small, wee Bear's breakfast, began to look about the room. Now Goldilocks had forgotten to put the hard cushion straight when she rose from the chair of the great, huge Bear.

SOMEBODY HAS BEEN SITTING IN MY CHAIR!

said the great, huge Bear, in his great, rough, gruff voice.

And Goldilocks had flattened down the soft cushion of the middle Bear.

SOMEBODY HAS BEEN SITTING IN MY CHAIR!

said the middle Bear, in her middle voice.

And you know what Goldilocks had done to the third chair.

SOMEBODY HAS BEEN SITTING IN MY CHAIR, AND HAS SAT THE BOTTOM OUT OF IT!

said the little, small, wee Bear, in his little, small, wee voice.

Then the Three Bears thought it necessary that they should make further search; so they went upstairs into their bedchamber. Now Goldilocks had pulled the pillow of the great, huge Bear out of its place—

See page 148

SOMEBODY HAS BEEN LYING IN MY BED!

said the great, huge Bear, in his great, rough, gruff voice.

And Goldilocks had pulled the bolster of the middle Bear's bed out of its place.

SOMEBODY HAS BEEN LYING IN MY BED!

said the middle Bear, in her middle voice.

And when the little, small, wee Bear came to look at his bed, there was the bolster in its place; and the pillow in its place upon the bolster; and upon the pillow was the head of Goldilocks—which was not in its place at all, for she had no business there.

SOMEBODY HAS BEEN LYING IN MY BED—AND HERE SHE IS!

said the little, small, wee Bear, in his little, small, wee voice.

Goldilocks had heard in her sleep the great, rough, gruff voice of the great, huge Bear, and the middle voice of the middle Bear, but only as if she had heard someone speaking in a dream. But when she heard the little, small, wee voice of the little, small, wee Bear, it was so sharp and so shrill that it awakened her at once. Up she started; and when she saw the Three Bears on one side of the bed she tumbled herself out at the other, and ran to the window.

Now the window was open, because the Bears, like

the good, tidy bears that they were, always opened their bedchamber window when they got up in the morning. Out Goldilocks jumped, and ran through the woods as fast as she could run—never looking behind her; and what happened to her afterward I cannot tell you. But the Three Bears never saw anything more of her again.   ROBERT SOUTHEY,
                                   L. LESLIE BROOKE COLLECTION

RUMPELSTILTZKIN

THERE WAS once upon a time a poor miller who had a very beautiful daughter. It happened one day that he had an audience with the King, and in order to appear a person of some importance he told His Majesty that he had a daughter who could spin straw into gold. "Now that is certainly a talent worth having," said the King to the miller. "If your daughter is as clever as you say she is, bring her to my palace tomorrow morning."

When the girl arrived the next day, the King led her into a room full of straw, gave her a spinning wheel and spindle and said, "Set to work and spin all night till early dawn, and if by that time you have not spun the straw into gold you shall die."

Then he closed the door behind him and left her alone inside.

So the poor miller's daughter sat down and did not know what in the world she was to do. She had not the least idea of how to spin straw into gold and at last became so miserable that she began to cry.

Suddenly the door opened, and in stepped a tiny little man who said: "Good evening, Miss Miller-Maid. Why are you crying so bitterly?"

"Oh," answered the girl, "I have to spin straw into gold for the King and I haven't a notion how it is done."

"What will you give me if I spin it for you?" asked the manikin.

"My necklace," replied the girl.

The little man took the necklace, sat himself down at the wheel, and whir, whir, whir, the wheel went around three times, and the bobbin was full. Then he put on another, and whir, whir, whir, the wheel went around three times, and the second too was full. And so it went on till the morning, when the whole room full of straw was spun away, and all the bobbins were full of gold.

As soon as the sun rose, the King came, and when he perceived the gold he was astonished and delighted, but seeing it only made him more greedy than ever for the precious metal. He had the miller's daughter put into another room full of straw, much bigger than the first, and bade her, if she valued her life, to spin it all into gold before the following morning.

The girl did not know what to do and began to cry. Then the door opened as before, and the tiny little man appeared, and said: "What will you give me if I spin the straw into gold for you?"

"The ring from my finger," answered the girl.

The manikin took the ring, and whir, around went the spinning wheel again, and when the sun rose he had spun all the straw into glittering gold. The King was pleased beyond measure at the sight, but he was still not satisfied, and he had the miller's daughter brought into a yet bigger room full of straw.

"You must spin all this away in the night," he said, "but if you succeed this time you shall become my wife." She's only a miller's daughter, he thought, but I could not find a richer wife if I were to search the whole world over.

When the girl was alone the little man appeared for the third time and said, "What will you give me if I spin the straw for you once again?"

"I've nothing more to give," answered the girl.

"Then promise me when you are Queen to give me your first child."

Who knows what may happen before that? thought

the miller's daughter, and, besides, she saw no other way out. So she promised the manikin what he demanded, and he set to work once more and spun the straw into gold. When the King came in the morning and found everything as he had desired, he straightway made her his wife, and the miller's daughter became a queen.

When a year had passed, a beautiful son was born to her. She had forgotten about the little man, till one day he suddenly stepped into her room and said, "Now give me what you promised."

The Queen was terribly upset, and offered the little man all the riches in her kingdom if he would only leave her the child.

But the manikin said, "No, a living creature is dearer to me than the finest treasures in the world." The poor Queen began to cry and sob so bitterly that the little man was sorry for her, and said: "I'll give you three days to guess my name, and if you discover it in that time you may keep your child."

Then the Queen pondered the whole night over all of the names she had ever heard and sent a messenger to scour the land to pick up far and near any names he should come across. When the little man arrived on the following day she began with Caspar, Melchior, Balthazar and every other name she had ever heard, but at each one the manikin called out, "That is not my name."

See page 154

The next day she sent to inquire the names of all the people in the neighborhood and had a long list of the most uncommon and extraordinary ready to ask the little man.

"Is your name, perhaps, Sheepshanks, Cruick-shanks, Spindleshanks?"

But he always replied, "That is not my name."

On the third day the messenger returned and announced: "I have not been able to find any new names; but as I came upon a high hill around the corner of the wood, where the foxes and hares bid each other good night, I saw a little house, and in front of the house burned a fire, and around the fire danced the most grotesque little man, hopping on one leg and crying:

> Tomorrow I brew, today I bake,
> And then the child away I'll take;
> For little deems my royal dame
> That Rumpelstiltzkin is my name!"

Imagine the Queen's delight at hearing the name—and when the little man stepped in shortly afterward and asked, "Now, my Lady Queen, what is my name?" she asked first: "Is your name Conrad?"

"No."

"Is your name Harry?"

"No."

"Is your name, perhaps, Rumpelstiltzkin?"

"Some demon has told you that! Some demon has told you that!" screamed the little man, and in his rage he drove his right foot so far into the ground that his leg sank in up to his waist. Then in a passion he seized his left foot with both of his hands and tore himself in two.

JAKOB AND WILHELM GRIMM, TRANSLATED BY MAY SELLAR

THE GOLDEN-HEADED FISH

ONCE UPON a time there lived in Egypt a King who had lost his sight from a bad illness. Of course he was very unhappy, and became more so as months passed and all the best doctors in the land were unable to cure him. The poor man grew so thin from misery that everyone thought he was going to die, and the Prince, his only son, thought so too. Great, therefore, was the rejoicing throughout Egypt when a traveler down the river Nile declared he was court physician to the king of a far country and would gladly, if he was allowed, examine the eyes of the blind man.

He was at once admitted into the royal presence and, after a few minutes of careful study, announced that the King's case, though very serious, was not entirely hopeless.

"Somewhere in the Great Sea," he said to the King, "there exists a golden-headed fish. If you can manage to catch this creature and bring it to me, I will prepare an ointment from its blood which will restore your sight. For a hundred days I will wait here, but if at the end of that time the fish should still not be caught, I must return to my own master."

The next morning the young Prince set forth in quest of the fish, taking with him a hundred men, each carrying a net. A little fleet of boats was awaiting them, and in these they sailed to the middle of the Great Sea.

For three months and more, they labored diligently from sunrise to sunset, but though they caught large multitudes of fishes not one of them possessed a golden head.

"It is quite useless now," said the Prince on the very last night, "for even if we find it this evening, the hundred days will be over in an hour, and long before we could reach the Egyptian capital the doctor will be on his way home. Still, I will go out and cast the net once more myself."

And the Prince did this, and at the very moment that the hundred days given him were up, he drew in his net and found the golden-headed fish entangled in its meshes.

"Success has come, but as often happens, it is too late," murmured the young man, who had studied in the schools of philosophy. "All the same, put the fish in that vessel full of water, and we will take it back. Then my father will know that we have done what we could." But when he drew near the fish, it looked up at him with such piteous eyes that he could not make up his mind to condemn it to death. For he knew well that, though the doctors of his own country were ignorant of the secret of the ointment, they would do everything in their power to extract something from the fish's blood.

He picked up the prize of so much labor and threw it back into the sea and then began his journey home to the palace. When at last the Prince reached it, he found the King in a high fever, caused by his disappointment, and he refused to believe the story told him by his son.

"Your head shall pay for it! Your head shall pay for it!" cried he, and bade his courtiers instantly summon the executioner to the palace.

Somebody ran at once to the Queen and told her of the King's order. She put common clothes on the Prince, filled his pockets with gold and hurried him on board a ship which was sailing that very night for a distant island.

"Your father will repent of this some day, and then he will be thankful to know that you are still alive," said she to her son. "But one last counsel will I give you: take no man into your service who desires to be paid every month."

The young Prince thought this advice rather odd. If a servant had to be paid anyhow, he did not understand what difference it could make whether it was by the year or by the month. However, he had many times learned that his mother was wiser than he, so he promised obedience.

After a voyage of several weeks, the Prince arrived at the island of which his mother had spoken. It was full of hills and woods and flowers, and beautiful white houses stood everywhere in gardens.

What a charming spot to live in, thought the Prince, and he lost no time in buying one of the prettiest of the dwellings.

Then servants came pressing to offer their services; but as they all declared that they must have payment at the end of every month, the young man declined to hire them.

At length, an Arab appeared one morning, begging the Prince to engage him.

"And what wages do you ask?" inquired the Prince, when he had questioned the newcomer and found him suitable.

"I do not want money," answered the Arab. "At

the end of a year you can see what my services are worth to you and can pay me in whatever way you like." The young man was pleased and took the Arab for his servant.

Now, although no one would have guessed it from the look of the part of the island where the Prince had landed, the other side was a complete desert, owing to the ravages of a horrible sea monster which devoured all the corn and cattle. The Governor had sent bands of soldiers to lie in wait for the creature in order to kill it, but, somehow, none ever happened to be awake at the moment that the ravages were committed. It was in vain that the sleepy soldiers had been punished severely—the same thing invariably occurred next time a group went on watch. At last, heralds went throughout the island to offer a great reward to the man who could slay the sea-beast.

As soon as the Arab heard the news he went straight to the Governor's palace. "If my master can succeed in killing the monster, what reward will you give him?" asked he.

"My daughter and anything besides that he chooses," answered the Governor.

The Arab shook his head.

"Give him your daughter and keep your wealth," said he. "But, henceforth, let her share in your gains, whatever they are."

"It is well," replied the Governor, and ordered a

deed to be prepared, which was signed by both of the men.

That night the Arab stole down to the shore to watch, but before setting out, he had rubbed himself with an oil which made his skin smart so badly that there was no chance of his going to sleep as the soldiers had done. Then he hid himself behind a large rock and waited. By and by a swell seemed to rise on the water and, after a few minutes, a hideous monster—part bird, part beast and part serpent—stepped noiselessly onto the rocks. It walked stealthily up toward the fields, but the Arab was ready for it and, when it passed, plunged his dagger into the soft flesh behind one ear. The creature staggered, gave a loud cry and then rolled over dead.

The Arab watched for a little while, in order to make sure there was no life left in his enemy. Since the huge body remained quite still, he quit his hiding place and cut off its ears. These he carried to his master, bidding him show them to the Governor and declare that he himself, and no other, had killed the monster.

"But it was you, and not I, who slew him," objected the Prince.

"Never mind; do what I bid you. I have a reason for it," answered the Arab. And, although the young man did not like taking credit for what he had not done, he finally gave in.

The Governor was so delighted at the news that he begged the Prince to marry his daughter that very day; but the Prince refused, saying that all he desired was a ship which would carry him to see the world. Of course this was granted him at once, and when he and his faithful Arab embarked, they found, heaped up in the vessel, stores of diamonds and many other precious stones which the grateful Governor had placed there for him.

So they sailed and they sailed and they sailed, and at length they reached the shores of a great kingdom. Leaving the Prince on board, the Arab went into the town to find out what sort of place it was. After some hours he returned, saying he had heard that the King's daughter was the most beautiful princess in the world and that the Prince would do well to ask for her hand in marriage.

The Prince listened to this advice and, taking some of the finest necklaces given him by the Governor, he mounted a splendid horse which the Arab had bought for him. He rode up to the palace, closely followed by his faithful attendant.

The strange King happened to be in a good humor, and they were readily admitted to his presence. Laying down his offerings on the steps of the throne, the Prince requested the King to grant him his daughter in marriage.

The monarch listened to him in silence, but finally

answered, "Young man, I will give you my daughter to wed, if that is your wish; but first I must tell you that she has already gone through the marriage ceremony with a hundred and ninety young men, and not one of them lived more than twelve hours. I advise you to think, while there is yet time."

The Prince was so frightened that he very nearly went back to his ship without any more words. But just as he was about to withdraw his proposal, the Arab whispered to him: "Fear nothing the King says, but take her."

"The luck must change some time," he said at last, "and who would not risk his head for the hand of the peerless Princess?"

"As you will," replied the King. "Since you wish it, I will give orders for the marriage to be celebrated tonight."

And so it was done. After the ceremony was performed the bride and bridegroom retired to their own apartment to sup by themselves, for such was the custom of the country. The moon shone bright, and the Prince walked to the window to look over the river and upon the distant hills, when his gaze suddenly fell on a silken shroud neatly laid out on a couch, with his name embroidered in gold thread across the front; for this was the pleasure of the King.

Horrified at the spectacle, he turned his head away, and this time his glance rested on a group of men digging busily beneath the window. It was a strange hour for anyone to be at work, and what was the hole for? It was a curious shape, so long and narrow, almost like——Ah, yes, that was what it was! It was his grave they were digging!

The shock of the discovery rendered him speechless, yet he stood fascinated and unable to move. At this moment a small black snake darted from the mouth of the Princess, who was seated at the table, and wriggled quickly toward him. But the Arab had hidden himself in the room and was secretly watching for something of the sort to happen. Seizing the serpent with a pair of pincers he had been holding in his left hand, he cut off its head with a sharp dagger.

The King could hardly believe his eyes when, early the next morning, his new son-in-law craved an audience with His Majesty.

"What, you?" he cried, as the young man entered his presence.

"Yes, I. Why not?" asked the bridegroom, who thought it best to pretend not to know anything that had occurred. "You remember I told you that the luck must turn at last, and so it has. But I came to ask whether you would be so kind as to bid the gardeners fill up a great hole right underneath my window; it spoils the view."

"Oh, certainly. Yes, of course it shall be done!" stammered the King. "Is there anything else?"

"No, nothing, thank you," replied the Prince, as he bowed and withdrew.

Now, from the moment the Arab cut off the snake's head, the spell, or enchantment—whatever it was— seemed to have been taken off the Princess, and she lived very happily with her husband. The days passed swiftly in hunting in the forests or sailing on the broad river that flowed past the palace, and when night fell she would sing to her harp, or the Prince would tell tales of his own country.

One evening, a man in strange garb, with a face burned brown by the sun, arrived at court. He asked to see the bridegroom and, falling on his face before the Prince, announced that he was a messenger sent by the Queen of Egypt, proclaiming him King in succession to his father, who was dead.

"Her Majesty begs you to set forth without delay, and your bride also, as the affairs of the kingdom are somewhat in disorder," ended the messenger.

Then the young man hastened to seek an audience with his father-in-law, who was delighted to find that his daughter's husband was not merely the Governor of a province, as he had supposed, but the King of a powerful country. He at once ordered a splendid ship to be made ready for the young couple, and in a week's time rode down to the harbor to bid farewell to the new ruler and his bride.

In spite of her grief for the dead King, the Queen

was overjoyed to welcome her son home, and commanded the palace to be hung with colorful banners to honor his bride. The people expected great things from their new sovereign, for they had suffered much under the harsh rule of the old one, and crowds presented themselves every morning with petitions which they hoped to persuade the King to grant.

Truly, the new King had enough to keep him busy; but he was very happy for all that, till one night the Arab came to him and begged permission to return to his own land.

Filled with dismay, the young man said, "Leave me? Do you really wish to leave me?"

Sadly, the Arab bowed his head. "No, my master, never could I wish to leave you! But I have received a summons, and I dare not disobey it."

The young King was silent, trying to choke down the grief which he felt at the thought of losing his faithful servant.

"Well, I must not try to keep you," he faltered at last. "That would be a poor return for everything you have done for me! Everything I have is yours; take what you will, for without you I should long ago have been dead!"

"And without you, I too should long ago have been dead," answered the Arab. "For I am the golden-headed fish."

ADAPTED BY FRÉDÉRIC MACLER, ANDREW LANG COLLECTION

HANSEL AND GRETEL

Once upon a time there dwelt on the outskirts of a large forest a poor woodcutter with his wife and two children; the boy was called Hansel and the girl Gretel. They had always little enough to live on, and once, when there was a great famine in the land, the woodcutter could not even provide them with daily bread.

One night, as he was tossing about in bed, full of cares and worry, he sighed and said to his wife, "What is to become of us? How are we to support our poor children, now that we have nothing more left even for ourselves?"

"Early tomorrow morning," answered the woman, who was the children's stepmother, "we will take Hansel and Gretel out into the thickest part of the woods. There we shall light a fire for them, give them each a piece of bread and go on to our work, leaving them alone. They will not be able to find their way home, and we shall thus be rid of them."

"No, wife," said her husband, "that I won't do. How could I find it in my heart to leave my children alone in the woods? The wild beasts would come and tear them to pieces."

"Oh," said she, "then we must all four die of hunger, and you may just as well go and prepare the boards for our coffins." And she left him no peace till he had consented.

"But I feel very sorry for the poor children just the same," said the husband.

The children, too, had not been able to sleep for hunger, and they overheard what their stepmother and father had said. Gretel wept bitterly, but Hansel whispered, "Don't fret, little Gretel. I will find a way to save us."

When the old people had fallen asleep he got up, slipped on his coat, opened the back door and stole out. The moon was shining brightly, and the white pebbles in front of the house glittered like bits of silver.

Hansel bent down and filled his pocket with as many of the stones as he could. Then he went back and said to Gretel, "Be comforted, dear sister, and go to sleep. God will not desert us." And he lay down in bed again.

At daybreak, even before the sun was up, the woman came and woke the two children. "Get up, you lazy things. We are going to the forest this morning to gather wood."

She gave them each a bit of bread and said, "There's

something for your luncheon, but do not eat it before, for it is all you will get."

Gretel put the bread into her apron pocket, as Hansel had the stones in his pocket. Then they set out together on the way to the forest.

After they had walked for a little while, Hansel stood still and looked back at the house, and this he did again and again.

His father observed him, and asked, "Hansel, what are you gazing at, and why do you always lag behind? Take care, and do not lose your footing."

"Oh, Father," said Hansel, "I am looking back at my white kitten, which is sitting on the roof, waving me a farewell."

The woman exclaimed, "What a donkey you are! That isn't your kitten, that is the morning sun shining on the chimney."

But Hansel had not been looking back at his kitten; he had been dropping the white pebbles out of his pocket onto the path.

When they reached the middle of the forest the father said, "Now, children, go and find some wood, and I will light a fire."

Hansel and Gretel heaped up brushwood till they had made a pile nearly the size of a small hill. The brushwood was set alight, and when the flames leaped high the woman said: "Now lie down by the fire, children, and rest yourselves. We are going into the forest to cut wood; when we have finished we will come back and fetch you."

Hansel and Gretel sat down beside the fire, and at midday ate their little bits of bread. They thought they heard the strokes of their father's axe close by. It was no axe they heard, however, but a bough on a dead tree blown about by the wind. And when they had sat for a long time their eyes closed with fatigue and they fell fast asleep. When they awoke at last they found it was pitch dark.

Gretel began to cry, and said, "How are we ever to get out of the wood?"

But Hansel comforted her. "Wait a bit," he said, "till the moon is up, and then we will find our way."

And when the full moon had risen he took his sister by the hand and followed the pebbles, which shone like silver and showed them the path. They walked all through the night, and at daybreak reached their father's house again. They knocked at the door and, when the woman opened it, she exclaimed, "You naughty children, what a long time you have slept in the forest! We thought you were never coming back." But the father rejoiced, for his conscience had tormented him for leaving his children.

Not long afterward there was again great scarcity in the land, and the children heard the woman say, "Everything is eaten up once more; we have only half a loaf of bread in the house. We shall lead them deeper into the woods this time so they cannot find their way out again."

The father's heart was filled with sadness as he pleaded with the woman, "Surely it would be better to share the last bite with one's children!" But if a man yields once he's done for.

When the old people were asleep Hansel wanted to go out and pick up pebbles again, as he had done the first time. The woman had barred the door, though, and he could not get out. But he consoled his little sister, and said, "Don't cry, Gretel. Sleep peacefully, for God is sure to help us."

At early dawn the woman came and made the children get up. They received their bit of bread, but it was even smaller than the time before. On the way to the woods Hansel crumbled it in his pocket, and every few minutes he stood still and dropped a crumb on the ground.

"Hansel, why are you stopping and looking about you?" said the father.

"I'm looking back at my little pigeon, which is sitting on the roof waving me a farewell," answered Hansel.

"That isn't your pigeon," said the woman, "it is the morning sun glittering on the chimney."

But Hansel gradually made a trail of crumbs to guide them home.

The woman led the children still deeper into the

forest, farther than they had ever been in their lives. Then a big fire was lit again, and she said, "Just sit down, children, and if you are tired you can sleep a bit. Your father and I are going into the forest to cut some wood and when evening comes we shall come back to fetch you."

At midday Gretel divided her bread with Hansel, for he had strewn his all along their path. Then they fell asleep, and it was evening, but nobody came for the poor children. They did not awake till it was pitch dark, and Hansel comforted his sister, saying, "Only wait, Gretel. When the moon rises, we shall see the crumbs I scattered along the path. They will show us the way back to the house."

When the moon rose they searched but found no crumbs, for the thousands of birds that fly about the woods and fields had picked them up. "Never mind," said Hansel, "we shall find a way out."

They wandered about the whole night, and the next day, from morning till evening, but they could not find a path out of the wood. They were very hungry, for they had eaten nothing but a few berries. And at last they were so tired they lay down under a tree and fell sound asleep.

On the third morning after they had left their father's house they were still wandering, and now they felt that if help did not come soon they must perish. At midday they saw a beautiful little snow-white bird sitting on a branch, which was singing so sweetly that they stopped to listen. When its song was finished it flapped its wings and flew on in front of them. They followed it and came to a little house, on the roof of which the bird perched. When they were quite near they saw that the cottage was made of gingerbread and covered with cakes, while the windows were made of transparent sugar.

"Now we can have a real feast," said Hansel. He reached up and broke off a bit of the roof to see what it was like, and Gretel went to a window and began to nibble at it. Thereupon a shrill voice called out from the room inside:

> Nibble, nibble, little mouse,
> Who is nibbling at my house?

The children answered:

> 'Tis Heaven's own child,
> The tempest wild,

and went on eating. Hansel, who thoroughly enjoyed the roof, tore down a big bit of it, while Gretel pushed out a whole round windowpane and sat down, the better to enjoy it. Suddenly the door opened, and an old woman leaning on a staff hobbled out. Hansel and Gretel were so terrified that they dropped what they had in their hands. But the old woman shook her head and said, "Oh, ho, you dear children! What has

brought you here? Just come in and stay with me; no harm shall befall you." She led them into the house and laid a sumptuous dinner before them—milk and sugared pancakes, pears, apples and nuts. After they had eaten, two beautiful little white beds were prepared for them, and when Hansel and Gretel lay down in them they felt as if they were in Heaven.

The old woman had appeared to be most friendly, but she was really an old witch. When anyone came into her power she cooked and ate him and held a regular feast day. Now witches have red eyes and cannot see far, but, like beasts, they have a keen sense of smell and know when human beings are nearby. When Hansel and Gretel fell into this witch's hands, she laughed maliciously and said, "I have them now. They cannot escape me."

Early in the morning, before the children were awake, she rose, and when she saw them both sleeping so peacefully, with their round, rosy cheeks, she muttered to herself, "They will make a dainty dish." Then she seized Hansel, carried him into a little stable and barred the door on him. He might scream as much as he liked; it would do him no good.

Then she went to Gretel, shook her awake roughly and cried, "Get up, you lazybones, fetch water and cook something for your brother. When he is fat I shall eat him." Gretel began to cry bitterly, but it was no use; she had to do what the witch bade her.

So the best food was cooked for poor Hansel, but Gretel got nothing but crab shells. Every morning the old woman hobbled out to the stable and cried, "Hansel, put out your finger that I may feel if you are getting fat or not."

But Hansel always stretched out a bone, and the old woman, because of her red eyes, never knew the difference and, always thinking it was Hansel's finger, wondered why he fattened so slowly.

When four weeks passed and Hansel still remained thin, she lost patience and determined to wait no longer. "Here! Gretel," she called to the girl, "be quick and get some water. Hansel may be fat or thin, I'm going to cook him tomorrow."

Oh, how the poor little sister sobbed as she carried the water, and how the tears rolled down her cheeks! "Kind Heaven, help us now!" she cried. "If only the wild beasts in the forest had eaten us, then at least we should have died together."

"Keep quiet," said the old witch, "crying won't help you."

That morning Gretel, as usual, had to hang up the kettle full of water and light the fire. "First we shall bake," said the old woman. "I have heated the oven and kneaded the dough." She pushed Gretel toward the oven. "Look in," said the witch, "and see if it is properly heated so we can shove in the bread." For when she had Gretel near the oven she meant to push

HANSEL AND GRETEL

her in and close the door and let the girl bake, that she
might eat her up too.

But Gretel knew what the old witch was up to, and
said, "I do not know how I am to do it. How do I get
my head in the oven?"

"You silly goose," said the witch, "the opening is
big enough. See, I could get in myself," and she
crawled toward it and poked her head into the oven.
Then Gretel gave her a shove that sent her right in. She
shut the iron door and drew the bolt. Gracious! How
the witch yelled! It was quite horrible, but Gretel fled,
and the wretched old woman was left there to perish
miserably.

Gretel flew straight to Hansel, opened the little
stable door and cried, "Hansel, we are free. The old
witch is dead." How they rejoiced and fell on each
other's necks and jumped for joy and kissed one
another! As they no longer had any cause for fear, they
went into the witch's house and there they found, in
every corner of the room, boxes with pearls and precious stones.

"These are even better than pebbles," said Hansel,
and crammed his pockets full of them.

"I, too, will bring something home." And Gretel
filled her apron.

"But now," said Hansel, "let us go well away from
the witch's forest."

When they had wandered about for some hours they

came to a big lake. "We cannot get over," said Hansel. "I see no bridge of any sort or kind."

"Yes, and there is no ferryboat either," answered Gretel. "But look, there swims a white duck; if I ask her she will help us." And she called out:

> Here are two children, mournful very,
> Seeing neither bridge nor ferry;
> Take us upon your downy white back,
> And row us over, quack, quack, quack!

The duck swam toward them, and Hansel got on her back and bade his sister sit beside him. "No," answered Gretel, "we should be too heavy a load for the duck. She shall carry us across separately." The good bird did this, and when they were landed safely on the other side and had gone on for a while, the wood became more and more familiar to them, and at length they saw their father's house in the distance. Then they set off at a run and, bounding into the front room, fell on their father's neck. The man had not passed a happy hour since he left them in the woods, and the woman had died. Gretel shook out her apron, and the pearls and precious stones rolled about the room, and Hansel threw down one handful after another from his pocket.

Thus all their troubles were ended, and they all lived happily ever afterward.

JAKOB AND WILHELM GRIMM, TRANSLATED BY MAY SELLAR

THE BRAVE LITTLE TAILOR

A TAILOR SAT in his work-room one morning, stitching away busily at a coat for the Lord Mayor. He whistled and sang so gaily that all the little boys who passed the shop on their way to school thought what a fine thing it was to be a tailor, and told one another that when they grew up they would be tailors, too.

"How hungry I feel, to be sure!" cried the little man at last. "But I'm far too busy to trouble about eating. I must finish His Lordship's coat before I touch a morsel of food," and he broke once more into a merry song.

"Fine new jam for sale!" sang out an old woman as she walked along the street.

"Jam! I can't resist such a treat," said the tailor, and, running to the door, he shouted: "This way, please! Show me a pot of your very finest jam."

The woman handed him jar after jar, but the tailor found fault with them all. At last he hit upon some jam to his liking.

"And how many pounds will you take, sir?"

"I'll take four ounces," he replied in a solemn tone, "and mind you give me a good weight."

The old woman was very angry, for she had expected to sell several pounds, at least; and she went off grumbling after she had weighed out the four ounces.

"Now for some food!" cried the little man, taking a loaf of bread from the cupboard as he spoke. He cut a huge slice and spread the jam on half an inch thick; then he suddenly remembered his work.

"It will never do to get jam on the Lord Mayor's fine coat," said he, "so I'll finish it before I take even one bite."

He picked up his work again, and his needle flew in and out like lightning.

I am afraid that the Lord Mayor later found some stitches in his garment that were almost a quarter of an inch long.

The tailor glanced at his slice of bread and jam once or twice, but when he looked the third time it was covered with flies, and a fine feast they were having from it.

This was too much for the little fellow. Up he jumped, crying, "So you think I provide bread and jam for you? Well, we'll soon see! Take that!" and he struck the flies such a heavy blow with a duster that no fewer than seven lay dead upon the table, while the others flew up hastily to the ceiling.

"Seven at one blow!" said the little man with great

pride. "Such a brave deed ought to be known all over the town, and it won't be my fault if folks fail to hear about it."

So he cut out a wide belt, and stitched on it in big golden letters the words "Seven at one blow." When this was done he put it on, crying, "I'm destined to be something better than a tailor, it's quite clear. I'm one of the world's great heroes, and I'll be off at once to seek my fortune."

He glanced around the cottage, but there was nothing of value to take with him. The only thing he possessed in the world was a small cheese. "You may as well come, too," said he, stowing away the cheese in his pocket, "and now I'll be on my way."

When he got into the street the neighbors all crowded around him to read the words on his belt. "Seven at one blow!" said they to one another. "What a blessing he's going! It wouldn't be safe to have a man about who could kill seven of us at one stroke."

You see, they didn't know that the tailor had only killed flies; they took it to mean men.

He jogged along for some miles until he came to a hedge where a little bird was caught in the branches. "Come with me," said the tailor. "I'll have you to keep my cheese company." So he caught the bird and put it carefully into his pocket with the cheese.

Soon he reached a lofty mountain, and he made up his mind to climb it and see what was happening on the other side. When he reached the top, there stood a huge giant, gazing down into the valley below.

"Good day," said the tailor.

The giant turned around, and seeing nobody but the little tailor there, he cried with scorn, "And what might you be doing here, might I ask? You'd best move along at once."

"Not so fast, my friend," said the little man, showing the giant his belt. "Read this."

"Seven at one blow," read the giant, and he began to wish he'd been more civil.

"Well, I'm sure nobody would think it to look at you," he replied. "But since you are so clever, do this," and he picked up a stone and squeezed it until water ran out.

"Do that! Why, it's mere child's play to me," and the tailor produced his cheese and squeezed it until the whey ran from it. "Now who is cleverer?" he asked. "You see, I can squeeze milk from a stone, while you get only water."

The giant was too surprised to utter a word for a few minutes. Then, taking up another stone, he threw it so high into the air that for a moment they weren't able to see where it went; then down it fell to the ground.

"Good!" said the tailor. "But I'll throw a stone that won't come back at all."

Taking the little bird from his pocket, he threw it

into the air, and the bird, glad to get away, flew right off and never returned.

This sort of thing didn't suit the giant at all, for he wasn't used to being beaten by anyone. "Here's something you'll never manage," said he. "Just come and help me to carry this fallen oak tree for a few miles."

"Delighted!" said the tailor. "I'll take the end with the branches, for it's sure to be heavier."

"Agreed," replied the giant, and he lifted the heavy trunk onto his shoulder, while the tailor climbed up among the branches at the other end and he sang as loud as he could, as though carrying a tree was but nothing to him.

The poor giant, who was holding the tree trunk and the little tailor as well, soon grew tired. "I'm going to drop it!" he shouted, and the tailor jumped down from the branches and pretended he had been helping all the time.

"The idea of a man your size finding a tree too heavy to carry!" laughed the little tailor.

"You are a clever fellow, and no mistake," replied the giant, "and if you'll only come and spend the night in our cave, we shall be delighted to have you."

"I shall have great pleasure in coming, my friend," answered the little tailor, and together they set off for the giant's home.

There were seven other giants in the cave, and each one of them was eating a roasted pig for his supper.

They gave the little man some food, and then showed him a bed in which he might pass the night. It was so big that after tossing about in it for half an hour the tailor thought he would be more comfortable if he slept in the corner, so he crept out of bed without being noticed.

In the middle of the night the giant stole up to the bed where he thought the little man was fast asleep. Taking a big bar of iron, he struck such a heavy blow at it that he roused all the other giants. "Keep quiet, friends," said he. "I've just killed the little scamp."

The tailor made his escape as soon as possible, and he journeyed on for many miles until he began to feel very tired. So he lay down under a tree and fell fast asleep. When he awoke, he found a big crowd of people standing around him. Up walked one very wise-looking old man, who was really the prime minister of the kingdom there. "Is it true that you have killed seven at one blow?" he asked.

"It is a fact," answered the little tailor.

"Then come with me to the King, my friend, for he's been searching for a brave man like you for some time past. You will be made captain of his army, and the King will give you a fine house to live in."

"That I will," replied the little man. "It is just the sort of thing that will suit me, and I'll come at once."

He hadn't been in the King's service long before everyone grew jealous of him. The soldiers were afraid that if they offended him he would make short work of them all, while the members of the King's household didn't fancy the idea of making such a fuss over a stranger.

So the soldiers went in a body to the King and asked that another captain be assigned to them, for they were afraid of this one. The King did not like to refuse, lest they would desert, and yet he did not dare get rid of the captain, in case such a strong and brave man should try to have his revenge.

At last the King hit upon a plan. In some woods close by, there lived two giants who were the terror of the countryside. They robbed travelers who were passing through, and if any resistance was offered they killed the men on the spot.

Sending for the little tailor, the King said, "Knowing you to be the bravest man in my kingdom, I want to ask a favor of you. If you will kill these two giants and bring me back proof that they are dead, you shall marry the Princess, my daughter, and have half my kingdom. You shall take one hundred men to help you, and you are to set off at once."

"One hundred men, Your Majesty! Pray, what do I want with one hundred men? If I can kill seven at one blow, I needn't be afraid of two. I'll kill them fast enough, never fear."

The tailor chose ten strong men and told them to await him on the border of the woods, while he went on alone. He could hear the giants snoring for half an hour before he reached them, so he knew in which direction to go.

He found the pair fast asleep under a tree, so he filled his pockets with stones and climbed up into the branches above their heads. He began to pelt one of the giants with the missiles, until after a few minutes he awoke. Giving the other a rough push, the giant cried, "If you dare to strike me like that again, I'll know the reason why."

"I didn't touch you," said the other giant crossly, and they were soon fast asleep once more.

Then the tailor threw stones at the other giant, and soon he awoke as the first one had done. "What did you throw that at me for?" said he.

"You are dreaming," answered the other, "I didn't throw anything."

No sooner were they fast asleep again, than the little man began to pelt the two of them afresh.

Up they both sprang and, seizing each other, they began to fight in earnest. Not content with using their fists, they tore up nearby trees by the roots and beat each other with these until very soon the pair lay dead on the ground.

Down climbed the little tailor, and taking his sword in his hand he plunged it into each giant, and then he went back to the edge of the forest where the ten men were waiting for him.

"They are as dead as two doornails," shouted the little man. "I don't say that I had an easy task, for they tore up trees by the roots to try to protect themselves, but of course it was no good. What are two giants to a man who has slain seven at one blow?"

The men wouldn't believe it until they went into the forest and saw the two dead bodies each lying in a pool of blood, while the ground was covered with uprooted trees. So they all told the King. But instead of handing over half his kingdom, as he had promised, His Majesty told the little tailor that there was still another brave deed for him to do before he got the Princess for his bride.

"Just name it, then; I'm more than ready," was the man's reply.

"You are to kill the famous unicorn that is running wild in the forest and doing so much damage. When this is done you shall have your reward at once."

"No trouble at all, Your Majesty. I'll get rid of him in a twinkling."

The tailor made the ten men wait for him at the entrance to the woods as they had done the first time and, taking a stout rope and a saw, he entered the forest alone once again.

Up came the unicorn, but just as it was about to rush at the man he darted behind a big tree. The unicorn dashed with such force against the tree that its horn was stuck quite fast in the trunk.

Taking his rope, the tailor tied it tightly around the animal, and, after sawing off the horn, back he went to the palace, leading the unicorn at his side.

But even then the King was not satisfied, and he demanded that the little man catch a wild boar that had been seen wandering in the woods. He took a party of huntsmen with him, but again he made them wait on the outskirts of the forest while he went on by himself.

The wild boar dashed at the little tailor, but the man was too quick for it. He slipped into a building close by, with the animal at his heels. Then, through a small window, he crawled out into the forest, while the boar inside the cabin was too big and clumsy to follow him. It stood gazing at the window where the man had disappeared, and the tailor ran around and closed the door, locking the animal inside. Then he called the hunters, who shot the boar and carried its body back to the palace.

This time the King was obliged to keep his promise. So the little tailor became a prince, and a grand wedding it was, too.

When they had been married for a few years, the Princess overheard her husband talking in his sleep one night. "Boy, take the Lord Mayor's coat to his home at once, or I'll box your ears," he said.

"Oh dear," cried the Princess, "to think that I've married a common tailor! Whatever can I do to get rid of him?"

See page 186

So she told her father the story, and the King said she need not worry, for he knew a way out of the difficulty. She was to leave the door open that night, and while the tailor was sleeping, the King's servants would steal into the room, bind the tailor and take him away to be killed. The Princess promised to see that everything was in readiness, and she tripped about all day with a light heart. She little knew that one of the tailor's servants had overheard their cruel plot and had carried the news straight to his master.

That night, when the Princess thought her husband was fast asleep, she crept to the door and opened it.

To her great terror, her husband began to speak. "Boy, take the Lord Mayor's coat to his home, or I'll box your ears. Haven't I killed seven at one blow? Haven't I slain two giants, a unicorn and a wild boar? What do I care for the men who are standing outside my door at this moment?"

At these words, off flew the men as though they had been shot from a gun, and no more attempts were ever made on the tailor's life. So the Princess had to make the best of a bad job.

He lived on, and when the old King died he ascended the throne in his stead. So the brave little tailor became ruler over the whole kingdom, and his motto throughout his whole life was, "Seven at one blow."

TRADITIONAL GERMAN TALE, COLLECTION OF
KATE DOUGLAS WIGGIN AND NORA ARCHIBALD SMITH

THE GINGERBREAD MAN

ONCE UPON a time there was a little old woman and a little old man, and they lived alone in a little old house. They didn't have any little girls or any little boys at all. So, one day, the little old woman made a boy out of gingerbread and she made a chocolate jacket and put cinnamon seeds in it for buttons. His eyes were made of fine, fat currants; his mouth was made of rose-colored sugar; and he had a gay cap of orange sugar-candy. When the little old woman had rolled him out, and dressed him up, and pinched his gingerbread shoes into shape, she put him in a pan. Then she put the pan in the oven and shut the door. Sitting there, she thought: Now I shall have a little boy of my own.

When it was time for the Gingerbread Boy to be done she opened the oven door and pulled out the pan. Out jumped the little Gingerbread Boy onto the floor and away he ran, out of the door and down the street! The little old woman and the little old man ran after him as fast as they could, but he just laughed and shouted:

Run! run! as fast as you can!
You can't catch me, I'm the Gingerbread Man!

And they couldn't catch him.

The little Gingerbread Boy ran on and on, until he came to a Cow by the roadside. "Stop, little Gingerbread Boy," said the Cow. "I want to eat you."

The little Gingerbread Boy laughed and said:

I have run away from a little old woman,
And a little old man,
And I can run away from you, I can!

And, as the Cow chased him, he looked over his shoulder and cried:

Run! run! as fast as you can!
You can't catch me, I'm the Gingerbread Man!

And the Cow couldn't catch him.

The little Gingerbread Boy ran on and on and on, until he came to a Horse in the pasture. "Please stop, little Gingerbread Boy," said the Horse, "you look very good to eat."

But the little Gingerbread Boy laughed out loud. "Oho! oho!" he said:

I have run away from a little old woman,
A little old man,
A cow,
And I can run away from you, I can!

And, as the Horse chased him, he looked over his shoulder and cried:

> Run! run! as fast as you can!
> You can't catch me, I'm the Gingerbread Man!

And the Horse couldn't catch him.

By and by the little Gingerbread Boy came to a barn full of threshers. When the threshers smelled the Gingerbread Boy, they tried to pick him up and said, "Don't run so fast, little Gingerbread Boy; you look very good to eat."

But the little Gingerbread Boy ran harder than ever and as he ran he cried out:

> I have run away from a little old woman,
> A little old man,
> A cow,
> A horse,
> And I can run away from you, I can!

And, when he found that he was ahead of the threshers, he turned and shouted back to them:

> Run! run! as fast as you can!
> You can't catch me, I'm the Gingerbread Man!

And the threshers couldn't catch him.

Then the little Gingerbread Boy ran faster than ever. He ran and ran until he came to a field full of mowers.

When the mowers saw how fine he looked, they ran after him, calling out, "Wait a bit! Wait a bit, little Gingerbread Boy, we wish to eat you!"

But the little Gingerbread Boy laughed harder than ever, and ran like the wind. "Oho! oho!" he said:

> I have run away from a little old woman,
> A little old man,
> A cow,
> A horse,
> A barn full of threshers,
> And I can run away from you, I can!

And when he found that he was ahead of the mowers, he turned and shouted back to them:

> Run! run! as fast as you can!
> You can't catch me, I'm the Gingerbread Man!

And the mowers couldn't catch him.

By this time the little Gingerbread Boy was so proud that he didn't think there was anybody at all who could catch him.

Pretty soon he saw a Fox coming across a field toward him. The Fox looked at the Gingerbread Boy and began to run.

But the little Gingerbread Boy shouted across to him: "You can't catch me!"

The Fox began to run faster, and the little Gingerbread Boy ran faster, and as he ran he chuckled:

See page 196

I have run away from a little old woman,
A little old man,
A cow,
A horse,
A barn full of threshers,
A field full of mowers,
And I can run away from you, I can!
Run! run! as fast as you can!
You can't catch me, I'm the Gingerbread Man!

"Why," said the Fox, "I would not catch you if I could. I would not think of disturbing you."

Just then, the little Gingerbread Boy came to a river. He could not swim across, and he wanted to keep running away from the Cow and the Horse and the people.

"Jump on my tail, and I will take you across," said the Fox.

So the little Gingerbread Boy jumped on the Fox's tail, and the Fox swam into the river. When he was a little way from shore he turned his head and said, "You are too heavy on my tail, little Gingerbread Boy, I fear I shall let you get wet; jump on my back."

The little Gingerbread Boy jumped on his back.

A little farther out, the Fox said, "I am afraid the water will cover you there. Jump on my shoulder."

The little Gingerbread Boy jumped on his shoulder.

In the middle of the stream the Fox said, "Oh, dear! Little Gingerbread Boy, my shoulder is sinking. Jump on my nose, so that I can hold you out of the water."

So the little Gingerbread Boy jumped on his nose.

The minute the Fox got on shore he threw back his head and gave a snap!

"Dear me!" said the little Gingerbread Boy, "I am a quarter gone!" The next minute he said, "Why, I am half gone!" The next minute he said, "My goodness gracious, I am three quarters gone!" And after that, the little Gingerbread Boy never said anything more at all.   TRADITIONAL ENGLISH TALE,
                                    RETOLD BY SARA CONE BRYANT

A HORNED GOAT

THERE WAS once a Goat, a wicked, horned Goat. She was at war with everyone, did mischief to all, butted with her horns, stamped her feet and threatened: "I, a hairy, horned Goat! Whoever touches me will fare badly! I will stamp him with my feet, I will beat him with my tail and I'll eat him up!"

All feared her because she threatened them terribly.

She grew bold, minded nobody and pillaged every garden. What she couldn't eat, she broke, stamped on and damaged. All suffered because all were afraid. One day she went into a tailor's garden where the tailor sat sewing at the window. When he spied the Goat among his cabbages, he jumped up shouting, but the Goat minded him not, just as if she hadn't heard him cry out.

"Oh, your hour has come! Do you think a tailor is afraid of a Goat?" shouted the master.

He caught up his big tailor's shears, jumped through the window and ran toward the Goat, opening and shutting his shears. The Goat saw a tailor for the first time; for the first time, also, she saw shears, and she became frightened at the brave tailor. She ran, and yet he followed her, opening and shutting his shears all the while.

The tailor was thin, lean and light, and he had long legs, but still the Goat ran faster on her four feet than the tailor could on his two. She escaped him, and the tailor fell on the grass, puffing.

"I am a hero. There is none braver than I," he said, and he went home a proud and haughty man.

The Goat kept on running. Leaving the road, she ran through a thick forest until, almost ready to drop from exhaustion, she fell into a Fox's den.

"I shall remain here; the tailor won't be able to find me," she said.

So she stayed, but she was so frightened that she trembled all over.

By this time Mrs. Fox had come home, but she could not get into her den because it was occupied by the Goat.

"Who's in there?" she called angrily.

The Goat was afraid, but she shouted loudly: "I, a hairy, horned Goat! Whoever touches me will fare badly! I will stamp him with my feet, I will beat him with my tail and I'll eat him up!"

Mrs. Fox almost fainted from fear. She went aside and sat, crying that she had no place to go. Soon Mr. Fox came home and, seeing his wife in distress, he asked her: "What has happened to you, Mother? Why do you cry?"

She answered: "A terrible misfortune has befallen us! Somebody went into our den, does not want to come out and threatens to eat us up!"

"Oh, who can it be?" said the Fox. "I will make him come out."

Together they went to the den. The Fox, knowing he was in the right, asked boldly in a deep voice: "Who is in there?"

The Goat was very much frightened, but she shouted with all her might: "I, a hairy, horned Goat! Whoever touches me will fare badly! I will stamp him with my feet, I will beat him with my tail and I'll eat him up!"

The Fox lowered his head, hung his tail between his hind legs and whispered: "I am not strong enough to make the creature come out. I can't help us!"

They went away into the forest, crying bitterly. A Hare met them and said, wonderingly: "This is news, this is news! Mr. Fox crying?"

"Oh, it's nothing! I have just tasted some strong tobacco," explained the Fox, wiping his eyes with shame.

"Tobacco? A Goat, and not tobacco! A Goat went into our den and will not come out. Where shall we go now, poor orphans?" cried Mrs. Fox.

The Hare, being kindhearted, felt sorry for Mr. and Mrs. Fox. He cried with them a little and then said: "Am I, a Hare of Hares, afraid of a foolish Goat? We shall see!"

He whisked past the Foxes to their den so fast that they could barely follow him and he called: "Who is in there? Come right out!"

The Goat became more and more frightened, because she knew there were many animals in the forest and, although some were afraid of her, there might come one that would chase her out of the den. And she thought that the tailor with his big shears waited outside the den. She stamped her feet and cried in a fearful voice: "I, a hairy, horned Goat! Whoever touches me will fare badly! I will stamp him with my feet, I will beat him with my tail and I'll eat him up!"

The Hare jumped aside and fled, as if a whole pack of greyhounds pursued him. When he saw that no one was after him, however, he felt ashamed and went back to the Foxes.

Now the Foxes were asking the Wolf to help them. Mrs. Fox sat under a bush, adding a word or two to the gentlemen's conversation. Mr. Fox, arm in arm with the Wolf, paced to and fro, putting the whole matter up to the Wolf.

"What shall we do now?" the Fox kept saying. "It is of no use looking for a new place, as all the dens, small holes and even last year's nests are occupied. Everything has its own corner and a roof over its head except us, poor orphans! We, Foxes of Foxes, that used to live comfortably, what shall we do when the little cubs come? Help us, Mr. Wolf, as you are our relative, friend and godfather, and I am helpless."

The Wolf listened patiently and said, gnashing his teeth: "You will be sleeping on that Goat's skin yet, you'll see. Lead me to your den; it is time to end this evil thing."

They went to the den, the Hare scampering after them. The Goat heard them coming and closed her eyes, thinking her last hour had come. The Wolf gnashed his teeth again, shouting: "Who is in there?"

The Goat, awaiting her death, at first could not make a sound, but then, in her terrible fright, she screamed in a voice she could not recognize as her own:

"I, a hairy, horned Goat!" and threatened as she had before.

When the Wolf heard that the Goat would stamp him with her feet and beat him with her tail, he became so frightened that he flattened his ears, stepped aside from the den and whispered to the Fox: "I can't help it; it is too much for me."

"Well, didn't I say so?" groaned the Fox. "Such is my misfortune to die without a home because of a horned Goat!"

They all wept and cried aloud. Going farther into the forest, they met a Bear, very much satisfied with himself, having just eaten a lot of sweet honey. He had been somewhat bitten by the bees who guarded their property; one part of his face was swollen, but he did not care, the hairy beast. Hearing so much lamentation, he stopped and asked what had happened.

They all began talking at the same time, making so much noise that the Bear covered up his ears and shouted to them to speak one at a time; otherwise, he said, he could not understand them and they would make him deaf.

Mrs. Fox had a greater ability for talking than the rest, so she described their sad affliction, saying unpleasant things about each and every helper. The Bear laughed heartily, repeating time after time: "They're afraid of a Goat, they're afraid of a horned Goat!"

The Fox and the Wolf resented the Bear's belittling

remarks, but they said nothing, as they wished him to help them. When the Bear had stopped laughing, he said: "All right, now. Let us go to the Goat. But I must take along my two helpers."

His two helpers were a Crab and a Porcupine. The Crab walked along slowly, moved his claws and threatened: "I am a Crab, and this is the way I pinch!"

The Porcupine rolled on his short feet, stuck out his needles and kept on saying: "I am a Porcupine, and this is the way I prick!"

The Bear called his helpers, and the whole crowd went to the den. The Bear asked the Goat: "How fare you in the den, my Nanny Goat?"

The Goat was terror-stricken, because she had never heard such a gruff voice, but she threatened as usual: "I will stamp you with my feet, I will beat you with my tail and I'll eat you up!"

"Oh, dear me!" laughed the Bear. "Eat up fast, don't delay! I'll send you down two!" Turning to those around him, he said to them: "The Crab and the Porcupine will go in to chase the Goat. The Wolf and I will wait at the mouth of the den to catch her. Mr. and Mrs. Fox had better wait on top of the hill to get her in case she should slip from our hands. The Hare, being the fastest, had better run to the other side of the hill. Should she pass us all, he won't let her go."

So the Crab pinched the Goat with all his strength and the Porcupine rolled with his needles over her

back, and the Goat whisked away from the den immediately, dashed past the Bear and the Wolf and ran up the hill so fast that the Foxes stepped aside. The Hare watched better than the rest; he jumped straight on her back and did not let her go. The whole crowd came running to mete out justice to the Goat.

"Well," said the Bear, "you got what you asked for. Your end has now come. Let the Foxes judge you, for they are the ones you wronged."

The Goat saw she was in trouble and that no one was afraid of her. So she began from a different angle. She stamped her feet, held her sides and mocked them: "What heroes you are! All of you together to get one Goat! A Bear and a Wolf, two Foxes and a Hare, and those other two have not reached me yet! Now you're so anxious to get to my skin! Hasten with my end; otherwise I'll make you known throughout the forest!"

They were ashamed and afraid that the other animals might hear the Goat shouting, and so the Wolf said: "All right, we will not go against you, a crowd against one. If you wish, we can have a proper war. Let us each gather an army and meet again in three days. Agreed?"

"Agreed!" shouted everybody. Even the Goat agreed, for what could she do? Just the same, she was glad that she gained three days' time. They parted to gather their armies. The Goat's enemies did not even try to find any allies, laughing at the thought of her army. The Bear, the Wolf and the Fox, just the three of them, were ready to fight the Goat, as it would not be becoming for Mrs. Fox to fight. The Crab and the Porcupine could not be found, and they were all ashamed to ask the Hare, for he had caught the Goat.

It went worse with the Goat. She was afraid of the tailor and she had accounts with other people. Where could she look for an army? She went hither and thither, but from each that she asked, a Dog or a Horse, she received the same answer: "You brewed the beer, drink it yourself!"

Besides, they were afraid to fight a Bear and a Wolf.

The Goat was desperate. She thought to herself: I will surely pay with my head, for I must keep my word and I cannot find anybody to help me.

But on the third day she came across Latek, a Dog with a scalded side, who was willing to help her.

He licked his side, saying: "I may just as well fight as not. I had one war with my master for killing his lamb and another war with my mistress for the lard she did not lock up in time. I may as well have a third war in the forest—I don't mind. Let us go!"

"There are not enough of us; we need at least one more," said the Goat.

"I'll bring along two more," promised the Dog. Soon he brought a dark gray Cat and a swaggering Rooster who was not afraid of anything.

"There are four of us now, and that makes a whole army," said the Dog. "Let us go." And they went into the forest.

The three left in the forest had grown tired of waiting so long for the Goat's army. The Fox at last begged the Bear: "Oh, brother, you know how to climb trees. Go up a pine, and you may be able to see them from that height."

The Bear climbed the pine, looked around and called down: "They're coming, they're coming! But—do you know?—it is a fierce-looking army! One shouts: 'Let me have him! Let me have him!' The second one crawls along the ground, scenting our tracks. The third one has a glistening sword hanging down his side. And this terrible Goat, to make matters worse! Well, my dears, you better look out for yourselves, for I am not coming down from this pine!"

At once the Wolf leaped aside and ran away. The Fox dug into the moss so that only the tip of his tail was seen. The Goat came with her army, looking for her enemies, but she found nobody. After a while the Cat spied the Fox's tail and grabbed it with his sharp claws. The Fox jumped out, shouting dreadfully, and in a fright the Goat's army ran in different directions. The Cat was frightened the most, and he ran up the tree to where the Bear sat.

They're after me! thought the terrified Bear. He let go of the branch where he sat and fell down to the ground with such a shock that the earth around trembled.

"Well, well," grumbled the Bear. "Now I may wander for three days and not meet anyone. My sides ache so I will not last without a massage. If I could only catch sight of the Hare! He would save me."

Somehow he got up and went along, moaning, when suddenly he heard nearby the Goat's doleful bleating.

If I could only get hold of you, I'd make your sides ache, too! thought the Bear to himself.

Just then the Goat appeared in front of him. The Hare sat on her back, holding her fast by her horns and threatening: "I will not let you go! You must be punished; you lost the war, since I caught you fleeing. Let the Fox judge you!"

"Oh, Mr. Hare!" called the delighted Bear. "Run, brother, bring me some mosquito fat, as I must be massaged after the war. My sides are so badly beaten that I can hardly stand. All my hope is in you, that you will save me, because I cannot go far by myself."

The Hare did not hesitate a moment; he jumped off the Goat's back and scuttled away for the mosquito fat. This was all the Goat needed. She knew the Bear could not chase her, so she leaped off and ran away. She ran one day, two, three; she ran six weeks and a year; and maybe she runs to this very day.

OLD POLISH TALE, TRANSLATED BY
LUCIA MERECKA BORSKI AND KATE B. MILLER

SEVEN SIMONS

FAR, FAR AWAY, beyond all the countries, seas and rivers, there stood a splendid city where lived King Archidej, who was as good as he was rich and handsome. His great army was made up of men ready to obey his slightest wish. He owned forty times forty cities, and in each city he had ten palaces with silver doors, golden roofs and crystal windows. His council consisted of the twelve wisest men in the country, each of whom was as learned as a whole college, and whose long white beards flowed down over their breasts. This council always told the King the exact truth.

Now the King had everything to make him happy, but he did not enjoy anything because he could not find a bride to suit him.

One day, as he sat in his palace looking out to sea, a great ship sailed into the harbor and several merchants came on shore. Said the King to himself, "These people have traveled far and beheld many lands. I will ask them if they have seen any princess who is as clever and as handsome as I am."

So he ordered the merchants to be brought before him. When they came, he said, "You have traveled much and visited many wonders. I wish to ask you a question and I beg you to answer truthfully.

"Have you anywhere seen or heard of the daughter of an emperor, king or prince, who is as clever and as handsome as I am and who would be worthy to be my wife and the Queen of my country?"

The merchants considered for some time.

At last the eldest of them said, "I have heard that across many seas, on the Island of Busan, there is a mighty King whose daughter, the Princess Helena, is so lovely that she can certainly not be plainer than Your Majesty and so clever that the wisest graybeard cannot guess her riddles."

"Is the island far off and which is the way to it?"

"It is not near," was the answer. "The journey would take ten years and we do not know the way. But even if we did, what use would that be? The Princess is no bride for you."

"How dare you say so?" cried the King angrily.

"Your Majesty must pardon us. Just think for a moment. Should you send an envoy to the island it will take him ten years to get there and ten more to return —twenty years altogether. Will not the Princess have grown old during that time and have lost all her beauty?"

The King reflected gravely. Then he thanked the

merchants, gave them leave to trade in his country without paying any duties and dismissed them.

After they were gone the King remained deep in thought. He felt puzzled and anxious, so he decided to ride into the country to distract his mind, and sent for his huntsmen and falconers.

The huntsmen blew their horns, the falconers took their hawks on their wrists, and they set out across country till they came to a green hedge. On the other side of the hedge stretched a great field of grain as far as the eye could see; the yellow tips swayed to and fro in the breeze like a rippling sea of gold.

The King drew rein and admired the field. "Upon my word," said he, "whoever dug and planted it must be good workmen. If every field in my kingdom were as well cared for as this, there would be more bread than my people could eat." And he wished to know to whom the field belonged.

Off rushed all his followers at once to do his bidding and found a nice, tidy farmhouse, in front of which sat seven peasants lunching on rye bread and water. They wore red shirts bound with gold braid, and were so much alike that one could hardly be told from another. The messengers asked, "Who owns this field of golden grain?"

The seven brothers answered, "The field is ours."

"And who are you?"

"We are King Archidej's laborers."

These answers were repeated to the King, who ordered the brothers to be brought before him at once. On being asked who they were, the eldest said, bowing low: "We, King Archidej, are your laborers, children of one father and mother, and we all have the same name—each of us is called Simon. Our father taught us to be true to our King, to till the ground and to be kind to our neighbors. He also taught each of us a different trade which he thought might be useful to us, and he bade us not to neglect Mother Earth, which would surely reward our labor."

The King was pleased with the honest peasant and said, "You have done well, good people, in planting your field and now you have a golden harvest. But I should like each of you to tell me what special trade your father taught you."

"My trade, O King," said the first Simon, "is not an easy one. If you will give me some workmen and materials I will build you a great white pillar that shall reach far above the clouds."

"Very good," replied the King. "And you, Simon the second, what is your trade?"

"Mine, Your Majesty," said the second Simon, "needs no great cleverness. When my brother has built the pillar I can climb it and, from the top, far above the clouds, I can see what is happening in every country under the sun."

"Good," said the King. "And Simon the third?"

"My work is very simple, sire. You have many ships built by learned men, with all sorts of new and clever improvements. If you wish it, I will build you quite a simple boat—one, two, three, and it's done! My plain little ship does not look grand enough for a king, but, where other ships take a year, mine makes the voyage in a day, and where they would require ten years, mine will do the distance in a week."

"Good," said the King again. "What has Simon the fourth learned?"

"My trade, O King, is really of no importance. Should my brother build you a ship, then let me embark in it. If we should be pursued by an enemy I can seize our boat by the prow and sink it to the bottom of the sea. When the enemy has sailed off I can draw it up to the top again."

"That is very clever of you," answered the King. "What does Simon the fifth do?"

"My work, Your Majesty, is mere blacksmith's work. Order me to build a smithy and I will make you a crossbow from which neither the eagle in the sky nor the wild beast in the forest is safe. The bolt hits whatever the eye sees."

"That sounds very useful," said the King. "And now, Simon the sixth, tell me your trade."

"Sire, it is so simple, I am almost ashamed to mention it. If my brother hits any creature I catch it quicker than any dog can. If it falls into the water I can pick it up out of the greatest depths; if it is in a dark forest I can find it even at midnight."

The King was much pleased with the trades and talk of the six brothers and said, "Thank you, good people. Your father did well to teach you all these things. Now follow me to the town, for I want to see what you can do. I need skillful people such as you about me, and when harvesttime comes I will send you home with royal presents."

The brothers bowed and said, "As the King wills."

Suddenly the King remembered that he had not questioned the seventh Simon, so he turned to him and said, "Why are you silent? What is your handicraft?"

And the seventh Simon answered, "I have no handicraft, O King: I have learned nothing; I could not manage it. And if I do know how to do anything it is not what might properly be called a real trade. It is, rather, a sort of performance which no one—not even the King himself—must watch me doing, and I doubt whether this performance of mine would please Your Majesty."

"Come, come," cried the King, "I will have no excuses! What is this trade?"

"First, sire, give me your royal word that you will not kill me when I have told you. Then you shall hear what it is."

"So be it, then. I give you my royal word."

Then the seventh Simon stepped back a little,

cleared his throat and said, "My trade, King Archidej, is such that a man who follows it in your kingdom generally loses his life and has no hope of pardon. There is only one thing I can do really well—that is to steal and to hide the smallest scrap of anything I have stolen. Not the deepest vault, even if its lock were enchanted, could prevent my stealing anything out of it that I wished to have."

When the King heard this he fell into a passion. "I will not pardon you, you rascal," he cried. "I will shut you up in my deepest dungeon, on bread and water, till you have forgotten such a trade. Indeed, it would be better to put you to death at once, and I've a good mind to do so."

"Don't kill me, O King! I am really not as bad as you think. Why, had I chosen, I could have robbed the royal treasury, bribed your judges to let me off and built a white marble palace with what was left. But though I know how to steal I don't do it. You yourself asked me my trade. If you kill me you will break your royal word."

"Very well," said the King, "I will not kill you. I pardon you. But from this hour you shall be shut up in a dark dungeon. Here, guards! Away with him to the prison! But you six Simons follow me and be assured of my royal favor."

So the six Simons followed the King. The seventh Simon was seized by the guards, who put him in chains and threw him into prison with only bread and water for food. Next day the King gave the first Simon carpenters, masons, blacksmiths and laborers, with great amounts of iron, mortar and the like. Simon began to build, and he built his great white pillar far, far up into the sky, as high as the nearest stars.

Then the second Simon climbed up the pillar and saw and heard all that was going on throughout the whole world. When he came down he had all sorts of wonderful things to tell. How one king was marching in battle against another and which was likely to be the victor. How, in another place, great rejoicings were going on, while in a third, people were dying of famine. In fact, there was not the smallest event going on over the earth that was hidden from him.

Next the third Simon began. He stretched out his arms, once, twice, thrice, and the wonder-ship was ready. At a sign from the King it was launched and floated like a bird on the waves. Instead of ropes it had wires for rigging, and musicians played on the wires with fiddle bows and made lovely music.

As the ship sailed about, the fourth Simon seized the prow with his strong hand and in a moment it was gone—sunk to the bottom of the sea. An hour passed, and then the ship was on top of the water again, drawn up by Simon's left hand, while in his right hand he carried a gigantic fish from the depths of the ocean for the royal table.

While this was going on, the fifth Simon had built his forge and hammered out his iron, and when the King returned from the harbor the magic crossbow was finished.

His Majesty went out into an open field at once, looked up into the sky and saw, far, far away, an eagle flying up toward the sun and looking like a tiny speck.

"Now," said the King, "if you can shoot that bird I will reward you."

Simon only smiled. He lifted his crossbow, took aim and fired, and the eagle fell. As it was falling, the sixth Simon ran up with a dish, caught the bird before it fell to earth and brought it to the King.

"Many thanks, my brave lads," said the King. "I see that each of you is indeed a master of his trade. You shall be richly rewarded. However, rest now and have your dinner."

The six Simons bowed and went to dinner. But they had hardly begun before a messenger came to say that the King wanted to see them. They obeyed at once and found him surrounded by all his court and councilors of state.

"Listen, my good fellows!" cried the King, as soon as he saw them. "Hear what my wise advisers have thought of. I am told that, far away, across many seas, is the great kingdom of the Island of Busan, and that the daughter of the King is the beautiful Princess Helena. As you, Simon the second, can see the whole world from the top of the great pillar, I want you to climb up and view the Island of Busan."

Off ran the second Simon and clambered quickly up the pillar. He gazed around, listened on all sides and then slid down to report to the King.

"Sire, I have obeyed your orders. Far away I saw the Island of Busan. The King is a mighty monarch but full of pride, harsh and cruel. He sits on his throne and declares that no prince or king on earth is good enough for his lovely daughter, that he will give her to none and if any king asks for her hand he will declare war against him and destroy his kingdom."

"Has the King of Busan a great army?" asked King Archidej. "Is his country far off?"

"As far as I could judge," replied Simon, "it would take you nearly ten years in fair weather to sail there. But if the weather were stormy it might be twelve. I saw the army being reviewed. It is not so very large— a hundred thousand men-at-arms and a hundred thousand knights. Besides these, he has a strong bodyguard and a good many crossbowmen. Altogether you might say another hundred thousand, and there is a picked body of heroes who reserve themselves for great occasions requiring particular courage."

The King sat for some time lost in thought. At last he said to the nobles and courtiers standing around, "I am determined to marry the Princess Helena, but how shall I do it?"

The nobles, courtiers and councilors said nothing, but tried to hide behind each other. Then the third Simon said: "Pardon me, Your Majesty, if I offer my advice. You wish to go to the Island of Busan? What can be easier? In my ship you will get there in a week instead of in ten years. But ask your council to advise you what you should do when you arrive—in one word, whether you will win the Princess peacefully or by war?"

But the wise men were as silent on this question as always.

The King frowned, and was about to say something sharp, when the court fool pushed his way to the front and said: "Dear me, what are all you clever people so puzzled about? The matter is quite clear. As it will not take long to reach the island, why not send the seventh Simon? He will steal the fair maiden fast enough, and then the King, her father, may consider how he is going to bring his army over here—it will take him ten years to do it! No less! What do you think of my plan?"

"What do I think? Why, that your idea is excellent and you shall be rewarded for it. Come, guards, hurry and bring the seventh Simon before me."

Not many minutes later, Simon the seventh stood before the King, who explained to him what he wished done, and also that to steal for the benefit of his King and country was by no means a wrong thing to do,

although it was very wrong to steal for his own advantage. The youngest Simon, who looked very pale and hungry, only nodded his head.

"Come," said the King, "tell me truly. Do you think you could steal the Princess Helena?"

"Why should I not steal her, sire? The thing is easy enough. Let my brother's ship be laden with rich brocades, Persian carpets, pearls and jewels. Send me in the ship. Give me my four middle brothers as companions and keep the two others as hostages."

When the King heard these words his heart became filled with longing for the Princess and he ordered all to be done as Simon wished. Everyone ran about to do his bidding, and in next to no time the wonder-ship was laden and ready to start.

The five Simons took leave of the King, went on board and had no sooner set sail than they were almost out of sight. The ship cut through the waters like a falcon through the air, and just a week after starting sighted the Island of Busan. The coast appeared to be strongly guarded, and from afar the watchman on a high tower called out to them: "Halt and anchor! Who are you? Where do you come from and what do you want?"

The seventh Simon answered from the ship, "We are peaceful people. We come from the country of the great and good King Archidej and we bring foreign wares—rich brocades, carpets and costly jewels—

which we wish to show to your King and the Princess. We desire to trade—to sell, to buy and to exchange."

The brothers launched a small boat, took some of their valuable goods with them, rowed to shore and went up to the palace. The Princess sat in a rose-red room, and when she saw the brothers coming near she told her lady-in-waiting to inquire who these people were and what they wanted.

The seventh Simon answered the lady-in-waiting. "We come from the country of the wise and good King Archidej," said he, "and we have brought all sorts of goods for sale. We trust the King of this country may condescend to welcome us and let his servants take charge of our wares. If he considers them worthy to adorn his followers, we shall be content."

This speech was repeated to the Princess, who ordered the brothers to be brought to the rose-red room at once. They bowed respectfully to her and displayed some splendid velvets and brocades, and opened cases of pearls and precious stones. Such beautiful things had never been seen in the island, and the ladies of the court stood bewildered by the magnificence. They whispered together that they had never beheld anything like that. The Princess, too, saw and wondered. Her eyes could not weary of looking at the lovely things nor her fingers of stroking the rich, soft velvets and of holding up the sparkling jewels to the light.

"Fairest of Princesses," said Simon, "be pleased to

order these gracious ladies to accept the silks and velvets and let them trim their headdresses with the jewels; these are no special treasures. But permit me to say that they are as nothing to the many-colored tapestries, the gorgeous stones and ropes of pearls in our ship. We did not like to bring more with us, not knowing what your royal taste might be. But if it seems good to you to give honor to our ship with a visit, you might condescend to choose such things as are pleasing in your eyes."

This polite speech pleased the Princess very much. She went to the King and said, "Dear Father, some merchants have arrived with the most splendid wares. I pray you to allow me to go to their ship and choose what I like."

The King thought and thought, frowned hard and rubbed his ear. At last he gave consent and ordered out his royal yacht, with a hundred crossbowmen, a hundred knights and a thousand soldiers to escort the Princess Helena.

Off sailed the yacht with the Princess and her escort. The brothers Simon came on board to conduct the Princess to their ship and, led by the brothers and followed by her lady-in-waiting and other women, she crossed the crystal plank which led from one vessel to the other.

The seventh Simon spread out his goods. He had so many curious and interesting tales to tell about them that the Princess forgot everything else in looking and listening, so she did not know that the fourth Simon had seized the prow of the ship and that all of a sudden it had vanished from sight and was racing along in the depths of the sea.

The crew of the royal yacht shouted aloud, the knights stood still with terror, the soldiers were struck dumb and hung their heads. There was nothing to be done but to sail back and tell the King of his loss.

How he wept and stormed! "Oh, light of my eyes," he sobbed, "I am indeed punished for my pride! I thought no one good enough to be your husband and now you are lost in the depths of the sea and have left me alone! As for all of those who saw this thing— away with them! Let them be put in irons and locked in prison while I think how I can best put them to death!"

While the King of Busan was raging and lamenting in this fashion, Simon's ship was swimming like a fish under the sea. When the island was well out of sight he brought the ship up to the surface again. At that moment the Princess recollected herself.

"We have been gazing at these wonders too long," she said to her lady-in-waiting. "I hope my father won't be vexed at our delay."

She tore herself away from the treasures and stepped on deck. Neither the yacht nor the island was in sight! Helena wrung her hands and beat her breast.

Then she changed herself into a white swan and flew up. But the fifth Simon seized his bow and shot the swan, and the sixth Simon did not let it fall into the water but caught it on the ship. Then the swan turned into a silver fish, but Simon lost no time and caught the fish, when, quick as thought, the fish turned into a black mouse and ran about the ship. It darted toward a hole, but before it reached it, Simon sprang upon it more swiftly than any cat, and then the little mouse turned once more into the beautiful Princess Helena.

Early one morning, just two weeks after the ship had left his kingdom, King Archidej sat thoughtfully at his window gazing out to sea. His heart was sad and he would neither eat nor drink. His thoughts were full of the Princess Helena, who was as lovely as a dream. When, suddenly—is that a white gull approaching the shore or is it a sail? No, it is no gull, it is the wonder-ship flying along with billowing sails. Its flags waved, all the fiddlers played on the wire rigging, the anchor was thrown out and the crystal plank laid from the ship to the pier.

The lovely Helena stepped across the plank. She shone like the sun, and the stars of heaven seemed to sparkle in her eyes.

Up sprang King Archidej in haste. "Hurry, hurry!" he cried. "Let us hasten to meet her! Let the bugles sound and the joyful bells be rung!"

The whole court swarmed with courtiers and servants. Golden carpets were laid down and the great gates of the palace were thrown open to welcome the Princess.

King Archidej went out himself, took her by the hand and led her into the royal apartments.

"Madam," said he, "the fame of your beauty had reached me, but I did not dare to expect such loveliness. Still, I will not keep you here against your will. If you wish it, the wonder-ship shall take you back to your father and your own country. But if you will consent to stay here, then reign over me and my country as our Queen."

What more is there to tell? It is not hard to guess that the Princess listened to the King's wooing, and that their betrothal took place with great pomp and rejoicings.

The brothers Simon were sent again to the Island of Busan with a letter to the King from his daughter to invite him to their wedding. And the wonder-ship arrived at the Island of Busan just as all the knights and soldiers who had escorted the Princess were being led to their execution.

Then the seventh Simon cried out from the ship: "Stop! Stop! I bring a letter from the Princess Helena!"

The King of Busan read the letter over and over again and ordered the knights and soldiers to be set free. He entertained King Archidej's ambassadors hospitably and told them to return to his daughter with his blessing, but he could not be persuaded to attend the wedding.

When the wonder-ship came home again, King Archidej and Princess Helena were enchanted with the news it brought.

The King sent for the seven Simons. "A thousand thanks to you, my brave fellows!" he cried. "Take whatever gold, silver and precious stones you want from my treasury. Tell me if there is anything else you wish for and I will give it to you, my good friends. Do you wish to be made nobles or to govern towns? Only speak."

Then the eldest Simon bowed and said, "We are plain folk, Your Majesty, and understand simple things best. What figures would we cut as nobles or governors? Nor do we desire gold. We have our fields which give us food and as much money as we need. If you wish to reward us, then grant that our land may be free of taxes, and of your goodness pardon the seventh Simon. He is not the first who has been a thief by trade and he will certainly not be the last."

"So be it," said the King, "your land shall be free of all taxes, and Simon the seventh is pardoned."

Then the King gave each brother a goblet of wine and invited them all to the wedding feast. And what a feast that was!

OLD HUNGARIAN TALE, ANDREW LANG COLLECTION

THE LITTLE MATCH-GIRL

IT WAS BITTERLY cold, snow was falling and darkness was gathering, for it was the last evening of the old year—it was New Year's Eve.

In the cold and gloom a poor little girl walked, bareheaded and barefoot, through the streets. She was wearing slippers, it is true, when she left home, but what good were they? They had been her mother's, so you can imagine how big they were. The little girl had lost them as she ran across the street to escape from two carriages that were being driven terribly fast. One slipper could not be found, and a boy had run off with the other, saying that he could use it very nicely as a cradle some day when he had children of his own.

So the little girl walked about the streets on her naked feet, which were red and blue with the cold. In her old apron she carried a great many matches, and she had a packet of them in her hand as well. Nobody had bought any from her, and no one had given her a single penny all day long. She crept along, shivering and hungry, the picture of misery, poor little thing! The snowflakes fell on her long golden hair which curled so prettily about her neck, but she did not think of her appearance now. Lights were shining in every window, and there was a glorious smell of roast goose in the street, for it was New Year's Eve, and she could not think of anything else.

She huddled down in a heap in a corner formed by two houses, one of which projected farther out into the street than the other, but though she tucked her little legs up under her she felt colder and colder. She did not dare to go home, for she had sold no matches nor earned a single penny. Her father would be sure to beat her, and besides it was so cold at home, for they had nothing but the roof above them and the wind whistled through that, even though the largest cracks were stuffed with straw and rags. Her thin hands were almost numb with cold. If only she could dare pull just one small match from the packet, strike it on the wall and warm her fingers!

She pulled one out—scr-r-ratch!—how it sputtered and burned! It had a warm, bright flame like a tiny candle when she held her hand over it—but what a strange light! It seemed to the little girl as if she were sitting in front of a great iron stove with polished brass knobs and brass ornaments. The fire burned so beautifully and gave out such a lovely warmth. Oh, how wonderful that was! The child had already stretched

her feet to warm them, too, when—out went the flame, the stove vanished and there she sat with a bit of the burned match in her hand.

She struck another—it burned clearly, and, where the light fell upon the wall, the bricks became transparent, like gauze. She could see right into the room, where a shining white cloth was spread on the table. It was covered with beautiful china and in the center of it stood a roast goose, stuffed with prunes and apples, steaming deliciously. And what was even more wonderful was that the goose hopped down from the dish, waddled across the floor with carving knife and fork in its back, waddled straight up to the poor child! Then—out went the match, and nothing could be seen but the thick, cold wall.

She struck another match, and suddenly she was sitting under the most beautiful Christmas tree. It was much larger and much lovelier than the one she had seen last year through the glass doors of the rich merchant's house. A thousand candles lit up the green branches, and gaily colored balls like those in the shop windows looked down upon her. The little girl reached forward with both hands—then, out went the match. The many candles on the Christmas tree rose higher and higher through the air, and she saw that they had now turned into bright stars. One of them fell, streaking the sky with light.

"Now someone is dying," said the little girl, for old

Granny, the only one who had ever been good to her but who was dead, had said, "Whenever a star falls, a soul goes up to God."

She struck another match on the wall. Once more there was light, and in the glow stood her old Granny, oh, so bright and shining, and looking so gentle, kind and loving. "Granny!" cried the little girl. "Oh, take me with you! I know you will disappear when the match is burned out; you will vanish like the warm stove, the lovely roast goose and the great glorious Christmas tree!"

Then she quickly struck all the rest of the matches she had in the packet, for she did so want to keep Granny with her.

The matches flared up with such a blaze that it was brighter than broad daylight, and her old Granny had never seemed so beautiful nor so stately before. She took the little girl in her arms and flew with her high up, oh, so high, toward glory and joy! Now they knew neither cold nor hunger nor fear, for they were both with God.

But in the cold dawn, in the corner formed by the two houses, sat the little girl with rosy cheeks and smiling lips, dead—frozen to death on the last evening of the old year. The dawn of the new year rose on the huddled figure of the girl. She was still holding the matches, of which a packet had been burned more than halfway down.

"She was evidently trying to warm herself," people said. But no one knew what beautiful visions she had seen and in what a blaze of glory she had entered with her dear old Granny into the heavenly joy and gladness of a new year.

HANS CHRISTIAN ANDERSEN, TRANSLATED BY PAUL LEYSSAC

EAST OF THE SUN
AND WEST OF THE MOON

ONCE UPON a time there was a poor countryman who had many children and little to give them either of food or clothing. They were all very pretty, but the prettiest was the youngest daughter.

Once, late on a Thursday evening in autumn, with wild weather outside, they were sitting together by the fireside, each busy with something or other, when suddenly someone rapped three times against the windowpane. The man went outside to see what could be the matter, and there in front of him stood a great big White Bear.

233

"Good evening to you," said the White Bear.

"Good evening," said the man.

"Will you give me your youngest daughter?" said the White Bear. "If you will, you shall be as rich as you are now poor."

Truly, the man had no objection to being rich, but he said to himself, "I must first ask my daughter about this." So he went in and told them all that a great White Bear was outside, who had promised to make them rich if he could have the youngest daughter.

But she said no, she would not hear of it. So the man went out again and settled with the White Bear that he should come again the next Thursday evening and get her answer. Then the man talked so much to her about the wealth they would have, and what a good thing it would be for herself, that at last she made up her mind to go, and washed and mended her rags to make herself as stylish as she could. Little enough had she to take away with her.

Next Thursday evening, the White Bear came to fetch her. She seated herself on his back with her bundle, and thus they departed. When they had gone a great part of the way, the White Bear said, "Are you afraid?"

"No, I am not," said she.

"Keep tight hold of my fur and then there is no danger," said he.

And thus she rode far, far away, until they came to

a great mountain. When the White Bear knocked on it, a door opened, and they went into a castle where there were many brilliantly lighted rooms which shone with gold and silver. There was a well-spread table, so magnificent it would be hard to make anyone understand how splendid it was.

The White Bear gave her a silver bell, which she had only to ring when she needed anything. After her supper she grew sleepy and thought she would like to go to bed. So she rang the bell, and scarcely had it sounded before she found herself in a chamber where a bed stood ready. It had pillows of silk, and curtains of silk fringed with gold, and everything in the room was of gold or silver. But when she had lain down and put out the light a man came and lay down beside her, and—behold!—it was the White Bear, who cast off the form of a beast during the night. She never saw him, however, for he always appeared after she had put out her light and went away before daylight.

So everything went well for a time, but then she began to be very sad and sorrowful. All day long she was alone; and she did so wish to go home to her father and mother and brothers and sisters. Then the White Bear asked what it was she wanted, and she told him it was because she could not see her brothers and sisters that she was so sorrowful.

"There might be a cure for that," said the White Bear, "if you would but promise me never to talk with your mother alone, as she will wish. If you do you will bring great misery on both of us."

So one Sunday the White Bear said they could now set out to see her father and mother. With the girl sitting on his back, they went a long, long way, and it took a long, long time. But at last they came to a large white farmhouse, and her brothers and sisters were running about outside, playing, and it was so pretty it was a pleasure to look at.

"Your parents dwell here now," said the White Bear. "But do not forget what I said to you, or you will do much harm both to yourself and me."

"No, indeed," said she, "I shall never forget." And as soon as she was at home the White Bear turned around and went away.

There were such rejoicings when she went in to her parents that it seemed as if they would never come to an end. Everyone thought he could never be sufficiently grateful to her for all she had done for them. Now they had everything they wanted, and everything was as good as it could be. All was well with her, too, she said, and she had everything she could want, but what other answers she gave did not tell them much about her.

In the afternoon, after they had dined at midday, it happened just as the White Bear had said. Her mother wanted to walk with her alone, but she remembered what the White Bear had told her and would on no account go. "What we have to say can be said at any time," she answered. But somehow or other her mother at last persuaded her, and she was forced to tell the whole story. She told how she continually went about in sadness, thinking how happy she would be if she could only see the White Bear when he was a man, and how all day long she was alone and it was so dull.

"Oh," cried the mother, in horror, "he is very likely a troll! You shall have a bit of one of my candles. Look at him with the candle when he is asleep. Take care, though, not to let any tallow drop upon him."

So she took the candle and hid it in her dress, and when evening drew near the White Bear came to take her away. When they had gone some distance, the White Bear asked her if everything had not happened just as he had suspected, and she had to admit to him that it had.

"Then, if you have done what your mother wished," he said, "you have brought great misery on both of us."

"No," she said, "I have not done anything at all."

When they reached home it was just the same as it had been before. A man came and lay down beside her, and late at night, when she knew he was sleeping, she rose and lit her candle. She saw he was the handsomest prince that eyes had ever beheld. She loved him so much it seemed she must die if she did not kiss him that moment. She did kiss him, but let three drops of hot tallow fall upon his shirt, and he awoke.

THE WORLD'S BEST FAIRY TALES

"What have you done now?" said he. "If you had just held out for the space of one year I should have been free. I have a stepmother who has bewitched me so I am a white bear by day and a man by night. Now all is at an end, and I must leave you and go to her. She lives in a castle which lies east of the sun and west of the moon. There is a Princess with a nose more than a yard long, and now she is the one I must marry."

She wept, but all in vain, for go he must. Then she asked him if she could not go with him. But no, that could not be. "Can you tell me the way then, and I will seek you—that I may surely be allowed to do!"

"Yes, you may do that," said he, "although there is no way to find it. It lies east of the sun and west of the moon, and never could you find your way there."

When she awoke in the morning, both the White Bear and the castle were gone and she was lying on a small green patch in the midst of a dark, thick wood. By her side lay the selfsame bundle of rags she had brought with her. When she had rubbed the sleep out of her eyes, and wept till she was weary, she set out on her way.

At last she came to a great mountain. At its foot an aged woman was sitting, playing with a golden apple. The girl asked her, "Do you know the way to the Prince who lives east of the sun and west of the moon, and who is to marry a Princess with a nose more than a yard long?"

"How do you happen to know about him?" inquired the old woman. "Maybe you are the one who should have had him."

"Yes, indeed, I am," she said.

"So it is you, then?" said the old woman. "I know only that he dwells in a castle east of the sun and west of the moon. You will be a long time reaching it, if ever you get there at all. But you shall have the loan of my horse. Ride on it to an old neighbor of mine; perhaps she can tell you. When you arrive there you must strike the horse beneath the left ear and bid it return home again. You may, however, take the golden apple with you."

The girl rode for a long, long way, and at last she came to another mountain, where an aged woman was sitting with a gold carding comb. The girl asked her if she knew the way to the castle which lay east of the sun and west of the moon. But she said what the first old woman had said: "I know nothing about it but that it is east of the sun and west of the moon, and you will be a long time in reaching it, if ever you get there at all. You shall have the loan of my horse to ride to the old woman who lives beyond me; perhaps she may know where the castle is. When you have reached her, just strike the horse beneath the left ear and bid it go home again."

Then she gave her the gold carding comb, for it might be of use to her, she said.

So the girl seated herself on the horse and rode a wearisome way onward again, and after a long, long time she came to a great mountain where an aged woman was sitting, spinning at a golden spinning wheel. She inquired if she knew the way to the castle which lay east of the sun and west of the moon.

"Maybe you should have had the Prince," said the old woman.

"Yes, I should have been the one," said the girl.

But this old crone knew the way no better than the others did.

It was east of the sun and west of the moon, she knew that. "And you will be a long time reaching it, if ever you get there at all," she said. "But you may have the loan of my horse, and I think you had better ride to the East Wind and ask him; perhaps he may know where the castle is and will blow you there. When you have reached him you must strike the horse beneath the left ear and he will come home again."

And then she gave her the golden spinning wheel, saying, "Perhaps you may find you have a use for it."

The girl had to ride for a great many days, for long hours, before she found the East Wind. But at last she did arrive, and then she asked him if he could tell her the way to the Prince who dwelt east of the sun and west of the moon.

"Well," said the East Wind, "I have heard tell of the Prince and his castle, but I do not know the way to it, for I have never blown so far. But, if you like, I will go with you to my brother the West Wind; he may know, for he is much stronger than I am. You may sit on my back and then I can carry you there."

She seated herself on his back, and off they went—so very swiftly! When they arrived, the East Wind went in and told his brother that the girl he had brought was the one who should have had the Prince at the castle which lay east of the sun and west of the moon, and now she was traveling about to find him again, and he had brought her to ask if the West Wind knew where the castle was.

"No," said the West Wind, "as far as that I have never blown. But, if you like, I will go with you to the South Wind, for he is much stronger than either of us and has roamed far and wide. Perhaps he can tell you what you want to know. You may seat yourself on my back and I will carry you to him."

They journeyed to the South Wind, nor were they long on the way, and the West Wind asked his brother if he could tell her the way to the castle that lay east of the sun and west of the moon, for she was the girl who should marry the Prince who lived there.

"Oh, indeed!" said the South Wind. "Well," said he, "I have wandered about a great deal in my time, and in all kinds of places, but I have never blown so far as that. If you like, however, I will go with you to my brother the North Wind. He is the oldest and strongest of us all, and if he does not know where the castle is, no one in the whole world will be able to tell you. You may sit upon my back and I will carry you there."

So she seated herself on his back, and off he went from his house in great haste, and they were not long on the way. When they came near his dwelling, the North Wind was so wild and frantic that they felt cold gusts long before they reached it.

"What do you want?" he roared out from afar, and they froze as they heard his voice.

Said the South Wind, "It is I, and this is the girl who should have had the Prince who lives in the castle which lies east of the sun and west of the moon. And now she wishes to ask you if you have been there and can tell her the way, for she would gladly find him."

"Yes," said the North Wind, "I know where it is. I once blew an aspen leaf there, but I was so tired that for many days afterward I was not able to blow at all. However, if you really are anxious to go there and are not afraid to go with me, I will take you on my back and try to carry you there."

"Go there I must," said she, "and if there is any way I will. I have no fear, no matter how fast you go."

"Very well then," said the North Wind, "but you must sleep here tonight, for we must have the day before us."

The North Wind woke her early the next morning,

and puffed himself up and made himself so big and so strong that it was frightful to see him, and away they went, high up through the air, as if they would not stop until they had reached the very end of the world. Below there was such a storm! It blew down woods and houses and, when they were above the sea, ships were wrecked by the hundreds.

Thus they tore on and on, and a long time went by, and then yet more time passed, and still they were above the sea, and the North Wind grew tired, and more tired, and at last so utterly weary he was scarcely able to blow any longer, and he sank and sank, lower and lower, until at last he went so low that the crest of the waves dashed against the heels of the poor girl he was carrying.

"Are you not afraid?" asked the North Wind.

"I have no fear," said she; and it was true.

They were not very far from land, and there was just enough strength left in the North Wind to enable him to throw her onto the shore, immediately under the windows of a castle which lay east of the sun and west of the moon. But then he was so weary and worn out he was forced to rest for several days before he could go to his own home again.

Next morning, the girl sat down beneath the walls of the castle to play with the golden apple, and the first person she saw was the maiden with the long nose who was to marry the Prince.

"How much do you want for that golden apple of yours, girl?" she asked, opening the window.

"It cannot be bought either for gold or money," answered the girl.

"If it cannot be bought either for gold or money, what will buy it? You may say what you please," said the Princess.

"Well, if I may go to the Prince who is here, and be with him tonight, you shall have it," said the girl who had come with the North Wind.

"You may do that," said the Princess, for she had made up her mind what she would do.

So the Princess got the golden apple, but when the girl went up to the Prince's apartment that night he was asleep, for the Princess had so contrived it by giving him a sleeping potion. The poor girl called to him and shook him, and between whiles she wept, but she could not wake him. In the morning, as soon as day dawned, in came the Princess with the long nose and drove her out again.

In the daytime she sat down once more beneath the windows of the castle and began to card with her golden carding comb; and then all happened as it had before. The Princess asked her what she wanted for it, and the girl replied it was not for sale, either for gold or money, but if she could have leave to go to the Prince and be with him during the night, she should have it. But when she went up to the Prince's room he was again asleep, and let her call him or shake him or weep as she would, he still slept on, and she could not put any life in him. When daylight came in the morning, the Princess with the long nose came too, and once more drove her away.

When day had come the girl seated herself under the castle windows, to spin with her golden spinning wheel, and the Princess with the long nose wanted to have that also. So she opened the window, and asked what she would take for it. The girl said what she had said on each of the former occasions—that it was not for sale either for gold or for money, but if she could have leave to go to the Prince who lived there, and be with him during the night, the Princess should have it. "Yes," said the Princess, "I will gladly consent to that."

In that palace there were some decent folk who had been sitting in the chamber which was next to that of the Prince and had heard how a woman had been there, weeping and calling on him two nights running, and they told the Prince of this. So that evening, when the Princess came once more with her potion, he pretended to drink but threw it away behind him instead, for he suspected that it was a sleeping drink. When the girl went into the Prince's room, this time he was awake, and she had to tell him how she had come to find her way there.

"You have come just in time," said the Prince, "for

I should have been married tomorrow. But I will not have the long-nosed Princess; and you alone can save me. I will say that I want to see what my bride can do and bid her wash the shirt which has the three drops of tallow on it. This she will consent to, for she does not know it is you who let them fall on it. No one can wash them out but one born of real folk; it cannot be done by a troll. Then I will say that no one shall ever be my bride but the woman who can succeed at this, and I know that you can."

There was great joy and gladness between them, and the next day, when the wedding was to take place, the Prince said to his stepmother, "I must see what my bride can do."

"That you may," said she.

"I have a fine shirt which I want to wear at my wedding, but three drops of tallow have got upon it which I want to have washed off, and I have vowed to marry no one but the woman who is able to do it. If she cannot, she is not worth having."

Well, that was a very small matter, they thought, and agreed to it.

The Princess with the long nose began to wash as well as she could, but the more she washed and rubbed, the larger the spots grew.

"Ah, you cannot wash at all," said the old troll who was her mother. "Give it to me."

But she too had not had the shirt very long in her

hands before it looked worse still, and the more she washed it and rubbed it, the larger and blacker grew the spots.

The other trolls had to come and wash, but the more they did, the blacker and uglier grew the shirt, until at length it was as black as if it had been up the chimney.

"Oh," cried the Prince, "not one of you is good for anything at all! There is a beggar girl sitting outside the window, and I'll be bound she can wash better than any of you! Come in, you girl there!" he cried.

So she came in.

"Can you wash this shirt clean?" he cried.

"Oh, I don't know," she said. "But I will try."

And no sooner had she taken the shirt and dipped it in the water than it was white as driven snow, and even whiter than that.

"I will marry you," said the Prince.

Then the old troll flew into such a rage that she burst, and the Princess with the long nose and all the little trolls must have burst too, for they have never been heard of since.

The Prince and his bride set free all the good people who were imprisoned there, and took with them all the gold and silver they could carry and moved far away from the castle which lay east of the sun and west of the moon. PETER C. ASBJÖRNSEN AND JÖRGEN E. MOE,
ANDREW LANG COLLECTION

THE MUSICIANS OF BREMEN

A CERTAIN MAN had a Donkey that had served him faithfully for many long years, but whose strength was so far gone that at last he was quite unfit for work. So his master began to consider how much he could get for the Donkey's skin, but the beast, perceiving that something was up, ran away along the road to Bremen. There, thought he, I can be town musician. When he had run some way, he found a Hound lying by the roadside, yawning like one who was very tired. "Why are you doing that, you big fellow?" asked the Donkey.

"Ah," replied the Hound, "because every day I grow older and weaker. I can no longer run with the hunt, and my master has almost beaten me to death. So I took flight, and now I do not know where to turn in order to earn my bread."

"Well," said the Donkey, "I am going to Bremen, to be town musician there. Suppose you go with me and take a share in the music. I will play the lute, and you shall beat the kettledrums." The Hound was pleased with the plan, and off they set.

Presently they came to a Cat, sitting in the middle of the path, with a face like three rainy days! "Now, then, Old Whiskers, what is bothering you?" asked the Donkey.

"How can one be merry when one's neck is in danger?" answered the Cat. "Because I am growing old, and my teeth are all worn to stumps, and because I would rather sit by the fire than run after mice, my mistress wanted to drown me; and so I ran away. But good advice is hard to find, and now I do not know what to do."

"Come with us to Bremen. You are an expert at night music, so you can be a town musician, too." The Cat agreed, and went along with them. The three vagabonds soon came to a farmyard, where a Cock was sitting on a barn door crowing with all his might. "Your crowing can pierce through marrow and bone," said the Donkey. "What do you do that for?"

"That is the way I prophesy fine weather," said the Cock. "But important guests are coming for Sunday dinner tomorrow and my mistress has told the cook to make me into soup. Tonight I shall lose my head, so I am crowing with a full throat as long as I can."

"Ah, but you, Red-Comb, should come away with us," replied the Donkey. "We are going to Bremen, to find something better than death. You have a good voice, and if we four make music together it will have full play."

The Cock was delighted with the idea, and so all four traveled on together.

They could not, however, reach Bremen in one day, and at evening they came to a forest, where they meant to pass the night. The Donkey and the Hound lay down under a large tree. The Cat and the Cock climbed up into the branches, but the latter flew right to the top, where he was most safe. Before he went to sleep he looked around the countryside and thought he saw a little spark in the distance; so, calling his companions, he said they were not far from a house, for he saw a light. The Donkey said, "If it is so, we had better get up and go toward it, for it's not very comfortable here in this place." And the Hound continued, "Yes, indeed! A couple of bones with meat on them would be very acceptable!"

So they made haste toward the spot where the light was, and which shone brighter and brighter, until they came to a well-lighted robber's den. The Donkey, as the biggest, went to the window and peeped in. "What do you see, Gray Horse?" asked the Cock.

"What do I see?" replied the Donkey. "I see a table laid out with savory meats and drinks, and robbers sitting around enjoying themselves."

"That would be the right sort of thing for us," said the Cock.

"Yes, yes, I wish we were sitting there," replied the Donkey. Then the animals took counsel together on how to drive away the robbers, and at last they thought of a plan.

The Donkey placed his forefeet upon the window ledge, the Hound got on his back, the Cat climbed up upon the Hound, and, lastly, the Cock flew up and perched upon the Cat. When this was accomplished, at a given signal they commenced to perform their music. The Donkey brayed, the Hound barked, the Cat meowed, and the Cock crowed; and they made such a tremendous noise that the windowpanes splintered and crashed. Terrified at these unearthly sounds, the robbers jumped up, thinking that some demons had burst in on them, and fled off into the forest. The four musicians immediately made themselves at home, and quickly ate all that was left, as if they had been fasting for six weeks.

As soon as they had finished, they put out the light, and each sought for himself a sleeping place according to his nature and custom. The Donkey stretched out upon some straw, the Hound behind the door, the Cat upon the hearth near the warm ashes, and the Cock flew up on a beam which ran across the room. Weary with their long walk, they soon went to sleep.

At midnight the robbers could see from their retreat that no light was burning in their house, and everything appeared quiet. The captain said, "We need not have been frightened into fits," and, calling one of the band, he sent him forward to reconnoiter. The

messenger, finding all still, went into the kitchen to strike a light, and, taking the glistening, fiery eyes of the Cat for live coals, he held a match to them, expecting the match to take fire. But the Cat flew in his face, spitting and scratching, and frightening him so dreadfully that he made for the back door; then the Hound, who lay nearby, sprang up and bit his leg; and as he limped over the straw where the Donkey was stretched out, it gave him a powerful kick with its hind foot. This was not all, for the Cock, awakened by the noise around him, cried from his perch on the beam, "Cock-a-doodle-doo, cock-a-doodle-doo!"

Then the robber ran back as fast as he could to his captain and cried, "Ah, my master, there dwells a horrible witch in the house, who spat on me and scratched my face with her long nails. In front of the door stands a man with a knife, who chopped at my leg, and in the yard there lies a black monster, who beat me with a great wooden club. In addition to all that, upon the roof sits a judge, who called out, 'Bring the knave up, do!'—so I ran away as fast as I could."

After this the robbers dared not go near their house again, but everything prospered so well with the four town musicians of Bremen that they never left their new home. And there they have been, from that day to this, for all I know.

OLD GERMAN TALE, COLLECTION OF
KATE DOUGLAS WIGGIN AND NORA ARCHIBALD SMITH

BLUE BEARD

THERE WAS once a man who had fine houses, both in town and country, a great deal of silver and gold plate, embroidered furniture and gilded coaches. But this man was unlucky enough to have a blue beard, which made him so frightfully ugly that all the women and girls ran away from him.

One of his neighbors, a lady of quality, had two daughters who were perfect beauties. He asked her for one of them in marriage, leaving to her choice which of the two she would bestow on him. Neither of them would have him. Another reason, besides the beard, for their disgust and aversion was his having been married to several wives; and nobody knew what had become of them.

To win their affection, Blue Beard took them, with their mother, three or four ladies of their acquaintance and some young people of the neighborhood, to one of his country houses, where they all stayed for a week. There was nothing but parties, hunting, fishing, dancing, mirth and feasting. Nobody went to bed, for they spent the night playing games and joking with one another. In short, everything went so well that the younger daughter began to think the master of the house was an agreeable gentleman after all.

As soon as they returned home, the marriage took place, and about a month afterward, Blue Beard told his wife he was obliged to take a journey for six weeks at least, about affairs of very great consequence. He begged her to amuse herself in his absence, and suggested that she invite some of her friends to the country, if she pleased, and to enjoy herself wherever she might be.

"Here," said he, "are the keys to the large storerooms wherein I have my best furniture; these are for my silver and gold plate, which is not in use every day; these open my strongboxes, which hold my money, both gold and silver; these, my caskets of jewels; and this is the master key to all my apartments. But this little one is the key to the closet at the end of the gallery on the ground floor. Open any of them you wish; you may go into every one, except that little closet, which I forbid you."

She promised to observe exactly what he had ordered. Then, having embraced her, he got into his coach and started on his journey.

Her neighbors and good friends did not wait to be sent for, so great was their impatience to see the rich furnishings of her house. Not daring to do so

while her husband was at home, they ran through the
rooms and looked into the closets and wardrobes, all
fine and rich.

They praised and envied the happiness of their
friend, who hardly greeted them—such was her eagerness to open the closet on the ground floor. She was
so driven by her curiosity that she went down a little
back staircase with such excessive haste that twice or
thrice she nearly broke her neck.

When she reached the closet door, she stopped for
some time, thinking of her husband's orders, but the
temptation was strong and she could not overcome it.
She took the little key and opened the door, trembling,
but could not at first see anything plainly, because the
shutters were closed. After some moments she perceived a bloodstained floor on which lay the bodies
of several dead women. These were the wives Blue
Beard had married and murdered, one after another.
She thought she would die of fear, and the key, which
she had pulled out of the lock, fell from her hand.

When she had somewhat regained her courage, she
picked up the key, locked the door and went upstairs
into her room to recover herself, but she could not,
so frightened was she. Having observed that the key
of the closet was stained with blood, she tried two
or three times to wipe it off. In vain did she wash it
and even rub it with soap and sand—but the blood
still remained, for the key was magical and she could

never make it quite clean. When the blood was gone from one side, it appeared again on the other.

Blue Beard returned from his journey that same evening, saying he had received letters on the way informing him the business matter had ended to his advantage. Next morning he asked her for the keys, which she gave him, but with such a trembling hand he easily guessed what happened. "What!" said he. "How comes this blood upon the key?"

"I do not know," cried the poor woman, paler than death.

"You do not know!" replied Blue Beard. "I know very well. You were resolved to go into the closet, were you not? Very well, madam, you shall go in and take your place among the ladies you saw there."

Hearing this, she threw herself at her husband's feet. She would have melted a rock, so beautiful and sorrowful was she, but Blue Beard had a heart harder than any rock!

"You must die, madam," said he, "and very soon."

"Since I must die," answered she, looking upon him with her eyes filled with tears, "give me some little time to say my prayers."

"I give you," replied Blue Beard, "half a quarter of an hour, but not one moment more."

When she was alone she called out to her sister, who was still visiting with her, and said, "Sister Anne, go up, I beg you, to the top of the tower, and look if our brothers are not coming. They promised me they would come today. If you see them, give them a sign to make haste."

Her sister Anne went up on the top of the tower, and the poor, afflicted wife called, "Anne, sister Anne, do you see anyone coming?"

And sister Anne said, "I see nothing but the sun, which makes a dust, and the grass, which looks green."

Meanwhile Blue Beard, holding a great saber in his hand, shouted to his wife, "Come down instantly, or I shall come up to you."

"One moment longer, if you please," said his wife. And then she cried out very softly, "Anne, sister Anne, do you see anyone coming?"

And sister Anne answered, "I see nothing but the sun, which makes a dust, and the grass, which is green."

"Come down quickly," cried Blue Beard, "or I will come up to you."

"I am coming, I am coming," answered his wife. And then she called, "Anne, sister Anne, do you not see anyone coming?"

"I see," replied sister Anne, "a great dust, which comes on this side here."

"Are they our brothers?"

"Alas, no, my dear sister, I see a flock of sheep."

"Will you not come down?" cried Blue Beard.

"One moment longer," said his wife. And then she

cried out, "Anne, sister Anne, do you see nobody coming?"

"I see," said she, "two horsemen, but they are still a great distance away."

"Heaven be praised," replied the poor wife joyfully. "They are our brothers; I will make a sign, as well as I can, for them to make haste."

Then Blue Beard bawled out so loud that he made the whole house tremble. The distressed wife came down and threw herself at his feet, all in tears, with her hair about her shoulders.

"This means nothing to me," said Blue Beard. "You must die." Then, taking hold of her hair with one hand and lifting up the sword with the other, he was about to take off her head. The poor lady, looking at him with pleading eyes, begged him for one moment more to collect herself. "No, no," said he, "commend yourself to God," and was just ready to strike.

At this very instant, there was such a loud knocking at the gate that Blue Beard stopped short. Two horsemen entered, drawing their swords. Blue Beard knew them to be his wife's brothers and he immediately dashed off to save himself. But the two brothers pursued so closely that they overtook him before he reached the steps, where they ran their swords through him and left him dead. The poor wife was almost as dead as her husband and had not strength enough to rise and welcome her brothers.

Blue Beard's wife became mistress of all his estate. She made use of one part of it to marry her sister Anne to a young gentleman who had loved her a long while; another part to buy captains' commissions for her brothers; and the rest to marry herself to a very worthy gentleman, who soon made her forget the ill time she had passed in the house of Blue Beard.

CHARLES PERRAULT, ANDREW LANG COLLECTION

THE PRINCESS
ON THE GLASS HILL

ONCE UPON a time there was a man who had a meadow which lay on the side of a mountain, and in the meadow there was a barn in which he stored hay. Every St. John's Eve, when the grass was at its height, it was all eaten clean up— just as if a flock of sheep had gnawed it down to the ground during the night. This happened once, and it happened twice, but then the man grew tired of losing his crop and said to his sons—he had three of them, and the third was called Cinderlad—that one of them must go and sleep in the barn on St. John's Eve, for it was absurd to let the grass be eaten up again, blade and stalk.

The eldest was quite willing to go to the meadow; he would watch the grass, he said, and he would do it so well that neither man nor beast nor even the devil himself should have any of it. So he went to the barn and lay down to sleep, but when night was drawing near there was such a rumbling and such an earthquake that the walls and roof shook, and the lad jumped up and took to his heels, and the barn remained empty again that year.

Next St. John's Eve, the second son was willing to show what he could do. He went to the barn and lay down to sleep, as his brother had, but when night fell there was a great rumbling, and then an earthquake, which was even worse. When the youth heard it, he was terrified and went off, running as if his life depended upon it.

The year after, it was Cinderlad's turn, but when he made ready to go, the others laughed at him. "Well, you are just the right one to watch the hay, you who have never learned anything but how to sit among the ashes and toast yourself by the fire!" said they. Cinderlad, however, did not trouble himself about what they said, and when evening drew near he rambled away to the outlying field.

He went into the barn and lay down, but in about

an hour's time the rumbling and creaking began, and it was frightful to hear. "Well, if it gets no worse than that, I can stand it," said Cinderlad. In a little time the creaking began again, and the earth quaked so that all the hay flew around the boy.

"Oh, if it gets no worse than that I can stand it," said Cinderlad. Then came a third rumbling and a third earthquake, so violent that the boy thought the walls and roof had fallen in; when that was over everything suddenly grew as still as death around him. Cinderlad thought the upheaval would come again, but everything was quiet, and everything stayed quiet. After a short time, he heard something that sounded as if a horse were chewing just outside the barn door. He crept to the door to see what it was, and there stood a horse eating away. It was so big and fat and fine a horse that Cinderlad had never seen one like it before; a saddle and bridle lay upon it, and a complete suit of armor for a knight, and everything was of copper so bright that it sparkled.

"Ha, ha! It is you who eats our hay then," said the boy. "I will stop that." So he made haste and took out his flint for striking fire, for it has a power over animals. He threw a spark over the horse, and then it could not stir from the spot and the boy could do what he liked with it. He mounted and rode away to a place no one knew of but himself, and tied the horse up. When he went home, his brothers laughed and asked how he had got on. "You did not lie long in the barn if you have been even as far as the field!" said they.

"I lay in the barn till the sun rose," said the boy. "What made you two so frightened?"

"Well, we shall soon see whether you have watched the meadow or not," answered the brothers. But they found the grass just as long and as thick as it had been the night before!

The next St. John's Eve, neither of the two older brothers dared go to the outlying field to watch the crop, but Cinderlad went, and everything happened exactly as before. There was a rumbling and an earthquake, and then there was another, and then a third. All three earthquakes were much, very much more violent than they had been the year before. Everything became still as death again, and the boy heard something chomping outside the barn. When he went to look. through a crack in the door, there was a horse standing close by the wall of the house, eating and chewing. It was far larger and fatter than the first horse, and it had a saddle on its back and a bridle, too, and a full suit of armor for a knight, bright silver and as beautiful as anyone could wish to see.

"Ho, ho!" said the boy. "Is it you who eats our hay in the night? I will put a stop to that." So he took out his flint for striking fire and threw a spark over the horse's mane, and the beast stood there as quiet as a lamb. Then the boy rode this horse, too, away to the place where he kept the other and then went back to his house again.

"I suppose you will tell us the grass hasn't been touched this time either," said the brothers.

"Well, so it hasn't," said Cinderlad. And there it was—the grass standing as high and as thick as it had been before; but that did not make them any kinder to Cinderlad.

When the next St. John's Eve came, neither of the older brothers was brave enough to go to the outlying barn to watch the grass, but Cinderlad dared to go. There were three earthquakes, each worse than the other, and the last flung the boy all the way across the barn, then everything suddenly became still as death. When he had lain quietly a short time, he heard the chewing sound outside the barn. He peeped through the crack in the door, and, behold—there stood a horse just outside, much larger and fatter than the two others he had caught. The saddle and bridle were gold, and there was a suit of golden armor, too.

"Ho, ho! It is you, then, who eats our hay this time," said the boy, "but I will put a stop to that." So he pulled out his flint for striking fire and threw a spark over the horse, and it stood as still as if it had been nailed to the field, and the boy could do just what he liked with it. He mounted the horse and rode away to the place where he kept the two others, and then he went home again.

The two brothers mocked him just as they had done before, but Cinderlad did not trouble himself about that, telling them to go to the field and see. This time, also, the grass was standing, looking as fine and as thick as ever.

Now it happened that the King had a daughter whom he offered to give to the one who could ride to the top of a very high hill of glass, slippery as ice, which stood close to his palace. Upon the top of this the King's daughter was to sit with three golden apples in her lap, and the man who was able to ride up and carry off the three apples could marry her and have half the kingdom. The King had this proclaimed throughout the whole kingdom, and in many other kingdoms, too.

The Princess was very beautiful, and all who saw her fell in love with her, in spite of themselves. It is needless to say that the princes and knights were eager to win her—and half the kingdom besides. They came riding from the ends of the world, dressed so splendidly that their raiments gleamed in the sunshine, and riding on horses which seemed to dance as they went. There was not one of these princes who did not think he was sure to win the Princess.

When the day of the contest arrived, there was such a host of knights and princes at the foot of the glass hill that it made one dizzy to look at them. Everyone who could walk or even crawl was there to see who would win the King's daughter. Cinderlad's two brothers were there too, but they would not hear of letting him go with them, for he was so dusty and grimy from sleeping among the ashes that they said everyone would laugh at them if they were seen in the company of such an oaf.

Then I will go by myself, thought Cinderlad.

When the two brothers appeared at the scene, the princes and knights were trying so hard to ride up the glass hill that their horses were in a foam. It was all in vain, for no sooner did the horses set foot upon the hill than down they slipped. Not one could get even so much as a couple of yards, for the hill was as smooth as a glass windowpane and as steep as the side of a house. But they were eager to win the King's daughter and half the kingdom, so they kept riding and kept slipping. At length all the horses were so tired they could do no more, and so hot that the foam dropped from them, and the princes and knights were forced to stop.

The King was just about to proclaim that the riding should begin afresh on the following day, when suddenly a knight came riding up on a horse of such beauty that no one had ever seen its like before. The knight had on armor of copper, and his bridle was of copper too, so bright that it sparkled. The other knights called out to him that he might just as well spare himself the trouble of trying to ride up the glass hill, for it was of no use; but he did not heed them and rode straight off to it and went up as if it were nothing at all. Thus he rode for a long time—it may have been a third of the way to the top—but turned his horse around and rode down again.

The Princess thought she had never seen so handsome a knight, and while he was riding up she was thinking: Oh, how I hope he will be able to come to the top! When she saw that he was turning his horse back, she threw down one of the golden apples after him, and it rolled into his shoe. But when he reached the bottom of the hill he rode away so fast no one knew what had become of him.

All the princes and knights were bidden to present themselves before the King that night in order that he who had ridden so far up the glass hill might show the golden apple which the King's daughter had thrown down. But no one had anything to show. One knight after another presented himself, and none could show the apple.

That same night, Cinderlad's brothers came back and had a long story to tell. At first, they said, there was no one able to get even so much as one step up the hill, but then came a knight who had armor of copper and a bridle of copper, and his armor and trappings were so bright they shone for a great distance, and it was a grand sight to see him riding. He rode one third of the way up the glass hill, and he could easily have ridden the whole of it if he had liked. But he had made up his mind that that was enough.

"Oh, I should have liked to see him too—that I should," said Cinderlad.

Next day, the brothers were about to set out again, and this time, too, Cinderlad begged to go with them and see who rode. But no, they said—he was not fit to do that, for he was much too ugly and dirty. Well, well, then I will go all by myself, thought Cinderlad. So the brothers went to the glass hill, and all the princes and knights began to ride again. Not one could even get so far as a yard up the hill. When they had tired out their horses so they could do no more, they again had to stop altogether.

Just as the King was thinking it would be well to proclaim that the riding should continue next day so they might have one last chance, he suddenly thought it would be well to wait a little longer to see if the knight in copper armor would come on this day, too. Nothing was to be seen of him, but just as they had stopped looking for him, a knight came riding up on a steed that was much, much finer than the one the knight in copper armor had ridden. This knight had silver armor and a silver saddle and bridle, and all were so bright they shone and glistened when he was still a long way off.

Again the other knights called to him and said he might just as well give up the attempt to ride up the glass hill, for it was useless to try. But the silver knight paid no heed to them and rode straight away to the glass hill, and went farther than the knight in copper armor had gone; when he had ridden two thirds of the way to the top, however, he turned his horse around and rode down again.

The Princess sat longing that he might be able to reach her, and when she saw him turning back she threw the second apple after him, and it rolled into his shoe also, and as soon as he reached the bottom of the glass hill he rode away so fast that no one could see what had become of him.

In the evening, when everyone was to appear before the King and Princess, one knight after another went in, but none of them had a golden apple to show.

The two brothers went home as they had the night before and told Cinderlad how everyone had ridden, but that no one had been able to get up the hill.

"But last of all," they said, "came a knight in silver armor, and he had a silver bridle on his horse and a silver saddle, and oh, but he could ride! He took his horse two thirds of the way up the hill, but then he turned back. He was a fine fellow indeed," said the brothers, "and the Princess threw the second golden apple to him!"

"Oh, how I should have liked to see him too!" said Cinderlad.

On the third day, everything happened as it had

before. Everyone waited for the knight in silver armor, but he was nowhere in sight. At last, after a long time, came a knight riding upon a horse that was so fine its equal had never yet been seen. The knight had golden armor, and the horse a golden saddle and bridle, and these were all so bright they shone and dazzled everyone, even while the knight was still at a great distance. The other princes and knights did not think to call to him how useless it was to try, so amazed were they at his magnificence. He rode straight away to the glass hill and galloped up as if it were no hill at all, and the Princess had no time even to wish he might reach the top. As soon as he had ridden to the top, he took the third golden apple from the lap of the Princess and then turned his horse around and rode down again. He vanished from sight before anyone was able to say a word to him.

When the two brothers came home that night, they had much to tell of how the riding had gone that day, and at last they told about the knight in the golden armor too.

"He was a grand fellow! Another such splendid knight is not to be found anywhere in the world!" said the brothers.

"Oh, how I should have liked to see him too!" said Cinderlad.

Next day, all the knights and princes were to appear before the King and the Princess so that he who had the third golden apple might produce it. They all went in turn, first princes, and then knights, but none of them had a golden apple.

"But somebody must have it," said the King, "for with our own eyes we all saw a man ride up and take it." So he commanded that every man in the kingdom should come to the palace, to see if he could show the apple. And one after the other they all came, but no one had the golden apple, and after a long, long time Cinderlad's two brothers came likewise. They were the last of all, so the King inquired of them if anyone else in the kingdom was left to come.

"Oh, yes. We have a brother," said the two, "but he couldn't have the golden apple! He never left the cinder heap on any of the three days."

"Never mind that," said the King. "As everyone else has come to the palace, let him come, too."

So Cinderlad was forced to go and appear at the King's palace.

"Have you the golden apple?" asked the King.

"Yes," said Cinderlad. "Here is the first, and here is the second, and here is the third, too." And he took all three apples out of his pocket and with that threw off his sooty rags and appeared before them in his bright golden armor, which gleamed as he stood.

"You shall have my daughter, and the half of my kingdom as well, and you have truly earned both," said the King.

So there was a wedding, and Cinderlad married the King's daughter, and everyone made merry at the feast. For all of them could make merry, though they could not ride up the glass hill; and if they have not left off their merrymaking they must be at it still.

PETER C. ASBJÖRNSEN AND JÖRGEN E. MOE,
ANDREW LANG COLLECTION

THE HALF-CHICK

THERE WAS once upon a time a handsome, black Spanish hen who had a large brood of chickens. They were all fine, plump little birds, except the youngest, who was quite unlike his sisters and brothers. This one looked just as if he had been cut in two. He had only one leg, and one wing, and one eye; and he had half a head and half a beak.

His mother shook her head sadly as she looked at him and said: "My youngest born is only a half-chick. He can never grow up a tall, handsome cock like his brothers. They will go out into the world and rule over poultry yards of their own. But this poor little fellow will always have to stay at home with his mother." And she called him Medio Pollito, which is Spanish for half-chick.

Now, though Medio Pollito was such an odd, help-less-looking little thing, his mother soon found he was not at all willing to remain under her wing and protection. Indeed, in character he was as unlike his brothers and sisters as he was in appearance. They were good, obedient chickens, and when the old hen called them they chirped and ran back to her side. But Medio Pollito had a roving spirit in spite of his one leg, and when his mother called him to return to the coop, he pretended he could not hear because he had only one ear.

When she took the whole family out for a walk, Medio Pollito would hop away by himself and hide among the Indian corn. His brothers and sisters had many an anxious moment searching for him, while his mother ran to and fro cackling in fear and dismay.

As he grew older, he became more self-willed and disobedient. His manner to his mother was often rude and his temper to the other chickens disagreeable.

One day, he had been out for a longer expedition than usual in the fields. On his return, he strutted up to his mother with a peculiar little hop and kick which was his way of walking and, cocking his one eye at her in a very bold way, he said: "Mother, I am tired of this life in a dull farmyard with nothing but a dreary corn-field to look at. I'm off to Madrid to see the King."

"To Madrid, Medio Pollito!" exclaimed his mother. "Why, you silly chick, it would be a long journey even for a grown-up cock; a poor thing like you would be tired out before you had gone half the distance. No, no. Stay here at home with your mother, and some day, when you are bigger, we will go on a little journey together."

But Medio Pollito had made up his mind. He would not listen to his mother's advice, nor to the prayers and entreaties of his brothers and sisters.

"What is the use of our crowding each other in this poky little place?" he said. "When I have a fine court-yard of my own at the King's palace, I shall perhaps ask some of you to come and pay me a short visit." And scarcely waiting to say good-bye to his mother and his brothers and sisters, away he stumped down the highroad that led to Madrid.

"Be sure you are kind and civil to everyone you meet," called his mother, running after him. But he was in such a hurry to be off he did not wait to answer her or even to look back.

A little later in the day, as he was taking a short cut through a field, he passed a stream. Now the stream was choked and overgrown with weeds and water plants so its waters could not flow freely. "Oh, Medio Pollito!" it cried, as the half-chick hopped along its banks. "Do come here and help me by clearing away these weeds."

"Help you, indeed!" exclaimed Medio Pollito, tossing his head and shaking the few feathers in his tail.
"Do you think I have nothing to do but waste my time
on such trifles? Help yourself, and don't trouble busy
travelers. I am off to Madrid to see the King." And hoppity-kick, hoppity-kick, hoppity-kick, away stumped
Medio Pollito.

A little later, he came to a fire that had been left by
some gypsies in a wood. It was burning very low and
would soon be out. "Oh, Medio Pollito," cried the fire
in a weak, wavering voice as the half-chick approached,
"in a few minutes I shall go out completely unless you
put some sticks and dry leaves upon me. Do help me
or I shall die!"

"Help you, indeed!" answered Medio Pollito. "I
have other things to do. Gather sticks for yourself and
don't trouble me. I am off to Madrid to see the King."
And hoppity-kick, hoppity-kick, away stumped Medio
Pollito.

The next morning, as Medio Pollito was nearing
Madrid, he passed a large tree in whose branches the
wind was caught and entangled. "Oh, Medio Pollito,"
called the wind, "do hop up here and help me get free
of these branches. I cannot tear myself away, and it is
so uncomfortable."

"It is your own fault for going there," answered
Medio Pollito. "I can't waste all my morning stopping
here to help you. Just shake yourself off and don't

hinder me, for I am off to Madrid to see the King." And hoppity-kick, hoppity-kick, away stumped Medio Pollito in great glee, for the towers and roofs of Madrid were now in sight.

When he entered the town, he saw before him a great splendid house, with soldiers standing before the gates. This he knew must be the royal palace, and he determined to hop up to the front gate and wait until the King appeared. But as he was hopping past one of the back windows, the King's cook looked out and saw him.

"Here is the very thing I want," he exclaimed, "for the King has just sent a message that he must have chicken broth for his dinner!" And, opening the window, he stretched out his arm, caught Medio Pollito and popped him into the soup pot standing next to the fire.

Oh, how wet and clammy the water felt as it went over Medio Pollito's head, making his feathers and his one wing cling to his side.

"Water, water," he cried in his despair, "do have pity upon me and do not wet me like this."

"Ah, Medio Pollito," replied the water, "you would not help me when I was a little stream away off in the fields, and now you must be punished."

Then the fire began to burn and scald Medio Pollito. He danced and hopped from one side of the pot to the other, trying to get away from the heat and crying out in pain: "Fire, fire! Do not scorch me like this. You cannot think how it hurts."

"Ah, Medio Pollito," answered the fire, "you would not help me when I was dying in the wood; and now you are being punished."

At last, just when the pain was so great Medio Pollito thought he was going to die, the cook lifted up the lid of the pot to see if the broth was ready for the King's dinner.

"Look here," he cried in horror, "this chicken is quite useless! It is burned to a cinder. I can't send it up to the royal table." And, opening the window, he threw Medio Pollito out into the street. But the wind caught him up and whirled him through the air so quickly that Medio Pollito could scarcely breathe, and his heart beat against his side till he thought it would surely break.

"Oh, wind," he gasped out, "if you hurry me along like this you will kill me. Do let me rest for just a moment, or ——" But he was so breathless he could not finish his sentence.

"Ah, Medio Pollito," replied the wind, "when I was caught in the branches of the tree you would not help me, and now you are being punished." And he swirled Medio Pollito over the roofs of the houses till they reached the highest church in the city, and there he left him fastened to the top of the steeple.

And there stands Medio Pollito to this day. If you

go to Madrid and walk through the streets till you come to the highest church, there you will see Medio Pollito perched on his one leg on the steeple, with his one wing drooping at his side, gazing sadly out of his one eye over the city.

OLD SPANISH TALE, ANDREW LANG COLLECTION

SLEEPING BEAUTY

THERE ONCE lived a King and a Queen who were sorry they had no children— so sorry that it cannot be expressed. They tried all the curative waters in the world, vows and pilgrimages, but to no purpose.

At last, however, the Queen gave birth to a daughter. There was a very fine christening; and the Princess had for her godmothers all the fairies they could find in the whole kingdom. They managed to locate seven, and so the Princess was endowed with all the perfections imaginable.

After the christening, the company returned to the King's palace, where a great feast was prepared for the fairies. Before every one of them was placed a magnificent casket of massive gold, wherein were a spoon, knife and fork of pure gold set with diamonds and rubies. But, as they were sitting down at table, they saw come into the hall a very old fairy who had not been invited. It was more than fifty years since she had been seen, and everyone believed that she was either dead or enchanted.

The King ordered a place set for her, but could not furnish her with a casket of gold because only seven had been made for the seven fairies. The old fairy felt she was intentionally slighted, and muttered some threats between her teeth. One of the young fairies, who sat by her, overheard her grumbling. Judging that she might give the little Princess some unlucky gift, the young fairy went, as soon as they rose from table, and hid herself behind the drapes so that she might speak last and repair, as much as she could, any evil which the old fairy intended.

Meanwhile all the fairies began to offer their gifts to the Princess. The youngest, for her gift, said that the Princess should be the most beautiful person in the world; the next, that she should have the wit of an angel; the third, that she should have wonderful grace in everything she did; the fourth, that she should dance perfectly; the fifth, that she should sing like a nightingale; and the sixth, that she should play all kinds of music to perfection.

The old fairy's turn came next. With her head shaking more with spite than age, she said that the Princess should have her hand pierced with a spindle and die of the wound. This terrible gift made the whole company tremble, and everybody began to weep.

At this very instant the young fairy came out from behind the drapes and spoke these words:

"Assure yourselves, O King and Queen, that your daughter shall not die. It is true, I have no power to undo entirely what my elder has done. The Princess shall indeed pierce her hand with a spindle. But instead of dying, she shall only fall into a profound sleep, which shall last for a hundred years. After that time a king's son shall come and wake her."

The King, to avoid the misfortune, immediately forbade spinning with a distaff and spindle, or to have so much as a spindle in the house.

About fifteen or sixteen years later, the King and Queen happened to be visiting one of their other castles, and the young Princess was diverting herself by running up and down the palace. She came into a little room at the top of the tower, where an old servingwoman was spinning with her spindle. This woman had never heard of the King's proclamation against spindles.

"What are you doing there, my good woman?" said the Princess.

"I am spinning, my dear child," said the old woman.

"Ha," said the Princess, "this is very pretty. How do you do it? Give it to me so I may see."

She had no sooner taken the spindle than it ran into her hand and she fell down in a swoon.

The good old woman cried out for help. People came and threw water upon the Princess' face, unlaced her dress and rubbed her hands and temples with perfume. But nothing would bring her to herself.

And now the King, who had returned to the palace, came up at the noise, remembered the prediction of the fairies and, judging very well that this must necessarily come to pass since the fairies had said it, had the Princess carried into the finest apartment in his palace and laid upon a bed all embroidered with gold.

One would have taken her for a little angel, she was so very beautiful. Her swooning had not dimmed her complexion, for her cheeks were carnation and her lips were coral. Indeed, her eyes were shut, but she was heard to breathe softly, which satisfied those about her that she was not dead. The King commanded that she be left to sleep quietly till her hour of awakening should come.

The good fairy who had saved the life of the Princess by condemning her to sleep a hundred years was in the kingdom of Matakin, twelve thousand miles off, when this accident befell the Princess. But she was instantly informed of it by a little dwarf who had boots with which he could go seven leagues in one stride.

The fairy came immediately, riding in a fiery chariot drawn by dragons.

The King handed her out of the chariot, and she approved everything he had done. But she touched with her wand everything in the palace—except the King and the Queen—governesses, maids of honor, ladies of the bedchamber, gentlemen, officers, stewards, cooks, undercooks, scullions, guards, pages, footmen. She likewise touched the horses in the stables, the great dogs in the courtyard and even pretty little Mopsey, the Princess' spaniel, which lay at the foot of her bed.

The minute she touched them they all fell asleep that they might not awake before their mistress and might be ready to wait upon her when she wanted them. The very spits at the fire, loaded with partridges and pheasants, fell asleep also, as did the fire. This was done in a moment, for fairies are not long in doing their magic.

And now the King and the Queen, having kissed their dear child without waking her, went out of the palace, and in a quarter of an hour's time there grew up all around about the park such a vast number of trees, great and small, bushes and brambles, twining so thickly one within another, that neither man nor beast could pass through. Nothing could be seen of the castle but the very tops of the towers, and those only from a great distance.

When a hundred years had passed, another family ruled the kingdom. The son of the king then reigning chanced to go hunting and asked about the towers which he saw in the middle of a great thick wood.

All answered according to the stories they had heard. Some said it was a ruined old castle, haunted by spirits; others that it was where sorcerers and witches held their night meetings. The common opinion was that it belonged to an ogre who carried there as many little children as he could catch.

The Prince was at a loss, not knowing what to believe, when a very aged countryman spoke to him: "May it please Your Royal Highness, about fifty years ago I heard from my father, who heard my grandfather say, there was in this castle a Princess, the most beautiful ever seen, who must sleep there a hundred years and should be awakened by a king's son."

The young Prince was fired by these words. Thinking it a gay and rare adventure and inspired by a wish for love and honor, he resolved that moment to look into it. Hardly had he advanced toward the wood when all the great trees, the bushes and brambles gave way of themselves to let him pass. He walked up a long avenue to the castle. What surprised him was that he saw none of his people could follow him. The trees closed behind him as soon as he had passed through. A young prince is always valiant, however, and he continued on his way.

He came into a spacious outer court, where everything he saw might have frozen the most fearless person with horror. There was a frightful silence, and nothing was to be seen but the stretched-out bodies of men and animals, all seeming to be dead. He knew, however, by the ruddy faces of the porters, that they were only asleep. And their goblets, wherein still remained some drops of wine, showed plainly that they had fallen asleep in their cups.

The Prince then crossed a court paved with marble, went up the stairs and came into the guardroom, where guards were lined up, their muskets upon their shoulders, and snoring as loudly as they could. After that he went through several rooms full of gentlemen and ladies, all asleep, some standing, others sitting. At last he came into a chamber gilded with gold, where he saw upon a bed, the curtains of which were open, the finest sight the young Prince ever beheld—a Princess, who appeared to be about fifteen or sixteen years old and whose radiant beauty had a somewhat unearthly quality. He approached, trembling with admiration, and fell down before her upon his knees.

And now, as the enchantment was at an end, the Princess awoke and, looking on the Prince with eyes more tender than a first glance might seem to admit, "Is it you, my Prince?" said she. "I have waited a long while."

The Prince, charmed with these words, and much

THE WORLD'S BEST FAIRY TALES

more with the manner in which they were spoken, knew not how to show his joy and gratitude. He assured her he loved her better than he did himself. There was little eloquence but a great deal of love in their talk. He was more at a loss than she, and we need not wonder at it. She had had time to think on what to say to him; for it is very probable—though history mentions nothing of it—that the good fairy, during so long a sleep, had given her very agreeable dreams. In short, they talked for hours together, and yet they said not half what they had to say.

Meanwhile the rest of the palace awoke; everyone went about his own business, and as they were not in love they were ready to die of hunger. The chief lady-in-waiting grew very impatient and told the Princess loudly that supper was served. The Prince helped the Princess to rise. She was dressed magnificently, but His Royal Highness took care not to tell her she was dressed like his great-grandmother in pictures he had seen—even to the lace band peeping over her collar. She looked not a bit less charming and beautiful for all that.

They went into the great hall of mirrors where they supped and were served by the Princess' officers. The musicians played old tunes, very excellently, even though it was now over a hundred years since they had touched their instruments. When supper was over they were married in the chapel of the castle, and though the bride was one hundred years older than the groom nobody would ever have guessed it.

A few days later the Prince took his bride to live with him in his own palace, and the enchanted castle and wood vanished, never to be seen again.

OLD FRENCH TALE, ANDREW LANG COLLECTION

THE MAGIC CARPET

THERE WAS a Sultan who had three sons and a niece The eldest of the Princes was called Houssain, the second Ali, the youngest Ahmed, and the Princess, his niece, Nouronnihar.

The Princess Nouronnihar was the daughter of the Sultan's younger brother, who had died when the Princess was very young. The Sultan took upon himself the care of his niece's education and brought her up in his palace with the three Princes.

To his dismay, he discovered one day that each of his sons loved the Princess passionately. He was very much concerned and devised a plan to settle the predicament. The next day he sent for all three together and said to them, "I think it would be advisable for each of you to travel separately into different countries. As you know, I have great curiosity and delight in everything that is unusual. I therefore promise my niece in marriage to him who shall bring me the most extraordinary rarity. For the purchase of the rarity and the expense of traveling I will give each of you a sum of money."

As the three Princes were always submissive and obedient to the Sultan's will and flattered themselves that Fortune might prove favorable to them, they consented. The Sultan gave them the money he had promised them; and that very day they gave orders for the preparations for their travels and took leave of their father.

Accordingly, they set out the next morning from the same gate of the city, each outfitted like a merchant, attended by an aide dressed like a slave, and all well mounted and equipped.

They went the first day's journey together and stopped at an inn where the road divided into three different directions. That night, when they were at supper, they agreed to travel for one year and meet in the inn at the end of that time. The first one who came should wait for the rest; since they had all taken their leave of the Sultan together, they would return together. The next morning, just as the sun was rising, after they had embraced and wished one another success, each mounted his horse and started off on a different road.

Prince Houssain, the eldest brother, arrived at Bisnagar, the capital of the kingdom of that name and the residence of its king. He lodged at an inn patronized by foreign merchants. Having learned that there were four principal sections in the city where merchants sold their various commodities, he went to one of these the next day.

He wandered through several streets, all vaulted and shaded from the sun, and yet very light too. He noted that those men who dealt in the same sort of goods lived in one street; as did the handicrafts men, who had their shops in the smaller streets.

The Prince's admiration was quickened when he beheld the multitude of shops stocked with a variety of merchandise, such as the finest linens from India, some painted in the most lively colors and representing beasts, trees and flowers; silks, brocades and tapestries from Persia and China; and porcelain from China and Japan. But when he came to the goldsmiths and jewelers he was in an ecstasy to behold such prodigious quantities of wrought gold and silver and was dazzled by the luster of the pearls, diamonds, rubies, emeralds and other jewels exposed for sale.

Another thing Prince Houssain particularly liked was the great number of rose sellers who crowded the streets, for the people of Bisnagar are such great lovers

THE WORLD'S BEST FAIRY TALES

of that flower that not one will stir without a nosegay in his hand or a garland on his head, and the merchants keep them in pots in their shops so the air is perfectly perfumed.

After Prince Houssain had gone through that first section street by street, he was very tired, and a merchant, noticing this, invited him to sit down in his shop. He accepted and had not been there long before he saw a peddler passing by with a piece of carpet, about six feet in length, on his arm, proclaiming its price at forty purses of gold.

The Prince called to the peddler and asked to see the carpet, which seemed to him to be valued at an exorbitant price not only for its size but for its inferior quality. When he had examined it well he told the peddler he could not comprehend how he could expect to sell so small and mediocre a piece of carpet at so high a price.

The peddler, who took Prince Houssain for a merchant, replied, "If this price seems so extravagant to you, your amazement will be greater when I tell you I have strict orders not to bargain and not to part with the carpet for anything less than the forty purses."

"Certainly," answered Prince Houssain, "it must have something very extraordinary in it, which I am not aware of."

"You have guessed it, sir," replied the peddler, "and you will admit its value when you come to know that whoever sits on this piece of carpet may be transported in an instant to wherever he desires to be, without being stopped by any obstacle."

When he heard this, the Prince, considering that the principal motive of his travel was to bring to the Sultan, his father, some singular rarity, thought he would never find anything in the world which would give him more satisfaction.

"If the carpet," said he to the peddler, "has the quality you assign it, I shall not think forty purses of gold too much for its price and I shall make you a present besides."

"Sir," replied the crier, "I have told you the truth, and it is an easy matter to convince you of it. With the permission of the owner of the shop we will go into the back and I will spread the carpet. When we have both sat down, you will form the wish to be transported to your room at the inn—if we are not taken to it there will be no sale and you are released from our bargain. As to your present, though I am paid for my trouble by the seller, I shall receive it as a favor and be very much obliged to you."

The Prince accepted the peddler's conditions and they concluded the bargain. Having the owner's leave, they went into the back of his shop, where they both sat down on the carpet.

As soon as the Prince had formed his wish to be transported to his room at the inn, he presently found himself and the peddler there. He needed no more proof of the value of the carpet and counted out forty purses of gold for the peddler, giving him twenty pieces for himself.

In this manner Prince Houssain became the possessor of the magic carpet and was overjoyed that he had found so rare a piece, which he never doubted would gain him the hand of Nouronnihar. In short, to him it appeared impossible for his younger brothers to find anything to compare with it. It was in his power, by sitting on his carpet, to be at the place of meeting that very day. But as he was obliged to wait there at the inn for his brothers and, being curious to see the King of Bisnagar and to inform himself of the strength, laws, customs and religion of the kingdom, he chose instead to spend some months in satisfying his curiosity. After traveling around Bisnagar for a time he transported himself and his aide to the inn where he and his brothers were to meet and where he passed for a merchant till they came.

Prince Ali, the middle brother, had decided to travel into Persia and joined a caravan three days after he parted from his brothers. After four days' travel he arrived at Shiraz, which was the capital of the kingdom of Persia. Here he decided to pass for a jeweler.

The morning after his arrival, Prince Ali, who had brought nothing but necessities along with him, took a walk into that part of the town which the natives called the bazaar.

Among all the peddlers who passed back and forth with various sorts of goods, he was surprised to see one who held in his hand an ivory telescope with black binding, about a foot in length and the thickness of a man's thumb, for sale at thirty purses of gold.

At first Prince Ali thought the peddler mad. To inform himself, he went to a shop and said to the merchant who stood at the door:

"Pray, sir, is not that man mad who hawks the ivory telescope at thirty purses of gold? If he is not, then I do not understand."

"Indeed, sir," answered the merchant, "he was in his right senses yesterday. I can assure you he is one of the ablest peddlers we have and the one most often employed when anything valuable is to be sold. If he asks thirty purses of gold for the ivory telescope it must be worth at least that much or more. He is sure to come by presently; we will call him and you shall be satisfied. But in the meantime sit down and rest yourself."

Prince Ali accepted the merchant's offer, and presently the peddler passed by. The merchant called to him by name and, pointing to the Prince, said, "This gentleman asked me if you were in your right senses. Tell him what you mean by selling an ivory telescope, which seems not to be worth much, at thirty purses of gold. I should be very much amazed myself if I did not know you."

The peddler, addressing himself to Prince Ali, said, "Sir, you are not the only person that takes me for a madman on account of this glass. You shall judge yourself whether I am or not. When I have told you its merits I hope you will value it as do those to whom I have shown it already, who had a worse opinion of me than you do.

"First, sir," pursued the peddler, presenting the telescope to the Prince, "observe that this pipe is furnished with a glass at both ends and consider that by looking through one of them you see whatever object you wish to behold."

"I am," replied the Prince, "ready to make you profound apologies if you will demonstrate the truth of what you said." The Prince glanced at both ends of the ivory telescope and added, "Show me through which of these ends I must look that I may be satisfied."

The peddler presently showed him, and he peered through, wishing at the same time to see the Sultan, his father, whom he immediately beheld in perfect health on his throne in the midst of his council. And, since there was nothing in the world so dear to him after his father as the Princess Nouronnihar, he wished to see her also, and beheld her seated at her dressing table, smiling, with her ladies-in-waiting grouped about her.

Prince Ali needed no other proof to be persuaded that this telescope was the most valuable thing in the world and believed that if he did not purchase it he would never meet again with such a rarity. He therefore took the peddler with him to the inn where he was lodging, paid him the money and received the telescope.

The Prince was overjoyed at his bargain. He persuaded himself that his brothers would not be able to meet with anything so rare and admirable, and therefore the Princess Nouronnihar would be his. So he visited the Court of Persia, incognito, seeing whatever was curious in Shiraz and thereabouts till he rejoined the caravan which was then returning to the Indies. The Prince arrived happily without accident or trouble at the place of rendezvous, where he found Prince Houssain, and both prepared to wait for Prince Ahmed.

When the three brothers had parted, Prince Ahmed took the road to Samarkand. The day after his arrival there, he went, as his brothers had done, into the great bazaar. He had not walked long before he heard a peddler, who had an artificial apple in his hand, offer it for sale at thirty-five purses of gold.

Upon hearing this, Ahmed stopped the man and said to him, "Let me see that apple and pray tell me what extraordinary properties it has to be valued at so high a price."

"Sir," said the peddler, putting it into his hand, "if you look at the outside of this apple it seems worthless, but if you consider the great use and benefit it is to mankind, you will say thirty-five purses of gold is no price for it and that he who possesses it is master of a great treasure. In short, it cures all sick persons of the most mortal diseases; if the patient is dying it will cause him to recover immediately and restore him to perfect health. And this is done in the easiest manner in the world—simply through the patient's smelling the apple."

"If I may believe you," replied Prince Ahmed, "the virtues of this apple are wonderful, and it is invaluable. But what ground have I, for all you tell me, to be persuaded of the truth of this matter?"

"Sir," replied the peddler, "the truth is known by the whole city of Samarkand. Without going farther, just ask all these merchants you see here and listen to what they say. You will find several who will tell you they would not be alive this day if they had not made use of this excellent remedy.

"And, that you may better comprehend what it is, I must tell you that this apple is the fruit of the experiments of a celebrated philosopher of this city, who applied himself during his entire lifetime to the study and knowledge of plants and minerals and at last attained this fruit, by which he performed such surprising cures in this town as will never be forgotten.

However, he died suddenly, before he could apply his own remedy, and left his wife and young children in difficult circumstances. She, to support her family and provide for her children, has resolved to sell the apple."

While the peddler informed Prince Ahmed of the virtues of the artificial apple, a great many persons surrounded them and confirmed what he said. One gentleman said he had a friend, dangerously ill, who was sure to die.

Here, the man suggested, was a favorable opportunity to show Prince Ahmed the experiment; upon which the Prince told the peddler that he would give him forty purses of gold for the apple if he cured the sick person.

The peddler, who was delighted at this generous price, said to Prince Ahmed, "Come, sir, let us go and make the experiment, and the apple shall become yours. I can assure you that it will always have the desired effect."

The experiment succeeded, and the Prince, after he had counted out to the peddler forty purses of gold and had received the apple, waited patiently for the first caravan that was returning to the Indies, and arrived in perfect health at the inn where the Princes Houssain and Ali waited for him.

When the Princes met, they showed each other their treasures. While peering through Prince Ali's tele-

scope, they saw that the Princess was dying. They all immediately sat down on the magic carpet, wished themselves with her and were there in a moment.

Prince Ahmed no sooner perceived himself in Nouronnihar's chamber than he rose from the carpet, as his brothers did also, went to the bedside and put the apple under the Princess' nose. Some moments afterward she opened her eyes and turned her head from side to side, looking at the people who stood around her. She then rose from the bed and asked to be dressed, just as if she had waked out of a sound sleep. Her ladies-in-waiting joyfully informed her that she was obliged to the three Princes for the sudden recovery of her health, especially to Prince Ahmed. Thereupon she immediately expressed her joy at seeing them and thanked them, and afterward thanked Prince Ahmed in particular.

While Princess Nouronnihar was dressing, the Princes went to throw themselves at the feet of the Sultan, their father, and to pay their respects to him. When they came before him they found he had already been informed by the chief of the Princess' eunuchs of their arrival and by what means the Princess had been perfectly cured. The Sultan embraced them with the greatest joy, both for their return and the recovery of his niece, who had been given up by the physicians.

After the usual ceremonies and compliments, each of the Princes presented his rarity: Prince Houssain

his magic carpet, Prince Ali his ivory telescope and
Prince Ahmed his artificial apple. And after each had
extolled his present when he put it into the Sultan's
hands, they begged him to pronounce their fate and
declare to which of them he would give the Princess
Nouronnihar as his wife.

The Sultan of the Indies, having heard without interrupting all that the Princes had to report about their
rarities, remained silent for some time as if he were
thinking of what answer he should make.

At last he broke the silence and said to them, "I
would declare for one of you children with a great
deal of pleasure if I could do it with justice, but consider whether I can do it or not. 'Tis true, Prince
Ahmed, the Princess is obliged to your artificial apple
for her cure, but I must ask you whether or not you
could have been so useful to her if you had not known
by Prince Ali's telescope the danger she was in and
if Prince Houssain's carpet had not brought you so
soon. Your telescope, Prince Ali, informed you and
your brothers that you were about to lose your cousin,
and so you are owed a great obligation. You must also
grant that the knowledge would have been of no service without the artificial apple and the magic carpet.

"And lastly, Prince Houssain, the Princess would
be very ungrateful if she did not show her appreci-
ation for your carpet, which was so necessary a means
toward her cure. But consider, it would have been of

little use if you had not learned of her illness through Prince Ali's glass and if Prince Ahmed had not applied his apple. Therefore, magic carpet, ivory telescope and artificial apple have not the least preference one before the other. In fact, there's a perfect equality, and I cannot grant the Princess to any one of you. All you have reaped from your travels is the glory of having equally contributed to restoring her health.

"If this be true," added the Sultan, "you see that I must have recourse to other means to determine the choice I ought to make among you. As there is time enough before nightfall, I'll do it today. Each of you is to get a bow and arrow and go out to the great plain where they exercise horses. I'll soon join you and I will give the Princess to him who shoots the farthest."

The three Princes had nothing to say against the Sultan's decision. When they had provided themselves with bows and arrows, they went to the appointed plain, followed by a great number of people.

The Sultan did not make them wait long for him. As soon as he arrived, Prince Houssain, as the eldest, took his bow and arrow and shot first; Prince Ali was next and shot much farther than his brother; and Prince Ahmed shot last of all. It so happened that nobody could see where Prince Ahmed's arrow fell; notwithstanding all the diligence used by himself and everybody else, it was not to be found far or near. And though it was believed that he had shot the far-

thest and therefore deserved the Princess Nouronnihar, it was, however, necessary that his arrow should
be found to make this certain. And, despite Prince
Ahmed's strong protests, the Sultan judged in favor of
Prince Ali and ordered preparations to be made for
the wedding, which was celebrated a few days later.

Prince Houssain would not honor the feast with his
presence. In short, his grief was so violent and in-
supportable that he left the court and, renouncing all
right of succession to the crown, became a hermit.

Prince Ahmed, also, did not go to the wedding of
Prince Ali and the Princess Nouronnihar, but he did
not renounce the world as Prince Houssain had done.
He still could not imagine what had become of his
arrow and he stole away from his attendants one night,
resolved to search for it, that he might not have anything to reproach himself with. He went to the place
where his brothers' arrows had been gathered up and,
going straight forward from there, searched carefully
on both sides of him. He went so far that at last he
began to think his labor was all in vain. Yet he
continued till he came to some steep, craggy rocks
which cut off his progress and were situated in barren
country about four leagues from where he had set out.

When Prince Ahmed came close to these rocks he
saw an arrow, which he picked up. After examining
it carefully he was greatly astonished to find it was the
same one he had shot off.

"Certainly," said he to himself, "neither I nor any man living could shoot an arrow so far." Having found it lying flat, not sticking into the ground, he judged that it had rebounded against the rock. There must be some mystery in this, he thought. Perhaps Fortune, to make amends for my loss of Nouronnihar, may have reserved a greater happiness for me.

The rocks were full of caves, some of them deep, and the Prince entered one. Looking about, he cast his eyes on an iron door which seemed to have no lock, but he feared it was fastened. When he thrust against it, the door opened and revealed an easy descent along an incline, down which he walked, carrying his arrow in his hand. At first it was very dark and difficult going, but presently a quite different light succeeded that out of which he came. Advancing into a spacious area he perceived a magnificent palace, which he had not then time enough to look at, for at the same moment a lady of majestic bearing appeared at the entrance, attended by a group of ladies so finely dressed and beautiful that it was difficult to distinguish which was the mistress.

The moment Prince Ahmed noticed the lady, he hastened to pay his respects. She, seeing him, said, "Come nearer, Prince Ahmed, you are welcome."

It was no small surprise to the Prince to hear himself named in a place he had never heard of and by a lady who was a stranger to him. At last he returned

THE WORLD'S BEST FAIRY TALES

the lady's compliment by throwing himself at her feet and, rising again, said to her, "Madam, a thousand thanks for the assurance you give me of a welcome to a place where I believe my curiosity has made me penetrate too far. But, madam, may I, without being guilty of ill manners, dare ask you by what chance you know me? And how you, who live in the same neighborhood with me, should be a stranger to me?"

"Prince," said the lady, "let us go inside. There I will gratify you in your request."

After these words the lady led Prince Ahmed into the great hall of the palace. Then she sat down on a sofa, and when the Prince, with her permission, had done the same, she said, "You are surprised, you say, that I should know you and not be known by you, but you will no longer be surprised when I inform you who I am.

"You are undoubtedly aware that the world is inhabited by genies as well as by men. I am the daughter of one of the most powerful and distinguished of genies. My name is Paribanou. You seemed to me to be worthy of a happier fate than that of marrying the Princess Nouronnihar. In order that you might attain it, I was present when you drew your arrow. I seized it in the air and gave it the necessary motion to strike against the rocks near which you found it. Now it lies in your power to make use of the favorable opportunity which presents itself to make you happy."

The fairy Paribanou pronounced these last words with a different tone and looked tenderly upon Prince Ahmed. It was therefore no hard matter for the Prince to comprehend what happiness she meant. He realized also that Princess Nouronnihar could never be his, and that the fairy Paribanou excelled her in beauty, wit and, as much as he could conjecture by the magnificence of the palace, in immense riches. He blessed the moment that he thought of seeking his arrow a second time and yielded to his love.

"Madam," replied he, "if all my life I should have the happiness of being your slave and the admirer of the many charms which ravish my soul, I should think myself the most blessed of men. Pardon the boldness which inspires me to ask you to admit into your court a Prince who is entirely devoted to you."

"Prince," answered the fairy, "will you not pledge your faith to me as I give mine to you?"

"Yes, madam," replied the Prince, ecstatically, "what can I do better and with greater pleasure? Yes, I'll give you my heart without the least reserve."

"Then," answered the fairy, "you are my husband and I am your wife. But I suppose you have eaten nothing today; a slight repast shall be served up for you while preparations are being made for our wedding feast tonight, and then I will show you the apartments of my palace and you shall judge if this hall is not the meanest part of it."

Some of the fairy's ladies-in-waiting who had come into the hall with them went out immediately, returning presently with some excellent meats and wines. When Prince Ahmed had eaten and drunk, Paribanou took him through all the apartments, where he saw diamonds, rubies and emeralds intermixed with pearls, agate, jasper and porphyry, together with the most precious marbles. There was such rich profusion throughout that the Prince said that he could not have imagined there was anything in the world that could come up to it.

"Prince," said the fairy, "if you admire my palace so much—it is very beautiful, indeed—I could also charm you with my gardens, but we will let that alone till another day. Night draws near, and it will soon be time to go to supper."

The next hall into which the fairy led the Prince, and where the table had been arranged for the wedding feast, was the only apartment he had not yet seen. He admired the infinite number of sconces of wax candles perfumed with ambergris, the multitude of which were placed with a symmetry that formed an agreeable and pleasant sight. A large side table was set out with all sorts of gold plate so finely wrought that the workmanship was much more valuable than the weight of the gold. Several choruses of beautiful women, whose voices were ravishing, began a concert, accompanied by many kinds of the most harmonious instruments.

When they were eating, the fairy Paribanou took care to serve Prince Ahmed with the most delicate meats, which the Prince found to be delicious. He found the same excellence in the wines, which neither he nor Paribanou tasted till the dessert, consisting of the choicest sweets and fruits, was served.

The wedding feast was continued the next day, and the days following the celebration were a continual round of feasts.

At the end of six months Prince Ahmed, who had always loved and honored his father, conceived a great desire to know how he was. He told Paribanou of it and asked if she would give him leave to visit his father, saying that he would return in a short time.

"Prince," she said, "go when you wish. But please don't take it amiss that I give you some advice. First, I don't think it proper for you to tell the Sultan, your father, of our marriage, nor of my quality, nor the place where you have been. Beg of him to be satisfied in knowing simply that you are happy, and let him understand that the sole purpose of your visit is to assure him of this."

She then appointed twenty gentlemen, well mounted and equipped, to attend him. When all was ready, Prince Ahmed took his leave of Paribanou, embraced her and renewed his promise to return soon. Then his horse, which was as beautiful a creature as any in the Sultan of the Indies' stables, was led to him, and he mounted it with extraordinary grace. After bidding Paribanou a last adieu he set forth on his journey.

It was not a great distance to his father's capital, and Prince Ahmed soon arrived there. The people, glad to see him again, received him with acclamations of joy and followed him in large crowds to the Sultan's palace. The Sultan received and embraced him with great rejoicing, complaining at the same time with a fatherly tenderness of the sadness his long absence had caused him, for he had feared the Prince might have committed some rash action.

Prince Ahmed told the story of his adventures, but without speaking of the fairy Paribanou, and added, "The only favor I ask of Your Majesty is to give me leave to come often in order to pay my respects and to know how you are."

"Son," answered the Sultan of the Indies, "I cannot refuse what you ask of me, but I should much rather you would resolve to stay with me. At least tell me where I may send for you if you should fail to come or when I may think your presence necessary."

"Sir," replied Prince Ahmed, "what Your Majesty asks of me is part of the mystery I spoke of. I beg of you to give me leave to remain silent on this point, for I shall come so frequently that I am afraid I shall sooner be thought troublesome than be accused of negligence in my duty."

The Sultan of the Indies pressed Prince Ahmed no

more but said to him, "Son, I penetrate no further into your secrets. However, I can tell you that your presence restores to me the joy I have not felt this long time. You shall always be welcome when you come, without interrupting your business or pleasure."

Prince Ahmed stayed three days at his father's court, and on the fourth returned to the fairy Paribanou, who did not expect him so soon.

A month after Prince Ahmed's return from his visit to his father, the fairy observed that the Prince, since the time that he gave her an account of his journey, never talked of the Sultan, as if there were no such person in the world, whereas before he was always speaking of him. She thought his silence was on her account; therefore she took an opportunity to say to him one day: "Prince, don't you remember the promise you made to go and see the Sultan, your father? I have not forgotten what you told me on your return and so I am reminding you not to delay too long in fulfilling your vow."

So Prince Ahmed went the next morning with the same attendants as before, but he himself was more magnificently mounted and dressed, and he was received by the Sultan with the same joy and satisfaction. For several months he constantly paid his visits, each time looking richer and finer.

At last some Viziers, the Sultan's favorites, who judged Prince Ahmed's grandeur and power by the figure he cut, made the Sultan jealous of his son, saying it was to be feared he might inveigle himself into the people's favor and dethrone him.

The Sultan of the Indies refused to believe Prince Ahmed capable of so evil a design as his favorites would make him believe, and he said to the Viziers, "You are mistaken. My son loves me, and I am certain of his tenderness and fidelity because I have given him no reason to be otherwise."

But the favorites went on defaming Prince Ahmed till the Sultan said, "Be it as it may, I don't believe my son Ahmed is as wicked as you would persuade me he is. However, I am obliged to you for your good advice and don't doubt that it proceeds from your good intentions."

The Sultan of the Indies said this in order that his favorites might not know the impression their charges had made on his mind. They had so alarmed him that he resolved to have Prince Ahmed watched, unknown to his Grand Vizier. He sent for a noted sorceress and said, "Go immediately. Follow my son and watch him so well that you find out where he retires. Then return and bring me word."

The sorceress left the Sultan and, knowing the place where Prince Ahmed had found his arrow, went there immediately and hid herself near the rocks in order not to be seen.

The next morning Prince Ahmed left at daybreak

to return to the fairy palace, without taking leave either of the Sultan or any of his court, according to the established custom.

The sorceress, seeing him coming, followed him with her eyes till suddenly she lost sight of him and his attendants. The rocks were steep and craggy, making an insurmountable barrier, and she judged that the Prince either retired into some cavern or an abode of genies or fairies.

Thereupon, the sorceress left the place where she had been hiding and looked carefully about on all sides. But she could detect no opening, certainly not the iron door that Prince Ahmed had discovered, which was to be seen and opened by none but men and only by those whose presence was agreeable to the fairy Paribanou.

The sorceress, who saw it was in vain for her to search any further, had to be satisfied with the discovery she had made and returned to give the Sultan an account.

The Sultan was well pleased with the sorceress' conduct and said to her, "Do as you think fit. I'll await the outcome patiently." And to encourage her he gave her a diamond of great value.

As Prince Ahmed had obtained the fairy Paribanou's leave to visit the Sultan of the Indies once a month, he never failed, and the sorceress, knowing the time of his visits, went a day or two before to the foot of the rock where she had lost sight of the Prince and his attendants, and waited there.

The next morning Prince Ahmed went out of the iron door, as usual, with the same attendants as before, and passed by the sorceress. Seeing her lying with her head against the rock, complaining as if she were in great pain, he took pity, turned his horse about and went to her. He asked what was the matter and what he could do to ease her pain.

The artful sorceress looked at the Prince in a pathetic manner, without ever lifting her head, and answered in broken words and sighs. She told him that she was on her way to the capital city, but had been taken by so violent a fever that her strength failed her and she was forced to lie down where he saw her, far from any habitation and without any hopes of assistance.

"Good woman," replied Prince Ahmed, "you are not so far from help as you imagine. I am ready to assist you and convey you to where you will meet with a speedy cure; only get up and let one of my people support you."

At these words the sorceress, who pretended sickness only to know where the Prince lived and what he did, accepted the charitable offer he made her. Two of the Prince's attendants, alighting from their horses, helped her up, set her behind another horseman and remounted, following the Prince, who turned back to the iron door, which was opened by one of his retinue who rode in front. And when he came into the fairy's outer court, without dismounting himself, he sent one of his attendants to tell her he wanted to speak with her.

The fairy Paribanou came with all imaginable haste, not knowing what made the Prince return so soon.

Without giving her time to ask the reason, he said, pointing to the sorceress, "Princess, I desire you would have compassion on this good woman. I found her in the condition you see her in and promised her assistance. I know that you, out of your goodness as well as upon my entreaty, will not abandon her."

Paribanou, who had her eyes fixed upon the sorceress all the time the Prince was talking to her, ordered two of her ladies-in-waiting to carry her into an apartment of the palace and take as much care of the woman as they would of herself.

While the two women executed the fairy's commands she went up to Prince Ahmed and whispered in his ear, "Prince, this woman is not sick as she pretends to be. I am very much mistaken if she is not an impostor who will be the cause of great trouble to you. But don't be concerned; be assured that I will deliver you out of all the snares that shall be laid for you. Go and pursue your journey."

This discourse of the fairy's did not in the least frighten Prince Ahmed. "My Princess," said he, "I do not remember ever doing anybody an injury and I cannot believe that anybody can have a thought of doing me harm. But if someone should, I shall nevertheless not forbear doing good whenever I have an opportunity." Then he started out again for his father's palace.

In the meantime, the two ladies-in-waiting had carried the sorceress into a richly furnished apartment. First they sat her down upon a sofa with her back supported by a cushion of gold brocade, while they made a bed for her; the quilt was finely embroidered with silk, the sheets were of the finest linen, and the coverlet cloth of gold. When they had put her into bed —for the old sorceress pretended that her fever was so violent she could not help herself in the least—one of the women went out and returned soon again with a china dish in her hand, full of a certain liquor, which she presented to the sorceress while the other helped her to sit up.

"Drink this," she said. "It is the Water of the Fountain of Lions and a certain remedy against all fevers whatsoever. You will feel the effect of it in less than an hour's time."

The sorceress, to dissemble the better, refused it despite a great deal of entreaty, but at last, holding back her head, swallowed down the medicine. When she was laid down again the women covered her up. "Lie quiet and get a little sleep if you can," they said.

"We'll leave you and hope to find you perfectly cured when we come again an hour from now."

When the two women returned they found the sorceress up and dressed, sitting upon a sofa. "O admirable potion!" she said. "It wrought its cure much sooner than you told me it would. I shall be able to continue my journey." The two fairies then conducted her through several apartments and into a large hall, the most elaborate and magnificently furnished of all the rooms in the palace.

Paribanou sat in this hall on a throne of massive gold, enriched with diamonds, rubies and pearls of extraordinary size, attended on each hand by a great number of beautiful fairies, all richly clothed. At the sight of so much majesty, the sorceress was not only dazzled but was so amazed that after she had prostrated herself before the throne she could not open her lips to thank the fairy as she proposed.

However, Paribanou saved her the trouble, and said to her, "Good woman, I am glad I had an opportunity to oblige you and to see you are able to continue your journey. I won't detain you, but perhaps it would please you to see my palace; follow my women and they will show it to you."

Then the sorceress went back and related to the Sultan of the Indies all that had happened and how very rich Prince Ahmed was since his marriage with the fairy, richer than all the kings in the world, and how there was danger that he might come and take the throne from his father.

Though the Sultan knew very well that Prince Ahmed's natural disposition was good, yet he could not help being concerned about the report made by the old sorceress. When she was taking her leave, he said, "I thank you for the pains you have taken and for your wholesome advice. I am so aware of its great importance that I shall deliberate upon it in council."

Now, the favorite Viziers warned that the Prince should be killed, but the sorceress advised differently. "Make him give you all kinds of wonderful things with the fairy's help," she said, "till she tires of him and sends him away. For example, every time Your Majesty goes into the field you are at great expense, not only in tents for your army but in mules and camels to carry their baggage. Now, persuade Prince Ahmed to use his influence with the fairy to procure you a tent which might be carried in a man's hand and would be large enough to shelter your whole army against bad weather."

When the sorceress had finished her speech the Sultan asked his favorites if they had anything better to propose. Finding them all silent, he determined to follow the sorceress' advice as the most reasonable and agreeable to him.

Next day the Sultan did as the sorceress had told him and asked his son for the tent. Prince Ahmed realized then that the old woman had informed the Sultan of his marriage to the fairy Paribanou. And, although he didn't know how great the power of genies and fairies was, he doubted whether it extended so far as to produce a tent such as his father desired.

At last he replied, "Though it is with the greatest reluctance imaginable, I will not fail to ask of my wife the favor Your Majesty desires but will not promise you to obtain it. If I should not have the honor to come again to pay you my respects, that shall be the sign I have not had success. But, beforehand, I desire you to forgive me and remember that you yourself have reduced me to this extremity."

"Son," replied the Sultan of the Indies, "I would be very sorry if what I ask of you should cause me the displeasure of never seeing you again. I find you don't know the power a husband has over a wife. Yours would prove that her love for you was very indifferent if she, with the power of a fairy, would refuse you so trifling a request. I desire you to ask this for my sake."

The Prince went back and was very sad for fear of offending the fairy. She kept pressing him to tell her what was the matter, and at last he said, "Madam, you may have observed that hitherto I have been content with your love and have never asked you any favor. Consider, then, that it is not I but the Sultan, my father, who unwisely, or at least so it seems to me, begs of you a tent large enough to shelter him, his court and his army from the violence of the weather, but which a man may carry in his hand. Remember it is my father who asks this favor."

"Prince," replied the fairy, smiling, "I am sorry that so small a matter should disturb you and make you as uneasy as you appear to be."

Then the fairy sent for her treasurer, to whom she said, "Nourgihan, bring me the largest tent in my treasury." Nourgihan returned presently with the tent, which she could hold in the palm of her hand when she shut her fingers, and presented it to her mistress, who gave it to Prince Ahmed to look at.

When Prince Ahmed saw the tent which the fairy called the largest in her treasury, a look of surprise appeared on his face.

Paribanou burst out laughing. "Prince," she cried, "do you think I jest with you? You'll see presently that I am in earnest. Nourgihan," she said to her treasurer, taking the tent out of Prince Ahmed's hands, "go and set it up, that the Prince may judge whether it is large enough for the Sultan, his father."

The treasurer immediately went out of the palace and carried the tent a great way off. When she had set it up, one end reached all the way to the palace. The Prince, after investigating it, found the tent was large enough to shelter two armies greater than his father's. He then said to Paribanou: "I ask my Princess a thousand pardons for my incredulity. After what I have seen I believe there is nothing impossible to you."

"You see," said the fairy, "that the tent is larger than your father may have occasion for, but you must know that it has one property—it is larger or smaller according to the army it is to cover."

The treasurer took down the tent and brought it to the Prince. Without staying any longer than the next day, he mounted his horse and went with the same attendants to visit his father.

The Sultan, who was persuaded there could not be any such tent as he had asked for, was greatly surprised at the Prince's diligence. He took the tent and admired its smallness. His amazement was boundless when it was set up in the great plain and he found it big enough to shelter an army twice as large as he could bring into the field. But the Sultan was not yet satisfied.

"Son," said he, "I have already expressed how much I am obliged for the present of the tent that you have procured for me. I look upon it as the most valuable thing in all my treasury. But you must do one thing more which will be just as agreeable to me. I am informed that the fairy, your spouse, makes use of a certain water, called the Water of the Fountain of Lions, which cures all sorts of fevers, even the most dangerous. Since I am perfectly certain that my health is dear to you, I don't doubt that you will ask her for a bottle of that water and bring it to me as a medicine which I may make use of when I have occasion. Do me this other important service and thereby complete the duty of a good son toward a tender father."

The Prince returned and told the fairy what his father had said.

"There's a great deal of wickedness in this demand," she answered, "as you will understand by what I am going to tell you. The Fountain of Lions is situated in the middle of a court of a great castle. The entrance is guarded by four fierce lions, two of which sleep alternately while the other two are awake. But don't let that frighten you; I'll give you means to pass by them without any danger."

The fairy Paribanou had several balls of thread by her side. She took up one and, presenting it to Prince Ahmed, said, "First, take this ball of thread. I'll tell you the use of it presently. Secondly, you must have two horses: one you are to ride yourself and the other you must lead; the latter must be loaded with a freshly slaughtered sheep cut into four quarters. Third, I will give you a bottle in which to bring back the water.

"Set out early tomorrow morning and, when you have passed the iron door, throw the ball of thread before you; it will roll till it comes to the gates of the castle. Follow it, and when it stops at the open gates, you will see the four lions; the two that are awake will wake the other two by their roaring, but don't be frightened. Throw each of them a quarter of the sheep and then clap spurs to your horse and ride to the fountain; fill your bottle without alighting and return here with speed. The lions will be so busy eating they will let you pass by them."

Prince Ahmed set out the next morning at the time appointed by the fairy and followed her directions carefully. When he arrived at the gates of the castle, he distributed the quarters of the sheep among the four lions and, passing among them bravely, went to the fountain, filled his bottle and got away from the castle safe and sound.

When he had gone a little distance from the castle gates he turned around and, seeing two of the lions coming after him, he drew his saber and prepared himself for defense. As he rode forward one of the lions turned off the road at some distance and showed that he had not come to do him harm but only to go before him, and the other lion stayed behind to follow. Guarded in this manner, Prince Ahmed arrived at the capital of the Indies, and the lions never left him till they had conducted him to the gates of the Sultan's palace. This done, they returned the same way they had come, but not without frightening all who saw them, even though they went in a very gentle manner and showed no fierceness.

A great many officers came to attend the Prince while he dismounted from his horse, and afterward they conducted him into the Sultan's apartment. Prince Ahmed approached the throne, laid the bottle at the Sultan's feet, kissed the rich tapestry which covered his footstool and then said: "I have brought you the healthful water which Your Majesty desired so much to keep among the other rarities in your treasury, but at the same time I wish you such extraordinary health as never to have occasion to make use of it."

After the Prince had paid his respects the Sultan placed him at his right hand and said to him, "Son, I am very much obliged to you for this valuable present. I am also aware of the great danger you have exposed yourself to upon my account, which I have been informed of by a sorceress who knows the Fountain of Lions. But do me the pleasure," he continued, "to inform me by what incredible power you have been so fortunate."

"Sir," replied Prince Ahmed, "I have no share in the compliment Your Majesty is pleased to make me; all the honor is due to my wife, whose good advice I followed." Then he informed the Sultan what those directions were and, by so doing, let him know how well he had behaved himself. When he had finished, the Sultan, who showed outwardly all the demonstrations of great joy but secretly was becoming more and more jealous, retired to a private apartment, where he sent for the sorceress.

The sorceress saved the Sultan the trouble of telling

her of the success of Prince Ahmed's journey; she had heard of it before she came and had prepared an infallible means to destroy the Prince. This she communicated to the Sultan, who declared it the next day to the Prince in the presence of all his courtiers. "Son," said he, "I have one thing more to ask of you, after which I shall expect nothing further. This request is that you bring me a man not above a foot-and-a-half high, whose beard is thirty feet long, who carries a bar of iron upon his shoulders weighing five hundred pounds, which he uses as a weapon."

Prince Ahmed, who did not believe there was such a man in the world as his father described, would gladly have excused himself. But the Sultan persisted in his demand and told him the fairy could do more incredible things.

The next day the Prince returned to his dear Paribanou, to whom he told his father's new demand, which he looked upon as more impossible than the first two. "For," he added, "I cannot imagine there is such a man in the world. Without doubt, my father has a mind to see whether or not I am so silly as to go about it, or he has a scheme for my ruin. How does he suppose that I can lay hold of such a man? If there are any means, I beg you will tell me them and let me come off with honor."

"Do not alarm yourself, Prince," replied the fairy. "You ran a risk in fetching the Water of the Fountain of Lions for your father. But there's no danger in finding this man, for he is my brother Schaibar. However, he is far from being like me though we both had the same father. He is of so violent a nature that nothing can prevent his showing cruelty for a slight offense; yet, on the other hand, he is so good as to oblige everyone in whatever they desire. He is made exactly as your father has described him and has no other weapon than a bar of iron of five hundred pounds' weight, without which he never stirs and which makes him respected. I'll send for him, and you shall judge the truth of what I am telling you. But be sure to prepare yourself against being frightened at his extraordinary figure when you see him."

"What, my Queen!" replied Prince Ahmed. "Do you say Schaibar is your brother? Let him be ever so ugly or deformed, I shall never be frightened at the sight of him, and as your brother I shall honor and love him."

The fairy ordered that a fire be set in a gold chafing dish placed in the courtyard of her palace. From a metal box she took a perfume and, after her throwing it into the fire, there arose a thick cloud of smoke.

Some moments afterward the fairy said to Prince Ahmed, "There comes my brother." The Prince immediately saw Schaibar approaching gravely, with his heavy bar on his shoulder, his long beard, which he held up before him, and a pair of thick mustaches, which were tucked behind his ears and almost covered his face. His eyes were very small and set deep in his head, which was far from being of the smallest size, and on his head he wore a grenadier's cap. Besides all this, he was very humpbacked.

If Prince Ahmed had not known that Schaibar was Paribanou's brother, he would not have been able to look at him without fear but, knowing first who he was, he stood by the fairy without the least concern.

Schaibar, as he came forward, looked at the Prince frightfully enough to have chilled the blood in his veins and asked Paribanou, when he first addressed her, who that man was.

To which she replied, "He is my husband, brother. His name is Ahmed. He is the son of the Sultan of the Indies. The reason I did not invite you to my wedding was because I was unwilling to divert you from an expedition you were engaged in and from which, I heard with pleasure, you returned victorious; so I took the liberty now to call for you."

At these words, Schaibar, looking on Prince Ahmed favorably, said, "Is there anything, sister, wherein I can serve him? It is enough for me that he is your husband to do for him whatever he desires."

"The Sultan, his father," replied Paribanou, "is curious to see you, and I desire the Prince may be your guide to the Sultan's court."

"He needs but lead the way: I'll follow him."

"Brother," replied Paribanou, "it is too late to go today, therefore stay till tomorrow morning. In the meantime, I will inform you of all that has passed between the Sultan of the Indies and Prince Ahmed since our marriage."

The next morning, after Schaibar had been informed of the affair, he and Prince Ahmed set out for the Sultan's court. When they arrived at the gates of the capital the people no sooner saw Schaibar than they ran and hid themselves; some shut up their shops and locked themselves in their houses, while others, fleeing, communicated their fear to all they met, who stayed not to look behind them but ran too. So that as Schaibar and Prince Ahmed went along they found the streets deserted till they came to the palace, where the porters, instead of minding the gates, also ran away. Prince Ahmed and Schaibar advanced without any obstacle to the council hall, where the Sultan was seated on his throne, giving audience. Here, likewise, the ushers at the approach of Schaibar abandoned their posts and gave them free admittance.

Schaibar went boldly and fiercely up to the throne, without waiting to be presented by Prince Ahmed, and accosted the Sultan of the Indies in these words: "You have asked for me. See, here I am. What would you have with me?"

The Sultan, instead of answering him, clapped his hands before his eyes to avoid the sight of so terrible an object. At this uncivil and rude reception Schaibar was so much provoked, after the Sultan had given him the trouble of coming this far, that he instantly raised his iron bar and killed the Sultan before Prince Ahmed could intercede in his behalf. All that he could do was to prevent Schaibar's killing the Grand Vizier, who sat not far from him, insisting that he had always given the Sultan, his father, good advice.

"These are the ones, then," said Schaibar, "who gave him bad advice," and as he pronounced these words he killed the other Viziers and favorites of the Sultan who were Prince Ahmed's enemies. Every time he struck he killed someone or other, and none escaped but those who were not so frightened as to stand staring and gaping and who saved themselves by flight.

When this terrible execution was over, Schaibar came out of the council hall into the middle of the courtyard with the iron bar upon his shoulder and, looking hard at the Grand Vizier who owed his life to Prince Ahmed, he said, "I know there is a certain sorceress who is a greater enemy of my brother-in-law than these base favorites I have chastised. Let the sorceress be brought to me."

The Grand Vizier immediately dragged her forward, and Schaibar struck her with his iron bar, saying, "Take the reward of your pernicious counsel and learn not to feign sickness again."

After that he said, "This is not yet enough; I will use the whole town after the same manner if it does not immediately acknowledge Prince Ahmed, my brother-in-law, as its Sultan and the Sultan of the Indies." Then all who were present made the air echo with the repeated acclamations of "Long life to Sultan Ahmed!" and, immediately after, he was proclaimed through the whole town.

Schaibar had him clothed in the royal vestments, installed him on the throne and, after he had caused everyone to swear homage and fidelity to Ahmed, went and brought his sister, Paribanou, with great pomp and grandeur, and made her be acknowledged Sultana of the Indies.

As for Prince Ali and Princess Nouronnihar, since they had had no hand in the conspiracy against Prince Ahmed and knew nothing of it, they were assigned a large province with a capital, where they spent the rest of their lives. The new Sultan sent an officer to Prince Houssain to acquaint him with the change and make him an offer of which province he liked best. But that Prince thought himself so happy in his solitude that he bade the officer give his brother thanks for the kindness he offered him, assuring the new Sultan of his submission and that the only favor he desired was to be given leave to live in retirement in the place he had chosen for his retreat.

ARABIAN NIGHTS, TRANSLATED BY ANTOINE GALLAND

JACK THE GIANT KILLER

IN THE REIGN of the famous King Arthur there lived in Cornwall a lad named Jack, who was a boy of bold temper and took delight in hearing or reading of conjurers, giants and fairies. He used to listen eagerly to the deeds of the knights of King Arthur's Round Table.

In those days there lived on St. Michael's Mount, off Cornwall, a huge giant, eighteen feet high and nine feet round. His fierce and savage looks were the terror of all who beheld him. His name was Cormoran and he dwelled in a gloomy cavern on the top of the mountain and used to wade over to the mainland in search of prey. He would throw half a dozen oxen upon his back, tie three times as many sheep and hogs around his waist and march back to his own abode. The giant had been doing this for many years when Jack resolved to destroy him.

Jack took a horn, a shovel, a pickaxe, his armor and a dark lantern and, one winter's evening, he went to the Mount. There he dug a pit twenty-two feet deep and twenty broad. He covered the top over to make it look like solid ground and then blew such a loud and long tantara that the giant awoke and came out of his den, roaring: "You saucy villain, you shall pay for this. I shall broil you for my breakfast."

He had scarcely spoken when, taking one step farther, he tumbled into the pit, and Jack struck him such a blow on the head with his pickaxe that he killed him. Jack then returned home to cheer his friends with the news.

When the townsfolk heard of this valiant action they declared that henceforth he should be called Jack the Giant Killer and gave him a sword and belt upon which was written in letters of gold:

> This is the valiant Cornishman
> Who slew the giant Cormoran.

Another giant, called Blunderbore, vowed revenge if ever he should have Jack in his power. This giant kept an enchanted castle which stood in the midst of a lonely wood. One day, some time after the death of Cormoran, Jack was passing through this wood while on his way to Wales and, being weary, sat down and went to sleep.

The giant, walking by and seeing the words on Jack's belt, carried him off to his castle, where he locked him up in a large room, the floor of which was covered with the bones of men and women. Soon after, he went to fetch his brother, likewise a giant, to make a meal of

Jack. Through the bars of his prison, Jack, terrified, could see the two giants approaching.

Perceiving in one corner of the room a strong cord, Jack took courage and, making a slipknot at each end, threw it over the giants' heads and tied it to the window bars. He then pulled with all his might till he had choked them. Quickly, he slid down the rope and stabbed them to the heart.

Jack next took a great bunch of keys from the pocket of Blunderbore and went into the castle again. He made a thorough search through all the rooms, and in one of them found three ladies tied up by the hair of their heads and almost starved to death. They told him their husbands had been killed by the giants, who then condemned them to be starved to death because they would not eat the flesh of their dead husbands.

"Ladies," said Jack, "I have put an end to the monster and his wicked brother. I give you this castle and all the riches it contains, to make some amends for the dreadful pain you have felt."

He then very politely gave them the keys of the castle and went farther on his journey. As Jack had but little money, he went on as fast as possible. At length he came to a handsome house, knocked at the door, and there came forth a Welsh giant. Jack said he was a traveler who had lost his way, at which the giant made him welcome and led him into a room where there was a good bed.

Jack took off his clothes quickly, but though he was weary he could not sleep. Soon after this he heard the giant walking back and forth in the next room, saying:

Though here you lodge with me this night,
You shall not see the morning light;
My club shall dash your brains out quite.

Well, thought Jack, so these are the tricks you play upon travelers? But I hope to prove as cunning as you.

Then, getting out of bed, he groped about the room, and at last found a large wooden log. He laid it in his own place in the bed and then hid himself in a dark corner of the room.

About midnight the giant entered the room and with his bludgeon struck many blows on the bed, in the very place where Jack had laid the log. Then he went back to his own room, thinking he had broken all Jack's bones.

Early in the morning Jack boldly walked into the giant's room to thank him for his lodging. The giant started when he saw him and began to stammer, "Oh, dear me, is it you? Pray, how did you sleep? Did you hear or see anything in the dead of the night?"

"Nothing worth speaking of," said Jack carelessly. "A rat, I believe, gave me three or four slaps with its tail and disturbed me a little. But I soon went back to sleep again."

The giant wondered more and more at this, yet he

did not answer a word, but went to bring two great bowls of hasty pudding for their breakfast. Jack wanted to make the giant believe he could eat as much as himself, so he contrived to button a leather bag inside his coat and slip the pudding into this bag while pretending to put it all into his mouth. When breakfast was over he said to the giant: "Now I will show you a fine trick. I can cure all wounds with a touch. I could cut off my head in one minute, and the next put it sound again on my shoulders. You shall see." He then took hold of a knife, with one stroke ripped up the leather bag, and all the pudding tumbled out upon the floor.

"I can do that myself!" cried the Welsh giant, who was ashamed to be surpassed by such a little fellow as Jack. So he snatched up the knife, plunged it into his own stomach and in a moment dropped down dead on the floor.

Having thus far been successful in all his undertakings, Jack resolved not to be idle in the future. He therefore furnished himself with a horse, a cap of knowledge, a sword of sharpness, shoes of swiftness and an invisible coat, the better to perform the wonderful enterprises that lay before him.

He traveled over high hills, and on the third day he came to a large and spacious forest through which his road lay. Scarcely had he entered the forest when he beheld a monstrous giant dragging along a handsome

knight and his lady by the hair of their heads. Jack alighted from his horse and, after tying him to an oak tree, put on his invisible coat, under which he carried his sword of sharpness.

When he came up to the giant he made several slashes at him. He could not reach his body, but wounded his thighs in several places. At length, putting both hands to his sword and aiming with all his might, Jack cut off both the giant's legs. Then, setting his foot upon his neck, he plunged his sword into the giant's body, and the monster gave a groan and expired.

The knight and his lady invited Jack to their house, to receive a proper reward for his services.

"No," said Jack, "I cannot be easy till I find out this monster's habitation." So he mounted his horse and soon after came in sight of another giant, who was sitting on a block of timber.

Jack alighted from his horse and, putting on his invisible coat, approached and aimed a blow at the giant's head, but he only cut off his nose. On this the giant seized his club and thrashed about unmercifully.

"Nay," said Jack, "if this be the case I'd better dispatch you!" So, jumping upon the block, he stabbed him in the back, and the giant dropped down dead.

Jack then proceeded on his journey and traveled over hills and dales. Arriving at the foot of a high mountain, he knocked at the door of a lonely house, where an old man let him in. When Jack was seated the hermit addressed him thus: "My son, on the top of this mountain is an enchanted castle kept by the giant Galligantus and a vile magician. I lament the fate of a Duke's daughter, whom they seized as she was walking in her father's garden, and brought here after transforming her into a deer." Jack promised that in the morning, at the risk of his own life, he would break the enchantment.

When he had climbed to the top of the mountain he saw two fiery griffins: but he passed between them without the least fear, for they could not see him in his invisible coat. On the castle gate he found a golden trumpet, under which were written these lines:

> Whoever can this trumpet blow
> Shall cause the giant's overthrow.

As soon as Jack had read this he seized the trumpet and blew a shrill blast which made the gate fly open and the very castle itself tremble.

The giant and the conjurer now knew their wicked course was at an end, and they stood biting their nails and shaking with fear. With his sword of sharpness Jack soon killed the giant, and the magician was then carried away by a whirlwind. Every knight and beautiful lady who had been changed into a bird or a beast returned to the proper shape. The castle vanished away like smoke, and the head of the giant Galligantus was sent to King Arthur.

The knights and ladies rested that night at the old man's hermitage, and the next day they set out for the court. Jack went up to the King and gave His Majesty an account of all his fierce battles.

Jack's fame had now spread through the whole country, and at the King's desire the Duke gave Jack his daughter in marriage, to the joy of the entire kingdom. After this the King gave him a large estate, on which he and his lady lived the rest of their days in joy and contentment.

OLD CHAPBOOK, ANDREW LANG COLLECTION

TWELVE DANCING PRINCESSES

ONCE UPON a time there lived in the village of Montignies-sur-Roc a little cowherd, without either father or mother. His real name was Michael, but he was always called the Star Gazer because he went along with his head in the air when he drove his cows over the meadows to seek pasture.

He had white skin, blue eyes and hair that curled all over his head, and the village girls used to cry after him, "Well, Star Gazer, what are you doing?" and Michael would answer, "Oh, nothing," and go on his way without even turning to look at them.

One morning about the middle of August, just at midday when the sun was hottest, Michael ate his dinner of a piece of dry bread and went to sleep under an oak tree. And while he slept he dreamed that a beautiful lady, dressed in a robe made of gold, came and said to him, "Go to the castle of Belœil, and there you shall marry a princess."

That evening the little cowherd told his dream to the farm people. But, as was natural, they only laughed at the Star Gazer.

The next day at the same hour he went to sleep again under the same tree. The lady appeared a second time, and said, "Go to the castle of Belœil, and there you shall marry a princess."

In the evening Michael told his friends that he had dreamed the same dream again, but they only laughed at him more than before.

"Never mind," he said to himself, "if the lady appears to me a third time, I will do as she tells me."

The following day, to the great astonishment of all the village, about two o'clock in the afternoon a voice was heard singing:

Raleô, raleô,
How the cattle go!

It was the little cowherd driving his cattle back to the barn.

The farmer began to scold him furiously, but he answered quietly, "I am going away." He made his clothes into a bundle, said good-bye to his friends and boldly set out to seek his fortune.

There was great excitement throughout the village, and on the top of the hill the people stood, holding their sides with laughter, as they watched the Star Gazer trudge bravely along the valley with his bundle at the end of his stick.

It was well known for full twenty miles around that in the castle of Belœil lived twelve Princesses of wonderful beauty, as proud as they were comely, and so sensitive and of such truly royal blood that they would have felt at once the presence of a pea in their beds, even if ten mattresses were laid over it.

They had twelve beds all in the same room, but what was very extraordinary was the fact that, though they were locked in by triple bolts, every morning their satin shoes were worn into holes. No noise was ever heard in the room, yet how could the shoes wear themselves out alone?

At last the Duke of Belœil ordered the trumpet sounded and a proclamation made that whoever could discover how his daughters wore out their shoes should choose one of them for his wife.

On hearing the proclamation, a number of Princes

arrived at the castle to try their luck. They watched all night at the door of the Princesses, but when the morning came the Princes had disappeared, and no one could tell what had become of them.

When he reached the castle, Michael went straight to the gardener and offered his services. Now it happened the garden boy had just been sent away, and though the Star Gazer did not look very sturdy, the gardener agreed to take him, as he thought his pretty face and golden curls would please the Princesses.

The first thing he was to do, when the Princesses awoke, was to present each one with a bouquet. So Michael placed himself behind the door of the Princesses' room, with the twelve bouquets in a basket. He gave one to each of the sisters, who took them without even deigning to look at the lad, except Lina, the youngest, who fixed on him her large black eyes as soft as velvet and exclaimed, "Oh, how pretty he is—our new flower boy!" The others burst out laughing, and the eldest said that a princess ought never to lower herself by looking at a garden boy.

Now Michael knew that all the Princes had disappeared, but the beautiful eyes of the Princess called Lina inspired him with a violent longing to try his fate. Unhappily he did not dare to come forward, being afraid he should only be jeered at or even turned away from the castle on account of his impudence.

Then the Star Gazer had another dream. The lady

in the golden dress appeared to him once more, holding in one hand two young laurel trees, a cherry laurel and a rose laurel, and in the other hand a little golden rake, a little golden bucket and a silken towel. She said, "Plant these two laurels in two large pots, rake them over with the rake, water them with the bucket and wipe them with the towel. When they have grown as tall as a girl of fifteen, say to each of them, 'My beautiful laurel, with the golden rake I have raked you, with the golden bucket I have watered you, with the silken towel I have wiped you.' Then, after you have done that, ask anything you choose, and the laurels will give it to you."

Michael thanked the lady in the golden dress, and when he woke he found the two laurel trees beside him. So he carefully obeyed the orders given to him by her.

The trees grew very fast and, when they were as tall as a girl of fifteen, he said to the cherry laurel, "My lovely cherry laurel, with the golden rake I have raked you, with the golden bucket I have watered you, with the silken towel I have wiped you. Teach me how to become invisible."

Instantly there appeared on the laurel a pretty white flower, which Michael gathered and stuck into his buttonhole and, true enough, it made him invisible.

That evening, when the Princesses went upstairs to bed, he followed them barefoot, so that he would

make no noise, and hid himself under one of the beds.

The Princesses began at once to open their wardrobes and boxes. They took out of them the most magnificent dresses, which they put on before their mirrors, turning themselves to admire their appearance. Michael could see nothing from his hiding place, but he could hear everything, and he listened to the Princesses laughing and talking with pleasure.

At last the eldest said, "Be quick, my sisters; our partners will be impatient."

When the Star Gazer peeped out, he saw the twelve sisters in splendid garments, with satin shoes on their feet, and in their hands the bouquets he had brought for them.

"Are you ready?" asked the eldest.

"Yes," replied the other eleven in chorus, and they took their places one by one behind her.

Then the eldest Princess clapped her hands three times and a trapdoor opened. All the Princesses disappeared down a secret staircase, and Michael hastily followed them. As he was following on the steps of the Princess Lina, he carelessly trod on her dress. "There is somebody behind me," cried the Princess, "holding my dress."

"You foolish thing," said her eldest sister, "you are always afraid of something. It is only a nail which caught you."

They went down, down, down, till at last they came

to a passage with a door at one end, which was only fastened with a latch. The eldest Princess opened it, and they found themselves immediately in a lovely little wood, where the leaves were spangled with drops of silver which shone in the brilliant light of the moon. Next they crossed another wood, where the leaves were sprinkled with gold, and after that still another, where the leaves glittered with diamonds.

At last the Star Gazer perceived a large lake, and on the shore were twelve little boats with awnings, in which were seated twelve Princes who, grasping their oars, awaited the Princesses.

Each Princess entered one of the boats, and Michael slipped in with the youngest. The boats glided along rapidly, but Lina's, being heavier, was always behind the rest.

"We never went so slowly before," said the Princess. "What can be the reason?"

"I don't know," answered the Prince. "I assure you I am rowing as hard as I can."

On the other side of the lake the Star Gazer saw a beautiful castle, splendidly illuminated, from which came the lively music of fiddles and kettledrums and trumpets. In a moment they touched land, and the company jumped ashore. The Princes, after having securely fastened their boats, gave their arms to the Princesses and conducted them to the castle.

Michael followed and entered the ballroom in their

train. Everywhere were mirrors, lights, flowers and damask hangings. The Star Gazer was quite bewildered at the magnificence of the sight.

He placed himself out of the way in a corner, admiring the grace and beauty of the Princesses. Some were fair and some were dark; some had chestnut hair, or curls darker still, and some had golden locks. Never were so many beautiful Princesses seen together at one time, but the one the garden boy thought the most beautiful and the most fascinating was the little Princess with the velvet eyes.

With what eagerness she danced! Leaning on her partner's shoulder she swept by like a whirlwind. Her cheeks flushed, her eyes sparkled, and it was plain that she loved dancing better than anything else. The poor garden boy envied those handsome young men with whom she danced so gracefully, but he did not know how little reason he had to be jealous of them.

The young men were really the Princes who, to the number of fifty at least, had tried to steal the Princesses' secret. The Princesses had made them drink a potion which froze the heart and left nothing but the love of dancing.

They danced on until the shoes of the Princesses were worn into holes. When the cock crowed the third time, the fiddles stopped, and a delicious supper was served, of sugared orange flowers, crystallized rose leaves, powdered violets, cracknels and wafers, which

349

are, as everyone knows, the favorite foods of princesses.

After supper, the dancers all went back to their boats, and this time the Star Gazer entered that of the eldest Princess. They crossed once again the wood with the diamond-spangled leaves, the wood with the gold-sprinkled leaves and the wood whose leaves glittered with drops of silver, and as a proof of what he had seen, the boy broke a small bough from a tree in the last wood. Lina turned as she heard the noise made by the breaking of the branch.

"What was that noise?" she asked.

"It was nothing," replied her eldest sister. "It was only the screech of the barn owl that roosts in one of the turrets of the castle."

While she was speaking, Michael managed to slip ahead and, running up the staircase, he reached the Princesses' room first. He flung open the window and, sliding down the vine which climbed up the wall, found himself in the garden just as the sun was rising and it was time for him to set to his work.

That day, when he made up the bouquets, Michael hid the branch with the silver drops in the nosegay intended for the youngest Princess. When Lina discovered it she was much surprised. However, she said nothing to her sisters, but when she met the boy while she was walking under the shade of the elms she suddenly stopped as if to speak to him. Then, changing her mind, she went on her way.

In the evening the twelve sisters went again to the ball, and once more the Star Gazer followed them, crossing the lake in Lina's boat. This time it was the Prince who complained that the boat seemed very heavy. "It is the heat," replied the Princess. "I, too, have been feeling very warm."

During the ball she looked everywhere for the garden boy, but she never saw him.

As they came back, Michael gathered a branch from the wood with the gold-sprinkled leaves, and now it was the eldest Princess who heard the noise it made in breaking.

"It is nothing," said Lina, "only the cry of the owl which roosts in the turrets of the castle."

The next morning Lina found the branch in her bouquet. When the sisters went down she stayed a little behind and said to the garden boy, "Where does this branch come from?"

"Your Royal Highness knows well enough," answered Michael.

"So you have followed us?"

"Yes, Princess."

"How did you manage it? We never saw you."

"I hid myself," replied the Star Gazer quietly.

The Princess was silent a moment and then said, "You know our secret—keep it! Here is the reward for your discretion." And she flung the boy a purse of gold.

"I do not sell my silence," answered Michael, and he went away without picking up the purse.

For three nights Lina neither saw nor heard anything extraordinary. On the fourth she heard a rustling among the diamond-spangled leaves of the wood. The next day there was a branch of the trees in her bouquet.

She took the Star Gazer aside and said to him in a harsh voice, "You know what price my father has promised to pay for our secret?"

"I know, Princess," answered Michael.

"Don't you mean to tell him?"

"That is not my intention."

"Are you afraid?"

"No, Princess."

"What makes you so discreet, then?"

But Michael was silent.

Lina's sisters had seen her talking to the garden boy, and ridiculed her for it.

"What prevents your marrying him?" asked the eldest. "You would become a gardener too; it is a charming profession. You could live in a cottage at the end of the park, and help your husband draw up water from the well, and bring us our bouquets."

The Princess Lina was very angry, and when the Star Gazer presented her bouquet she received it in a disdainful manner. Michael behaved most respectfully. He never raised his eyes to her, but nearly all day she felt him at her side without ever seeing him.

One day she made up her mind to tell everything to her eldest sister. "What!" said she. "This rogue knows our secret and you never told me! I must lose no time in getting rid of him."

"But how?"

"Why, by having him taken to the tower with the dungeons, of course."

For this was the way in old times that beautiful princesses rid themselves of people who knew too much. But the astonishing part of it was that the youngest sister did not seem to relish this method of stopping the mouth of the garden boy, who, after all, had said nothing to their father. They agreed to ask their ten sisters. Each was on the side of the eldest. Then the youngest sister declared that, if they laid a finger on the garden boy, she would herself go and tell their father the secret of the holes in their shoes.

At last it was decided that Michael should be put to the test; they would take him to the ball, and at the end of supper would give him the potion which was to enchant him like the rest. They sent for the Star Gazer and asked him how he had contrived to learn their secret, but still he remained silent. Then, in commanding tones, the eldest sister gave him the order they had agreed upon. He only answered, "I will obey."

He had been present, invisible, at the council of Princesses and had heard all. But he had made up his mind to drink of the potion and sacrifice himself for the happiness of her he loved. Not wishing, however, to cut a poor figure at the ball by the side of the other dancers, he went at once to the laurels and said, "My lovely rose laurel, with the golden rake I have raked you, with the golden bucket I have watered you, with the silken towel I have wiped you. Dress me like a prince."

A beautiful pink flower appeared. Michael plucked it, and in a moment found himself clothed in velvet which was as black as the eyes of the little Princess, with a cap to match, a diamond aigrette and a blossom of the rose laurel in his buttonhole.

Thus dressed, he presented himself that evening before the Duke of Belœil and obtained leave to try and discover his daughters' secret. He looked so distinguished that hardly anyone would have known who he was.

The twelve Princesses went upstairs to bed. Michael followed them and waited behind the open door till they gave the signal for departure. This time he did not cross in Lina's boat. He gave his arm to the eldest sister, danced with each in turn and was so graceful that everyone was delighted with him. At last the time came for him to dance with the little Princess. She found him the best partner in the world, but he did not dare speak a single word to her. When he was taking her back to her place she said to him in a mocking voice, "Here you are at the summit of your wishes; you are being treated like a prince."

"Don't be afraid," replied the Star Gazer gently. "You shall never be a gardener's wife."

The little Princess stared at him with a frightened face, and he left her without waiting for an answer.

When the satin slippers were worn through, the fiddles stopped and they were at the banquet table, Michael was placed next to the eldest sister and opposite the youngest.

They gave him the most exquisite dishes to eat and the most delicate wines to drink; and in order to turn his head more completely, compliments and flattery were heaped on him from every side.

At last the eldest sister made a sign, and one of the pages brought in a large golden cup. "The enchanted castle has no further secrets for you," she said to the Star Gazer. "Let us drink to your triumph."

He cast a lingering glance at the little Princess and without hesitation lifted the cup.

"Don't drink!" the Princess Lina suddenly cried out. "I would rather marry a gardener." And she burst into tears. Michael flung the contents of the cup behind him, sprang over the table and fell at Lina's feet. The rest of the Princes fell likewise at the knees of the Princesses, each of whom chose a husband and raised him to her side. The charm was broken.

The twelve couples embarked in the boats, which

crossed back many times in order to carry over the other Princes. Then they all went through the three woods, and when they had entered the underground passage a great noise was heard as if the enchanted castle were crumbling to the earth.

They went straight to the room of the Duke of Belœil, who had just awakened. Michael held in his hand the golden cup and he revealed the secret of the holes in the shoes. "Choose, then," said the Duke, "whichever one you prefer."

"My choice is already made," replied Michael, and he offered his hand to the youngest Princess, who blushed and lowered her eyes.

The Princess Lina did not become a gardener's wife; on the contrary, it was the Star Gazer who became a prince. But before the marriage ceremony the Princess insisted that Michael tell her how he came to discover the secret.

So he showed her the two laurels which had helped him, and she, being a prudent girl and thinking they gave him too much advantage over his wife, cut them off at the root and threw them into the fire.

And this is why the country girls go about singing:

> We won't go to the woods anymore,
> The laurel trees are cut—

and dance in summer by the light of the moon.

OLD GERMAN TALE, ANDREW LANG COLLECTION

HERE WERE two men in one village, both of whom had the very same name. They were both called Claus, but one of them owned four horses, and the other only one; so to tell them apart, people called the man who had four horses Big Claus and the man who had only one horse Little Claus. We are going to hear what happened to these two, for this is a true story.

The whole week long, Little Claus had to plow for Big Claus and lend him his one horse; in return, Big Claus lent him his four horses, but only once a week, and that was on Sundays. Hooray! How Little Claus did crack his whip over all the five horses, for they were as good as his own on that one day. The sun shone brightly, and the church bells rang merrily as the people passed by. Dressed in their best clothes and with their prayer books under their arms, they were on their way to hear the parson preach. They looked at Little Claus plowing away with all the five horses, and he was so happy that he cracked his whip and shouted, "Gee up, all my good horses!"

"I don't want you to shout that," said Big Claus. "Only one of the horses is yours, remember!"

But when some more people passed by on their way to church, Little Claus forgot, and he shouted again, "Gee up, all my good horses!"

"Look here; kindly stop that," said Big Claus. "If you say that once again, I'll knock your horse on the head and kill him on the spot, and that will be the end of him."

"All right, I won't say it again," said Little Claus, but when another lot of people went by and nodded "Good morning," it pleased him so much and he thought he looked so grand to be plowing with five horses that he cracked his whip once more and shouted, "Gee up, all my good horses!"

"I'll gee up your horses for you!" said Big Claus, and he took the tethering mallet and gave Little Claus's only horse such a knock on the head that it fell down, stone dead.

"What a shame! Now I haven't got any horse at all!" said Little Claus, and he began to cry. By and by he flayed the horse and took the hide and let it dry thoroughly in the wind. Then he stuffed the skin into a bag, which he slung over his shoulder, and went off to town to sell it.

He had a very long way to go and had to pass through a big, gloomy forest. Presently a terrible storm came up. He lost his way, and before he could find it again it was too far for him to get either to the town or back home before night fell.

Close to the road there was a large farmhouse; the shutters had already been put up over the windows for the evening, but a ray of light still escaped at the top. I suppose they won't mind letting me spend the night here, thought Little Claus and he knocked at the front door.

The farmer's wife opened it, but when she heard what he wanted, she told him to go away. Her husband was not at home, and she wasn't having any strangers on the place.

"Very well, then I shall have to sleep out of doors," said Little Claus, and the farmer's wife slammed the door in his face.

Close by stood a big haystack, and between this and the house was a little shed with a flat thatched roof.

"I can sleep up there," said Little Claus when he saw the roof. "It will make a fine bed. I hope the stork won't fly down and bite my legs!"—for a real live stork was standing on the roof, where it had its nest.

Little Claus climbed up onto the shed, and he tossed and turned about until at last he found a comfortable position. When he faced the farmhouse, he could see that the wooden shutters didn't quite fit the windows at the top, and so he was able to look straight into the dining room of the house.

There was a large table laid with wine and roast

meat and a delicious-looking fish. The farmer's wife and the parish clerk were sitting at the table; she kept helping him to wine, and he kept helping himself to the fish—for it was one of his favorite dishes.

"If only I could get a bite of that!" said Little Claus and he poked his head quite close to the window. Heavens, what a glorious cake he could see now! That was a feast and no mistake!

Suddenly he heard someone riding along the road toward the house. It was the woman's husband coming back home.

He was an excellent man, but he had one strange prejudice—he couldn't for the life of him bear the sight of a parish clerk; if he ever set eyes on one he got mad with rage. That's why the parish clerk had come to pass the time of day with the farmer's wife, knowing that her husband would be away; and the good woman had put before him the best food she had in the house. All of a sudden they heard the husband coming, and they were so frightened that the woman begged the clerk to creep into a great empty chest which stood against the wall. He did as he was told, for he knew very well how the poor husband felt at the sight of a parish clerk. The woman quickly hid the delicious food and wine in her oven, for if her husband were to see it he would certainly ask what it all meant.

"Oh, dear," sighed Little Claus up on the shed, when he saw all the food disappear.

"Is there anybody there?" asked the farmer, looking up at Little Claus. "What are you doing on the roof? You'd better come inside with me."

Little Claus then told him how he had lost his way, and asked if he might stay the night.

"Why, certainly!" said the farmer. "But first let's have a bite to eat."

The farmer's wife welcomed them in a most friendly way, laid the long table and gave them a large bowl of porridge. The farmer was hungry and set to with right good will, but Little Claus couldn't help thinking about the delicious roast meat, the fish and the cake which he knew were in the oven.

He had put the bag with the horsehide under his feet—for you remember he had left home to sell the horsehide in the town. He had no appetite at all for porridge, so he trod on the bag and the dry hide gave quite a loud squeak.

"Ssh!" said Little Claus to his bag, but at the same time treading on it again, and it squeaked much louder than before.

"Why, what on earth have you got in your bag?" asked the farmer.

"Oh, it's a wizard," said Little Claus. "He tells me that we shouldn't be eating porridge, when he's conjured the whole oven full of meat, fish and cake."

"You don't say so!" said the farmer, and in less than no time he had opened the oven and seen all the delicious food his wife had hidden—but he thought it was the wizard in the bag who had conjured it there. The wife didn't dare say a word but at once she put the food on the table, and they had their fill of the meat, the fish and the cake.

Little Claus again trod on his bag and made the hide squeak.

"What does he say now?" asked the farmer.

"He says," answered Little Claus, "that he's also conjured up three bottles of wine, and that they are in the oven too." Then the wife had to bring out the wine she had hidden, and the farmer drank and got quite merry. He thought what fun it would be to have a wizard like the one Little Claus had in his bag.

"Can he conjure up the devil too?" asked the farmer. "I should like to see him, for now I'm just in the mood for it."

"Certainly," said Little Claus. "My wizard can do anything I ask him to. Can't you?" he asked, and he trod on the bag so that it squeaked again. "Did you hear? He said 'Yes!' But the devil is so terrifying to look at that I should advise you not to try."

"Oh, I'm not a bit afraid. I wonder what he looks like."

"Well, he's going to appear in the shape of a parish clerk."

"Ugh!" said the farmer. "How horrible! I can't bear the sight of parish clerks. But never mind—so long as I know it's the devil, I can stand it better. I've plucked up my courage now, but don't let him come too close."

"Just let me ask my wizard," said Little Claus, treading on the bag and putting his ear up against it.

"What does he say?"

"He says you must open the chest over there against the wall, and you'll see the devil crouching inside, but mind you hold on to the lid, otherwise he'll slip out."

"Will you help me to hold it?" asked the farmer, going to the chest in which his wife had hidden the real clerk, who was trembling with fear.

The farmer lifted the lid ever so little and peeped under it. "Ugh!" he gasped out, jumping backward. "I did see him; he looked exactly like our own clerk. It was too awful!"

So they had to have another go at the wine, and then another one after that, and there they sat drinking till late into the night.

"You must sell me that wizard," said the farmer. "Ask as much as you like for him. I'll give you a whole bushel of money right away."

"No, I couldn't do that," said Little Claus. "Just think how useful this wizard can be to me."

"Oh, but I must have him," said the farmer, and he went on insisting.

"Well," said Little Claus, giving in at last, "as you've been kind enough to give me a night's lodging, all right. You shall have the wizard for a bushel of money, but you must give me full measure."

"Don't worry about that," said the farmer, "but you'll have to take the chest away with you. I won't keep it in the house another hour. The devil might still be in it."

So Little Claus gave the farmer the bag with the dried hide in it, and got a whole bushel of money— and full measure too—in exchange for it. The farmer also gave him a big wheelbarrow to take away the money and the chest.

"Good-bye," said Little Claus, and off he went with his money and the chest with the clerk still in it.

On the other side of the wood ran a deep river; the current was so strong that it was hardly possible to swim against it, and a fine new bridge had been built over it. Little Claus stopped halfway across, and said loud enough for the clerk to hear him: "What good is that stupid chest to me? It's heavy enough to be full of stones. I shall be tired out if I wheel it any longer. I'll just throw it into the river; if it sails home to me, well and good; but if it doesn't, no matter!"

Then he took hold of the chest with one hand and lifted it up a little as if he meant to throw it into the water.

"Stop! Stop!" shouted the clerk inside. "Let me out first!"

"Oh!" exclaimed Little Claus, pretending to be

THE WORLD'S BEST FAIRY TALES

frightened. "He's still there! I'd better be quick and push the chest into the river and let him drown."

"Oh, no, no!" screamed the clerk. "I'll give you a whole bushel of money if you don't."

"Well, that's another story," said Little Claus, opening the chest. The clerk crept out at once and pushed the empty chest into the water. They went off to his home, where Little Claus got his bushel of money. Since he'd already gotten a bushel from the farmer, he now had his whole wheelbarrow quite full of money.

"Anyway, I call that a good price for my horse," he said to himself when he got home to his room and emptied all the money in a heap on the floor. "Big Claus will be as cross as two sticks when he hears what a lot I've made out of my one and only horse, but I'm not going to tell him the whole truth about it."

Then he sent a boy over to Big Claus to borrow a bushel measure.

What can he want with that? thought Big Claus, and he smeared tar on the bottom of it, so that a little of whatever was being measured might stick to it. And that's exactly what happened, for when the measure was returned to him there were three silver coins sticking to the bottom.

"What's this?" said Big Claus, and he immediately went rushing over to Little Claus's home. "How did you get all that money?"

"Oh, I got it for my horsehide which I sold last night," Little Claus explained.

"My word, that's a thundering good price, I must say!" exclaimed Big Claus. Then he ran home, took an axe and knocked all his four horses on the head, ripped off their hides and drove off to the town with them.

"Hides! Hides! Who'll buy hides?" he shouted through the streets.

The shoemakers and tanners came running up and asked him how much he wanted for them.

"A bushel of money apiece!" said Big Claus.

"Are you mad?" they all said. "Do you think we've got money by the bushel?"

"Hides! Hides! Who'll buy hides?" he shouted again, and to everyone who asked him the price, he answered, "A bushel of money."

"He's trying to make fools of us," they all said, and the shoemakers took their straps, and the tanners their leather aprons, and they all began to beat Big Claus.

"Hides, hides!" they mocked at him. "Yes, we'll give your hide a good tanning! Out of the town with him!" they shouted, and Big Claus ran away as fast as he could, for he'd never received such a beating in his life before.

"Well," he said when he got home, "Little Claus shall pay for this. I'll slay him for it."

Now at Little Claus's home his old grandmother had died; true enough, she had been bad-tempered and nasty to him, but all the same he was very sorry, so he took the dead woman and put her into his own warm bed, to see if she might not possibly come to life again. She was to lie there until morning, while he himself meant to sit in the corner and sleep in a chair, as he had often done before.

As he sat there in the night, the door opened and Big Claus came in with an axe. He knew well enough where to find Little Claus's bed, so he went straight up to it and knocked the dead grandmother on the head, thinking she was Little Claus.

"There now," he said, "you won't fool me any-more." And he went home again.

"What a wicked man he is, wanting to kill me," said Little Claus. "It's lucky for poor old Granny that she was dead already, otherwise he would have finished her off."

Then he dressed his old grandmother in her Sunday best and, having borrowed a horse from his neighbor, harnessed it to his cart and planted her bolt upright on the back seat in such a way that she couldn't possibly fall out when the horse began to trot—and off they bowled through the woods. When the sun rose, they were near a big inn. Little Claus pulled up and went in to get something to eat.

The innkeeper had heaps and heaps of money, and was quite a good sort, but he was very hot-tempered, almost as if he were filled with pepper and snuff.

"Good morning," he said to Little Claus. "You've got into your Sunday best early today."

"Yes," said Little Claus. "I'm going to town with my old grandmother. She's out there in the cart; I can't get her to come in. Would you mind taking her a glass of cider? But you'll have to speak pretty loud, for she's hard of hearing."

"Right you are!" said the innkeeper, and he filled a large glass full of cider and took it out to the dead grandmother, who was still propped up in the cart.

"The young man has sent you a glass of cider," said the innkeeper, but the dead woman never uttered a word or moved.

"Can't you hear?" shouted the innkeeper just as loud as he could. "The young man has sent you a glass of cider!"

Once more he shouted the same thing, and then again for the fourth time, but when she never even stirred, he lost his temper and flung the glass right into her face, so that the cider ran down her nose, and she tumbled over backward into the cart, for she was only propped up, and not tied at all.

"Hi! What are you doing there?" shouted Little Claus, rushing out and grabbing the innkeeper by the throat. "You've killed my grandmother. Just look, there's a great hole in her forehead."

"Oh, what a tragedy!" cried the innkeeper, clasping his hands in despair. "It's all because of my hot temper. Dear Little Claus, I'll give you a whole bushel of money and have your grandmother buried as if she was my own; but mum's the word, or they'll cut my head off, and that's very unpleasant, you know."

So Little Claus got another bushel of money, and the innkeeper buried the old grandmother as if she'd been his own.

When Little Claus came back home with his money, he immediately sent his boy over to Big Claus to borrow a bushel measure.

"What the devil does this mean?" exclaimed Big Claus. "Didn't I kill him after all? I'd better go and find out for myself." And he went over to Little Claus with the measure.

"Where in the world did you get all that money from?" he asked, opening his eyes wider and wider when he saw the money that had been added to Little Claus's heap.

"It was my grandmother you killed, not me," said Little Claus, "so I have just sold her for a bushel of money!"

"My word, that's a thundering good price!" said Big Claus, so he hurried home, took an axe and quickly killed his own old grandmother. Then he put her in his cart, drove to the hospital in town and asked a doctor if he wanted to buy a dead body.

"Who is it and where did you get it from?" asked the doctor.

"It's my grandmother," said Big Claus. "I've killed her to get a bushel of money."

"Good Lord!" said the doctor. "You must be raving, man! You'd better not say that, or they'll have your head off." And then he told him what a terribly wicked thing he had done, and what a scoundrel he was, and that he ought to go to prison. At this Big Claus got so frightened that he dashed straight from the hospital into his cart, whipped up the horses and galloped home. But the doctor and everyone else thought he must be mad, so they let him drive wherever he liked.

"You shall pay for this," said Big Claus, once he had reached the highroad. "Yes, indeed, you shall pay for this, Little Claus." So as soon as he got home he took the biggest sack he could find, went over to Little Claus's home and said, "You've fooled me again. First I killed my horses and now I've killed my old grandmother. It's all your fault, but you shan't make a fool of me anymore." Then he grabbed Little Claus by the middle, thrust him into the sack and threw him over his shoulder, shouting, "Now I'm going to take you out and drown you!"

The river was some distance away, and Little Claus wasn't at all light to carry. The road went past the church, where the organ was playing and the people were singing very beautifully. Big Claus put the sack down close to the church door and thought it might be a good thing to go in and hear a hymn before he went any farther. There was no chance for Little Claus to get out of the sack, and everybody else was in church, so in he went.

"Oh, dear, oh, dear!" sighed Little Claus in the sack. He twisted and turned, but he couldn't manage to loosen the cord. At that very moment, an old cattle drover with chalk-white hair passed by, leaning on a big stick. He was driving a whole herd of cows and oxen in front of him, and they bumped into the sack in which Little Claus was sitting and pushed it over.

"Oh, dear!" sighed Little Claus. "I'm so young to go to Heaven already."

"And poor me," said the drover, "I'm so old and yet I can't get there!"

"Open the sack!" shouted Little Claus. "Crawl in and take my place, and you'll be in Heaven before you know it."

"That's just what I want!" said the cattle drover, and he untied the sack for Little Claus, who jumped out at once.

"You'll take care of the cattle for me, won't you?" said the old man, and he crawled into the sack. Little Claus tied it up again and went off with all the cows and oxen.

Soon after this, Big Claus came out of church and threw the sack over his shoulder again. He couldn't help noticing that it had gotten very light during his absence, for the old drover was not more than half the weight of Little Claus.

"How light he is to carry now! I'm sure it must be because I've been listening to a hymn." Then he went to the broad, deep river, threw the sack with the old drover in it into the water and shouted after him, thinking that it was Little Claus, "There now! You shan't fool me anymore."

So he started off for home, but when he came to the crossroads he met Little Claus coming along with all the cattle.

"I'll be blowed!" exclaimed Big Claus. "Didn't I drown you?"

"To be sure you did!" said Little Claus. "You threw me into the river less than half an hour ago."

"But where on earth did you get all these fine cattle from?" asked Big Claus.

"They're sea cattle," said Little Claus. "I'm going to tell you the whole story, and I'm going to thank you for drowning me. I'm at the top of the ladder now; I'm really rich, I tell you. I was scared to death in the sack when the wind whistled about my ears as you threw me down from the bridge into the cold water. I sank straight to the bottom, but I didn't hurt myself, for the finest soft grass grows down there. I fell on that, and the sack was opened at once. The loveliest maiden in snow-white garments, with a green wreath on her wet hair, took my hand and said, 'Is that you,

373

Little Claus? Here are some cattle for you to begin with. Four miles farther up the road there's another herd of them which I will also give you for a present.' Then I discovered that the river is a great highroad for the sea people. Down there at the bottom they walk straight in from the sea and far up into the land, where the river is lost to sight. It was lovely down there with flowers and the freshest of grass. Fishes darted past my ears as birds do in the air up here. I can't tell you how nice looking the people were, and what a lot of cattle there were grazing along the ditches and fences!"

"But why have you come back so soon?" asked Big Claus. "I shouldn't have done that if it was so beautiful down there."

"Why," said Little Claus, "that's where I've been very clever! Don't you remember what I told you? The sea maiden said that four miles farther up the road—and by the road she meant the river, for she can't get anywhere else—there was another herd of cattle waiting for me. But I know how the river meanders in and out; it would be a terribly roundabout way. No, the shortest way, if you can manage it, is to come up on land and go straight across to the river again. It saves about two miles, and so I get to my sea cattle that much more quickly."

"Oh, you are a lucky fellow," said Big Claus. "Do you think I shall get some sea cattle too, if I go down to the bottom of the river?"

"I'm sure of it," said Little Claus, "but I can't carry you in the sack to the river, you're too heavy. If you'll go there yourself and crawl into the sack, I'll throw you in with the greatest of pleasure."

"Thanks very much," said Big Claus, "but if I don't find any sea cattle when I get down there, I'll give you a walloping such as you'll never forget."

"Now don't be so hard on me!" said Little Claus— and down they went to the river.

When the thirsty cattle saw the water, they ran as fast as they could to reach it and drink.

"Look what a hurry the cattle are in," said Little Claus. "They're longing to go down to the bottom of the river again."

"Yes, but help me first," said Big Claus, "or you'll get a good beating." And then he crawled into the big sack which had been lying across the back of one of the oxen.

"Put a stone in it, or I'm afraid I shan't sink," said Big Claus.

"You'll sink fast enough," said Little Claus, but still he put a good big stone in the sack, tied the rope tight and gave it a good push—plump! There was Big Claus out in the river, and he sank straight to the bottom.

"I'm afraid he won't find his cattle," said Little Claus, and he drove home the ones he had.

HANS CHRISTIAN ANDERSEN, TRANSLATED BY PAUL LEYSSAC

Long, long ago, as far back as the time when animals spoke, there lived a community of cats in a deserted house not far from a large town. They had everything they could possibly desire for their comfort. They were well fed and well lodged, and if by any chance an unlucky mouse was stupid enough to venture in their way, they caught it, not to eat but for the pure pleasure of catching it.

The old people of the town related how they had heard their parents speak of a time when the whole country was so overrun with rats and mice that not so much as a grain of corn was to be gathered in the fields; and it might be out of gratitude to the cats who had rid the country of these plagues that their descendants were allowed to live in peace.

No one knows where the cats got the money to pay for everything, or who paid it, for all this happened so very long ago. But one thing is certain: they were rich enough to keep a servant, for though they lived very happily together and did not scratch or fight more than human beings would have done, they were not

clever enough to do the housework themselves and pre-
ferred at all events to have someone to cook their meat,
which they scorned to eat raw.

Not only were they very difficult to please about the
housework, but most women quickly tired of living
alone with only cats for companions, and consequently
they never kept a servant long. It had become a saying
in the town, when anyone found herself reduced to her
last penny: "I will go and live with the cats," and
many a poor woman actually did so.

Now Lizina was not happy at home, for her mother,
who was a widow, was much fonder of her elder
daughter. Often the younger one fared very badly and
had not enough to eat, while her sister could have
everything she desired, and if Lizina dared to complain
she was certain to receive a good beating.

At last the day came when she was at the end of her
patience, and she exclaimed to her mother and sister,
"Since you hate me so much, you will be glad to be rid
of me—so I am going to live with the cats!"

"Away with you!" cried her mother, seizing an old
broom handle from behind the door.

Poor Lizina did not wait to be told twice, but ran
off at once and never stopped till she reached the door
of the cats' house. Their cook had left them that very
morning with her face all scratched, the result of such
a quarrel with the head of the house that he had nearly
clawed out her eyes. Lizina therefore was warmly wel-

comed, and she set to work at once to prepare the dinner, not without many misgivings as to the tastes of the cats and whether she would be able to satisfy them.

Going to and fro about her work, she found herself frequently hindered by a constant succession of cats who appeared one after another in the kitchen to inspect the new servant. She had one in front of her feet, another perched on the back of her chair while she peeled vegetables, a third sat on the table beside her and five or six others prowled about among the pots and pans on the shelves against the wall.

The air resounded with their purring, which meant they were pleased with their new maid, but Lizina had not yet learned to understand their language, and often she did not know what they wanted her to do. However, as she was a good, kindhearted girl, she set to work to pick up the little kittens which tumbled about on the floor, she patched up quarrels and nursed on her lap a big tabby—the oldest of the community—which had a lame paw.

All these kindnesses could hardly fail to make a favorable impression on the cats, and it was even better after a while, when Lizina had become accustomed to their strange ways. Never had the house been kept so clean, the meats so well served nor the sick cats so well cared for.

Some weeks later they had a visit from an old cat whom they called their father, who lived by himself in a barn at the top of the hill and came down from time to time to inspect the little colony. He too was much taken with Lizina, and on seeing her, asked, "Are you well served by this nice, black-eyed little person?" and the cats answered with one voice, "Oh, yes, Father Gatto, we have never had so good a servant!"

At each of his visits the answer was always the same; but after a time the old cat, who was very observant, noticed that the little maid was looking sadder and sadder.

"What is the matter, my child—has anyone been unkind to you?" he asked one day, when he found her almost crying in her kitchen.

She burst into tears and answered between her sobs, "Oh, no! They are all very good to me. But I long for news of home and I pine to see my mother and sister."

Gatto, being a sensible old cat, understood the little servant's feelings. "You shall go home," he said, "and you shall not come back here unless you please. But first you must be rewarded for your kind services to my children. Follow me down into the inner cellar, where you have never been before, for I always keep it locked and carry the key away with me."

Lizina looked around her in astonishment as they went down into the great vaulted cellar underneath the kitchen. Before her stood two big earthenware water jars, one of which contained oil, the other a liquid shining like gold.

"Into which of these jars shall I dip you?" asked Father Gatto, with a grin that showed all his sharp white teeth, while his mustaches stood out straight on either side of his face.

The little maid looked at the two jars from under her long dark lashes. "In the oil jar!" she answered timidly, thinking to herself, I could not ask to be bathed in gold.

But Father Gatto replied, "No, no; you have deserved something better than that." And seizing her in his strong paws he plunged her into the liquid gold.

Wonder of wonders! When Lizina came out of the jar she shone from head to foot like the sun in the heavens on a fine summer's day. Her pretty pink cheeks and long black hair alone kept their natural color, but otherwise she had become like a statue of pure gold.

Father Gatto purred loudly with satisfaction. "Go home," he said, "and see your mother and sister; but take care if you hear the cock crow to turn toward it; if on the contrary the donkey brays, you must look the other way."

The little maid, having gratefully kissed the white paw of the old cat, set off for home. Just as she got near her mother's house the cock crowed, and quickly she turned toward it. Immediately a beautiful golden star appeared on her forehead, crowning her glossy black hair. At the same time the donkey began to bray,

but Lizina took care not to look over the fence into the field where the donkey was feeding. Her mother and sister, who were in front of their house, uttered cries of admiration and astonishment when they saw her, and their cries became still louder when Lizina, taking her handkerchief from her pocket, drew out a handful of gold also.

For some days the mother and her two daughters lived very happily together, for Lizina had given them everything she had brought away except her golden clothing, for that would not come off, in spite of all the efforts of her sister, who was madly jealous of her good fortune. The golden star, too, could not be removed from her forehead. But the gold pieces she drew from her pockets had found their way to her mother and sister.

"I will go now and see what I can get out of the pussies," said Peppina, the elder girl, one morning, as she took Lizina's basket and fastened her purses into her own skirt. I should like some of the cats' gold for myself, she thought, as she left her mother's house before the sun rose.

The cat colony had not yet hired another servant, for they knew they could never get one to replace Lizina, whose loss they had not ceased to mourn. When they heard that Peppina was her sister, they ran to meet her. "She is not the least like her," the kittens whispered among themselves.

"Hush, be quiet!" the older cats said. "All servants cannot be pretty."

No, decidedly she was not at all like Lizina. Even the most reasonable and generous of the cats soon acknowledged that.

The very first day she shut the kitchen door in the faces of the tomcats, who used to enjoy watching Lizina at her work, and a young and mischievous cat who jumped in by the open kitchen window and alighted on the table got such a blow with the rolling pin that he squalled for an hour.

With every day that passed the household became more and more aware of its misfortune.

The work was as badly done as the servant was surly and disagreeable. Heaps of dust collected in the corners of the rooms; spiders' webs hung from the ceilings and in front of the windowpanes; the beds were hardly ever made; and the feather beds, so beloved by the old and feeble cats, had never once been shaken since Lizina left the house. At Father Gatto's next visit he found the whole colony in a great state of uproar.

"Caesar has one paw so badly swollen that it looks as if it were broken," said one. "Peppina kicked him with her great wooden shoes. Hector has an abscess on his back where a wooden chair was flung at him, and Agrippina's three little kittens have died of hunger beside their mother, because Peppina forgot them in their basket up in the attic. There is no putting up with the creature—do send her away, Father Gatto! Lizina herself would not be angry with us; she must know very well what her sister is like."

"Come here," said Father Gatto in his most severe tones to Peppina. And he took her down into the cellar and showed her the same two great jars that he had shown Lizina. "Into which of these shall I dip you?" he asked; and she made haste to answer, "In the liquid gold," for she was no more modest than she was good and kind.

Father Gatto's yellow eyes darted fire. "You have not deserved it," he uttered in a voice like thunder and, seizing her, he flung her into the jar of oil, where she was nearly suffocated.

When she came to the surface screaming and struggling, the vengeful cat seized her again and rolled her in the ash heap on the floor; then when she rose, dirty, blinded and disgusting to behold, he thrust her from the door, saying, "Begone! When you meet a braying donkey be careful to turn your head toward it."

Stumbling and raging, Peppina set off for home, thinking herself fortunate to find a stick by the wayside with which to support herself. She was within sight of her mother's house when she heard the voice of a donkey loudly braying in the meadow on the right. Quickly she turned her head toward it, and at the same time put her hand up to her forehead where, waving like a plume, was a donkey's tail. She ran home to her mother at full speed, yelling with rage and despair; and it took Lizina two hours with a big basin of hot water and two cakes of soap to wash off the layer of oil and ashes with which Father Gatto had adorned her. As for the donkey's tail, it was impossible to get rid of that; it was as firmly fixed on her forehead as was the golden star on Lizina's.

Their mother was furious. She first beat Lizina unmercifully with the broom. Then she took her to the mouth of the well and lowered her into it. She went away, leaving her stranded at the bottom, weeping and crying for help.

Before this happened, however, the King's son in passing the mother's house one day had seen Lizina sitting and sewing in the parlor and had been dazzled by her beauty. After coming back two or three times, he at last ventured to approach the window and to whisper in the softest voice, "Lovely maiden, will you be my bride?"

And she had answered, "I will."

Next morning, when the Prince arrived to claim his bride, he found her wrapped in a large white veil. "It is thus that maidens are received from their parents' hands," said the mother, who hoped to make the King's son marry Peppina in place of her sister, and had fastened the donkey's tail around her head like a lock of hair under the veil. The Prince was young and a little timid, so he made no objections, and he seated Peppina in the carriage beside him.

Their way led past the old house inhabited by the cats, who were all at the window, for the report had got about that the Prince was going to marry the most beautiful maiden in the world, on whose forehead shone a golden star, and they knew that this could only be their adored Lizina. As the carriage slowly passed in front of the old house, where cats from all parts of the world seemed to be gathered, a song burst from every throat:

> Mew, mew, mew!
> Prince, look quick behind you!
> In the well is fair Lizina,
> And you have nothing but Peppina.

When he heard this, the coachman, who understood the cats' language better than the Prince did, stopped his horses and asked, "Does Your Highness know what the grimalkins are saying?"

The song broke forth again, louder than ever.

With a turn of his hand, the Prince threw back the white veil and discovered beneath it the puffed-up, swollen face of Peppina, with the donkey's tail twisted around her head.

"Ah, traitoress!" he exclaimed, quivering with rage, and, ordering the horses to be turned around, he drove the elder daughter back to the woman who had sought to deceive him. With his hand on the hilt of his sword he demanded Lizina in so fierce a voice that the mother hastened to the well to draw her prisoner out.

Lizina's clothing and her star shone so brilliantly that when the Prince led her home to the King, his father, the whole palace was lit up. Next day they were married, and lived happily ever after; and all the cats, headed by old Father Gatto, were at the wedding.

ITALIAN FAIRY TALE, ANDREW LANG COLLECTION

SINDBAD THE SAILOR

IN THE TIMES of Caliph Haroun al Raschid there lived in Baghdad a poor porter named Hindbad who, on a very hot day, was sent to carry a heavy load from one end of the city to the other. Before he had accomplished half the distance, he was so tired that, finding himself in a quiet street where the pavement was sprinkled with rosewater and a cool breeze was blowing, he set his burden upon the ground and sat down to rest in the shade of a grand palace.

Very soon he decided he could not have chosen a pleasanter place; a delicious perfume of aloes wood and pastilles came from the open windows and mingled with the scent of the rosewater which steamed up from the hot pavement. Within the palace he heard music, as of many instruments cunningly played, and the melodious warble of nightingales and other birds; and by this, and the appetizing smell of many dainty dishes, he judged that feasting and merrymaking were going on.

He wondered who lived in this magnificent place he had never seen before, the street in which it stood being one which he seldom had occasion to pass. To satisfy his curiosity he went up to one of the splendidly dressed servants who stood outside the door and asked the name of the master of the mansion.

"What," replied he, "do you live in Baghdad and not know that here lives Sindbad the Sailor, that famous traveler who has sailed over every sea upon which the sun shines?"

The porter could not help feeling envious of one whose lot seemed to be as happy as his own was miserable. Casting his eyes up to the sky he exclaimed aloud: "Consider, Mighty Creator of all things, the difference between Sindbad's life and mine. Every day I suffer a thousand hardships and misfortunes and have hard work to get even enough barley bread to keep myself and my family alive, while the lucky Sindbad spends money right and left and lives upon the fat of the land! What has he done that you should give him this pleasant life—what have I done to deserve so hard a fate?"

Saying this, he stamped upon the ground like one beside himself with misery and despair. Just at this moment a servant came out of the palace and, taking him by the arm, said, "Come with me. The noble Sindbad, my master, wishes to speak to you."

Hindbad was not a little surprised at this summons and feared that his unguarded words might have drawn upon him the displeasure of Sindbad, and he tried to excuse himself upon the pretext that he could not leave the burden which had been entrusted to him in the street. However, the lackey promised him it should be taken care of and urged him to obey the call so pressingly that, at last, the porter was obliged to yield.

He followed the servant into a vast room, where a great company was seated around a table covered with all sorts of delicacies. In the place of honor sat a tall, grave man whose long white beard gave him a venerable air. Behind his chair stood a crowd of attendants ready to minister to his wants. This was the famous Sindbad himself.

Sindbad, making a sign to him to approach, caused him to be seated and heaped many choice morsels upon his plate. Presently, when the banquet drew to a close, he addressed the noble company and the humble porter.

"Since you have, perhaps, heard but confused accounts of my seven voyages, and the dangers and wonders that I have met with by sea and land, I will now give you a full and true account of them, which I think you will be well pleased to hear."

As Sindbad was relating his adventures chiefly on account of the porter, he ordered, before beginning his tale, that the burden which had been left in the street should be carried by some of his own servants to the place for which Hindbad had set out at first, while he remained to listen to the story.

First Voyage

I inherited considerable wealth from my parents and, being young and foolish, I squandered it recklessly upon every kind of pleasure. But before long, finding that riches speedily take to themselves wings if managed as badly as I was managing mine, and remembering also that to be old and poor is misery indeed, I began to think of how I could make the best of what still remained to me. I sold all my household goods by public auction, joined a company of merchants who traded by sea and embarked with them at Balsora in a ship which we had fitted out among us.

We set sail and took our course toward the East

Indies by the Persian Gulf, having the coast of Persia upon our left hand and upon our right the shores of Arabia Felix. I was at first much troubled by the uneasy motion of the vessel but speedily recovered my health, and since that hour have been no more plagued by sickness.

From time to time we landed at various islands where we sold or exchanged our merchandise, and one day when the wind dropped suddenly we found ourselves becalmed close to a small island which rose only slightly above the surface of the water. Our sails were furled, and the captain gave all who wished permission to land for a while and amuse themselves. I was among the number, but when, after strolling about for some time, we lighted a fire and sat down to enjoy a repast, we were startled by a sudden and violent trembling of the island. At the same moment those left upon the ship set up an outcry, bidding us come on board for our lives, since what we had taken for an island was nothing but the back of a sleeping whale. Those who were nearest to the boat jumped into it, others leaped into the sea, but before I could save myself, the whale plunged suddenly into the depths of the ocean, leaving me clinging to a piece of wood which we had brought to make our fire.

Meanwhile a breeze had sprung up, and in the confusion of hoisting the sails and collecting those who were near the boat and clinging to its sides, no one missed me and I was left at the mercy of the waves. All that day I floated, now beaten this way, now that, and when night fell I despaired for my life. But weary and spent as I was, I clung to my frail support, and great was my joy when the morning light showed that I had drifted against an island.

The cliffs were high and steep, but luckily for me some tree roots protruded in places, and by their aid I climbed up at last and stretched myself upon the turf at the top, where I lay, more dead than alive, till the sun was high in the heavens. By that time I was very hungry, but after some searching I came upon edible herbs and a spring of clear water, and much refreshed I set out to explore the island.

Presently I reached a great plain where a grazing horse was tethered and, as I stood looking at it, I heard voices talking, apparently underground. In a moment a man appeared who asked me how I had come to be on the island.

I told him my adventures and heard in return that he was one of the grooms of Mihrage, the King of the island, and that each year they came to feed their master's horses on this plain. He took me to a cave where his companions were assembled. When I had eaten the food they set before me, they bade me think myself fortunate to have come upon them when I did, since they were going back to their master, the King, on the following day and without their aid I could certainly never have found my way, alone, to the inhabited part of the island.

Early the next morning we accordingly set out, and when we reached the capital I was graciously received by the King, to whom I related my adventures. He ordered that I should be well cared for and provided with such things as I needed. The capital was situated upon the seashore and was visited by vessels from all parts of the world. Being a merchant, I sought out men of my own profession, particularly those who came from foreign countries, as I hoped in this way to hear any news from Baghdad and find some means of returning there.

In the meantime I heard many curious things and answered many questions concerning my own country, for I talked with everyone who came to me. Also, to while away the time of waiting, I explored a little island named Cassel, which belonged to King Mihrage and was supposed to be inhabited by a spirit named Deggial. Indeed, the sailors assured me that often at night the playing of timbals could be heard upon it. However, I saw nothing strange on my voyage, saving some fish that were a full three hundred feet long, but were fortunately even more in dread of us than we of them, and fled from us if we did but strike upon a board to frighten them. Other fishes there were only a cubit long and these had heads like owls.

One day, down on the quay, I saw a ship which

had just cast anchor and was discharging her cargo, while the merchants to whom it belonged were busily directing the removal of it to their warehouses. Drawing nearer I presently noticed that my own name was marked upon some of the packages and, after having carefully examined them, I felt sure that they were indeed those which I had put on board our ship at Balsora. I then recognized the captain of the vessel, but as I was certain that he believed me to be dead, I went up to him and asked who owned the packages at which I was looking.

"There was on board my ship," he replied, "a merchant of Baghdad named Sindbad. One day he and several of my other passengers landed upon what we supposed to be an island but which was really an enormous whale floating asleep upon the waves. No sooner did it feel the heat of the fire which had been kindled upon its back, than it plunged into the depths of the sea. Several of the people who were upon it perished in the waters and, among others, was this unlucky Sindbad. This merchandise is his, but I have resolved to dispose of it for the benefit of his family should I ever chance to meet with them."

"Captain," I said, "I am that Sindbad whom you believe to be dead, and these are my possessions!"

When the captain heard these words he cried out in amazement, "Lackaday! What is the world coming to? In these days there is not an honest man to be met with. Did I not with my own eyes see Sindbad drown, and now you have the audacity to tell me that you are he! I should have taken you to be a just man, and yet for the sake of obtaining what does not belong to you, you are ready to invent this horrible falsehood."

"Have patience and do me the favor of hearing my story," said I.

"Speak then," the captain replied to me, "I am all attention."

So I told him of my escape and of my fortunate meeting with the King's grooms and how kindly I had been treated at the palace. Very soon I began to see that I had made some impression upon him, and after the arrival of some of the other merchants who showed great joy at once more seeing me alive, he declared that he also recognized me.

Throwing himself upon my neck, he exclaimed, "Heaven be praised that you have escaped from so great a danger. As to your goods, I pray you take them and dispose of them as you please."

I thanked him and praised his honesty, begging him to accept several bales of my merchandise in token of my gratitude, but he would take nothing. Of the choicest of my goods I prepared a present for King Mihrage, who was amazed, having known that I had lost all of my possessions. When I explained how my bales had been miraculously restored to me, he accepted my gifts and in return gave me many valuable things. I then took leave of him and, exchanging my merchandise for sandal and aloes wood, camphor, nutmegs, cloves, pepper and ginger, I embarked upon the same vessel and traded so successfully during our homeward voyage that I arrived in Balsora with about one hundred thousand pieces of gold.

My brothers and sisters received me with joy. I bought land and slaves, and built a great house in which I resolved to live happily and, in the enjoyment of all the pleasures of life, to forget my past sufferings.

Here Sindbad paused and commanded the musicians to play again, while the feasting continued until evening. When the time came for the porter to depart, Sindbad gave him a purse containing one hundred pieces of gold, saying, "Take this, Hindbad, and go home, but tomorrow come again and you shall hear more of my adventures."

The porter retired, quite overcome by so much generosity, and you may imagine that he was well received at home, where his wife and children thanked their lucky stars that he had found such a benefactor as the wealthy Sindbad.

The next day, Hindbad, dressed in his best, returned to the voyager's house and was received with open arms. As soon as all the guests had arrived the banquet began as before, and when they had feasted long and merrily, Sindbad addressed them.

"My friends, I beg that you will give me your attention while I relate the adventures of my second voyage, which you will surely find even more astonishing than the first."

Second Voyage

I had resolved, as you know, on my return from the first voyage, to spend the rest of my days quietly in Baghdad, but very soon I grew tired of such an idle life and longed once more to find myself upon the sea. I procured, therefore, goods that were suitable for the places I intended to visit and embarked for the second time in a good ship with other merchants whom I knew to be honorable men.

We went from island to island, often making excellent bargains, until one day we landed at a spot which appeared to possess neither houses nor people. While my companions wandered here and there gathering flowers and fruit, I sat down in a shady place and, having heartily enjoyed the provisions and the wine I had brought with me, I soon fell asleep, lulled by the murmur of a brook which flowed by.

How long I slept I know not, but when I opened my eyes I perceived with horror that I was alone and the ship was gone. I rushed to and fro like one distracted, uttering cries of despair, and when I saw the vessel under full sail just disappearing upon the horizon, I wished bitterly enough that I had been content to stay at home in safety.

Since wishes could do me no good, I presently took courage and looked about me for a means of escape. I climbed a tall tree and first of all directed my anxious glances toward the sea; but, finding nothing hopeful there, I turned landward and my curiosity was excited by a huge dazzling white object, so far away that I could not make out what it might be.

Descending from the tree, I hastily collected what remained of my provisions and set off as fast as I could. As I drew near, it seemed to me to be a white ball of immense size and height, and when I could touch it I found it marvelously smooth and soft. Since it was impossible to climb—for it presented no foothold—I walked around it, seeking some opening, but there was none. I counted, however, that it was at least fifty paces round.

By this time the sun was near setting, but quite suddenly something like a huge black cloud came swiftly over me, and I saw with amazement that it was a bird of extraordinary size which was hovering near. Then I remembered I had often heard the sailors speak of a wonderful bird called a roc, and it occurred to me that the white object which had so puzzled me must be its egg.

Sure enough the bird settled slowly down upon it, covering it with its wings to keep it warm, and I cowered close beside the egg in such a position that one of the bird's feet, which was as large as the trunk of a tree, was just in front of me. Taking off my turban, I bound myself securely to the foot with the linen in the hope that the roc, when it took flight next morning, would bear me away with it from the island. And this was precisely what did happen.

As soon as the dawn appeared, the bird soared into the air, carrying me up and up till I could no longer see the earth and then suddenly descended so swiftly that I almost lost consciousness. When I became aware that the roc had settled and I was once again upon solid ground, I hastily unbound my turban from its foot, and not a moment too soon; for the bird, pouncing upon a huge snake, grasped it with its powerful beak, rose into the air and soon had disappeared from my view. After I had looked about me I began to doubt if I had gained anything at all by quitting the desolate island.

The valley in which I found myself was deep and narrow and surrounded by mountains which towered into the clouds and were so steep and rocky there was no way of climbing up their sides.

As I wandered about, seeking for some means of escaping from this trap, I observed that the ground was strewn with diamonds, many of them of an astonishing size.

This sight gave me great pleasure, but my delight

was speedily dampened when I also saw numbers of horrible snakes so long and so large that the smallest of them could have swallowed an elephant with ease. Fortunately for me they seemed to hide in caverns in the rocks by day, and only came out by night, probably because of their enemy the roc.

All day long I wandered up and down the valley, and when it grew dusk I crept into a small cave. Having blocked up the entrance to it with a stone, I ate part of my little store of food and lay down to sleep, but all through the night the serpents crawled to and fro, hissing horribly, so that I could scarcely close my eyes for terror.

I was thankful when the morning light appeared and, when I judged by the silence that the serpents had retreated to their dens, I came tremblingly out of my cave and wandered up and down the valley once more, kicking the diamonds contemptuously out of my path, for I felt that they were indeed vain things to a man in my situation.

At last, overcome with weariness, I sat down upon a rock, but I had hardly closed my eyes when I was startled by something which fell to the ground with a thud close beside me.

It was a huge piece of fresh meat, and as I stared at it several more pieces rolled over the cliffs in different places. I had always thought that the stories the sailors told of the famous Valley of Diamonds, and of the cunning way which some merchants had devised for getting at the precious stones, were mere travelers' tales invented to give pleasure to the hearers, but now I perceived that they were surely true.

These merchants came to the valley at the time when the eagles, which keep their aeries in the rocks, had hatched their young. The merchants then threw great lumps of meat into the valley. These, falling with so much force upon the diamonds, were sure to take up some of the precious stones with them when the eagles pounced upon the meat and carried it off to their nests to feed their hungry broods. Then the merchants, scaring away the parent birds with shouts and outcries, would secure their treasures.

Until this moment I had looked upon the valley as my grave, for I had seen no possibility of getting out of it alive, but now I took courage and began by picking up all the largest diamonds I could find and storing them carefully in the leather pouch which had held my provisions; this I tied securely to my belt. I then chose the piece of meat which seemed most suited to my purpose, and with the aid of my turban bound it firmly to my back. This done, I lay down upon my face and awaited the coming of the eagles. I soon heard the flapping of their mighty wings above me, and had the satisfaction of feeling one of them seize upon the meat and me with it, and rise slowly toward his nest, into which he presently dropped me.

Luckily for me the merchants were on the watch and, setting up their usual outcries, they rushed to the nest, scaring away the eagle. Their amazement was great when they discovered me, also their disappointment, and with one accord they fell to abusing me for having robbed them of their usual profit.

Addressing myself to the one who seemed most aggrieved, I said, "I am sure, if you knew all I have suffered, you would show more kindness toward me, and as for diamonds, I have enough here of the very best for you and me and your entire company." So saying I showed them to him.

The others all crowded around me, wondering at my adventures and admiring the device by which I had escaped from the valley. When they had led me to their camp and examined my diamonds, they assured me that, in the many years they had carried on their trade, they had seen no stones to be compared with them for size and beauty.

I found that each merchant chose a particular nest, so I begged the one who owned the nest to which I had been carried to take as much as he would of my treasure, but he contented himself with one stone and that by no means the largest, assuring me that with such a gem his fortune was made and he need toil no more. I stayed with the merchants several days, and then, as they were journeying homeward, I gladly accompanied them.

Our path lay across high mountains and came at last to the seashore. We sailed to the Isle of Roha, where the camphor trees grow to such size that a hundred men could shelter under one of them with ease. The sap flows from an incision made high up in the tree into a vessel hung there to receive it and soon hardens into the substance called camphor, but the camphor tree itself withers up and dies when it has been so treated.

In this same island we saw the rhinoceros, an animal smaller than the elephant and larger than the buffalo. It has a horn a foot and a half long which is solid but has a furrow from the base to the tip. Upon it is traced in white lines the figure of a man. The rhinoceros fights with the elephant and, transfixing him with his horn, carries him off upon his head, but becoming blinded with the blood of his enemy, he falls to the ground. Then comes the roc and he clutches them both in his talons, taking them to feed his young.

This doubtless astonishes you, but if you do not believe my tale go to Roha and see for yourself. For fear of wearying you, I pass over in silence many other wonderful things which we saw on this island. Before we left I exchanged one of my diamonds for much goodly merchandise by which I profited greatly on our homeward way. At last we reached Balsora, whence I hastened to Baghdad, where my first action was to bestow large sums of money upon the poor, after which I settled down to enjoy tranquilly the riches I had gained with so much toil and pain.

Having thus related the adventures of his second voyage, Sindbad again bestowed a hundred pieces of gold upon Hindbad, inviting him and all the other guests to return on the following day and hear how he fared upon his third voyage. The other guests also departed for their homes but returned at the same hour the next day, including the porter, whose former life of hard work and poverty already seemed to him like a bad dream. Once more, when the feast was over, Sindbad claimed the attention of his guests and began the account of his third voyage.

Third Voyage

After a very short time, the pleasant, easy life I led made me quite forget the perils of my two voyages. So once more providing myself with the rarest and choicest merchandise of Baghdad, I set sail with other merchants of my acquaintance for distant lands. We had touched at many ports and made much profit, when one day upon the open sea we were caught by a terrible wind which blew us completely out of our reckoning and lasted for several days, finally driving us into harbor on a strange island.

"I would rather have come to anchor anywhere than

here," cried our captain. "This island and those adjoining it are inhabited by hairy savages who are certain to attack us. Whatever these dwarfs may do we dare not resist, since they swarm like locusts, and if one of them is killed the rest will fall upon us and speedily make an end of us."

These words caused great consternation among all the ship's company and only too soon we were to find out that the captain spoke truly. There appeared a vast multitude of hideous savages, not more than two feet high and covered with reddish fur. Throwing themselves into the waves, they surrounded our vessel. Chattering meanwhile in a language which we could not understand, and clutching at ropes and gangways, they swarmed up the ship's side with such speed and agility that they almost seemed to fly.

You may imagine the terror that seized us as we watched them, neither daring to hinder them nor able to speak a word to deter them from their purpose, whatever it may be. Of this we were not left long in doubt. Hoisting the sails and cutting the anchor cable, they sailed our vessel to an island which lay a little farther off, where they drove us ashore. Then, taking possession of the ship, they made off to the place from which they had come, leaving us stranded upon a shore avoided with horror by mariners for a reason you will learn before long.

Turning away from the sea we wandered miserably

inland, finding as we went various herbs and fruits which we ate, feeling that we might as well live as long as possible though we had no hope of escape. Presently we saw in the distance what seemed to be a splendid palace, toward which we turned our weary steps. When we reached it we saw that it was a castle, lofty and strongly built. Pushing back the heavy ebony doors we entered the courtyard, but upon the threshold of the great hall beyond it we paused, frozen with horror at the sight which greeted us. On one side lay a huge pile of bones—human bones, and on the other numberless spits for roasting!

Overcome with despair we sank trembling to the ground and lay there without speech or motion. The sun was setting when a loud noise aroused us, the door of the hall was violently burst open and a hideous giant entered. He was as tall as a palm tree and had but one eye, which flamed like a burning coal in the middle of his forehead. His teeth were long and sharp and he grinned horribly, while his lower lip hung down upon his chest, and he had ears like elephant's ears, which covered his shoulders, and his nails were like the claws of some fierce bird.

At this terrible sight our senses left us and we lay like dead men. When at last we came to ourselves the giant sat examining us attentively with his fearful eye. Before long, having looked at us enough, he came toward us and, stretching out his hand, took me by the back of the neck, turning me this way and that, but feeling that I was mere skin and bone he set me down again and went on to the next, whom he treated in the same fashion. At last he came to the captain and, finding him the fattest of us all, he took him up in one hand and stuck him upon a spit and proceeded to kindle a huge fire at which he presently roasted him. After the giant had supped he went to sleep, snoring like the loudest thunder, while the rest of us lay shivering with horror the whole night through. When day finally broke the giant awoke and went out, leaving us alone in the castle.

When we believed him to be really gone, we started up, bemoaning our horrible fate until the hall echoed with our despairing cries. Though we were many and our enemy was alone, it did not occur to us to kill him. Indeed we should have found that a hard task even if we had thought of it, but no plan could we devise to deliver ourselves. So at last, submitting to our sad fate, we spent the day in wandering up and down the island, eating such fruits as we could find, and when night came we returned to the castle, having sought in vain for any other place of shelter.

At sunset the giant returned, supped upon one of our unhappy comrades, slept and snored till dawn and then left us as before. Our condition seemed to us so frightful that several of my companions thought it would be better to leap from the cliffs and perish in the waves at once, rather than await so miserable an end; but I had a plan of escape which I now unfolded to them, and which they immediately agreed to attempt with me.

"Listen, my brothers," I said, "you know that plenty of driftwood lies along the shore. Let us make several rafts and carry them to a suitable place. If our plot succeeds, we can wait patiently for the chance of some passing ship which would rescue us. If it fails, we must quickly take to our rafts; frail as they are, we have more chance of saving our lives with them than we have if we remain here."

All agreed with me, and we spent the day in building rafts, each capable of carrying three persons. At nightfall we returned to the castle, and very soon in came the giant, and one more of our number was sacrificed. As soon as he had finished his horrible repast, he lay down to sleep as before, and when we heard him begin to snore, I, and nine of the boldest of my comrades, rose softly. Each of us took a spit, which we made red-hot in the fire, and then at a given signal we plunged it with one accord into the giant's eye, completely blinding him.

Uttering a terrible cry, the giant sprang to his feet reaching about in every direction to try to seize one of us, but we had all fled different ways as soon as the deed was done and thrown ourselves flat upon the ground in corners where he was not likely to touch us with his feet. After a vain search he fumbled about till he found the door leading from the castle and fled out of it, howling frightfully. As for us, my companions and I immediately made haste to leave the fatal place and, stationing ourselves beside our rafts, we waited to see what would happen.

Our idea was that if, when the sun rose, we saw nothing of the giant and no longer heard his howls, which still came faintly through the darkness, growing more and more distant, we should conclude that he was dead and that we might safely stay on the island and need not risk our lives upon the frail rafts. But alas, morning light showed us our enemy approaching, supported on either hand by two giants nearly as large and fearful as himself, while a crowd of others followed close upon their heels. Hesitating no longer, we clambered onto our rafts and rowed out to sea as fast as we could.

The giants, seeing their prey escaping them, seized huge pieces of rock and, wading into the water, hurled them after us. So good was their aim that all rafts except the one I was on were swamped and their luckless crews drowned, without our being able to do anything to help them. Indeed, I and my two companions had all we could do to keep our own raft beyond the reach of the giants, but by dint of hard rowing we at last gained the open sea. Here we were at the mercy of the winds and waves, which tossed us to and fro that entire day and night, but the next day we found ourselves near an island, upon which we gladly landed.

There we picked delicious fruits and, having satisfied our hunger, we presently lay down to rest upon the shore. Suddenly we were aroused by a loud rustling noise and, starting up, saw that it was caused by an immense snake which was rapidly gliding toward us over the sand.

So swiftly it came that it had seized one of my comrades before he had time to fly and, in spite of his struggles and cries, speedily crushed him in its mighty coils and proceeded to swallow him.

By this time my other companion and I were running for our lives to some place where we might hope to be safe from this new horror. Seeing a tall tree, we climbed up into it, having first provided ourselves with a store of fruit from the surrounding bushes. When night came I fell asleep, only to be awakened once more by the terrible snake, which coiled itself around the tree and, finding my comrade who was perched just below me, swallowed him and crawled away, leaving me half dead with terror.

When the sun rose I crept down from the tree, with hardly a hope of escaping the dreadful fate which had overtaken my comrades; but life is sweet, and I determined to do everything I could to save myself. All day long I toiled with frantic haste and collected quantities of dry brushwood which I bound with reeds and, making a circle of them under my tree, I piled them firmly one upon another until I had a kind of tent in which I crouched, like a mouse in a hole when she sees the cat coming.

You may imagine what a fearful night I passed, for the snake returned eager to devour me and glided around and around my frail shelter seeking an entrance. Every moment I feared that it would succeed in pushing aside some of the brushwood, but happily for me it held together, and when it grew light my enemy retired, baffled and hungry, to his den. As for me, I was more dead than alive!

Shaking with fright and half suffocated by the poisonous breath of the monster, I came out of my tent and crawled down to the sea. I felt that it would be better to plunge from the cliffs and end my life at once than pass another night of such horror. But to my joy and relief I saw a ship in the distance and, shouting wildly and waving my turban, I managed to attract the attention of her crew.

A boat was sent to rescue me, and very soon I found myself on board surrounded by a wondering crowd of sailors and merchants eager to know by what chance I found myself on that desolate island. After I had told my story they regaled me with the choicest food the ship afforded, and the captain, seeing that I was dressed in rags, generously bestowed upon me one of his own coats. After sailing about for some time and touching at many ports the ship came at last to the Island of Salahat, where sandalwood grows in great abundance.

Here we anchored, and, as I stood watching the merchants preparing to sell or exchange their goods, the captain came up to me and said, "I have here some merchandise belonging to a passenger of mine who has died. Will you do me the favor to trade with it, and when I meet with his heirs I shall be able to give them the money, though it will be only just that you shall have a portion for your trouble."

I consented gladly, for I did not like standing by idle. Whereupon he pointed the bales out to me and sent for the person whose duty it was to keep a list of the goods that were upon the ship. When this man came he asked in what name the merchandise was to be registered.

"In the name of Sindbad the Sailor," replied the captain.

At this I was greatly surprised but, looking carefully at him, I recognized him to be the captain of the ship upon which I had made my second voyage, though he had altered much since that time. As for him, believing me to be dead, it was no wonder that he had not recognized me.

"So, captain," said I, "the merchant who owned those bales was called Sindbad?"

"Yes," he replied, "he was so named. He was from

Baghdad and joined my ship at Balsora, but by mischance he was left behind upon a deserted island where we had landed to fill up our water casks, and it was not until four hours later that he was missed. By that time the wind had freshened and it was impossible to put back for him."

"You suppose him to have perished, then?" said I.

"Alas, yes," he answered.

"Why, captain," I cried, "look well at me! I am that Sindbad who fell asleep upon the island and awoke to find himself abandoned."

The captain stared at me in amazement, but was presently convinced that I was indeed speaking the truth and rejoiced greatly at my escape.

"I am glad to have that piece of carelessness off my conscience at any rate," said he. "Now take your goods and the profit I have made for you upon them, and may you prosper in the future."

I took them gratefully and, as we went from one island to another, I laid in stores of cloves, cinnamon and other spices. In one place I saw a tortoise which was twenty cubits long and as many broad, also a fish that was like a cow and had skin so thick it was used to make shields. Another fish I saw was like a camel in shape and color. By degrees we came back to Balsora, and I returned to Baghdad with so much money that I could not myself count it, besides treasures without end. I gave largely to the poor and bought much land to add to what I already possessed, and thus ended my third voyage.

When Sindbad had finished his story he gave another hundred pieces of gold to Hindbad, who then departed with the other guests. The next day, when they had all reassembled and the banquet was ended, their host continued his adventures.

Fourth Voyage

Rich and happy as I was after my third voyage, I could not make up my mind to stay at home altogether. My love of trading and the pleasure I took in anything that was new and strange made me set my affairs in order and begin my journeying again. I took ship at a distant seaport, and for some time all went well, but at last, being caught in a violent hurricane, our vessel became a total wreck and many of our company perished in the waves. I, with a few others, had the good fortune to be washed ashore clinging to pieces of the wreck, for the storm had driven us near an island, and, scrambling up beyond the reach of the waves, we threw ourselves down to wait for morning.

At daylight we wandered inland and soon saw some huts, to which we directed our steps. As we drew near, their inhabitants swarmed out in great numbers and surrounded us, and we were led to their houses and divided among our captors. I with five others was taken into a hut, where we were made to sit upon the ground, and certain herbs were given to us which our captors made signs for us to eat.

Observing that they themselves did not touch them, I was careful only to pretend to taste my portion; but my companions, being very hungry, rashly ate all that was set before them, and very soon I had the horror of seeing them become perfectly mad. Though they chattered incessantly, I could not understand a word they said, nor did they heed when I spoke to them. The savages now produced large bowls full of rice prepared with coconut oil, of which my crazy comrades ate eagerly, but I tasted just a few grains, understanding clearly that the object of our captors was to fatten us speedily for their own eating, and this was exactly what happened.

My unlucky companions, having lost their reason, felt neither anxiety nor fear and ate greedily whatever was offered them. So they were soon fat and there was an end of them, but I grew leaner day by day, for I ate but little, and even that little did me no good by reason of my fear of what lay before me. However, as I was far from being a tempting morsel, I was allowed to wander about freely, and one day, when the savages had gone off upon some expedition, leaving only an old man to guard me, I managed to escape from him and plunged into the forest, running faster the more he cried to me to come back, until I completely outdistanced him.

For seven days I hurried on, resting only when the darkness stopped me, and living chiefly upon coconuts, which afforded me both meat and drink; and on the eighth day I reached the seashore and saw a party of men gathering pepper, which grew abundantly. I advanced toward them and they greeted me in Arabic, asking who I was and whence I came. My delight was great on hearing this familiar speech, and I willingly satisfied their curiosity, telling them how I had been shipwrecked and captured.

"But these savages devour men!" said they. "How did you escape?" I repeated to them what I have just told you, at which they were mightily astonished. I stayed with them until they had collected as much pepper as they wished, and then they took me back to their own country and presented me to their King. To him also I had to relate my adventures, which surprised him much, and when I had finished he ordered that I should be supplied with food and raiment and treated with consideration.

The island on which I found myself abounded in all sorts of desirable things, and a great deal of traffic went on in the capital, where I soon began to feel at home and contented. Moreover, the King treated me with special favor and in consequence of this everyone, whether at the court or in the town, sought to make life pleasant for me.

One thing I remarked which I thought very strange: from the greatest to the least, all men rode their horses without bridle or stirrups. One day I presumed to ask His Majesty why he did not use them, to which he replied, "You speak to me of things of which I have never before heard!"

This gave me an idea. I found a clever workman and made him cut out, under my direction, a bridle, reins and the foundation of a saddle, which I wadded and covered with choice leather, adorning it with rich gold embroidery. I then had a locksmith make me a bit, stirrups and a pair of spurs after a pattern that I drew for him, and when these things were completed I presented them to the King and showed him how to use them.

When I had saddled one of his horses he mounted it and rode about, quite delighted with the novelty, and to show his gratitude he rewarded me with many gifts. After this I had to make saddles for all the principal officers of the King's household, and as they gave me rich presents I soon became very wealthy and quite an important person in the city.

One day the King sent for me and said, "Sindbad, I am going to ask a favor of you. Both I and my subjects esteem you, and wish you to end your days among us. Therefore, I desire you to marry a rich and beautiful lady I will find for you, and think no more of your own country."

As the King's will was law I accepted the charming bride he presented to me and lived happily with her. Nevertheless, I had every intention of escaping at the first opportunity and going back to Baghdad. Things were thus going prosperously with me when it happened that the wife of one of my neighbors, with whom I had struck up quite a friendship, fell ill and presently died. I went to his house to offer my consolations and found him in the depths of woe.

"Heaven preserve you," said I, "and send you a long life!"

"Alas!" he replied. "What is the good of saying that when I have but an hour left to live!"

"Come, come!" said I. "Surely it is not so bad as all that. I trust that your life may be spared for many years."

"I hope," answered he, "that your life may be long, but as for me, all is finished. I have set my house in order, and today I shall be buried with my wife. This has been the law upon our island from the earliest ages—the living husband goes to the grave with his dead wife, the living wife with her dead husband. So did our fathers and so must we do. The law changes not and all must submit to it!"

As he spoke, the friends and relations of the unhappy pair began to assemble. The body, decked in rich robes and sparkling with jewels, was laid upon an open bier, and the procession started, making its way to a high mountain at some distance from the city; the wretched husband, clothed from head to foot in a black mantle, followed mournfully.

When the burial place was reached, the corpse was lowered, just as it was, into a deep pit. Then the husband, bidding farewell to all his friends, stretched himself upon another bier, on which were laid seven little loaves of bread and a pitcher of water, and he was also let down, down, down to the depths of the horrible cavern. A stone was then laid over the opening, and the melancholy company wended its way back to the city.

You may imagine that I was no unmoved spectator of these proceedings. All the others were accustomed to it from their youth up, but I was so horrified that I could not help telling the King how it struck me.

"Sire," I said, "I am more astonished than I can express to you at the strange custom which exists in your dominions of burying the living with the dead. In all my travels I have never before met with so cruel and horrible a law."

"What would you have, Sindbad?" he replied. "It is the law for everybody. I myself should be buried with the Queen if she were the first to die."

"But, Your Majesty," said I, "dare I ask if this law applies to foreigners also?"

"Why, yes," replied the King, smiling in what I could but consider a very heartless manner, "they are no exception to the rule if they have married in the country."

From that time forward my mind was never easy. If only my wife's little finger ached I fancied she was going to die, and sure enough before very long she fell really ill and within a few days she had breathed her last.

My dismay was great, for it seemed that to be buried alive was even a worse fate than to be devoured by cannibals. The body of my wife, arrayed in her richest robes and decked with all her jewels, was laid upon the bier. I followed it, and after me came a great procession, headed by the King and all his nobles, and in this order we reached the fatal mountain, one of a lofty chain bordering the sea.

Here I made one more frantic effort to excite the pity of the King and those who stood by, hoping to save myself at this last moment, but it was of no avail. No one spoke to me, they even appeared to hasten over their dreadful task, and I speedily found myself descending into the gloomy pit, with my seven loaves and pitcher of water beside me. Almost before I reached the bottom the stone was rolled into its place above my head, and I was left to my fate.

A feeble ray of light shone into the cavern through some chink, and when I had the courage to look about me I could see that I was in a vast vault, strewn with the bones of the dead. I even fancied that I heard the expiring sighs of those who, like myself, had come into this dismal place alive. All in vain did I shriek aloud with rage and despair, reproaching myself for the love of gain and adventure which had brought me to such a pass; but at length growing calmer, I took up my bread and water and, wrapping my face in my mantle, groped my way toward the end of the cavern, where the air was fresher.

Here I lived in darkness and misery until my provisions were nearly exhausted. One day I fancied that I heard something near me which breathed loudly. Turning to the place from which the sound came I dimly saw a shadowy form which fled at my movement, squeezing itself through a cranny in the wall. I pursued it as fast as I could and found myself in a narrow crack among the rocks, along which I was just able to force my way. I followed it for what seemed to me many miles and, at last, saw before me a glimmer of light which grew clearer every moment until I emerged upon the seashore with a joy which I cannot describe.

When I was sure that I was not dreaming, I realized that it was doubtless some little animal which had found its way into the cavern from the sea and when disturbed had fled, showing me a means of escape which I could never have discovered for myself. I hastily surveyed my surroundings and saw that I was safe from all pursuit from the town.

The mountains sloped sheer down to the sea and there was no road across them. Being assured of this I returned to the cavern and amassed a rich treasure of diamonds, rubies, emeralds and jewels of all kinds which were scattered over the ground. These I made up into bales, stored them in a safe place upon the beach, then sat down and waited hopefully for the passing of a ship.

I had looked out for two days, however, before a single sail appeared, so it was with much delight that I at last saw a vessel not very far from the shore, and by waving my arms and uttering loud cries succeeded in attracting the attention of the crew. A boat was sent off to me, and in answer to the questions of the sailors as to how I came to be in such a plight, I replied that I had been shipwrecked two days before but had managed to scramble ashore with the bales which I pointed out to them.

Luckily for me they believed my story and, without even looking at the place where they found me, took up my bundles and rowed me back to the ship. Once on board, I soon saw that the captain was too much occupied with the difficulties of navigation to pay much heed to me, though he generously made me welcome and would not even accept the jewels with which I offered to pay my passage.

Our voyage was prosperous, and after visiting many lands and collecting in each place a great store of goodly merchandise, I found myself at last in Baghdad once more with unheard-of riches of every description.

Here Sindbad paused, and his audience took their leave, followed by Hindbad, who had once more received a hundred pieces of gold and with the rest had been bidden to return next day for the story of the fifth voyage.

When the time came all were in their places and, when they had eaten and drunk what was set before them, Sindbad began his tale.

Fifth Voyage

Not even all that I had gone through could make me contented with a quiet life. I soon wearied of its pleasures and longed for change and adventure. Therefore I set out once more, but this time in a ship of my own; but as I did not intend carrying enough goods for a full cargo, I invited several merchants of different nations to join me. We set sail with the first favorable wind, and after a long voyage upon the open seas we finally landed upon an unknown island which proved to be uninhabited.

We determined to explore it, but had not gone far when we found a roc's egg, as large as the one I had seen before and evidently very nearly hatched, for the beak of the young bird had already pierced the shell.

In spite of all I could say to deter them, the merchants who were with me fell upon it with their hatchets, breaking the shell and killing the young roc. Then, lighting a fire upon the ground, they hacked morsels from the bird and proceeded to roast them while I stood by, aghast.

Scarcely had they finished their ill-omened repast, when the air above us was darkened by two mighty shadows. The captain of my ship, knowing by experience what this meant, cried out to us that the parent birds were coming and urged us to get on board with all speed. This we did, and the sails were hoisted, but before we had made any headway, the rocs reached their despoiled nest and hovered about it, uttering frightful cries when they discovered the mangled remains of their young one. For a moment we lost sight of them and were flattering ourselves that we had escaped, when they reappeared and soared into the air directly over our vessel, and we saw that each held in its claws an immense rock ready to crush us.

There was a moment of breathless suspense, then one bird loosed its hold and the huge block of stone hurtled through the air, but thanks to the presence of mind of the helmsman, who turned our ship violently in another direction, it fell into the sea close beside us, cleaving it asunder till we could nearly see the bottom. We had hardly time to draw a breath of relief before the other rock fell with a mighty crash right in the midst of our luckless vessel, smashing it into a thousand fragments and hurling passengers and crew into the sea.

I myself went down with the rest, but had the good fortune to rise unhurt and, by holding on to a piece of driftwood with one hand and swimming with the other, I kept myself afloat and was presently washed up by the tide onto an island. Its shores were steep and rocky, but I scrambled up safely and threw myself down to rest upon the green turf.

When I had somewhat recovered I began to examine the spot in which I found myself, and truly it seemed to me that I had reached a garden of delights. There were trees everywhere, laden with flowers and fruit, while a crystal stream wandered in and out under their shadow. When night came I lay down and slept in a cozy nook, though the remembrance that I was alone in a strange land made me sometimes start up and look around me in alarm, and then I wished heartily that I had stayed at home.

The morning sunlight restored my courage and I once more wandered among the trees. I had penetrated some distance into the island when I saw an old man, bent and feeble, sitting upon the river bank. At first I took him to be some shipwrecked mariner like myself. Going up to him I greeted him in a friendly way but he only nodded his head at me in reply. I then asked what he did there, and he made signs to me that he wished to get across the river to gather some fruit and seemed to beg me to carry him on my back.

Pitying his age and feebleness, I took him up and, wading across the stream, I bent down that he might more easily reach the bank and bade him get down. But instead of allowing himself to be set upon his feet, this creature, who had seemed so decrepit, leaped nimbly upon my shoulders and, hooking his legs around my neck, gripped me so tightly that I was well-nigh choked, and so overcome with terror that I fell insensible to the ground.

When I recovered, my enemy was still in his place, though he had released his hold enough to allow me breathing space, and seeing me revive he prodded me adroitly first with one foot and then with the other, until I was forced to get up and stagger about with him under the trees while he gathered and ate the choicest fruits. This went on all day, and even at night, when I threw myself down half dead with weariness, the terrible old man held on tight to my neck. Nor did he fail to greet the first glimmer of morning light by drumming upon me with his heels, until I perforce awoke and resumed my dreary march with rage and bitterness in my heart.

It happened one day that I passed a tree under which lay several dry gourds. Catching one up I amused myself with scooping out its contents and pressing into it the juice of several bunches of the grapes which hung from every vine. When it was full I left it propped in the fork of a tree, and a few days later, carrying the hateful old man that way, I snatched at my gourd as I passed it and had the satisfaction of a draught of excellent wine so good and refreshing that I even forgot my detestable burden and began to sing and caper.

The old monster was not slow to perceive the effect which my draught had produced and that I carried him more lightly than usual, so he stretched out his skinny hand and, seizing the gourd, first tasted its contents cautiously, then drained it to the very last drop. The wine was strong and the gourd capacious, so he also began to sing after a fashion. Soon I had the delight of feeling the iron grip of his goblin legs unclasp, and with one vigorous effort I threw him to the ground, from which he did not move again. I was so delighted to have at last got rid of this old man that I ran leaping and bounding down to the seashore where, by the greatest good luck, I met with some mariners who had anchored off the island to enjoy the delicious fruits and to renew their supply of water.

They heard the story of my escape with amazement, saying, "You fell into the hands of the Old Man of the Sea, and it is a mercy that he did not strangle you as he has everyone else upon whose shoulders he has managed to perch himself. This island is well known as the scene of his evil deeds, and no merchant or sailor who

lands upon it cares to stray far away from his comrades."

After we had talked for a while they took me back with them on board their ship, where the captain received me kindly. We soon set sail, and after several days reached a large and prosperous-looking town where all the houses were built of stone. Here we anchored, and one of the merchants, who had been very friendly to me on the way, took me ashore with him and showed me a lodging set apart for strange merchants. He then provided me with a large sack and pointed out to me a party of other men equipped in like manner.

"Go with them," he said, "and do as they do, but beware of losing sight of them, for if you stray your life would be in danger."

I set out with my new companions and soon learned that the object of our expedition was to fill our sacks with coconuts. The crowns of the coco palms were alive with monkeys, big and little, which skipped from one to the other with surprising agility, seeming to be curious about us and disturbed at our appearance. I was at first surprised when my companions, after collecting stones, began to throw them at the lively creatures, which seemed to me quite harmless. But very soon I saw the reason of it and joined them heartily, for the monkeys, annoyed and wishing to pay us back in our own coin, began to tear the nuts from the trees and cast them at us with angry gestures, so after little labor on our part our sacks were filled with the fruit which we could not otherwise have obtained.

As soon as we had all the coconuts that we could carry, we went back to the town, where my friend bought my share and advised me to continue the same occupation until I had earned money enough to carry me to my own country. This I did and before long had amassed a considerable sum.

Just then I heard that there was a trading ship ready to sail. Taking leave of my friend I went on board, carrying with me a goodly store of coconuts; and we sailed first to the islands where pepper grows, then to Comari where the best aloes wood is found and where men drink no wine by an unalterable law. Here I exchanged my nuts for pepper and aloes wood, and went searching for pearls with some of the other merchants, and the divers I engaged were so lucky that very soon I had an immense number of pearls and those very large and perfect. With all these treasures I came joyfully back to Baghdad, where I disposed of them for large sums of money, of which I did not fail as before to give the tenth part to the poor, and after that I rested from my labors and comforted myself with the many pleasures that my riches could give me.

Having thus ended his story, Sindbad ordered that one hundred pieces of gold should be given to Hindbad, and the guests then withdrew; but after the next day's feast he began the account of his sixth voyage.

Sixth Voyage

It must be a marvel to you how, after having five times met with shipwreck and unheard-of perils, I could again tempt fortune, but evidently it was my fate to rove, and after a year of repose I prepared to make a sixth voyage. Instead of going by the Persian Gulf, I traveled a considerable way overland and finally embarked from a distant Indian port with a captain who meant to make a long voyage. One day we fell in with stormy weather which drove us completely off our course, and for many days neither the captain nor the pilot knew where we were nor where we were going.

When they did at last discover our position we had small ground for rejoicing, for the captain, casting his turban upon the deck and tearing his beard, declared that we were in the most dangerous spot upon the whole wide sea and had been caught by a current which was at that minute sweeping us to destruction. It was too true! In spite of all the sailors could do we were driven with frightful rapidity toward the foot of a mountain which rose sheer out of the sea, and our vessel was dashed to pieces upon the rocks at its base, not, however, before we had managed to scramble onto the shore, carrying with us the most precious of our possessions.

When we had done this the captain said to us, "Now that we are here we may as well begin to dig our graves at once, since from this fatal spot no shipwrecked mariner has ever returned."

This speech discouraged us much, and we began to lament over our sad fate.

The mountain formed the seaward boundary of a large island, and the narrow strip of rocky shore upon which we stood was strewn with the wreckage of a thousand gallant ships, while the bones of luckless mariners shone white in the sunshine, and we shuddered to think how soon our own would be added to the heap.

All around, too, lay vast quantities of the costliest merchandise, and treasures were heaped in every cranny of the rocks, but these things only added to the desolation of the scene. It struck me as very strange that a river of clear fresh water, which gushed from the mountain not far from where we stood, instead of flowing into the sea as rivers generally do, turned off sharply and flowed out of sight under a natural archway of rock. When I went to examine it more closely, I found that inside the cave the walls were thick with diamonds and rubies and masses of crystal and the floor was strewn with ambergris.

Here, then, upon this barren shore we abandoned

ourselves to our fate, for there was no possibility of scaling the mountain, and if a ship had appeared it could only have shared our doom. The first thing our captain did was to divide equally among us all the food we possessed, and then the length of each man's life depended on the time he could make his portion last. I myself could live upon very little.

Nevertheless, by the time I had buried the last of my companions my stock of provisions was so small I hardly thought I should live long enough to dig my own grave. I regretted bitterly the roving disposition which was always bringing me into such straits and thought longingly of all the comfort and luxury I had left. But luckily the fancy took me to stand once more beside the river where it plunged out of sight into the depths of the cavern, and as I did so an idea struck me.

This river which hid itself underground doubtless emerged again at some distant spot. Why should I not build a raft and trust myself to its swiftly flowing waters? If I perished before I could reach the light of day again I should be no worse off than I was now, for death was staring me in the face. I decided at any rate to risk it, and speedily built myself a stout raft of driftwood and strong cords, of which enough and to spare lay strewn upon the beach. I then made up many packages of rubies, emeralds, rock crystal, ambergris and precious stuffs, and bound them upon my raft. Then I seated myself upon it and loosed the cord which held it to the bank.

In the strong current my raft flew swiftly under the gloomy archway, and I found myself in total darkness, carried smoothly forward by the rapid river. On I went, as it seemed to me, for many nights and days. Once the channel became so small that I had a narrow escape from being crushed against the rock roof, and after that I took the precaution of lying flat upon my precious bales. Though I ate only what was absolutely necessary to keep myself alive, the inevitable moment came when, after swallowing my last morsel of food, I began to wonder if I must, after all, die of hunger.

Then, worn out with anxiety and fatigue, I fell into a deep sleep and when I again opened my eyes I was in the light of day. A beautiful country lay before me, and my raft, which was tied to the riverbank, was surrounded by friendly dark men. I rose and saluted them, and they spoke to me in return, but I could not understand a word of their language. But one of the natives, who spoke Arabic, came forward, saying, "My brother, be not surprised to see us; this is our land, and as we came to get water from the river we noticed your raft floating down it, and swam out and brought you to the shore. We have waited for your awakening; tell us whence you come and where you were going by that dangerous way?"

I replied that nothing would please me better than

to tell them, but that I was starving and would like to eat something first. I was soon supplied with all I needed and, having satisfied my hunger, I told them faithfully what had befallen me.

They were lost in wonder at my tale when it was interpreted to them and said that adventures so amazing must be related to their King only by the man to whom they had happened. So, procuring a horse, they mounted me upon it, and we set out, followed by several strong men carrying my raft just as it was upon their shoulders. In this order we marched into the city of Serendib, where the natives presented me to their King, whom I saluted in the Indian fashion, prostrating myself at his feet and kissing the ground; but the monarch bade me rise and sit beside him, asking what was my name. "I am Sindbad," I said, "whom men call 'the Sailor,' for I have voyaged much on many seas."

"And how come you here?" asked the King.

I told my story, concealing nothing, and his wonder and delight were so great that he ordered my adventures to be written in letters of gold and laid up in the archives of his kingdom.

Presently my raft was brought in, the bales were opened, and the King declared that in all his treasury there were no such rubies and emeralds as those which lay in great heaps before him.

Seeing that he looked at them with interest, I ventured to say that I myself and my possessions were at

his disposal, but he answered me, smiling, "Nay, Sindbad. Heaven forbid that I should covet your riches; I
will rather add to them, for I desire that you shall not
leave my kingdom without taking with you some
tokens of my goodwill."

After many days I petitioned the King that I might
return to my own country, to which he graciously consented. Moreover, he loaded me with rich gifts, and
when I went to take leave of him he entrusted me with
royal presents and a letter to the Commander of the
Faithful, our sovereign lord, saying, "I pray you give
these to the Caliph Haroun al Raschid, and assure him
of my friendship."

I accepted the charge respectfully and soon embarked upon the vessel which the King himself had
chosen for me. The King's letter to the Caliph was
written in beautiful blue characters upon a very rare
and precious skin of yellow color, and these were the
words of it:

The King of the Indies—before whom walk a
thousand elephants, who lives in a palace, the
roof of which blazes with a hundred thousand
rubies, and whose treasurehouse contains twenty
thousand diamond crowns—to the Caliph Haroun al Raschid sends greeting. Though the offerings we present to you are unworthy of your
notice, we pray you to accept them as a mark of
the esteem and friendship which we cherish for

you, and of which we gladly send you these tokens, and we ask of you a like regard if you deem
us worthy of it. Adieu, brother.

The presents consisted of a vase carved from a single
ruby, six inches high and as thick as my finger; this
was filled with the choicest pearls, large and of perfect
shape and luster; secondly, a huge snakeskin which
would preserve from sickness those who slept upon it;
then quantities of aloes wood, camphor and pistachio
nuts; and, lastly, a beautiful slave girl, whose robes
glittered with precious stones.

After a long and prosperous voyage we landed at
Balsora, and I made haste to reach Baghdad. Taking
the King's letter I presented myself at the palace gate,
followed by the beautiful slave and various members
of my own family, bearing the treasure.

As soon as I had declared my errand I was conducted into the presence of the Caliph Haroun al
Raschid, to whom, after I had made my obeisance, I
presented the letter and the King's gifts. When he had
examined these closely he demanded of me whether
the King of Serendib was really as rich and powerful
as he claimed to be.

"Commander of the Faithful," I replied, again bowing humbly before him, "I can assure Your Majesty
that the King of Serendib has in no way exaggerated
his wealth and grandeur. Nothing can equal the magnificence of his palace. When he goes abroad, his throne

is prepared upon the back of an elephant, and on either side of him ride his ministers, his favorites and courtiers. On his elephant's neck sits an officer, his golden lance in his hand, and behind him stands another bearing a pillar of gold, at the top of which is an emerald as long as my hand.

"A thousand men in cloth of gold, mounted upon richly caparisoned elephants, go before him, and as the procession moves onward the officer who guides his elephant cries aloud, 'Behold the mighty monarch, the powerful and valiant Sultan of Serendib, whose palace is covered with a hundred thousand rubies, who possesses twenty thousand diamond crowns. Behold a monarch greater than Solomon and Mihrage in all their glory.' Further, my lord, in Serendib no judge is needed, for to the King himself his people come for justice."

The Caliph was well satisfied with my report. "From the King's letter," said he, "I judge that he is a wise man. It seems that he is worthy of his people, and his people of him." So saying he dismissed me with rich presents and I returned in peace to my own house.

When Sindbad had done speaking, his guests withdrew, Hindbad having first received a hundred pieces of gold; but all returned next day to hear the story of the seventh voyage. Sindbad thus began.

Seventh Voyage

After my sixth voyage I was determined to go to sea no more. I was now of an age to appreciate a quiet life and I had run risks enough. I only wished to end my days in peace. One day, however, when I was entertaining a number of my friends, I was told that an officer of the Caliph wished to speak to me. When he had been admitted he bade me follow him into the presence of Haroun al Raschid, which I did.

I saluted him, and the Caliph said, "I have sent for you, Sindbad, because I need your services. I have chosen you to bear a letter and gifts to the King of Serendib in return for his message of friendship."

The Caliph's commandment fell upon me like a thunderbolt. "Commander of the Faithful," I answered, "I am ready to do all that you command, but I humbly pray you to remember that I am utterly disheartened by the sufferings I have undergone. Indeed, I have made a vow never again to leave Baghdad."

"I admit," said he, "that you have indeed had some extraordinary experiences, but I do not see why they should hinder you from doing as I wish. You have only to go straight to Serendib and give my message, then you are free to come back and do as you will. But go you must; my honor and dignity demand it."

Seeing there was no help for it, I declared myself

willing to obey; and the Caliph, delighted at having his own way, gave me a thousand gold pieces for the expenses of the voyage. I soon embarked at Balsora and sailed quickly and safely to Serendib. Here, when I had disclosed my errand, I was well received and brought into the presence of the King, who greeted me with joy.

"Welcome, Sindbad," he cried. "I have thought of you often, and rejoice to see you once more."

After thanking him for the honor he did me, I displayed the Caliph's gifts: first a bed with complete hangings of cloth of gold, and another like it of crimson stuff; fifty robes of rich embroidery; a hundred fine white linens from Cairo, Suez, Kufa and Alexandria; an agate vase carved with the figure of a man aiming an arrow at a lion; and finally a costly table which had once belonged to King Solomon.

The King of Serendib received with satisfaction the assurance of the Caliph's friendliness toward him. And now my task being accomplished I was anxious to depart, although it was some time before the King would think of letting me go. At last, however, he dismissed me with many presents and I lost no time in going on board a ship, which sailed that very hour, and for four days all went well.

On the fifth day we had the misfortune to come upon pirates, who seized our vessel, killing all who resisted and making prisoners of those who were prudent enough to submit at once, of whom I was one. When they had despoiled us of all we possessed, they forced us to put on vile raiment and, sailing to a distant island, there sold us for slaves.

I fell into the hands of a rich merchant, who took me home with him, clothed and fed me, and after some days sent for me and questioned me about what I could do. I answered that I too was a rich merchant, who had been captured by pirates, and therefore did not know a trade.

"Tell me," said he, "can you shoot with a bow?"

I replied that this had been a pastime of my youth, and that doubtless with practice my skill would come back to me.

Upon this he provided me with a bow and arrows and, mounting me with him upon his own elephant, took the way to a vast forest which lay far from the town. When we had reached the wildest part of the forest, we stopped, and my master said, "This forest swarms with elephants. Hide yourself in this great tree and shoot at any that pass you. When you have succeeded in killing one, come and tell me."

So saying he gave me a supply of food and returned to the town. I perched myself high up in the tree and kept watch. That night I saw nothing, but just after sunrise the next day a large herd of elephants came crashing by. You may be sure that I immediately let fly several arrows, and at last one of the great animals fell to the ground, dead. The others retreated, leaving me free to come down from my hiding place and run back to tell my master of my success, for which I was praised and regaled with good things. Then we went back to the forest together and dug a mighty trench in which we buried the elephant I had killed, in order that when it became a skeleton my master might return and secure its tusks.

For two months I hunted thus, and no day passed without my getting an elephant. Of course I did not always station myself in the same tree, but sometimes here, sometimes there. One morning as I watched the coming of the elephants I was surprised to see that, instead of passing the tree I was in, as they usually did, they paused and completely surrounded it, trumpeting horribly and shaking the very ground with their heavy tread. When I saw that their eyes were fixed upon me I was terrified, and my arrows dropped from my trembling hand.

I had indeed good reason for my terror when, an instant later, the largest of the animals wrapped his trunk around the tree, and with one mighty effort tore it up by the roots, bringing me to the ground entangled in its branches. I thought now my last hour was surely come; but the huge creature, picking me up gently enough, set me upon its back, where I clung more dead than alive. Then, followed by the whole herd, it turned and crashed into the dense forest.

It seemed to me a long time before I was once more set upon my feet, and I stood as if in a dream watching the herd which trampled off in another direction and were soon hidden in the heavy underbrush. Then, recovering myself, I looked about me and found that I was standing upon the side of a great hill, strewn as far as I could see on either hand with bones and tusks of elephants. "This then must be the elephants' burying place," I murmured to myself, "and they must have brought me here that I might cease to persecute them, seeing that I want nothing but their tusks, and here lie more than I could carry away with me in a lifetime."

Whereupon I turned and made for the city as fast as I could go, not seeing a single elephant as I went. This convinced me that they had retired deeper into the forest to leave the way open to the ivory hill, and I did not know how to admire their sagacity sufficiently. After a day and a night I reached my master's house and was received by him with joyful surprise.

"Ah, poor Sindbad," he cried, "I was wondering what could have become of you. When I went to the forest I found the tree newly uprooted, the arrows lying beside it, and I feared I should never see you again. Pray tell me how you escaped death."

I soon satisfied his curiosity, and the next day we went together to the ivory hill, and he was overjoyed to find that I had told him nothing but the truth. When we had loaded our elephant with as many tusks as it could carry and were going back to the city, he said: "My brother—since I can no longer treat as a slave one who has enriched me thus—take your liberty and may Heaven prosper you. I will no longer conceal from you that these elephants have killed numbers of our slaves. You alone have escaped their wiles; therefore you shall not only receive your freedom, but I will also bestow fortune and honors upon you."

So I stayed with him till the time of the monsoon, which would bring the ivory ships, and every day we added to our store of ivory till his warehouses were overflowing with it. By this time the other merchants knew the secret, but there was enough and to spare for all. When the ships finally arrived, my master put on board for me a great store of choice provisions, also ivory in abundance and some of the costliest curiosities of the country.

I left the ship at the first port we came to, not feeling at ease upon the sea after what had happened to me by reason of it. Having disposed of my ivory for much gold and having bought many rare and costly presents, I loaded my pack animals and joined a caravan of merchants. Our journey was long and tedious, but I bore it patiently, reflecting that at least I had not to fear tempests, nor pirates, nor serpents, nor any of the other perils from which I suffered before. After a time we reached Baghdad.

My first care was to present myself before the Caliph and give him an account of my journey.

By his orders this story and the others I had told him were written by his scribes in letters of gold and laid up among his treasures. I took my leave of him, well satisfied with the honors and rewards he bestowed upon me; and since that time I have rested from my labors and given myself up wholly to my family and my friends.

Thus Sindbad ended the story of his seventh and last voyage. Turning to Hindbad he added, "Well, my friend, what do you think now? Have you ever heard of anyone who has suffered more or had more narrow escapes than I have? Is it not just that I should now enjoy a life of ease and tranquillity?"

Hindbad drew near and, kissing his hand respectfully, replied, "Sir, you have indeed known fearful perils; my troubles have been nothing compared to yours. Moreover, the generous use you make of your wealth proves that you deserve it. May you live long and happily in the enjoyment of it."

Sindbad then gave him a hundred pieces of gold and henceforward counted Hindbad among his friends. Also he caused him to give up his profession as a porter and to eat daily at his table that he might all his life remember Sindbad the Sailor.

ARABIAN NIGHTS, TRANSLATED BY ANTOINE GALLAND

ACKNOWLEDGMENTS Collected and edited by Andrew Lang: RAPUNZEL, TWELVE DANCING PRINCESSES, from *Red Fairy Book*, © 1948; DICK WHITTINGTON AND HIS CAT, RUMPELSTILTZKIN, HANSEL AND GRETEL, EAST OF THE SUN AND WEST OF THE MOON, BLUE BEARD, THE PRINCESS ON THE GLASS HILL, SLEEPING BEAUTY, JACK THE GIANT KILLER, from *Blue Fairy Book*, © 1948; THE EMPEROR'S NEW CLOTHES, THE STEADFAST TIN SOLDIER, THE SIX SWANS, from *Yellow Fairy Book*, © 1948; JORINDA AND JORINGEL, LITTLE ONE EYE, LITTLE TWO EYES AND LITTLE THREE EYES, THE HALF-CHICK, from *Green Fairy Book*, ©1948; ALADDIN AND THE WONDERFUL LAMP, THE MAGIC CARPET, SINDBAD THE SAILOR, from *Arabian Nights*, © 1898, 1946; the aforementioned books are copyrighted and published by David McKay Company, Inc. THE GOLDEN-HEADED FISH, from *Olive Fairy Book*, first published by David McKay Company, Inc., in 1950. All the aforementioned books are published in Great Britain by Longmans, Green & Co. Ltd. SEVEN SIMONS, THE COLONY OF CATS, from *Crimson Fairy Book*; both first published by Longmans, Green & Co. Ltd. in 1951.

DOCTOR KNOW-IT-ALL, from *Tales From Grimm*, © 1936, Wanda Gág; THE RED SHOES, THE LITTLE MATCH-GIRL, LITTLE CLAUS AND BIG CLAUS, from *It's Perfectly True and Other Stories*, by Hans Christian Andersen, translated by Paul Leyssac, © 1937, Paul Leyssac; renewed, 1965, Mary Rehan, published by Harcourt, Brace & World, Inc. THE THREE LITTLE PIGS, from *English Fairy Tales*, by Joseph Jacobs, published by G. P. Putnam's Sons. THE SHOEMAKER AND THE ELVES, THE BRAVE LITTLE TAILOR, THE MUSICIANS OF BREMEN, from *Tales of Laughter*, edited by Kate Douglas Wiggin and Nora Archibald Smith, © 1908, 1926 and published by Doubleday & Company, Inc. BILLY BEG AND HIS BULL, from *Chimney Corner Stories*, by Veronica S. Hutchinson, © 1925 and published by G. P. Putnam's Sons. PUSS IN BOOTS, from *Perrault's Complete Fairy Tales*, translated by A. E. Johnson and others, © 1961 and published by Dodd, Mead & Company, Inc. and Constable & Ltd. SNEGOURKA, THE SNOW MAIDEN, from *Favorite Fairy Tales Told in Russia*, by Virginia Haviland, © 1961, Virginia Haviland, published by Little, Brown and Co. and the Bodley Head Ltd. THE THREE BEARS, from *The Golden Goose and the Three Bears*, by L. Leslie Brooke, published by Frederick Warne and Co. Ltd. THE GINGERBREAD MAN, from *Stories to Tell to Children*, by Sara Cone Bryant, © 1907, Sara Cone Bryant, published by Houghton Mifflin Company and George G. Harrap & Co. Ltd. A HORNED GOAT, from *The Jolly Tailor and Other Fairy Tales*, translated by Lucia Merecka Borski (Lucia Merecka Szczepanowice) and Kate B. Miller, © 1928 and published by Longmans, Green & Co. Ltd.